7613
6-8-79

D0903780

The
Last
Mandarin

Books by Stephen Becker

NOVELS
The Season of the Stranger
Shanghai Incident
Juice
A Covenant with Death
The Outcasts
When the War Is Over
Dog Tags
The Chinese Bandit
The Last Mandarin

BIOGRAPHY
Marshall Field III

HISTORY
Comic Art in America

TRANSLATIONS
The Colors of the Day
Mountains in the Desert
The Sacred Forest
Faraway
Someone Will Die Tonight in the Caribbean
The Last of the Just
The Town Beyond the Wall
The Conquerors
Louis-Philippe's American Diary

The Last Mandarin

Stephen Becker

Random House
New York

Rare
PS
3552
.E26
L37
1979

Copyright © 1979 by Stephen Becker
All rights reserved under International and Pan-American Copyright
Conventions.
Published in the United States by Random House, Inc., New York, and
simultaneously in Canada by Random House of Canada Limited, Toronto.

Library of Congress Cataloging in Publication Data
Becker, Stephen D., 1927-
The last mandarin.
I. Title.
PZ4.B396Las [PS3552.E26]   813'.5'4   78-23844
ISBN 0-394-49927-1

Manufactured in the United States of America
9 8 7 6 5 4 3 2
First Edition

For JMF

寶 I

Peking

愛 1

There were many bodies in the street that winter, and Aunt Chi reported an unusual number of virgins sold into the penny brothels. Men and women starved and froze in Chicago too, and Paris, and Moscow, but they were often drunk or sick and could be counted by dozens or scores, while in Peking they were men, women and children of all talents and aspirations, though naturally of low degree, and they had to be stacked on corners, and wagons were dispatched to remove the corpses.

The enemy was driving down from the north and east to ring the city.

The yellow wind had long since come and gone. Each year in November there was a yellow day, when a blast from the northwest blew Mongolia's yellow dust far south of the Great Wall and tinted the sky, and brought frost. Measured against the phases of the moon, the yellow wind might be an early yellow wind or a late yellow wind, and the severity of frost was important: this year a late yellow wind and heavy frost indicated, according to the astrologers, a long and cold winter. In Small Palisade Street, and under Cattail Bridge, low scamps and vagabonds huddled and cursed. It was necessary now to steal garments from the freshly dead.

There were more bodies on the street that winter than nature made.

It was not true that men raised cats for meat. Dogs, however, were eaten. That was only fair. They were fat on corpses.

The organized beggars congregated in ill-heated sheds or disused shops; lone wolves and amateurs skulked and shivered.

The ricksha men bundled up, and bound cloth across their faces when the wind cut too shrewdly.

Students rioted, and the unemployed. The police and the army vied in suppressing them.

The rich made plans to flee; but where?

In the sealed ammunition well of an abandoned Japanese bunker in the Cemetery of the Hereditary Wardens of the Thirteen Gates, two skeletons lay embraced. The place inspired dread, so only the dregs and scum—the beggars, the poorer than beggars, and those who were too poor to entertain even superstition—spent an occasional night in the bunker to take shelter from the blast. They knew nothing of the ammunition well, so the last mandarin rested in peace.

Sons cursed fathers, and the people cursed the ministers, and the ministers cursed the leader; how, then, could the state thrive?

The Nationalists within, some said, were vice and anarchy and the foreign glove; the Communists without, others said, were virtue and tyranny but the Chinese hand.

This was the winter of 1949, and the worst of times: the unknown evil was finally preferable to the known.

寶 2

"An astrologer warned me I'd die in China," Burnham told the colonel. "He was a little round fellow, pockmarked, and he was wearing a dunce cap decorated with squirrels' paws. I paid him two cash." Outside the Dai-Ichi Mutual Life Insurance Building a gray rain dripped through the twilight. Windows glimmered dolefully among Tokyo's ruins and rebuildings.

"Superstition," the colonel said. "You've been fully briefed?"

"Kanamori Shoichi. First-class war criminal. Been spotted in Peking—maybe."

"Been tried and found guilty."

"And sentenced to death in absentia. I am supposed to do something about the absentia." Burnham was tall and bearish, with curly brown hair and a strong, crooked nose broken at least once.

"A sadist, a killer, a rapist and a major," the colonel said. "Queer people, these Japs."

"We've probably got some sadists, killers and rapists too," Burnham said, "and some of them may be majors by now. No offense, Colonel."

"None taken, Major." The colonel was dapper and barbered.

"Major, hell. I'm retired. I'm a civilian now, and I outrank you. I want respect from the rude and licentious soldiery."

" 'Rude and licentious' is very funny, coming from you. As I recall your service record, it consisted largely of shack-ups, AWOLs and reprimands."

Burnham blazed: "You mean to say they put my love life in my army records?"

"Not exactly in. More like alongside."

Burnham almost spat. "Eunuchs. No class."

"Anyway, they handed you this one. I suppose it's an honor."

"Honor! They picked me because I can live on a handful of rice and have no brains. Also I speak both languages and I found Isuzu for them in '45. I don't know why the Chinese can't find this fellow Kanamori, but I suppose you want him for a showcase execution. Sanctimonious press releases, just about the time we announce some new superbomb."

"Yours not to reason why."

"Maybe you only want an excuse to run a plane in there," Burnham went on. "Maybe your pilots are running opium out, or politicians, or rich traitors, or sweatshop tycoons. Or maybe I'm a diversion, and they've got another man, a Chinese probably, who's going to nab Kanamori while everybody stares at this big tall foreign son of a bitch."

"Then why do it?" the colonel asked. "Do you hate the Japs so much?"

"Oh for Chrissake." Burnham groaned. "I was *born* here. Until I was six I spoke Japanese better than English. Listen, do you know about the old Japanese left wing? The union people? Don't be scared, now. MacArthur's in Kobe at the Peerless Mixed Baths."

"No. What about them? Radicals and agitators?"

"Goddam heroes," Burnham said. "Kanamori probably tortured a few of them too, for practice. Like the National Guard back home shooting at strikers."

"You talk too much," the colonel said sharply.

"Sorry, champ." Burnham's smile was fuzzy, and he swallowed a yawn. "Four days in the air, snoozing, reading rotten magazines, eating junk and fending off fools. There was a Christian on one of those planes. With tracts."

"I understood your parents were missionaries."

"There you are," Burnham said. "A man is capable of just so much piety in one lifetime. I'm thirty-five, and my quota was exhausted a long time ago. So I told this fellow I was an atheist. He went snow-white. Staggered back to his seat and prayed over the engines." Again Burnham squinted out at the rain and gathering darkness. This colonel bored him. In Tokyo were dim cellars, lutanists with painted faces, stately dancers in silk, and afterward a formal courtship, honorifics, even the language differentiated, male and female. "Afraid I must be going," he said. "My country needs me."

"I wish I could be sure which country you meant," the colonel said. "You've got your travel orders for Seoul and Peking. Do you need weapons?"

"Thank you, no. I ha' ma wee kit wi' me." Burnham rose. An unseasonal thirst was upon him. Time zones played hell with the inner clock.

"You'll want a pass for the officers' mess."

"Sorry," Burnham said. "Previous engagement. Five days without fornication, you know. Bad for the complexion. Sludge gathers."

Smiling without joy, the colonel said, "There's good and evil out there, Burnham. Life's not all jokes."

Burnham slipped into his parka. "There's no more good and evil, Colonel. There's only good and bad, and pretty soon convenient and inconvenient."

"Then why bother with Kanamori?"

Burnham's face hardened. He swung the duffel bag over his shoulder. "Kanamori was rude to some friends of mine," he said. "I'll see you, Colonel. Thanks for the plane ticket."

Burnham seemed to be stumbling down the social ladder. A lieutenant colonel met him at the airport in Seoul, showed him to a bachelor officer's room and supplied him with whiskey and magazines. At dawn a major woke him, or tried to, and after awkward efforts to interest him in food, escorted him—groggy, in pain, tongue furred, eyes in aspic—to a DC-3, where a captain welcomed him aboard. The major tossed Burnham's duffel bag through the passenger door, shook hands gently with him, wished him luck, and transferred the patient to the captain.

This was a Captain Moran, freckled and wholesome, yet with some experience of the world, as was immediately obvious. "Right here, old friend." He steered Burnham to a bucket seat. "Sit very still, don't move your head, and we'll have a mug of coffee for you in no time."

"A trifling excess of Old Stump Remover," Burnham mumbled.

"We understand," Moran said. "It is in the highest tradition of the American military."

Burnham was much moved. "Moran, God will reward you. If in the meantime you need money—"

"No tipping," Moran said. "Air Force policy." Shortly he served black coffee. "I have to drive now."

"Nng." Burnham sucked and slurped. Engines barked, stirred, roared, hummed. Burnham's stomach rumbled in sympathy. The coffee scalded. It was a cold morning, and the aircraft was still freezing; he huddled into the hood of his parka and embraced the hot mug with both hands. The DC-3 trundled forward. He glanced sadly out a port: a clear day, the brightest of northern mornings, the purity of winter, and old Burnham rancid as usual.

Toward the tail four enlisted men sprawled. One was already asleep, one deep in a comic book. No one seemed to notice that they were in the air. The plane's interior glowed black, silver, olive, and smelled of canvas and oil. Burnham buried his nose in the cup and inhaled. Shortly Moran joined him and they sat companionably silent. Moran rattled a cigarette from a cellophaned pack and gestured toward Burnham, who raised a large palm in refusal. He smoked other vegetables, price and custom permitting. Since leaving China he had abstained without unbearable gripes or unseemly yearning, and he could survive another day or two.

Moran asked, "Where you from?" Obligatory.

"San Francisco."

"Long way."

"Worse. Washington and back, first. Then Tokyo by way of Dutch Harbor. Dutch Harbor in January."

"Hell of a time to go to Peking," Moran said. "Mukden's gone, Kalgan went Christmas Eve, and Mao's about a bicycle ride from Peking and Tientsin both."

"It's always the wrong time when they send me in," Burnham said gloomily.

"Been in before, then."

"Hell, I lived there almost twenty years. Then they dropped me in back in '44, and it was hairy and scary."

"Dropped you where?"

"Manchuria. With the guerrillas."

"Oh Christ, Reds," Moran said.

"Guerrillas. Not all Reds. And let me tell you, those were hard guys. Out all night, twenty below, cut your throat before breakfast. They could curse you to death at five miles." Burnham enjoyed a small surge of good cheer; memory had its uses. "We had a little town up there once for a day or so, and the phones worked. Japanese efficiency. So I called the Japanese in Tsitsihaerh and jabbered away at them. Scared hell out of them. They put planes in the air and all, flying off in the wrong direction."

"By golly, a war hero," Moran said. "Got a medal, I bet."

"Indeed and indeed. A shiny little medal. Last I saw it, it was way out there at the tip of a full Angora sweater. Jesus," he moaned, "I'm wasting my life. A goddam do-gooder."

"Do-gooder, hell. If you volunteered for Manchuria in '44 you must enjoy these excursions."

"Volunteer?" Burnham was outraged. "Enjoy? Listen, that idiot MacArthur dropped me in there. 'You may have to improvise,' he said. 'Remember, you bear the flag. Stay in uniform at all times. Orientals respect only force.' Know what that means? It means MacArthur respects only force. No brains, believe me."

"Glad he's not my boss," Moran said.

"Well, he was mine, all right. When I came out of Manchuria he asked me what I thought. So I told him. Jesus. How dumb can a major be?" Burnham winced in bitter mirth, pain, ironic wonder. "So I was expelled from the race of man. Hah! All I said was, the Communists are going to win. I figured anybody over the age of three knew that already. He looked down his parrot's nose at me and he said, 'Burnham, I don't like quitters.'"

"An anarchist," Moran said. "A free lance. What have you been doing since? Making bombs? Robbing post offices?"

"I am a graduate electrical engineer," Burnham said, "and have built a powerhouse north of the Arctic Circle."

"Where you got that jacket. Eskimo clothes."

"Good parka. Won it in a card game in Fairbanks. Three fours. Those small three of a kinds take courage."

"What else you done?"

"Kicked around some. Organized for the Democrats and got old Harry Truman elected."

"At least it wasn't Henry Wallace."

"Nothing wrong with old Henry," Burnham said. "Just ahead of his time, is all. So after the election I caught up on my drinking, and then those fools in Washington called and I was summoned from a warm and crowded bed to fly into a doomed city and root out an animal who may or may not be there. If I don't find him I will shortly be drowning in Communists, and if I do find him he will doubtless scramble my giblets."

"A warm and crowded bed." Moran scowled. "I suppose you have one of those bachelor apartments."

"You know the sort of thing," Burnham said airily. "The bidet seats six."

"Don't talk like that. I'm a married man."

"You're luckier than you know," Burnham said. "You wouldn't believe how boring it can be to wake up with a different woman every week."

Moran was aghast. "I got to spell the co-pilot. You can lie to *him* for a while."

The co-pilot was more mechanically inclined, a trim man who showed no emotion or even interest until it transpired that Burnham had jumped from DC-3s and even flown one for an hour or two. This established the social level, and the co-pilot allowed a smile. Toward the tail, the enlisted men played cards.

By midmorning Burnham was in fair command of all bodily functions, sat sprawled rather than huddled, and chewed with growing interest on a ham-and-cheese sandwich. Moran rejoined him. Burnham washed down the last crumbs with coffee, set his mug on the next seat and glanced out a starboard port for the tenth time. He saw land, and held his breath.

Moran noticed. "What you lookin at out there?"

"Lü Shun K'ou."

"No kiddin'. What's that in Merkin?"

"Port Arthur."

Moran squinted at his wristwatch. "Right on time. Your old hometown, or something?"

"Never been there."

"You plan to be long in Peking?"

"Can't say."

"Reason I ask," Moran said, "we may not be able to fly in there forever."

"Fly anything out?"

"Big shots. Bags of gold, probably. Antiques. What the hell do I know? But it's a good run. Peking's a nice old town."

A nice old town!

"So there goes China," Moran said sadly.

"No," Burnham said. "She'll be right where she always was. Any flak along here?" He stretched to retrieve his duffel bag.

"None. Peaceful. You mind if I ask what line of work you're in?"

Burnham freed the lock and rummaged. "Kidnapping." He dumped garments, cloth shoes. He brandished a round winter hat, heavily ruffed in rabbit fur.

"Good pay?"

"Civil service."

"Pension."

"Benefits." Burnham took off his parka, sweater and khaki shirt. Aft, the murmuring died; they were watching him. He removed his mukluks and trousers, and stood tall in socks and skivvies.

Moran asked, "Do you do this on commercial flights?"

Burnham drew on the padded dark-blue Chinese trousers. The waistband was forty-four inches; he folded it over in front and belted it with a red silk sash. He donned a heavy cotton shirt, cream-colored, the collar Prussian but rounded, the buttons of cloth, knots that slipped into loops. Then the quilted gown, dark blue; then the overgown, dark blue; and the black shoes with many-layered cotton soles. He bowed. Moran and the others applauded. He transferred his wallet, passport and bandanna to mysteriously located pockets, like a magician preparing surprises, stuffed his Western clothes into the duffel bag, locked it, then sat back and set the winter hat square on his head. He rolled down the furry ruff; it fell to his shoulders.

"Come on out," Moran said.

Burnham tugged the hat off and rolled up the ruff. "You can cut holes for eyes."

They gossiped for a while then, Did-you-ever-know-Dale-Ball-No-but-how-about-Phil-Hanes, so that Burnham almost forgot his destination, but at the sudden sight of the Chinese landscape he prickled, and his blood sang.

"I bet you do just fine with those Chinese women," Moran was saying. Burnham grunted, gazing down on snowy fields. "Millions and millions of 'em," Moran said, "and you sweet-talkin' in their language and showin' real money."

Burnham ignored him. He saw a river and a fisherman's boat and a village in a hollow, half misted over.

It was one thing, Burnham knew, to love Peking from the air on a shiny winter morn: to glimpse the massive city walls from a thousand feet, the Temple of Heaven, the Forbidden City, the tiny rise of Coal Hill, the shifting sparkle of sunlight off tiled roofs, bright red, some blue, most green—little yellow now and he missed it, the warm imperial yellow of old Peking—the darker blue lakes, and the black lines of canals and railroad tracks.

It was another thing, he knew, to be a Pekinger, man or woman, and never to see all that. To be someone for whom Peking was not the glittering Cambaluc but a nest of squalid alleys, or perhaps worse, the grimy corner of a foul room off one of those alleys. Where the poor of Peking lived, the alleys reeked of excrement, dead animals and, on lucky days, opium; and in them swarmed tens of thousands whose lives darkened quickly from trachoma, who hobbled and lurched from rickets, whose ancestors had vanished in flood or famine and whose near and dear in plague and war, leaving no tablets to be revered, no land, no silver, no pigs or pots, whose bellies were clenched fists, who sucked the dry bones of despair and were too empty to weep.

Yet this superman's sight of China excited him; he almost shook. This was home. In his mind English faded away and the great Eastern voice rose: the voice of the Middle Kingdom, ancient and musical, the song of pied birds and fat gods, of archers and empresses, of the cardinal points and the eight winds, of moon gates and pagodas, and the same song a dirge for myriad upon myriad of men, women and children whose bones filled the Great Wall, and fertilized whole provinces, and paved riverbeds. The anthem of a land where civil officials of the fifth grade had formerly worn as a badge of rank not a star, thunderbolt, dagger or death's-head, but a silver pheasant.

The aircraft banked and swooped. Shanties bloomed below, and fields patchy with snow. Then a wall, a runway, a row of lights mute now at noon, a bump, a squeal. They taxied past the low terminal, crawled among fighters and transports and halted.

Burnham clambered down the steel ladder and set foot once more in China.

3 獅

Toward the end of 1937 the Japanese crushed the worm people along the Yangtze River. They left behind a pale and terrified Shanghai, millions of worm people—and better yet, thousands of paper-colored foreigners—trembling like moths. They swept west, all units—units with names like Nakajima, Hatanaka, Minoura, Inoki, and many more—and raced to the Purple Mountain at Nanking, two hundred miles in one month.

Their impatience was understandable. They had waited decades. In 1931 they had finally conquered Manchuria ("self-defense," they said). In 1932 they had invaded Shanghai and withdrawn when asked by the League of Nations ("statesmanship," they said). Their moment came in July of 1937, when they took advantage of a minor incident outside Peking to vent half a century of frustration: they committed themselves to the conquest of all China, seized Shanghai firmly and started west (Asia for the Asiatics, they called it, and later the Greater East Asia Co-Prosperity Sphere).

On the road to Nanking Sublieutenant Kanamori Shoichi made a wager with Sublieutenant Kurusu Kiyoshi: that he would set foot first on the Purple Mountain and piss down on Nanking. Thus soldiers spoke and laughed and swaggered. With Kurusu he made another wager, and soon the whole division spoke of it, and later the *Asahi* and the *Japan Advertiser* and the whole world: the winner would be he who first killed one hundred Chinese in combat with the sword. Women and children would not count. For most Japanese officers this was the first campaign offering scope to the sword.

The Chinese inflicted forty thousand casualties. Between Shanghai and Nanking, knowing themselves vanquished, fighting without transport, wielding kitchen utensils, firing obsolete, pitted and homemade rifles, they still felled forty thousand. A worm would peer over a mud wall, fire one round, and then be disintegrated by Japanese fire. But his one round would have killed or wounded a monkey. Some of the Chinese had been trained by Germans. This was perhaps an irony, but ironies were the way of Asia. German-trained Chinese machine-gunners would form a suicide squad and open heavy fire on a Japanese column or truck convoy. The squad would be wiped out. The Japanese advance was inexorable; why then did the worms resist? The Japanese became less jolly and more angry.

It is crowded country west of Shanghai, many villages along the river and many small farms. The Japanese swept along the river and also overland, through martyred villages and towns and cities called Ch'ang-chou and Tan-yang and Chü-jung. The weather held clear for the most part, though there were days of autumn rain. As the Japanese advanced along the river the screen of rain would part and on the river would be a sampan or a small fishing boat, the fisherman at the sweep. These were fine targets, with the challenge of bad light, haze, rain and only the brief moment. Several shots would sound, and as the soldiers laughed the fisherman would seem to slide down his sweep and into the Yangtze like a fisher of pearls or an ungainly cormorant.

On 20 November 1937, thirty miles from Nanking, Kanamori killed his first man with the sword. The man was trapped and had no choice. He stood panting and his eyes darted like mice, but he made an effort. Kanamori lunged and feinted left; the man parried like a child. Kanamori lunged and feinted right; the man lurched and hunched. Kanamori leaped forward, shouted "Ima!" ("Now!") and sliced through the neck. This was Kanamori's dance, to the left, to the right, and slash; and it became known as Kanamori's three-step. Afterward he sat to bow his head and pray. He prayed thanks to his father, though his father, who had killed four Russians in one day with the sword during the battle of the River Sha thirty-three years before, was still alive. Until this first killing by sword Kanamori had in truth scarcely felt like a soldier. On the blade near the hilt was his name: Kanamori Shoichi.

He was a warrior but he was not insensible to the humor of war.

A fall day, overcast, and the fields dun, here and there a burnt-out farmhouse, a village leveled, smoking still, the women and children afraid even to beg for their lives. His platoon surrounded six Chinese soldiers obviously cut off and making their way like frogs along an irrigation ditch. "Up, up, up!" cried the Japanese, and the Chinese stumbled up from the ditch—raw young men, farmers and no true fighters—and stood shivering in the dank breeze. Already the Japanese were laughing, and Sergeant Ito called out, "Which one first, Lieutenant?"

"Let them decide."

Ito knew some Chinese; he spoke. (Kanamori's Chinese was fluent, but his men never learned this.) The Chinese did not understand; that is, they understood the words but not the proposal. Kanamori drew his saber; he slashed the air and thrust.

The Chinese jabbered. Ito pointed. The shortest of the lot blinked up. His eyes darted and scurried like beetles. "Very well," Kanamori announced. "We begin with the mouse and proceed by stages to the lion." His men cheered.

Ito placed a saber in the little one's hand. The little one wagged it this way and that. Kanamori cried "Ha!" and placed himself on guard. The little one blinked, and spoke to Ito. Kanamori stepped toward him and raised the saber. The little one only squinted in wonder. Again Kanamori cried "Ha!" The little one raised his sword tentatively. Kanamori touched it once with his own: the proprieties. He lunged and feinted left; his men chorused "Left!" He lunged and feinted right; his men chorused "Right!" He then chopped the little one's head half off; his men chorused "Ima!" The bones of the neck were obstinate; the little one's head flopped to one side and lay along his shoulder. Only then did he fall. His knees bent and he hunkered for a moment before the collapse.

Ito cleaned the saber and passed it to the next man. This one knew that he was to die, and that hope was foolish; he rushed Kanamori. A tough little rat. He rushed and swung for the neck. No time now for the Kanamori three-step. Kanamori ducked and parried in one motion, then brought his sword down across the kidneys. The man screamed, and would not turn; Kanamori walked around him, looked him in the eye and pierced him through. The man seemed relieved, and died upon the blade.

They searched the bodies. Nothing, a few cash. Ito called out, "This one is a woman!"

"Curse it!" Kanamori cried. "I cannot count her, then."

"We had better use for her," Ito said.

Kanamori said to the men, "I owe you a woman. You will remind me in Nanking."

And the men cheered: "We shall remind you!"

The rain quit. The sky cleared. Cold promised. The Japanese swept on, stumbled, took casualties. Between the mountains and Nanking the Chinese stiffened and were stubborn. But the Japanese were wondrous in war. The earth trembled with the weight of them. They assaulted Chü-jung, and Chü-jung fell. Colonel Wakizaka of the 9th Foot honored Kanamori with a message: Prince Asaka himself had heard of the wager with Kurusu, and wished them both luck and glory. Prince Asaka! General Matsui commanded the entire force, General Yanagawa the Tenth Army, Prince Asaka the Shanghai Expeditionary Army. This last was to proceed directly to Nanking. The Tenth under Yanagawa was to take Wuhu first and then join the assault. All this was in accordance with the orders of General Matsui, "The Way of Capturing the Walled City of Nanking." Kanamori read the orders again and again. They were a work of genius.

He read them prickling, with an acceleration of the blood, as though Nanking were a dragon to be slain. Also in Nanking were foreigners. Westerners, large hairy creatures lacking passion and nobility. They spoke always as if to servants. In Shanghai Kanamori had accompanied his colonel to a social meeting with several British. These British were of an unpleasant sandpaper color. It was soon apparent that their only concern was the interruption of commerce. Only one spoke of the women and children, of the random bombardments, and declined to drink, and turned angrily and left. The others apologized for him. Kanamori could not have said which he disliked more. They had a way of laughing. There were French, too, and Germans, and Americans. Kanamori scorned them all. The Chinese were an inconsequential people, true; killing them was like crushing lice or burning ant hills. Yet they were of Asia.

Kanamori's head count was sixty-five and his blade was nicked. A tall Chinese officer had fought back. Kanamori's men formed the customary circle, and offered this officer the customary sword, of the same length and weight as Kanamori's though surely inferior in workmanship. The Chinese took up the sword, slashed the air, examined the edge. His behavior was exemplary; he bowed, as did Kanamori. The Chinese offered to remove his helmet if Kanamori would do the same. Kanamori declined, and allowed him to remain covered. This officer's helmet was little more than a cooking pot; Kanamori laughed aloud. He remembered tales of the Chinese army twenty, even ten, years before, swarming to battle with a teapot and a paper umbrella hanging from the belt.

But this one fought. He danced and parried. He was larger than Kanamori and heavier, though surely not as strong. His gaze did not falter, nor his wrist tire. Kanamori's men fell silent. Kanamori panted but maintained a victorious air. The Chinese too huffed and puffed. Kanamori feinted, let his left foot seem to slip; the Chinese leaped and thrust, but Kanamori was already out of range, and as the weight of the sword carried the Chinese through his stroke Kanamori flew at him with the two-handed chop. The saber sliced through the Chinese helmet, skull, neck and some of the breast. It was the finest stroke Kanamori had ever delivered. The thrill of it raced through his arms, and to his heart. Even years later he felt it. But the helmet, or an angry human bone, nicked his blade. In the forging the steel of that blade had been folded double twenty times: a million bondings and more! And yet that nick!

Nevertheless Kanamori did not omit his prayer of thanks. As if to forgive the nick he uttered thanks to Yamato. There was no sword like a Yamato sword.

That was number sixty-five. Kurusu was on the right wing and they were too busy fighting, with no time for diversion and gossip. Kanamori would of course believe whatever figure Kurusu reported; Japanese officers did not lie.

This village was deserted. The Japanese had been cheated. They stormed through every house, even the reed huts. They smashed chairs and pots. Ito and Kyose set fires. In one house they found painted tiles of old men with wispy white beards. They smashed them with rifle butts. The men carried Arisaka 38's. Kanamori carried the carbine, the type 44. Two men tended a type-99 light machine gun. It was useless half the time, on the march, but in the occasional true skirmish it was invaluable. Supply was always a problem. The trucks and ammunition trains tried to keep pace, and each evening units tried to find them and restock.

In one hut they heard a cry. All came running, eager and ready. They heard movement then, and waited. Beside Kanamori, Ito hissed and hissed. He was a burly man who carried hissing too far, but Kanamori's breath too came thin and quick.

A creature emerged. The men shouted in rage and bafflement, and then all guffawed. It was a pig, a scrawny but brave pig. He charged two steps, then halted, then lunged this way and that. He shrieked. Kyose stalked him in the evening light, a scene from the comic opera, and the men cheered him on as he flung himself upon the animal. Tateno, a former apprentice butcher, cut the pig's throat. Bleeding copiously, the pig walked a few steps more. He walked calmly, even reflectively, like a skinny old gentleman out to enjoy the sunset, and then fell. Kanamori ordered Tateno to quarter him. They would not stop here; there was still twilight; when they did stop, they would cook pork. Fresh pork! It was little enough. The men's impatience was noticeable now. A mood was rising day by day.

Chü-jung was perhaps thirty kilometers from Nanking, and the assault on it offered more scope to conquerors. Here they found food, porcelain, buried silver, men to kill and women to enjoy.

Kanamori's head count reached eighty-nine. He was scrupulous. There were many boys of uncertain age. None below sixteen fell to his sword; those went to his men. Kojima preferred other sport: he released young men and shot them running. Day by day he increased the handicap; at first he caught them quickly, for the efficiency of it, but soon he gave them fifty yards, or a hundred, for the sport of it. The men held impromptu games. They released three at a time, left, center and right, and three would wait for Kanamori's signal, then fire. Success was not their object. If the three fell simultaneously, the game was won; if one missed, the target was allowed to escape. It seemed fair.

In Chü-jung they allowed themselves a foretaste of delights to come. The able-bodied men had fled. The Japanese felt justified in believing that they had fled to fight again, and therefore punished the remainder. Old men and old women were shot or bayoneted. Infants and young girls were bayoneted or spared capriciously. Women of a proper age—the definition was generous—were raped. Kanamori's platoon had only the one night. They took their pleasure for some hours, both doing and watching. Some women screamed and thrashed and had to be clubbed. Others lay like statues. Others wept. They were faceless. Ito claimed that those who resisted gave more pleasure. As if their beans were jumping, the vulgar phrase for a woman seized by sexual excitement. Ito would shout it at them: "Mame wa pinpin desu ka?" and then plunge and rip.

In the morning they were a tired but happy band. The surviving adults had to be killed, including all those women. They were the enemy. One knife, one hidden pistol, could cost the life of a Japanese soldier.

It was at Chü-jung that Kanamori felt the first swell of true conquest, of the deep inner meaning of war. There seemed a mysterious connection, a correspondence, among land, sky, houses and people. A village taken was a further patch of sky for Japan. A woman raped was a house burned. Stolen food tasted richer. Degrees and distinctions vanished. What had been Chinese became Japanese, and was thus ennobled. To suck at the

Japanese root was for these women all they would ever know of strength and valor, was to rise above the squalid nullity of their swarming insects' lives. Kanamori and his men shared a vision: the Imperial Armies sweeping west, an eternal invincible cavalry thundering across China as the Mongols had, subduing endless fetches of primitive land, countless villages, rivers, pagodas, shrines, stamping this decayed civilization everywhere with the sharp indelible seal of Japanese might, Japanese style, Japanese will, Japanese vigor, Japanese accomplishment!

Also, they would be the first to resist absorption, corruption, mongrelization. They would rule, purify. Out of this cesspool, this swamp, a new China, a new Asia!

Later they heard that the winter crop around Chü-jung had been destroyed, and the spring seed was not sown because there was none to sow, and bodies clogged the streets and alleys for some weeks. The population had been fifteen or twenty thousand. The Japanese boasted that the city had been seventy-two percent destroyed. No one ever knew precisely what this meant. Seventy-two percent of all buildings? of all commerce? of all labor? of all food and water? of all lives?

4 愛

Not one to pester customs and immigration, Burnham made his discreet way among the hangars and assorted aircraft. Duffel bag on his shoulder, he proceeded to the main terminal, a low, functional, ugly building, nothing Oriental about it. Inside, he saw Chinese air force officers, unexplained women of style and beauty, maintenance men. In a corner two wiry, ragged porters squatted, puffing alternately on one cigarette. Wooden folding chairs stood scattered; he thought of missionary congregations in the open air.

"Mr. John Ames Burnham, by any fortune?"

The man was scrawny. Tight features, clean-shaven, a few gray hairs. In a gown he would have been ordinary, but he was wearing a gray sharkskin suit. Burnham noted the white shirt, the dark-blue silk tie knotted by a miniaturist, the waistcoat, the trouser cuffs. Politely he answered in English, "Yes. I'm Burnham."

The man bowed a hair's-breadth. "Welcome. And I am name Inspector Yen of Peking police."

"Your fame has preceded you," Burnham said in Chinese. "Is your esteemed name the Yen of the nine divisions?"

Yen gaped, then blinked. "No," he managed. "My unworthy name is the Yen of two fires."

"Ah, the Yen of glowing fiercely," Burnham said, bowing now in his turn and making, he hoped, spaniel's teeth. "Of yen yen hei hei."

"But this is a pleasure. The last one had many orders to give and was deficient in the proprieties."

"My deficiencies are those of ignorance, and it is a mean guest who instructs his host."

"Those are fine words," Yen said slyly, "and your appearance is agreeable."

Burnham was ready: " 'Fine words and an insinuating countenance are seldom associated with virtue.' "

"Yü!" Yen was overjoyed. His eyes gleamed. "Now this is a

wonder! My life has taken a sharp turn for the better!"

Burnham went on gravely: " 'The progress of the superior man is upwards; the progress of the mean man is downwards.' "

"But this is not to be believed," Yen said. "Come." He gestured sharply. The two young smokers—little more than boys—dashed toward them, babbling. They were quoting prices. They could not know what the job was to be, and their price—they were old hands, and named the same figure—was about a penny American. "The sadness is not to be borne," Burnham said to Yen, "the looms are empty," which was an old phrase for hard times.

"But if one tear escape, there is no end to the weeping." Yen chose one of the boys and said, "Remove the gentleman's bag to the green car out front." The boy snatched up the bag and whisked away. The other stood resigned, then padded back to his place. Burnham wondered if at day's end they pooled their meager take; or were they believers in free enterprise and rugged individualism?

Outside again, Burnham rejoiced in the clear, frosty Chinese air, and the sky of Chinese blue. He knew about loving places. There were many place-mistresses, where one wasted money on intoxications and sweet dishes. And there was one place-wife, where tea was tastier than wine elsewhere, and rice than duck. "You wear no coat?"

"Bah," Yen said. "I have lived through wartime winters in Manchuria. The cold is my friend."

Burnham too had lived through a wartime winter in Manchuria, but withheld comment. His comrades in arms had been what Yen might call raffish elements. It was even possible that Burnham and his merry band of pickpockets, muggers and agrarian reformers had fought against Yen, or Yen's minions. Manchuria in 1945 had been cosmopolitan, a land of many skins.

Yen's car was, or seemed to be, a green 1939 Packard. Battered and peeling, it looked as if its owner had spent his Manchurian winters in it. The coolie had stowed the bag, and stood waiting. Burnham dug for money. "No, no," Yen protested, and tossed the boy a sheaf of the old bills, saying bitterly to Burnham, "it is worthless. As you say, the looms are empty. I gave him ten ten thousands in the old bills. It will buy him a bowl of noodles from some equally poor vendor."

They settled in, and Yen ran through a pre-flight check. He banged at the dashboard. He tapped the horn. He tested the lights. He inserted a key. The motor ground, shrieked, caught. "A miracle," Yen said. "I am not really so indifferent to the cold, you know. Why am I not as smart as you? Why do I not wear the quilted clothes of my own people? I have been corrupted by imperialism and persuasive tailors. I wore this suit to honor you, and am now paying the price. You have been in Japan recently? Do the Japanese now wear Western clothes?"

"They have begun to."

"A bad thing. And those are your own clothes that you wear? From a previous time?"

"I bought them here in 1945," Burnham said. "I was assured that they were the height of fashion."

Yen chuckled briefly. "They are still the height of fashion. They were also the height of fashion some centuries ago. Will you be overwarm if I activate the heater?"

"Not at all."

"In this antique spirit-cart the heater is the only reliable element."

"The car is perhaps what the Americans call a lemon."

"A lemon. But why a lemon?" Yen was pleased.

"Perhaps because its very essence is sour; perhaps because it sets the teeth on edge."

"Indeed! You see? You hear? Another miracle. My lemon shudders, barks, howls, and in the fullness of time even moves."

"After the first miracle, disbelief is vulgar," Burnham said solemnly.

They cut across a runway. Yen leaned on the horn; a work crew scattered. Burnham had known all his life that in China cars were driven by horn, yet he found himself wishing that Yen had driven around these men at work. He rebuked himself: that was a Western wish. Liberty, equality and fraternity were not Oriental inventions.

"You must tell me all about yourself," Yen said. The car banged into a pothole, rebounded, and chugged on. In this land of innumerable laborers, the airport road had once been smooth, and now it was pits and ruts. Rickshas crawled, veering aside at Yen's blasts. Burnham saw few real rickshas, the man-pulled ones; there were mainly the bicycle rickshas, the pedicabs, called in Peking three-wheelers, san-lun, except that in Peking endings were musically slurred, so it was san-luerh. He saw porters, farmers driving geese and sheep; even in winter, even outside a doomed city, even in a land with confetti for money, men and women cut cloth, contrived lanterns, farmed, bought, sold; life ran on, whatever the rules, climate or state of the roads. China was perhaps like Yen's lemon. Repairs to the national machine were made by hairpin, rubber band and string; yet it ran on.

Burnham recognized the onset of humility, or perhaps merely proportion. "I am of no interest," he said. "Only in that the lord of all under heaven saw fit to set me down in China."

"Then you are an adopted son of Han."

Burnham saw a Peking cart, and brightened: a covered cart pulled by a pony. In one of those he had traveled to see the Ming tombs. A quarter century ago! But what was a quarter century here?

They passed a teahouse, and he thirsted. There would be wooden stools and a long wooden table, and at the back a counter and many shelves, and on the shelves cheerfully colored canisters or paper cylinders full of tea; green tea from the southern provinces, and a little black tea, kept because near the airport an occasional exigent foreigner would stop in, and red tea for the hot months. Red tea being the hottest of teas cooled the exterior by a process of contrast. And the proprietor would bow and bustle, not like a lackey but like a man of worth. The world shimmered; a little boy's excitement swept over Burnham.

After a short time and some further chat, a village or two,

smoke rising, playful ruddy children in padded rags, Yen said, "As to the matter at hand."

"I know only that he has been seen. He has *perhaps* been seen."

"In the glove compartment is a report," Yen said. "I presumed to translate it into English, though my skill is less than rude. Or should I say more than rude? I hope you are not offended."

"Indeed I am not offended," Burnham said lightly. "I am grateful."

"In intent it was a courtesy."

"As it is in effect."

"It is not much to go on," Yen said gloomily, "but it is all we have."

1. 24/12/48 student of Peita, Tsing Hua and Yenching University, as well also minor institute of learning, go to street in Peking. More student than common in winter holiday because many student can not go home because occupation of town or province by red bandits.

2. Student manifest impatient on usual many matter. Many banner. Slogan are shouted. Oratory take place. Demand to treat with red bandits; supply coal to poor; raise money of lower worker; bring into city food from out side. Such are student, under influence of propaganda: not knowing lack of food is also out side!

3. Such parade and talking clearly inflame. Action of evil nature become probably, to wit, running in street, smashing, or invading government office.

4. Student attack police line and into office of National Judiciary on Wu-tiao Street.

5. Police and soldier forced to commence fire.

6. Student attack in great mass and some return fire. With forbidden arm and ammo.

7. This is *riot*. Crowd carry self, also moved by menace of police and army, to Square of May 4rd.

8. 9 student killed. 2 police. 4 police and army wunded.

Burnham asked, "Would they not vent their anger and disperse peacefully if ignored?"

"No." Yen was positive. "The city is almost surrounded, and is full of enemy agents. They inflame the students. Their goal is chaos."

That was surely true. Burnham read on. A Lieutenant Pao had been shot in the chest and beaten. Doctors and nurses had come running from the nearby Rat's Alley Children's Clinic, also known as the Beggars' Hospital. Dr. Nien Hao-lan was in charge, and the nurses, orderlies and stretcher bearers were of both sexes. Lieutenant Pao was half-conscious but recalled being rolled, or dumped, onto a stretcher; he looked up into the face of a beautiful woman—and also saw, gazing down at him with fierce and melancholy concern, the face of Kanamori Shoichi, who had once interrogated him after fighting in the hills of Anhui, and whose portrait even now adorned, or blemished, posters.

Medical and military officials assumed that Pao was delirious and hallucinating. An after-image of the posters, perhaps, the shock that followed a serious wound. But Pao's account rang true. It rang true to Burnham also. "Yes, I was raving. I recall raving. But there was no doubt. I had been set upon the stretcher. I saw the hills of Anhui and I also saw my hundredth year." Burnham loved this language: "after my hundredth year" was the elegant version of "when I am dead." He read on. "Yet I was not so confused as to be unaware of confusion, and Kanamori was no dream. No ghost. No phantom. His hair was long. He was wearing a surgical mask as so many do in the streets, but there was no doubt. I did not *think* it was Kanamori. I simply saw Kanamori." Lieutenant Pao was a soldier of valor and probity. Kanamori had not been seen for three years and more, but was known to have been in Peking when the war ended.

"I thank you for the translation," Burnham said, "and I believe Lieutenant Pao."

"So do I," said Yen. "Have you read the beggar's report?"

"No. I have just come to the advice and opinions of Dr. Nien."

Yen snorted.

Interrogated, Dr. Nien Hao-lan recalled nothing and no one out of the ordinary. The personnel who left the hospital were the personnel who returned. The doctor had never heard of Kanamori. There were so many war criminals. A friend of the doctor had been raped by an American marine. The marine had been sentenced to twenty years in jail after serious student demonstrations. Shipped back to the United States, he had been reprimanded and released. Why should a Kanamori be more momentous? Money was worthless and the populace starving: why should a Kanamori matter at all? The government was collapsing, the students were rioting, the generals were preparing to sell the city; what if a Kanamori lived or died? Through ten years of war Chinese regiments had broken, dissolved, scampered home, leaving whole provinces defenseless against these Kanamoris; who was more at fault? The army had just lost thirty divisions in Manchuria, half of them American-equipped; what was a Kanamori? Dr. Nien had spoken in unseemly terms.

"Now I come to the beggar," Burnham said. "Tell me about the beggars."

"About the beggars?" Yen was amazed. "They are the scum of the earth, and that is all there is to say. They are of many nations. I myself have seen beggars with light hair and blue eyes," he added in undisguised and creamy satisfaction. "There are a hundred thousand. They should be eliminated."

In May of 1946 a beggar called One Foot One Hand had presented himself at the police house off Lantern Street, near West Station, in the Chinese City.

"Almost three years ago," Burnham said. "Was this reported at the time?"

"It was not. Nor even set down in writing and filed. I learned of it only this week, from the Meng you will read of."

Filthy and lousy, and unprepossessing at his best, One Foot One Hand had been detained outside by the guards, but he blew the mustache—soared into a state of high excitement—and jabbered that he had seen a famous Japanese, and would tell the story to the proper official for the proper remuneration. There were many Japanese who had elected to remain in north China and Manchuria; the guards scoffed. A uniformed official emerged, sparkling with medals and insignia of rank. ("Formally bedecked, I cowed him," was the best translation of Superintendent Meng's remark, jotted in hasty grass script in the margin.) One Foot One Hand then demanded an enormous sum for the information, the equivalent of ten American dollars. Superintendent Meng had feigned amazement and outrage, but had scented truth, and finally promised some payment.

One Foot One Hand thereupon reported that in the time of his youth, some three years before, he had been an assassin, specializing in the Japanese who occupied Peking. He was then hale and hearty, and had not yet been maimed and mangled by an exploding boiler. He alone had accounted for six Japanese, and not one was an easy job.

Superintendent Meng instructed him to cease blowing the cow —bragging—and get on with his story.

One Foot One Hand stated that Major Kanamori of the Japanese occupation forces was now a beggar; that he had been gravely injured in a manner unknown to One Foot One Hand, sheltered and restored to health by the beggars, and permitted to remain as one of them. One Foot One Hand knew the face because he had spied upon Kanamori in 1945, thinking what a prize this one would be. Of course the beggar bureaucracy knew that the man was Japanese, but in the ancient tradition of beggars had asked no questions. Perhaps in all Peking only One Foot One Hand was certain of this identification.

And where was Kanamori now?

Alas, he had run to earth, none knew where.

Superintendent Meng scoffed. And was that the full extent of this anecdote?

Alas, it was.

Superintendent Meng gave One Foot One Hand the equivalent of ten cents American. One Foot One Hand protested and cried out to heaven at this injustice. Superintendent Meng ordered the sentries to drive him off. The sentries kicked the beggar's crutch out from under him and pushed him roughly. Superintendent Meng returned to his office and dismissed the incident from his mind. He had no idea what had become of the beggar or his banknote.

Burnham could guess.

Well, it was little enough. But Burnham's instincts spoke strongly. Kanamori was in Peking. Perhaps it was only a hope. Still. "I think Kanamori is in Peking," he said.

"Good," said Yen. "I too think so. And there is the Hsi Chih Men."

Burnham saw it half a mile off, the great arched gate in the massive city wall, the battlements above, and the tower. This was a moment of magic and solemnity. He was about to enter Peking, his place-wife. In summer, he remembered, there was usually a woman at work in the coalyard outside Hsi Chih Men. She shoveled coal dust and dirt from great heaps to small heaps, and then shaped coal balls. She was perhaps forty-five and worked naked to the waist; it was easier later to wash the layers of dust and grime off a body than out of a garment. To Burnham she had come to stand for the true China: sweating, matted black, denied by stark need even the rudimentary dignity of a shirt to cover her womanhood. She, and One Foot One Hand, and the boy porters at the airfield. China.

Now at the gate he saw shops and stalls, rickshas, more children, the bustle of small commerce: porters pushing small carts; an old man like a scholar seated at a low table covered with a mosaic of cloth scraps, wooden buttons, cigarettes loose and in packs; an outdoor barber, with a pan of water steaming over a brazier; a seller of steamed dough.

Then they were within the cavernous gate and the croak of the engine echoed off the walls like thunder, and then they were through, and in the Imperial City, and Burnham looked for an omen, the first living soul within the gates.

He saw two immediately: boys of about thirteen, in bits and pieces of uniform, carrying submachine guns.

Soon they rode beneath the West Four P'ai-lou, ornate arched

structures over the avenue, like frozen banners, and the lesser
p'ai-lou farther down, where in summer there had always stood
a vendor of persimmons. Now there was a seller of hot chestnuts,
and Burnham wondered if this was the same man.

"So," Yen asked, "what do you propose?"

"First that we work separately," Burnham said. "Among my
friends the presence of a policeman might require delicate and
time-consuming explanations."

"That was to be expected, and is acceptable," Yen said. "Nor
will I interest myself in their goings, comings or practices."

"What is this Rat's Alley Children's Clinic?"

"An improvised hospital. Its personnel seem less than respectable, though they do good work. Radicals, perhaps. The belief is
that somehow the beggars' union supports it, or at any rate con-
tributes."

"Have you investigated?"

Yen hissed uneasily, and pressed the horn; a cart full of pottery
swerved away. "The fact is," Yen said angrily, "that my superiors,
including the division of war crimes, show little interest in war
criminals. This time I went directly to the Americans with my
information."

"And they came directly to me." Burnham sighed, briefly re-
calling abandoned frolics. "And what causes this lack of interest?"

"I should think," Yen said judiciously, "a certain blurring of
the lines."

"Ah." Burnham spoke bluntly: "A certain Chinese presence
among the Japanese occupiers."

"Yes. In the sad book of war, some chapters are better left
closed."

"Then we are opening the book at a bad page."

"Yüü," Yen said, and glancing at him Burnham saw the classic
face of the disillusioned cop: weary, bitter, half regretting the
honorable and narrow path trod, the bribes not taken, the low
pay, the sandy rice and weak tea.

"There are sons of turtles everywhere," Burnham said gloomily.
"We have them too. Our own little fascists in high places, cheap

and greedy bastards well below the salt, who think themselves above the law."

"Ours are doomed," Yen said, "at least in Peking. A matter of weeks, months at most. But so am I."

"Will you stay in Peking?"

"Where could I go? I am a man of Peking. I am also a poor but honest policeman, and not an important official."

"Well, it may not be so bad."

"It will be barbarous," Yen said. "But as to the matter at hand."

"As to the matter at hand," Burnham said, "I propose to go to the beggars, and to the hospital. It is all we have to work with."

"Good. I will come to you tomorrow. At what time?"

"Six in the evening. In a crisis, anytime."

"One thing more. Not a thing: a person. We have a famous hater of Japanese in Peking. His name is Sung Yun and he is a merchant, councillor and member of the chamber of commerce."

"A distinguished gentleman. Why should he not detest the Japanese?"

"As you say. He is also a director of the Sino-American Amity Association. Beyond that one does not ask. He grew overnight like a mushroom. He is not a Pekinger. In 1944 the Japanese put a price on his head. A thousand pieces of gold. That is a memorable sum and commands attention; overnight the man was famous. But no one knew him. He surfaced just after the war and was a tycoon in no time."

"The underground hero and the tycoon were one and the same man?"

"Your mind works like mine. Somewhere in you lives a cop. Yes, it was Sung Yun. From down around the Yangtze somewhere. Plenty of friends in the government, and they all vouched for him. He basked in the praise of his fellow patriots. He is a great contributor of reward money, and is still basking. He, ah—"

"He would like to welcome me to Peking."

"Precisely." Yen was relieved. "He is— I have your confidence?"

"To the death."

"You exaggerate," Yen reproached him. "At any rate, Sung Yun is a bit of a busybody. He is a city father and a connoisseur of this and that, and surrounds himself with the beautiful things of life, including women, and now he must flee. He would obviously be out of place in whatever collective purgatory awaits China. He has asked to meet you."

"I am no more than a humble laborer in the vineyards of justice," Burnham intoned. "To be bathed in the light of the sun and the moon may blind me."

"Do not make fun of me. All cities suffer these benefactors." Yen's tone altered: "And he is not to be mocked. He is a rather powerful man."

And I can just see him, Burnham thought. He is short and round as a grape and not a wrinkle on him, and he wears a little red hat and a smile, but his eyes are bullets. His wife, if any, eats in the kitchen. "Whither does he flee?"

"Shanghai, one assumes."

"That will not be far enough, you know."

"It is but a way stop." Yen braked. "Defile it!"

"Exquisite courtesy," Burnham said. "I was not sure that you owned brakes."

"That is a honey cart," Yen said. "I am here to welcome you, not to bury you in night soil."

"My heartfelt thanks."

Carefully Yen accelerated. "So then, you will soon have an invitation. I hope you will accept it, if only because of my own association with the eminent gentleman. He has a male secretary who speaks perfect colloquial English. Of course," he added hastily, "in your case that is a superfluity."

"But it came in handy with the American military, in buy-sell, and the relief organizations, and maybe for a little social life with the diplomats."

"One sees that you have traveled a thousand li," Yen said smoothly, "and spoken with princes."

"Like all of us," Burnham said, "I have smiled at fools for a bowl of rice. One more will do no harm."

Yen growled assent, and they sat companionably silent as they passed through the gate with two names. They were leaving the Imperial City—most of Peking, with the colleges and institutes, the offices and yamens, the lakes, parks, churches, temples, hotels, foreigners—and entering the Chinese City, where stood the flea-bags but also the Temple of Heaven; many whorehouses but also the Temple of Agriculture; the Model Prison but also the Temple with the Tablet to the Foreign Dead of World War I. Much of the Chinese City was specialty streets; Bead Street, Embroidery Street, Gold Street, the whole street given over to one commerce, fifty yards of competitors eyeing one another shrewdly and fixing prices when possible. In the Chinese City were many beggars, thieves and opportunists, also deserters, exiles and lepers.

To Burnham it was home. The Imperial City was modern and mannered, with much running water and electricity. The Chinese City was timeless and real and raunchy.

"It is not the neighborhood foreigners choose," Yen ventured.

"Probably the neighborhood chose me," Burnham said. They proceeded down Red Head Street, named not for a trade but for a notorious swindler of the Ming Dynasty, and entered Stone Buddha Alley by the east mouth. It was barely wide enough for the car. "There," Burnham said. "With the small balcony." In the old days there had been a small balcony opposite also, an easy jump for a fleeing thief or a tracked husband, and many decades ago on those balconies painted women had sat in summer, cooing and coy, chirping at passers-by, and Burnham's destination was still called the Willow Wine Shop. Why the willow stood for venery was an ancient Chinese mystery. Venery! The hunt! A tickle of lust regaled him in this city of sweet foxes. Tally-ho!

"My number," said Yen, passing him a scrap of paper.

"There will be few telephones in this quarter."

"Nevertheless. Now, as to Kanamori's appearance—"

"I know what he looks like."

"You have seen photographs?"

"I have seen Kanamori," Burnham said.

Sunday, 12 December 1937. At dawn Kanamori stood on the slopes of the Purple Mountain and pissed down at Nanking. At the tomb of Sun Yat-sen. A correspondent from *Nichi-Nichi* came to interview him. Kanamori told of the nicked blade, of the enemy cropped like wheat, of rising emotion among the men, a quickening of the breath and blood as when the leopard nears the hart. Smoke drifted to them, and the reporter was alarmed. Kanamori calmed him: a unit below was burning brush to smoke out the Chinese rats. Bullets hummed and buzzed; the two men withdrew, Kanamori reassuring the reporter: Kanamori was invulnerable.

By now Kurusu claimed a score of one hundred and six. Kanamori claimed but one hundred and five. How to say who passed one hundred first? Impossible. "You will put this down," Kanamori said. "Kanamori demands that the goal be extended by fifty. Ha!" The pencil flew.

Kanamori could see museums, universities, tile roofs everywhere, railroad stations, factories, canals, hotels, an airport. And the great highway, the Yangtze. All this falling to the Imperial Armies. The 9th Mountain Artillery Regiment. The 36th. T'ai-p'ing Gate below. Chung-shan Gate. Two blimps riding the sky. City walls. His men trembling. "Temples," Tateno said. "There will be temples. Objects of gold."

"There will be women," Kyose said. They were on the march now, and had stopped to rest at a bus station. Posters: *Resist the Invader! Water the land of your ancestors with the blood of the monkeys!* "There will be rows and rows of women," Kyose said, "all on their backs with the legs apart, and on the great hairy bush a little sign that says 'Japanese spoken here.' "

The joke and the laughter spread like a fever. Men rolled and slapped and shouted "Japanese spoken here." A car rattled up to them and halted, and they saw their captain and major, and the major asked why the laughter. Kanamori stepped forward, saluted and stood like a stake. He told the truth; the captain and the major clucked. How many heads, Kanamori? One hundred and five. And Kurusu? One hundred and six. Then who—? We cannot know. The new goal is one hundred and fifty. The captain and the major approved, and even smiled. The car raised dust. "Oh laughers," Kanamori said to his men, "now be killers."

They entered the T'ai-p'ing Gate, Ito sprinting beside Kanamori. Ito potted an old man fleeing down an alley. The old man fell on his face, possibly in a patch of oil or excrement, and slid forward. The Japanese fired at all interesting targets: anyone who ran, any distant figure on a rooftop. The city resounded, like a city in festival, with the stuttering, racy rhythms of the twentieth century: boom-crack-boom-crackcrackcrack. Kyose took the first woman. This and not the city was their triumph. The woman was of no description, forty or fifty. They broke into a bead-and-bauble shop and the men held her for Kyose, who rammed her, "Aha! Aha!" It was turn and turn about then, and the woman barely conscious; but not for long. There was work to do. A piece of bridgework and two wooden teeth fell from the woman's mouth. Someone shot her and they went on. They skirmished to the rendezvous, to the open place where the Chu-chiang-lu met the Tung-ha-lu, and there the captain and major were waiting. Light casualties. The men drawn up, at ease, and the announcement then, the major breathing victory like a dragon breathing fire, and his voice like a temple bell: anchored in the Yangtze, an American gunboat called the *Panay* had been sunk by Japanese aircraft.

The silence was overwhelming; the men were stunned. Even the firing seemed to cease. Then arose a great shout, a roll of Japanese thunder, and thrice they roared "Banzai!" and thrice more, and thrice more, and men were weeping, Kanamori among them.

At the Willow Wine Shop Burnham refreshed body and soul. He sat opposite a scroll of ancient warriors on the march, or was it a funeral procession? Noon was well past, and he empty as a wine barrel after the wedding. Other diners stared once and then ignored the foreigner. He ordered Huang Hsiao-chieh ts'ai, or Miss Huang mixed vegetables; also Tientsin water buffalo, which was fresh fish; and beef with lotus root. With these he ate pickled turnips and drank hot yellow wine. In time his balances were restored, and his tides and breezes swirled harmoniously. Still thirsty, he called the waiter: "Huo-chi!"

The slim, attentive waiter hurried to him.

"Such food is for beggars," Burnham said. "I demand to see the proprietor."

"It is fresh," the young man protested. "For the gods! Prepared by the master himself! This is unjust!"

"Your greasy rat is an amateur," Burnham said firmly. It was an old phrase for the cook, and not much of an insult.

The waiter flung up his hands in outrage. "Then I will fetch him. But this is crazy. Perhaps one is a perfectionist," he muttered, padding away. "Perhaps one seeks horns on a newborn ram."

Burnham composed himself.

The waiter returned, still muttering. Behind him waddled a medium-sized middle-aged man of imposing girth, his face frozen in anger. "Now, where is this barbarian?"

The fat man stopped dead, then shouted what Burnham had known he would shout: "Defile you! Burnham! Bugger you twice over, you great foreign whore!"

Burnham was up and striding forward; before the dazed waiter and a few interested, villainous patrons, the two men embraced.

The landlord of the Willow Wine Shop was called Hai Lang-t'ou. Strictly speaking, that was not a name. It meant "Sea Hammer" and designated harsh, tough-talking men of the fishing villages outside Tientsin. But this one had chosen to discard his earlier name or names, surely for reasons of prudence and jurisprudence. He seemed an average, amiable fat man; Burnham had watched him dispatch Japanese prisoners, and knew he was not average. Nor was the Willow Wine Shop an average restaurant, but a house of major advantages: discretion, a loyal landlord and half a dozen exits.

"Still hammering," Burnham said.

"And you still poking the big nose into Chinese matters."

"What a welcome! You have a room?"

"The best. Ground floor back. Out the window and you have four alleys in seconds. If you are killed on the premises I cannot promise elaborate rites. Or perhaps," Hai asked wistfully, "you are merely a tourist this time?"

"Not a tourist," Burnham said. "But with luck there will be no violence."

"You said that outside Tsitsihaerh, and we lost a good handful."

"And the Japanese lost a power station."

"True." The word was spoken grudgingly but was close to praise. "Such an explosion that was! A glorious day. Nevertheless, seeing you here I wish I belonged to a burial society."

Burnham scoffed and complimented: "You have never thought twice about death."

"Or once," said Sea Hammer, "except at Tsitsihaerh. So." Hai looked him over. "You are three years older, and much sadder."

"And you are three years older and much fatter. You have put on twenty kilos, you old murderer. You rifleman. No more acrobatics on a stolen horse."

"Never again," Hai said sadly. "It comes of peace, and owning a restaurant. You will recall, however, that only the virtuous fatten."

"True. You are a good man, and deserve fat."

"Who knows? But in the old days we were all good men."

"They were good days. Fighting purifies."

"It does," said Sea Hammer. "These days it is all politics. A man feels useless and therefore lazy."

Burnham smiled; his heart was big with memories. "Come and sit. A cruet of yellow wine."

"Yellow wine! No, no. The white. And hot." Hai sent the waiter scurrying.

"Good," Burnham said, "but no competitions. A cup or two only."

"Oho. You have work to do. What can it be, with no more Japanese to slaughter?"

"Well, there is one more," Burnham said, "named Kanamori."

For some seconds Hai did not speak. Then he repeated the name. "Kanamori."

"Yes. But first we speak of you. Have you married? Are you surrounded by little Hais?"

"It would require more to surround me than could be got in three years," Hai said ruefully. "No, no wife. But"—he waved carelessly—"a woman or two. And you? You went home a hero, and married and begot?"

"Ha!" Burnham snorted fiercely and made dragon's eyes. "I was sent home with one medal and one rebuke. The medal for doing my job with you and those other cutthroats. The rebuke for maintaining that the wily Chinese should be left to find their own destiny. I told this to a general."

"To a general!" Hai was frankly shocked. "Then you deserve the reprimand. Courage is commendable; recklessness endangers all. And a wife?"

Burnham shook his head. "I have thought of it, but—"

"But courage is commendable," Hai repeated dryly, "and recklessness endangers all."

"I am not yet fully mature," Burnham explained. "I have not seen all the green willows, nor heard all the lutes."

"Green willows indeed," Hai said. "You were always a notable weasel, hankering for the young ones."

"Ah well, the young ones," Burnham said. "No more. In my country the young ones go on and on about their parents. Or their young men. They are winsome and cuddly but mistrust the bed and make excuses."

"Barbarous. No wonder you are sadder! We never told you this, but we called you Upper Fish, because at critical moments you were always to be found—if you were to be found at all—making the fish with two backs."

Burnham was vastly pleased. "I think 'superior fish' would have been kinder," he said reproachfully. "How quickly we come to the subject! Is there nothing else to speak of?"

"There is plenty to speak of," Hai said glumly. The waiter set down a cruet and two small porcelain cups, and poured. "There is bad money and a useless war, and trade has fallen off." He raised his cup: "Kan i pei!"

"Dry cup!"

They tossed them off. The liquor was a hundred and fifty proof and almost boiling. Burnham had accustomed himself to thinner potations; when this rammed his belly he swelled like a volcano and erupted immediately. "Woff!" he said, and tears sprang to his eyes.

"Good stuff," Hai said. "How was your meal, in truth?"

"The best. You were always hungry. Skinny as a snake and ravenous. A restaurant seemed the natural thing. But if anything, the food has improved in three years."

"I am unworthy." Hai bowed in place. "Hsü! You are back."

"And glad of it," Burnham said. "For Peking men there is no other city."

"True." Hai hesitated. "And you have work to do."

Burnham nodded.

"Then I suppose it must be done quickly."

"Yes," Burnham said. "Before—"

"Before the posts crack and the lintel falls. Well, let us see now: who owes who?" Hai replenished the cups; they sipped.

"Memory dims," Burnham said. "You pulled me out of the freezing river."

"You held the monkeys off at that monastery."

"You persuaded Li Tu to trust me."

Hai shrugged. "You took a bullet meant for me. I owe you a life."

Burnham too shrugged. "We are surely even."

"Then let us begin again. How can I help?"

"You know that Kanamori has been seen?"

Again Hai was silent for some seconds. "Yes, I heard that."

"I am to find him."

"And?"

"And take him back."

"Do you know why?"

"Why?" Burnham showed surprise. "He is a famous villain."

"And that is all?"

Now Burnham set down the cup. "Ah. Then there is more. What are you telling me?"

"That you must not hunt a tiger with bird shot."

"And what more?" Burnham drank. "Listen, old Hai, this is a serious matter. Do not send a blind man to pluck this tiger's whiskers."

"I have never seen Kanamori. I have heard that he is here. Also that he has something—or knows something. A villain, yes, but villains are a copper a peck nowadays."

"And how have you heard this?"

"One hears. A customer here, an old friend there."

"And what does he know? Or what does he have?"

Hai frowned. "Your own people have not told you?"

"Not a word."

"Yü! A blind man indeed."

"Then unseal my eyes."

"I wish I could," Hai said. "Listen, there are always rumors, and the years exaggerate them. We had our own Kanamoris, you know; perhaps it is merely that he knows who they were, and has much to tell. I heard also that he had amassed wealth."

"Wealth? And carries it about in a bag?"

"No. Not money. What, I cannot say. Jewels? A hoard. He is said to have had a Chinese look about him."

"Yes."

Hai looked up sharply. "You have seen him."

"Yes."

"Ah. And if he passes for Chinese, how will you find him?"

Burnham shrugged. "Do you know a policeman called Yen Chieh-kuo? An inspector."

Hai made the mouth of a man who would spit. "A turtle egg. An unforgiving man and full of hate. A good policeman nevertheless. How do you know him?"

"He is the local expert on Kanamori."

Hai's face grew fatter, and he laughed like a goat. "Eh, eh, eh." His flesh trembled. "He is, is he? But my dear friend, no one will ever tell Yen the truth. He has not that easy way with common people. He is too stiff from bowing to his superiors, too canny from much desiring rank and emoluments."

"You know much."

"One hears."

"Is he to be trusted?"

"No. You should work alone." Hai was positive. "You move well by instinct. You found Isuzu."

"That was easy," Burnham said. "Journeying from town to town, handed along by men of good bones, drawing the countryside tight like a seine. Besides, he was afraid of the Russians. He bolted into my snare like a rabbit."

"Yet in his time he was a dragon. A scourge."

"No longer."

"Times change," Hai said. "Perhaps the wily Chinese should be left to find their own destiny."

Burnham did not answer immediately. "Kanamori was an animal," he said at last.

"So were we all. Dragons. Hares. Wolves and tigers. Weasels." Hai quaffed his wine and poured again. "Well, I will help all I can. Tell me, old friend, how long have you graced Peking?"

Indignantly Burnham said, "Not two hours. Would I let the sun set on old friends?"

"Old friends," Hai murmured.

Burnham let the silence hang, and sipped at his firewater. Hai seemed to pout, and went on slowly: "To see you is joy. You must not misunderstand."

"It is not that I misunderstand, but that I do not understand at all. You cannot want Kanamori to roam free."

"It is only . . ." Hai poured more wine.

"I am a mere barbarian," Burnham said, "and unpracticed in delicacies of speech."

"We owe the Americans so much. Perhaps too much." Burnham said, "Ah."

"How pleasant," Hai said, "how just, how inspiring, if we could now doctor our own horses."

"Yet this horse," Burnham said, "has not been found, much less doctored."

"After years of battle, herds of fallen steeds dot the field. Here and there one screams or whickers. To make him well, or to ease him out of life, is for those whose field it is."

"Then I insult your soup by pouring my own spices into it."

"You could never insult our soup," Hai said, "you who saved the pot. And yet. Listen, my friend: if your own life were at stake I would fling away my apron and take up my bow. But the Kanamoris of this world must settle their accounts with us and with no others. Understand, I know nothing, only rumor. But my heart whispers warnings and rebukes. You have slain your thousands by our side; to let you do more would be ungenerous, and would taste of shame."

"Yen was less sensitive."

"Yen is perhaps stirring a different soup."

"Ah."

"Kanamori is of no importance to the Americans," Hai said gently. "It is what he knows, or has. And that is more important to us, to us Chinese. It was Chinese, in China, that he killed and raped and robbed. Still"—Hai brightened—"I will do what I can. You will go doctor your horse, and when he is well, or dead, you will return here, and we will eat walnut soup and nutty pheasant, and carouse like warriors."

"Of course," Burnham answered, "without fail," and each man

masked the moment with a smile. "Now show me this famous room."

They crossed a tiny courtyard, ten steps, and entered the rear wing. Sea Hammer opened a wooden door, ushered Burnham into a pleasant room and demonstrated: he jammed the door shut behind them and shot the bolt. Burnham approved, and tossed his duffel bag on the huge bed. "A wooden bed. A stitched mattress. The bridal suite."

"As in a way it is"—Sea Hammer chuckled—"when I rent it by the hour. And a footlocker, and a chest of drawers, and a dandy little stove and a teapot—you see, 'The wine cups have been polished, and are impatient.' "

"Why, that is nobly said. You are kind to an old comrade."

"So. It is yours. I suppose you will be in and out at all hours. And I suppose"—he sighed dolefully—"you will entertain a lovely friend or two."

"You wrong me," Burnham protested.

"Ha! A bet?"

"No bet."

"What is your wish about unexpected visitors?"

Burnham considered briefly. With so little to go on he decided to welcome complications and possibilities. "Let them in. But warn me."

"As you say. Try to respect the reputation of the house. No dynamite or messy torture."

"I am a guest in your land," Burnham said solemnly.

"No, no, you are at home," Hai said, "you have made yourself one of us," and added, "as if floods and famine were not enough," and let himself out, with a last shake of the head and a mournful "Yüü!"

Burnham unpacked. He was not a tidy man but preferred not to live out of a duffel bag. The chest of drawers sufficed; he would reserve the footlocker for corpses and souvenirs. He stripped off the padded gown, tossed it on the bed, and went down the hall to the convenience. An Oriental toilet in a minuscule dungeon. Two little starting blocks for the feet, and you hunkered, and if you were lucky there was a chain somewhere to pull. He returned to his room, made his .38 comfortable in a shoulder holster, donned the gown, and practiced his draw. About five seconds minimum; the pistol was, for practical purposes, in storage. But he was an errand boy and not a cowhand. The knife, however, lodged in his left sleeve, might be useful. He bowed, crossed hands up his sleeves in the Chinese manner, and drew the knife with a flourish.

He stashed his money in an inner pocket and left his new home. No one molested him in the courtyard; he passed through the restaurant, nodded at the slim waiter, and stepped out into Stone Buddha Alley beaming in the cold glow like a village idiot. He drew his fur hat snug; a west wind whistled through the alley. He turned onto Red Head Street and was assailed by rickshas.

Only five pedicabs, really, but they surrounded him and the jabber was fierce. He waited. In time they quieted; it was after all necessary to learn the foreigner's destination before whacking him with a price.

"I would go to the Beggars' Hospital in Rat's Alley near the Eastern Handy Gate."

The screaming commenced. It was half an hour's ride at most. They were competing for a nickel. Four cents. Shrill cries. Jostling. Three cents.

Only one did not speak or move. He was a tall man, well-timbered and young, and beneath his tattered cloth hat his eyes were steady and even contemptuous.

"And what is your price?" Burnham asked him.

The others fell silent, shocked.

The large man did not answer for some seconds. He wore a short, padded black jacket, and black trousers bound by a legging at the ankle, and tattered cloth shoes bound to his feet by rags. His black hair hung lank.

"One half an American dollar," he said.

"That is a great deal."

"It is a long trip on a cold day. Good grazing makes fast horses."

Burnham nodded. "It will do." He stepped to the pedicab, a commodious double.

"What!" cried one, and then all of them: "What! Hsüü! Madness! A trick!" One voice detached itself: "Why, sir, why?" Burnham settled in. "It is not a trick. I am honoring pride."

"Pride!" They buzzed and exclaimed, and finally the voice rose again: "One whole dollar, then!" And in a cheerful chorus, "One dollar and a half! Two dollars!"

Burnham's man hopped to the seat and leaned into the pedals. They skirted the group and struck off down the street. Behind him Burnham heard a last wail: "An ounce of gold, foreign devil!" But by then his pedicab was warping smoothly into a calm sea of traffic.

Burnham sat back and inhaled Peking, rubbernecking his way to K'uang An Men Street and noting cloth shops, lamp shops, meat shops, a small shop specializing in white vegetables, a shop for small gods—so the sign said: SMALL GODS. Probably large gods had to be ordered in advance. He saw shops without signs. Soldiers patrolled in pairs. A bus racketed past, ancient, perhaps a week to live; fenders clanked and clattered, gouts of yellowish smoke stained its wake. Burnham saw a foreigner in Chinese clothes, and a Chinese in a velvet-collared overcoat, a surgical mask over his mouth. Two young men walked hand in hand. It was the Chinese way. In San Francisco they would be mocked or arrested. Smells came to him, the rich medley of the Orient. When he was out of China almost nothing was good enough to remind him of China, but now and then, once a year, he would pass a restaurant in a poor neighborhood, unsanitary, and a little whiff of the East would bruise his heart.

The pedicab lurched. Burnham heard a slap-slap-slap, and the screech of dry brakes; they halted. The driver sat. After a moment he dismounted heavily, and went to look at his front tire. He made a queer noise. Startled, suddenly disturbed, Burnham recognized a sob.

He stepped out. "What has happened?"

The man gestured. Burnham saw the tire, shredded.

"You have no spare?"

"Spare!" The voice was heavy with bitterness. "And now the wheel is bent."

Burnham joined him. "It cannot be repaired?"

"Repaired! Look at it. Defile it!" Tears stood bright in the man's eyes, but his gaze was steady on Burnham.

"You cannot patch it?"

"For the tenth time? Look again! Which is tire, and which is patch?"

Another pedicab whispered to a stop beside them, and its driver said, "Sir. You will transfer."

Squatting, his hand on the broken wheel, Burnham's driver scowled. "Go," he said. "The gentleman owes me nothing."

Burnham nodded. To the second driver he said, "Move along. I will stay."

The second man shrugged and pedaled away.

Again Burnham's driver said, "Defile it! Not even God sees the ricksha man."

"If I pay you now," Burnham said, "will you buy a new tire?"

"A new tire! A new tire is twice that." The driver defiled this misbegotten bugger of a wheel. He then defiled his government, his day of birth, and money too fragile even for use behind. "I will beg the price of a hank of rope," he finished, "and hang myself and have done with it."

"I think not."

"I am a large man and in two days have eaten but one bowl of noodles," the squatting man said angrily. "I have killed many men and now cannot keep myself alive!"

"What is your esteemed name?"

"My miserable name is Feng. It is not a lucky name."

"Well then, Feng," Burnham said, "we will walk to a bicycle shop and buy you a new tire, and have the wheel repaired."

Feng stood quickly. His chin rose, his eyes narrowed. "And then what? What does the gentleman want of me?"

"I want to go to the Beggars' Hospital in Rat's Alley," Burnham said reasonably.

Feng wiped his face with his sleeve. The bones of his face were strong; he reminded Burnham of the hardy Manchurians up by the Russian border. "The gentleman means this," Feng said.

"I mean it," Burnham said. "Without the poor, there would be no rich; the rich are therefore indebted."

"By the lord of all under heaven! I have lost a sheep and found an ox!" Feng drew himself up even straighter: "Foreign gentleman, I am yours to command."

Peking was dotted with bicycle shops; they were like bars in San Francisco. Burnham wondered how many pedicabs the city supported. Many thousands. The two men walked only two blocks. "My ricksha barn is over by the East Station," Feng said. "Fortunately, that is too far. They would only kick me and tell me not to return."

"Then the san-luerh is not yours?"

"Mine!" Feng went so far as to laugh. "Good sir, if I worked for a year, and did not eat, and went naked, and did without a roof, then perhaps I could buy a san-luerh. But by then," he added gloomily, "the money would be worthless."

"Well, you are in luck."

" 'When bad fortune reaches its natural limit, good fortune must follow,' " Feng said. "Though I do not believe that. It sounds well, but I do not believe it."

"It is the remark of an educated man," Burnham said.

"I learned it from my father," Feng said. "My father was a tiler."

"An artisan."

"And a good one."

"What became of him?"

"The Japanese," Feng said. "My father would not lick piles, so they killed him."

There were times when Burnham preferred English: "kissing

ass" was so much more genteel. "A tragedy," he said. "And your mother?"

"We had no money and no food and no nothing," Feng said sadly. "Shortly she went to the dark dwelling."

"Bad," Burnham said. "Defile them all, it is bad. Good men and women plant a willow slip and do not live to enjoy the shade of the tree."

" 'The morning cannot guarantee the evening,' " Feng said. "But here we are. 'Tun Kuan-kuang, bicycles and repairs.' "

Together they opened the wooden door and pushed the san-luerh into the shop. "Busy, busy!" cried a voice from the back. "Not today! Too busy."

Unabashed, Burnham enjoyed the fruits of imperialism. "Nevertheless," he said loudly, "you will repair this san-luerh immediately."

"Dogs defile your get!" the voice called. A figure loomed out of the shadows. "Moreover, be off— But sir!" Tun bowed. "If I had known! Please. You do infinite honor to my contemptible shop."

"I will do even more honor by paying in foreign money," Burnham said.

"A dazzling notion," said Tun, and then asked swiftly, "Of what country?"

"America."

Tun bowed low. " 'The flowers blush, and the moon hides her face.' "

"You fool!" Burnham said. "That was said of a beautiful woman, not of a rich man."

Tun bowed again. "You are no American, sir, and not even a foreigner. You are of course a scholar."

" 'He who lives by flattery,' " Burnham said coldly, " 'works harder than the peasant.' "

"Sir." Tun bowed a third time. "You have but to express your wishes."

"My man will explain," Burnham said.

Feng stiffened for a moment, but quickly saw that this was

Burnham's joke; he turned to Tun and said, "Now see here. We require the wheel to be straightened and weak spokes replaced, and then a new front tire."

"Without delay," Tun said. He knelt to examine the catastrophe. "Half an hour," he said. "Perhaps less."

"We shall return," Burnham said, and to Feng, "Come along."

Outside, Feng asked, "Where does the gentleman take me?"

Burnham pointed across the street. "My horse needs oats."

Feng hung his head. "But I cannot. This passes the bounds."

"I need to drink tea," Burnham said. "While drinking tea I need someone to chat with. There is no reason why you should not enjoy a bowl of pork-liver-rice-soup while you oblige me. Come. We will drink and peck."

Feng heaved a great moan, and followed Burnham to the dingy restaurant.

It was the kind of place Burnham had always loved: dark, dirty, the wooden tables and stools worn shiny even in the gloom, the proprietor bald, the customers shabby. There was, as this foreigner entered, the customary sharp, total hush, followed by the customary awkward resumption of low gossip. Burnham and Feng took a table and ordered. Waiting, Burnham eavesdropped. A man who could not eavesdrop was not truly at home in any language. The customers were speaking of money, or the lack of it; of the Communists, or the lack of them; and of heating, or the lack of it.

Feng devoured his meat soup and several cups of tea in what seemed a few seconds. Burnham clucked and ordered another for him. Embarrassed, Feng asked, "Will the gentleman not?"

"No. I have eaten, and sworn a vow not to stuff myself like a foreign pig."

"Vows must be kept."

"You too have sworn vows?"

Feng made big teeth. "I vowed to kill five Japanese for my father, and five for my mother."

"And did you keep that vow?"

"I am one short."

Well, I may be able to help you, Burnham thought. "And the enemy has departed."

"The Lord of all under heaven will forgive me."

"And what of the future?"

Feng shrugged. "One must wait."

"What is the gossip?"

"Oh, the city will fall. It is already sold." With two fingers Feng made the sign for the number eight.

Burnham nodded recognition. The Red Army, after a reorganization in 1937, had become the Eighth Route Army. They, and later the New Fourth Army, had fought hard against the Japanese; men and units had died in their tracks if need be. Some of the Nationalists also had fought well, but more often whole regiments vanished like dew in the heat of war. It was a bitter joke, perhaps a slander but much circulated, that the only time Chiang Kai-shek attacked was when he attacked the Eighth Route and New Fourth. Then too he was beaten.

The proprietor slid a fresh bowl before Feng.

"And how do you know that the city is sold?" Burnham asked.

"Well"—Feng addressed his soup more sedately this time— "perhaps two months ago the government in Nanking announced that Peking would hold out to the last man." He waved his chopsticks. "That was customary and meaningless. The gentleman surely knows about such matters."

"It is international practice."

"So, so. What is more important, General Fu said the same thing last month."

"That is Fu Tso-yi."

"That is Fu Tso-yi. A Shansi man and a shrewd country boy, though being a general he is now over fifty." Feng smacked his lips. "Words cannot express the savor of this soup. Chu kan t'ang fan! Rice is scarce, you know. In the south is nothing but rice. Not so here."

"Go on about Fu," Burnham said.

"Well, when he says Peking will be defended to the last man, he means that the Communists must pay a stiff price for it. The Communists said immediately that they could walk into Peking when they chose. That meant, Fu must not expect too much. Well, they are all around us now, out past the Summer Palace, out by the Western Hills, and the railway to Tientsin is useless. So in a week or two or three, or two months if the weather is bad and movement difficult, the Communists will come marching in, and General Fu will greet them, and will be made a general in their armies and placed in charge of boots, or cooking."

"And what will happen to you?"

Feng slumped, blew a great razzing whicker, tapped his chopsticks level on the wooden table and scratched his head with them. Finally he said, "I will drive a san-luerh. Nothing will change for the poor. Nothing has ever changed for the poor."

Outside the restaurant Burnham was approached by two beggars, both male, both in tatters, scruffy, doubtless diseased. Feng moved swiftly, interposing himself and crying, "Be off! Be off!"

"Wait," Burnham said.

The beggars stood humbly, with cupped hands.

Burnham was uncertain, but took the plunge. "Here," he said, "is money," and he passed them a bill each. "I am living at the Willow Wine Shop in Stone Buddha Alley off Red Head Street, and I have come to Peking to speak with Head Beggar. Do you understand me? The kai-t'ou. The chi-t'ou."

Feng made round eyes.

The beggars might have been deaf.

"You will tell the others," Burnham said. "I have money for Head Beggar."

The beggars exchanged a glance and cringed.

Burnham shrugged. "Feng: you too. Let Peking nourish this report: there is a foreigner who seeks Head Beggar."

"It is madness," Feng mumbled.

"Probably," Burnham laughed. "Now let us chaffer with Master Tun."

*   *   *

The san-luerh was ready. The bill came to two dollars. Burnham offered two American bills, and Tun almost jigged in delight. He rushed to the greasy window and held the bills to the glow. "This I recognize," he said. "Your Confucius, and the number one. Sir, it has been my pleasure. I trust I have given satisfaction, and that you will one day renew your custom."

Feng was inspecting the wheel. "It is well," he said.

Burnham announced regally, "My expert says it is well. Why should I not renew my custom? I thank you, Master Tun."

"My poor shop is honored."

"The satisfaction is mine." And murmuring this and smiling that, Burnham and Feng drove out the wide door.

At the Beggars' Hospital Burnham offered Feng his fare. Feng scowled, muttered and finally blew his nose onto the street. "No, I will not," he said, and then shook his head, unable to explain.

Nor did he have to. Burnham had not expected this tough one to accept money now. "Well, it was a small justice," he said. "You lost father and mother. You work like a horse. One tire seems little enough recompense."

"Justice should not be the gentleman's burden alone," Feng said.

"You have been a good omen on my first day. I owe you for that."

"No, no, no," Feng said, and then did an unusual thing, daring, unheard of. He set a hand on Burnham's shoulder. "Long life and prosperity," he said. "I will burn paper for this."

"Strength and courage," Burnham said, "and no more talk of hanks of rope, hey? See you again."

"See you again," Feng said. It was the traditional farewell in Peking, and in most of China, and Burnham always marveled at the optimism of it.

7

In Nanking all resistance ceased on the night of Monday 13 December 1937. The Japanese armies had successfully completed one of the most brilliant campaigns of modern warfare. But the men were bitter to hear that resistance had ceased. The rifle was loaded and cocked, the finger on the trigger; peace was too much to bear. Victory alone was not enough; some historic accumulation of repressed savagery demanded slaughter. A city of one million, and no one to be found who would resist! More: the foreigners—a handful, righteous, tireless, arrogant even—had designated a Safety Zone, as if their embassies and universities and missions were holy places not to be defiled by rude Japanese. The major said to pay no attention.

Anyone running in the street was shot or bayoneted. Small fires persisted. The city smoldered.

In squads and platoons the Japanese patrolled. They sought the mark of the military hatband, and on the hands the rifleman's calluses. Firing squads were formed and re-formed. The crackle of rifle fire was incessant, resistance or no resistance.

Also they drank. They smashed wine shops. They found rice wine, and the stronger kao-liang wine, red wine and white made by the foreign fathers, whiskey and gin and brandy. Kanamori remembered much local brandy, plum brandy and even banana brandy. They did not drink to stupefaction, nor stagger and fall; they drank to exhilaration, and their strength grew. Tireless and lawless and heartless, they roamed and swaggered.

They bashed in doors at random. Families huddled. They shot the men and raped the women. They raped girls of ten and grandmothers of seventy. Akata raped a dumb girl. She rasped and shrieked "Khee khee khee khee," and at last only a bubbling gurgle. In one house they shot the owner and a man kneeling for mercy behind him. The wife struck Tateno; he bayoneted her. There were two daughters about fifteen, and the men stripped them. A grandmother emerged and hobbled on bound feet to embrace the girls. One of them had a pimple on her face, high on the cheekbone, beside the eye. Kanamori saw that pimple for years. They shot the grandmother. They raped the girls turn and turn about. Kyose found a bamboo flute and raped one with that. Then he blew a tune on the flute. The younger girl screamed and screamed; they stabbed her. Then they were hungry. They left the girls, probably dead.

In the street they found civilians milling, darting, seeking shelter. Some they shot; from some they took wristwatches, fountain pens, jewelry. One day Kanamori took charge of forty Chinese soldiers now claiming to be coolies. He roped them together, doused them with gasoline and set fire to them. Good sport. Bayonet practice, too; they nailed men to wooden doors by the hands and feet for bayonet drill. They prodded fifty women onto trucks and drove them to a factory yard—a large pottery—where they performed a festival of rape in the open air. And from the Judicial Yüan where three hundred disarmed policemen awaited orders, Kanamori marched them to the West Gate. The policemen were ordered to sit inside the gate, hands on heads. Outside the gate a steep slope dropped off to the canal. The police were divided into groups of one hundred. Outside the gate machine guns were positioned for crossfire. The policemen were forced through the gate at a trot and taken in the crossfire. They tumbled into the canal. Those who did not tumble were bayoneted. Next some thousand male civilians were taken to Hsia Kuan on the bank of the Yangtze. They were seated facing a battery of machine guns at forty meters. After an hour a major arrived and ordered the gunners to open fire.

Families tried to cross the river in small boats. Kimaya of the 9th, an acquaintance of Kanamori, commanded a small motor launch and intercepted them. One time his squad took a boat and raped some daughters before the whole family. A brother attacked the squad and was dumped overboard; they paused to watch him thrash and drown. Then they ordered the father to rape his daughter. The family jumped as one and was drowned.

One girl's parents were killed as she was raped, all three in full view of one another. Small groups of men were surrounded and ordered to wrestle. The losers were bayoneted; the winners were to wrestle Japanese. The first to wrestle a Japanese lost and was freed. Thus encouraged, the next contestant scarcely fought; they shot him. Thus encouraged, the next fought like a tiger and won; they shot him.

The Chinese were to uncover at the sight of a Japanese. The Chinese were to yield sidewalks to the Japanese. The Chinese were to call the Japanese "sir." Those who did not were shot or bayoneted, some few stabbed with a knife or their throats cut. By the third day the streets were lined with corpses.

The Bible schools were favored settings for rape. Altogether twenty thousand women were raped. One woman was raped thirty-seven times.

Near the north mouth of Rat's Alley the hospital gate stood open; on the stone wall beside it a small plaque proclaimed CHILDREN'S CLINIC. Burnham entered. The building was without character, and might have been a warehouse or the home of some municipal department. It stood two stories high, a large square paved courtyard at its center, and in the courtyard were only a bench, a distressed and naked tree, the glow of smooth stone, and a cumbersome two-wheeled wagon, as would be drawn by a donkey or pushed or pulled by a man.

Burnham hesitated. At the sound of a car he turned; in the alley a jeep passed—soldiers or police, he could not tell. To either side of the entryway a door: to the right EMERGENCY, to the left ADMISSIONS. Burnham faced left and knocked. After a moment he turned the knob. Modern and foreign: a knob, not a latch. He entered an office. One feeble bulb, tables, filing cabinets, a desk, an empty room. Within, above, he heard faint stirrings. He waited.

He waited ten minutes, went outside, and crossed to the emergency entrance. He did not knock, but let himself in. It was a room much like the other, but with two rude treatment tables and many cabinets. At one of the cabinets stood a woman, dumpy, wearing a gown and a surgical mask and cap; she turned, and her glasses glittered at him. "What is it?" she asked sharply.

"I am looking for Dr. Nien Hao-lan," he said.

"Dr. Nien is very busy," the woman said.

"This is important," Burnham said.

"Important! Are you sick? Bleeding? Wounded?"

Burnham was shocked at the harsh, direct address; it was un-Chinese. "No," he said.

"Then come back in the evening," the woman said. "Dr. Nien has wounded students to treat."

"Evil times," Burnham said.

"Evil times! Rotten police! Corrupt soldiers! There is no time now. Come back later."

Burnham was oddly appalled; this woman was not even intrigued by the presence of a foreigner. "I can wait," he said.

"No, you may not wait!" she cried. "Dr. Nien has no time now for conversation. Dr. Nien needs plasma! Dr. Nien needs antibiotics!"

Burnham saw with dismay that she was weeping; behind her glasses tears flowed.

"Dr. Nien needs gut and anesthetics!" the woman went on, shouting and sobbing at once. "Dr. Nien is treating a twelve-year-old girl for venereal disease, with the primary lesion in the armpit! The *armpit*, do you understand? We have rickets and kala-azar and dead children in every ward! We have frostbite and malnutrition and we are all worked to death and have no time for foreign tourists! Now go away! Go away! Will you please go away!"

"Forgive me," Burnham said, feeling for a moment that it was truly all his fault; and he went away.

He stepped out into Rat's Alley, grieving for a whole nation, and saw a pedicab and knew that it was Feng's. Feng sprawled at ease in the passenger's seat, but hopped down immediately and bowed.

"I was not fooled," Burnham said. "And this is kindness indeed, but you must not spend a lifetime thanking me."

"To leave the gentleman to others is to sully my family name," Feng said. "Where would the gentleman go now? To the Willow Wine Shop, perhaps?"

"Not at all. Start for the old Pei-t'ang Cathedral." Burnham settled into the pedicab and said, "Sooner or later you will have to take money. You will have to eat and sleep."

"That is prophecy. Each hour is new and uncertain." Feng mounted his bicycle.

The air was cool on Burnham's face. "You will be cold."

Feng turned to make big teeth: "Not for long. The gentleman is large."

They rolled off west. Burnham asked, "How did you kill the Japanese?"

Feng said, "With the knife."

"Well, you have the look of a fine villain."

"It is as the gentleman says."

Burnham cursed himself. This man in rags could not return banter for banter, could not afford humor, possibly could not recognize it. To a slave who has been hungry long enough, a rich man's laugh is one more cold wind. "Have you a knife now?"

"I sold it," Feng said, "to eat."

"Then stop at a cutler's," Burnham said.

Now Feng turned. "May I ask, how many years has the gentleman?"

"Thirty-five," said Burnham. "And my horse?"

"Twenty-two. The gentleman is therefore a decade wiser and more, and we shall stop at a cutler's."

"Perhaps a cutler who does not cater to emperors."

"But to the worm people."

It was the old, galling game of the common folk. "To the worm people," Burnham said.

"A sinister future looms," Feng said. "I trust the gentleman will see to my enlightenment."

"The gentleman himself walks in darkness."

Feng groaned into his work. Over his shoulder he asked, "Is it the cathedral that the gentleman wishes?"

"No," Burnham said. "It is another sort of religious house. A convent, you might say."

Feng cackled. "With a mother superior. Is that it?"

"That is it." Burnham made wolf's teeth in the late light.

"Then perhaps I know the place. It is the only such house so far north. The rest are down south in Whore Street."

"A row of chapels. There were ninety of them before the war."

"Every religion has its truth, and every truth has its religion," Feng said. "Is the gentleman a Christian?"

"No. The Christian in me died young."

"Christians are good people."

Burnham was scandalized. 'What do I hear?"

"They give away hot soup."

"There is much to be said for that," Burnham conceded.

"I think perhaps the Christian in the gentleman is not yet dead," Feng ventured.

"Do not confuse Christianity with decency or goodness," Burnham said severely. "I am a nice fellow. That does not make me a Christian. Christians have been killing each other and everybody else for two thousand years. They once gathered together thirty-five thousand of their own children for a distant campaign to recover their holy places. They assembled the children in a seaport. They then sold them into slavery."

"But who does not? Still, thirty-five thousand is a large number. And who bought these slaves? Other Christians?"

"Well, no," Burnham said. "Mohammedans."

"Ah, Mohammedans. Here we have many," Feng said. "From the northwest they come, and they despise dogs and do not eat pork. I carried a rich Mohammedan once." He paused.

"Go on."

"The gentleman does not object to conversation?"

"The gods have granted me little else this day." Burnham sighed. "Go on."

"Well, he grew hungry, and ordered me to halt by a seller of meat patties. On the seller's tray were three rows of patties. 'And what is this row?' asked the Mohammedan. 'Pork,' said the vendor. 'And this one?' 'Pork,' said the vendor. 'And this one?' 'Pork,' said the vendor. My Mohammedan returned to the first row. 'And this one?' Now the vendor looked one swift look at the man's face and clothing. 'Oh, that is beef,' said the vendor. 'Oh, beef,' said the Mohammedan, 'and why did you not tell me so? I will have two beef patties.' So much for religion."

"So much for religion," Burnham agreed, laughing; it was an old story but still funny, and enriched by artful telling. "And that is why I will do my praying at Aunt Chi's convent in the Street of the Blind Weaver."

As Feng pedaled through the dark streets, rich odors gratified Burnham; his belly growled. Here and there a sequin of light glittered, or a shaft shot from an open window. "If the gentleman offend against heaven," Feng offered, "to whom will he pray?"

"The question is reasonable," Burnham said. "But you will turn me grumpy. At the moment I pray for silence."

Feng pedaled on; his new tire whispered and hissed.

Outside Aunt Chi's, Burnham tried again to force money on Feng; again it was refused. "If I am not with you again in half an hour," Burnham cautioned him, "do not wait. You must eat. Where do you sleep?"

"If the gentleman does not return I must find another fare and eat on that. I can sleep in the ricksha shed." Feng was adamant: no money.

Burnham feigned disgust. "What can be done with such a horse?"

"If it is to be the morning, then at what hour and where?"

"I cannot tell," Burnham said. "Perhaps eight. At the Willow Wine Shop. But first wait here for half an hour."

"As the gentleman says."

Burnham tugged at a bell. Again Feng ranged his ricksha along the wall, clambered aboard, sprawled, and seemed to sleep. Beyond the heavy wooden gate a voice called, "Who is it?" and Burnham returned the traditional answer: "It is I."

The gate creaked open a crack; a small boy peered out, held up a lamp, and sucked in his breath at this apparition: a foreign devil in local garments.

Burnham asked, "Who are you?"

The young one drew himself tall: "Number One Boy," he said in English.

"Oh God, and you're proud of it," Burnham said. "Towel boy in a Peking hussy hut, and you're in the upper tenth economically. You'll miss the dirty foreigners, won't you? You're a ranking anti-Communist, aren't you? How old are you? Seven? Eight?" He said all this in English. The boy goggled, and finally bowed.

Burnham went on in Chinese: "Is Aunt Chi alive and well? Is she here?"

"She is within," the boy said, "and is my benefactress." Defiance crossed his face.

"She is my benefactress too," Burnham said soothingly. "Indeed, more; I hope I may call her my friend."

The boy mellowed, and stood aside. "Please come in."

Burnham brushed past him into a small courtyard. Aunt Chi's was a functional residence: no spirit wall, no lacy carvings, no airy compound, only a little front garden and the Chinese equivalent of a three-story brownstone. It had perhaps been a rectory once, or a dormitory for traveling civil servants.

Burnham crossed the garden, and in those few steps he warmed; his eyes brightened; his blood fluttered, thickened; he seemed to swell. He had come home. He walked in Peking at dusk, and there was no city as beautiful by day, or as mysterious and overwhelming at night. In the shadowed garden spirits prowled. Silence crouched. He held his breath. He had come so far, and now approached the magician's booth, and enchantment. His mind drew no images, but he walked through a dim gallery of women, and of womanly delights: the sweet round faces, the sweet smooth skin, the sweet small breasts, the surpassing warmth of thighs, the molten moment of union. He was approaching the finite but unbounded universe of the senses, and the stars above him seemed hung from a low and private sky; here he was safe, and could seek the only love he knew or trusted, the shared annihilation. Here he was not foreign; here he was little boy Burnham, offering the dewy, downy, silken submission of the soul, the ultimate, brimming fusion of yang and yin. He stepped softly toward a luminous dream.

And entered a parlor, and a nightmare. Once gold, the room stood gray, even in lamplight; once richly painted, richly hung with scrolls and drawings, the bare walls shed flakes and curls of cheap plaster. The chill room repelled him. He turned sharply to the boy: "You say Aunt Chi is well?"

"I will fetch her," the boy assured him, and padded away.

Burnham rubbed his hands and wrinkled his nose in dismay. He sniffed: a faint mist of tea, of cooked meats and spices. One lamp only. Where were the rosewood tables, the cloisonné cigarette boxes? And here in the parlor, the antechamber, the scrolls had been decorous: finches, bamboo, calligraphy, a mountain in a red-gold mist. All gone.

The far door quavered open and he saw her, a little heron of a woman, ancient yet ageless, face and hair all cobwebs, blouse and trousers always red silk, her feet bound, shoes not four inches long. He was assailed by pity—this old bawd, silenced, impoverished, doomed—and did not know what to say.

Not so Aunt Chi. "Burnham!" she shouted, like a bull bellowing. "Oh you weasel! Oh rutting elephant! Oh liar! Oh thief of sweets! Oh scourge of maidenheads! You owe me twenty dollars!"

Burnham strode forward, his arms open: "Oh my dowager empress! My forger of virginities! My second mother! You old bustard!"

She tottered a step or two and suffered his embrace; she had suffered worse. Pulling away to read her features, Burnham saw that her deep brown eyes were clouded, and her lips drawn farther back from black gums. On her left cheek rode the mole he remembered, sprouting two hairs like antennae.

"Nn, nn, nn," she agreed. "I age. It is better than not aging. And you? Your health? I suppose you are covered with plum blossoms?"

These being chancres, Burnham chuckled and winced at once. "You never change. You are the most evil and cynical bawd it has ever been my good luck to know."

"Bawd, is it! A business like any other, my son. Younger Brother"—she turned to the boy—"tea in the salon."

The boy had lingered in the doorway, and his astonishment was obvious; he scurried away.

For a moment they did not stir or speak.

"Times are bad," he said at last.

"We have fallen low," she said. "No more singing girls. Only t'u-ch'ang."

Local whores. "But I see none here."

"I am a madam, not a procuress. Bustard indeed! So I retired. Come into the other room."

He followed her.

"Close the door," she told him. "Heat flees."

This room too was dead—the grand salon, once a long room and jolly, with real wallpaper in a pattern of golden grass and the walls hung with works of art: *The Magistrate's Wife, Disheveled, Pleading with her Mongol Captors; The Monk and His Pretended Novice; The Virgin's First Sight of the New Household God; The Four Wives Instruct the Fifth (with the Aid of a Handsome Wine Merchant from Loyang).* Burnham saw traces of the wallpaper, stained, peeling.

Aunt Chi hobbled to a plain wooden chair and sat. Before her, a barrel and a board served as table. Burnham's cloth shoes scuffed the stone floor. He, too, sat; for a moment they mourned the past. "Tell me."

The old woman shrugged. "They left. I can hire all the t'u-ch'ang I want, but t'u-ch'ang are not my way, with a dozen in one room and every street vendor paying a penny for three minutes. You recall Li-li?"

"Who could forget Li-li?"

"Ah, yes." Aunt Chi smiled; her head trembled. "That famous behind. She ran off to Shanghai with a textile tycoon."

"And Han-chen?"

"Of the extravagant globes. The foreigners' delight. Gone south." Aunt Chi's wave dismissed her. "She had a baby and disgraced herself."

"She bathed the baby?" It was the gentle way to say "drowned."

"No, no. Playfully she squirted milk at a client. I swear to this. An American. He was offended." Aunt Chi drew breath; she seemed to pant through her wide nostrils.

"And Mei-tzu the acrobat?"

"With a colonel. It was fate. This was a house of quality, and women of quality will not stay in rotten times. Rotten, rotten,

rotten times. First the money went rotten. Then last year in August they gave us new money, the gold yuan, four of them to one dollar of yours. By then the old money was about twelve million to one of yours, so at the least the new money was easier to carry. With the old money clients brought bags of it for an hour's pleasure. But the new money too—ai! in a month it was twenty to one. Now it is a thousand to one and doubling every week. That would be—what?—three thousand million of the old money to one of your dollars! And the old money is still much in use, and who can count so high? Who can grasp? Who can conceive?"

"It is a horror," Burnham agreed. "Why do I owe you twenty dollars?"

Aunt Chi giggled. "Perhaps you do not. It is a thing one says. Who knows? A bad conscience pays untendered bills."

"You old bandit," he said softly. "Then you are alone."

She nodded. "Only the boy stays. I could rent the rooms, but who can pay rent? Ah, this money! It is garbage! Ju pu fu ch'u!"

Outgo exceeds income! But it was lovely and almost funny in the melodic Mandarin. He could not laugh in the face of his crabbed old friend's hot-eyed distress; yet he could not feel the anguish, not fully and perhaps not at all.

"Paper," she was muttering. "Endless banknotes. Printed in your Philadelphia."

"I know. Shipped to Shanghai. Boatloads."

The quiet room spoke. Shabby genteel. Decayed whorehouse. Faded lives. Silenced echoes. "Then how do you live?"

A gleam of the old mischief, a flash of teeth: "I trade a little. Buy-sell."

"Ah." Perfect understanding flowed instantly between them. "First-class stuff?"

"Of many origins but one quality." She grew suddenly cheerful, a hostess remiss: "And you? What is your life? Have you taken a dustpan and broom?"

"A stupid and thorny? No, I am not married. Such phrases for wives!"

"Men made the language," she said, still cheerful. "Women were forbidden to read or write, and could be sent away for daring to learn. What phrase would you prefer? 'Within woman'?"

"Not even that," Burnham said. " 'My within woman.' As if she were let out of a small box twice a day."

"Oh well, women," she said. "When did you arrive?"

"Only this afternoon. Would I wait to see my true love?"

She cackled. "Your true love! Many women were your friends, but your true love was a juicy cunt." The boy had entered; he set down the tray. "I remember them shouting 'Burnham! Burnham!' like a cageful of birds."

"Birds of paradise," he sighed, and he too remembered them, hopping forward like wind-up toys to shelter in his hug; remembered the glee in his soul, as if he were a collector among rare porcelains, or—credit where credit is due—a man of warm affections among many old friends. The beauty of young women, the loose blouses, khaki shirts, high-slit tunics, a breast bobbling here and a muff flashing there; the lovely faces, soft features, full lips, gentle noses and long black hair, often with red glints. An image teased him: Han-chen's round face, and the hair whipping as she danced. She wore a whore's scanty robe, a sleazy print loosely belted, and as she whirled she offered and withdrew her glories, breasts fuller than most Chinese breasts, ivory thighs, an exuberant bush, a jungle. Often he had lit a campfire in that jungle, and even now he could remember the taste of her broad, perfumed nipples, and the waft of ginger on her breath.

"No gratitude," Aunt Chi grumbled. "Without me they would have been good women and starving, or slaves to some impotent old guzzler, or hasting toward the long sleep in a military brothel."

He remembered Mei-tzu in a long fly-fronted silk shirt, just one gold button at the navel. Tall Li-li of the classic rump, hauntingly handsome in tunics. Shrieks of laughter, glimpses, caresses, protests, their joy in the hair on his chest.

"I can find you a girl if you want," Aunt Chi said. "I can send out."

"No, no. I came to see you."

They sipped. Aunt Chi pulled a box of cigarettes from her pocket and waved it at him; he shook his head, but reached for her matches and offered fire. "Thank you," she said. "You always did have a manner." She squinted through the smoke. "You are up to something."

"Younger Brother," Burnham said, "my san-luerh is outside. Will you tell him to wait?"

The boy hurried off.

Burnham swallowed more tea, and told the woman about Kanamori.

"Will it never end?"

"It is the quest for justice."

"Justice does not exist," she said flatly, and he was reminded that the Manchus had forbidden the binding of feet but could not enforce the prohibition. Those twisted, clawed, agonized feet were deemed sexually exciting. "All men know that justice does not exist. Surely all women know it. If one steals a bowl of rice, why is that worth a year in prison? Why not a week? Or ten years? If one bathes the baby nothing is said. What is justice? Who decides? Where is the justice in being born what one is, a daughter of Han or a son of your American gold? It is accident, not justice."

"The man must be punished," Burnham said. "Do you know of him?"

"Know of him! Hsüü!" She grimaced, a death's-head.

He waited.

"Yü," she said, "vile, vile." She muttered; he did not catch the words. She spat on the floor. "Do you remember O-lu-ka with the dyed red hair?"

"The White Russian? Olga?"

"Her. She came here from Nanking, where she had a house once. We gossiped, she and I. Bustards love gossip. Olga knew many Japanese. The White Russians were contemptuous of the Japanese, but even more contemptuous of the Chinese."

"And Kanamori was her friend?"

"Friend? Men like Kanamori have no friends. But she knew his secret. His mother was Chinese."

"Chinese!" So much for American military intelligence. Burnham was not easily shocked, but he felt as if the world were slipping from his grasp. "Chinese! But he . . . he raped! He killed! He was cold-blooded, uncontrollable! A Chinese mother!"

Aunt Chi shrugged. "Men! Listen now: that was his disgrace. For a Japanese officer a secret shame. He was killing the worst of himself." She cocked her head, a wizened hen. "Did he rape? You are sure?"

Burnham was stopped cold. It was an axiom, an eternal verity, a truism: Kanamori raped. Now he reconsidered. He recalled no testimony or evidence that Kanamori himself had raped. "He led gangs of rapists. He kidnapped."

"Ah, but the man himself." Aunt Chi shuddered. "Less than human." She brooded.

"Tell me."

"Patience. One does not speak willingly of such filth."

Burnham was confused and impressed. What there was to know of men's filth, Aunt Chi knew; what gave her pause must be momentous.

"He required to be whipped," Aunt Chi said. "Olga told me this. She supervised the whipping, so this animal would not go too far and die in her house. This skinny Japanese with welts on his back would fall naked to his hands and knees, and his pizzle drooped long like an old horse's, and the girls would whip him, and he would cry out in Chinese, always in Chinese, and his pizzle would rise. A madman. At the moment of fulfillment he would weep and wail and hang on the tit."

Gagging slightly, Burnham protested: "This was a hero. A great fighter, even in single combat."

"So much for heroes," Aunt Chi said. "Then this hero would threaten brutal revenge against any who gossiped. He threatened Olga with mass rape and then flaying. Ah, the officer's mind! As time passed he needed more and more whipping. A hero! Because he commanded rapists? Because he executed helpless men? Olga was losing weight and had stomach trouble, and between his fancy notions of love and his wild-eyed threats she began to vomit at the sight of him. This was less than courtly."

"And what became of him? Did Olga tell you?"

"He disappeared." She hesitated. "He is dead."

"Do you know this?"

"I know this."

"You saw?"

"Well," she said, "I heard. There are a few like him still here, the dregs. Also in Tientsin, and in the northeast. This country is full of Japanese." She waved in dismissal of those invaders. "But I no longer hear anything. I am no longer at the center of society."

"Do you know an inspector of police called Yen Chieh-kuo?"

She laughed harshly. "Him I know. Who does not? A famous guardian of morals, a flogger of students. Is he also after this Japanese?"

"Yes."

"Then I am on the side of the Japanese."

"Yüü!"

Aunt Chi snorted rudely: "There is little difference between one man and another. With the exception of my foster son Burnham they are all nasty brutes, and I care very little what they do to one another."

"But you did not know Kanamori yourself?"

"No. I tell you the truth."

"You always did. Listen: I have spoken to others about this one. They know more than they will say."

"So you did not come here first." She grinned, evil and sly.

"I make my important visits late in the day."

"You always did."

"And none more important than you."

"Even now?"

"Even now." He patted her hand.

She grunted, but her smile softened. "Well, then."

Younger Brother entered: the ricksha man was well and would wait. Was more tea desired? "Go be warm in the kitchen," Aunt

Chi said. The boy left. "And what do your friends tell you?"

"The usual murky poetry, the usual coded secrets. The Americans told me too little; there must have been more. My Chinese friends tell me politely to go home. I am perhaps to make a friend of the beggars."

Aunt Chi radiated astonishment: "Beggars! Beggars of the street?"

"Beggars. I want to see Head Beggar."

She shrugged. "These I do not know. These do not—did not —come here."

"Nevertheless, help me if you can. Do you know the place they call the Beggars' Hospital?"

Now she nodded. "I know of it. In the lower city. It heals those no one else will heal."

"Is it Christian?"

"No."

"Government?"

"No." She scowled, in the annoyance of the gossip balked. "A clinic. The very poor go. Chiefly for children."

"And whence flows the money?"

Again the scowl. "I do not know. It is perhaps . . ." She made the finger sign for eight.

"That would surprise me. What do you think of them?"

"The Communists?" Again she waved in impatience and scorn; how many governments had come and gone in her lifetime! "We need *something,* " she grudged. "But these Communists are ungenerous with their seed! They do not differentiate between yang and yin! They hump principles!"

"Will they harm you?"

"Who can tell? I am an old woman with bound feet. They will show me and make speeches. I will eat and be warm. I do little more now."

"You have money, surely."

She peered, as if to verify his identity: yes, it was old Burnham, the goat with two pizzles, who had drunk and pranced and scattered gold. "I have money," she said. "Why do we speak of my money?"

"If you truly sell," he said reasonably, "it behooves old friends to buy."

"You sweet boy," she sympathized. "What do you need?"

" 'Need' is perhaps too strong. 'Desire.' Stylet, pipe, a hundred pellets—what sort have you?"

"Heavy yang-t'u," she said immediately, "from the Plaine des Jarres, and light ch'uan-t'u."

"Ch'uan-t'u? They still run it up from Szechuan, do they?"

"Roundabout. The caravans march always, nothing stops the caravans. And goods arrive at staging points. It is like a great river and many small tributaries. And winter, as you know, is the good season. In summer opium stinks, and the officials pounce on hidden stores."

"It will be banned, you know, when the Communists win. A matter of weeks," Burnham said smoothly.

"What is this now?" Aunt Chi pretended outrage.

"It will be illegal and troublesome to possess," Burnham cautioned her. "In truth I do you a favor to take it from you."

"Hsüü! Trader! Thus you dicker with your second mother!" She glowed with the fun of this. "Men died to bring it here! I risk execution for your pleasure!"

"You risk execution if your inventory comes to light," he said. "Furthermore, I offer hard currency."

"Hard currency is in your favor," she conceded. "But you save time and trouble dealing with old friends; you spare yourself wanderings and chafferings; moreover, you can trust the goods."

"All that is in your favor," he grumbled. "I might go twenty dollars."

Aunt Chi all but split a gusset. Her laughter trilled and echoed in the bare room. "Burnham," she said finally, "you were always a man of great good humor. Many a jape," and she shook her head, and swabbed at tears.

"Now, now," he said. "After all, this is not a yen kuan, not a low opium den where addicts yearn and clutch. I can do without."

"The Communists occupy the countryside, and will not accept squeeze. Little comes through, only by the caravans. And where there are no Communists there are rapacious officials. The bribes are extortionate. My last such sale was a hundred dollars. Perhaps a hundred and ten; memory dims. I might consider less; you are my foreign son."

"Only filial affection offers thirty. One does not offer one's mother gritty rice."

"Fifty must do," Aunt Chi said firmly. "Think what you have saved by the absence of singing girls."

"Fifty is impossible," Burnham said. "It is too soon gone, too soon smoke, and after the easy doze, the empty purse. No. Forty, all told."

"That cannot be," she said sadly. "There is a question of principle, of morals. To maintain pride and to regulate the traffic. Even overpowering fondness is no excuse: you are the son of my heart, but if I lose on the deal, I have allowed you to cheat your mother. Yet I have an idea!" Her brows flew up, her mouth opened in silent glee. "I sell you the pellets at fifty. It is my bottom price. But because you are my son, I *give* you the pipe! A good one I have. Of brass, with a jade mouthpiece."

Burnham was overcome: "But that is too honest." His voice trembled. "That is watering your horse and throwing cash into the river."

"For you," she said, "I would do more, if only this world were not jang-jang chiao-chiao. We have seen some good times together."

"That we have," Burnham said. The deal was not bad, and with MacArthur's money at that, or Truman's. Odd: he could almost smell the stuff, yet he wanted whiskey more. Also he was tired. A long day. He seemed to have been in Peking at least a week. "About that other matter: if gossip comes your way, I can reward it."

"What I hear is yours. But no one comes to see me."

Firmly he said, "I shall come to see you."

"You prince. Let me go now and make a package for you. One

thing I did hear." She rose, creaking gracefully, all in red, old but imperishable. "The students will march and riot. The streets will not be safe."

"I too heard. Aunt Chi: one thing."

She spread her hands. "I am yours."

"Do not mind. It is only that I think of you often, and wonder. How did you start your life of hospitality?"

Her cobwebbed smile was all mischief. "You ask how I became an old bustard."

"No. A young bustard."

"Well, it is not an indelicate question. When my husband was killed, you see, I was first wife, and had charge of four others."

"Like the painting!" Burnham was delighted.

"The painting was no accident. We had it done years ago. At any rate, there we were, penniless and the house looted, four ladies of quality and fashion, with only one talent. Thanks to my rabbit of a husband, the talent was notable. Yü! I took charge; we rented a small house; we began humbly but always with style, the best wine, fresh fish, Kansu melons. Those were great days, with gold and silver for money, and strings of cash." Now she shrugged. "So."

"So. You survived."

"And had some good times. None of us regretted the life. Our husband had been a gangster of sorts, and the house was always swarming with knaves."

"A rare woman," Burnham said. "When was he killed?"

"In the Boxer times. He was a great friend of the foreigners."

"Boxer times!" Burnham was truly shocked; it was as if she had said "the Middle Ages."

She understood. "Oh yes. I am about eighty, you know."

"Hsü. One would not know. The mind is sage, but the body flows with youthful grace."

"I am about eighty," she repeated thoughtfully, "and you are the biggest liar I ever met."

9 獅

In December of 1937 only two or three dozen foreigners remained in Nanking. Some of the most concerned, who fought hardest for decency and humanity—or at least mercy—were Germans. Letters streamed, memorials, protestations. The Japanese command ordered its men not to molest foreigners. The order rankled. Why, Kanamori wondered, was a French or American woman less to be violated than a Chinese woman? Not that foreign women were in themselves alluring, with their long legs and crinkled hair and eagles' noses. Motor cars. Servants. Houses of many rooms.

The Safety Zone was a mile square, between the great lake and the great river. Within it lay many government offices, the Supreme Court, embassies, the Drum Tower and the Overseas Club. The boundaries were sketched for every company of soldiers: Hankow Road, Chung Shan Road, Sikang Road. There were a quarter of a million refugees in this square mile. Ginling College, the Bible Teachers' Training School, the War College and the Law College, the great Nanking University. Rumor said that six thousand disarmed soldiers had sought haven in the Zone.

The Japanese entered the Zone, ignoring the orders they knew they were intended to ignore. By midweek Nanking was a Japanese city. They flooded in: tanks, artillery, trucks, cavalry, swarms of impatient infantry. Shopfronts, whole neighborhoods, were systematically destroyed. Kanamori and Ito commandeered a wagon and four coolies. On the wagon they piled coal, small stoves, a drum of oil, bolts of brocade, bags of rice, bags of rings and bracelets, stone jugs of wine, bottles of foreign spirits, a crate of dressed ducks, small chests and ornamental boxes, and a rain of silver: coins, knives, picture frames, platters, goblets. They were barracked in a post office. Behind a counter they heaped their booty.

At first staff officers led a tentative invasion of the Zone in search of the disarmed Chinese soldiers. They announced in the name of the High Command that these soldiers would not be harmed. The foreigners published their promise. Kanamori assumed that even Chinese soldiers would prefer to die fighting, but these believed the foreigners' assurances and turned in their arms. The Japanese then removed thousands, and further announced that ex-soldiers who volunteered for the Military Labor Corps would be amnestied. One afternoon they took two hundred such volunteers from the Zone and executed them. Of the thousands more—those they were obliged to ferret out—they disposed of many by machine-gun fire. They bound others in large groups and used them for bayonet drill. Some they bound in packed circles, and as the outer ranks sagged they thrust over them; those at the center were shot. Others were roped in long dense lines and attacked from both sides; one Japanese soldier was killed across such a line by a friendly bayonet. Smaller bound groups were doused with gasoline and set afire. Still smaller groups were sabered. Little piles of heads accumulated. Kanamori did not participate in the sabering, feeling that Kurusu would scoff; Kurusu, he learned later, had refrained for a similar reason.

The foreigners protested. The Chinese protested. The Red Swastika Burial and Safety Society smuggled men and women to freedom, and gathered up corpses.

It was ordered that all Chinese bow to all Japanese.

The Japanese cut open the bank vaults.

The foreigners demanded food for the Safety Zone; the refugees were starving.

Then the Japanese invaded the Zone in force. They despoiled houses, colleges, courts. They rounded up more thousands, men and women. Kanamori and Ito entered one fine house and found a dozen women, teachers and students. The oldest of the women squawked angrily, and Ito knocked her down. Kanamori called in the squad. As the women were removed to a truck, a foreigner drove up, the American flag flapping from his radiator cap. He was a long gray-haired man wearing silver glasses. His name was Burnham, but Kanamori did not know that and would not have cared. Burnham leaped out to protest. Ito held him while Kanamori slapped him. "Fuck you! Go!" That was much of Kanamori's English: hello, good-bye, come, go, fuck you, passport, dollar, Roosevelt. The man stood by his car weeping and shouting, perhaps cursing.

They tore down foreign flags.

They burned a YMCA.

They executed the servants of foreigners. It was not meet that Asians serve whites. It was difficult to make the Chinese understand this.

They went to Ginling College. The men cheered; their eyes glittered. They were tipsy and skylarking. They took a truck to one of the dormitories. Tonight they would select, not herd. The city was all excitement, everywhere streaks and billows of flame, the tang of smoke, and the streets lined with corpses, many headless. The truck picked its way among clumps of dead. Smashed carts, everywhere smashed carts, spokes like fingers reaching into the headlamps.

At Ginling College a foreign woman came to the door and they pushed her inside. Women were packed in, bedding on the floor, as if assembled for Japanese pleasure. Oil lamps flickered. They rounded up twenty or thirty, marched them outside, and ordered them to strip for inspection. The rape was nothing without the humiliation. In the glare of headlamps they disrobed. Some were slow; these the soldiers struck. A dance, a ceremony, theater. Gowns and robes off, bloomers off, and the breast halters, foreign, coarse cloth like a fruit seller's sling. Naked, the women huddled and sobbed, and the foreign woman raged. It was a spectacle to quicken the blood: a score and more of youthful Chinese women naked in the harsh light. Ito and Kyose and others moved among them like buyers, prodding and cupping.

The same car drew up. Again the American flag. Two men this time, the long one with silver glasses and another, younger and angrier, whose eyes darted to the women. He too! Kanamori rejoiced: he too! It was Jack Burnham. He cursed the soldiers in Japanese, defiling them for monkeys, promising them that they would die in fire, their flesh wither, their balls pop. With a rifle butt Ito knocked him down. To Kanamori's pleasure, the foreigner's nose bled.

Burnham was full of hate. For days and nights, helpless, he had watched the unreasoning slaughter. The rapes above all. To interrupt the rape of a servant or a friend, and see the beast laugh. Soldiers of Japan with drool on their chins and trousers about their knees. Twice he was held at bayonet point and forced to watch. His old amah was raped. Fourteen years he had known her. From her he had first learned Chinese. Her brother had taught him to ride a horse. She was sixty, a woman of Peking, and had not wanted to come along on this ill-timed excursion to Nanking. At the house where the Burnhams stayed the fish pond was clogged with bodies, and the fish floated dead beside them. The Burnhams had roamed from house to house protecting whom they could.

Sprawled and bleeding, Burnham spoke: " 'If you affect valor and act with violence,' " he said in Japanese, " 'the world will in the end detest you and look upon you as wild beasts.' Do you recognize that? You—the sublieutenant."

"It is from the Imperial Precept," Kanamori said angrily. "The old General Orders."

"Wild beasts," Burnham said. "Nameless cowards."

"My name is Kanamori Shoichi," Kanamori said, "and you stared at the women. I saw you! Animal! Kyose, take one here for the edification of the foreigners. Ito, if this one moves, bash him again."

Burnham did not move. Beside him he heard his father praying. Kyose took one of the girls and Tateno held her down. Kyose dropped his trousers and showed his swollen member to the foreign woman, who turned away with a cry. Burnham did not know the girl, but for a moment she was all Chinese girls. Burnham had never needed to rape. Foreigners charmed and seduced. Young lust, he had thought, was brother to joy, not to rape. Now he wept.

When Kyose finished they prodded all the women onto the

truck, took them to the post office and caroused. The women screamed and bled and then were silent.

Next day Kanamori's unit was ordered into fresh uniforms. General Matsui held a religious service for the dead. He made a statement of sympathy for those who had suffered the evils of war, but now, he said, the Imperial Way had come to offer rebirth to China. He urged the Chinese to consider the advantages of order and Asian solidarity. (General Matsui was later decorated for meritorious service on this campaign. He was angry that foreigners had spread vicious rumors about the Japanese army. Still later he was hanged for war crimes.)

Kanamori saw the long man with silver glasses and gray hair once more. There was work to do, a city to administer, and electricity was essential. Kanamori's regimental colonel sent for him, asked his head count, and was jovial. Kanamori informed him respectfully that he had not added to his head count in Nanking, which was not truly combat. The colonel approved, and invited Kanamori to accompany him on a visit of protest to the foreigners; they had sheltered trained technicians, and must now give them up for the good of Nanking and its beleaguered citizens.

There were half a dozen of those foreigners in a library, one of them the long man with silver glasses. He did not seem to recognize Kanamori.

The colonel was cold and firm. In particular he required the release of electrical engineers and technicians to restart the power plant at Hsia Kuan.

The long man with silver glasses made proud teeth and stood tall. His gray hair was cut short, and his face was gentle, lined and sorrowful. "You killed them," he said. "You took them from their refuge, stood them on the bank of the Yangtze, and killed them with machine guns for no reason."

The colonel was taken aback. To save face he turned upon Kanamori. "Is this true, Kanamori?"

Before Kanamori could speak, the American said, "Ah, Kanamori. Is that Kanamori Shoichi?" And looked at him with those outlandish blue eyes.

The colonel was pleased. "You see! Kanamori is famous! You must tell Kurusu!"

The American said no more, nor did Kanamori. The colonel grew fierce and blustered, but then led his men away. The engineers and technicians were indeed dead.

Two days later Kanamori was sent west of the river to combat, and this was a relief but it came too late. He had entered the last house for one last rape or robbery, shot a husband, and was raping the pregnant wife when she went into labor. Kanamori Shoichi, sublieutenant, of the village of Saito on the River Omono near Akita, son of a noted warrior and heir to all the samurai, broke the bag of waters with his virile member.

He hung there on his knees, at first annoyed, and as the sticky fluid welled his annoyance became discomfort, and as the canal distended his discomfort became horror, which was a new emotion. He shrank away, and the horror became fury, and he plunged his knife into the woman's belly again and again. He breathed curses. He cursed all Chinese. He cursed his mother. He scrambled to his feet and left the three of them dead. He returned to headquarters talking to himself, heated water and bathed. In the morning he went to the post office and learned that he was posted to combat with Ito and Kyose and Tateno and the lot. "Ah, this was a time!" Ito said. The men cheered Kanamori and wished him well, and he laughed with them, but the laughter was tinny in his own ears.

Combat! He thanked the gods for combat! For months then he fought like a hero. He met Kurusu; they agreed to omit Nanking, and he beat Kurusu to one hundred and fifty. He was mentioned in dispatches and was decorated; there was talk of a promotion. He dreamed confused dreams. He dreamed one dream many times, of that child, who was born and was a man immediately, and challenged Kanamori to battle with the saber, and Kanamori was afraid, and woke up cold and shivering. But combat cleansed him somewhat; other corpses supervened. In the end he was not destroyed. No immediate remorse crippled him; his soul did not soften, nor did doubts enfeeble him.

In June of 1938 Kanamori was wounded, but remained in the line. In July he and his men were returned to Nanking for rest and reassignment, and he learned that he was to be transferred to the General Staff, where important responsibilities awaited him.

Gunfire pattered as they rode south. In the night sky Burnham saw bursts and tracers; a distant siren sang. He imagined the scene: dark streets thronged with chanting students, a bonfire of flickering orange light, bullet-chipped government buildings, shattered windows, men in leather and olive drab, the police uncaring, obeying orders. Some would die, perhaps many, and in a month the Reds would be here, and the battle, the fury, the lives cut short, would lose all meaning.

Feng's way wound through shadow and tangle, and the alleys were almost empty. In the ivory glow of a full moon Burnham's breath blew white; a cloud blanked the moon, and he sniffed coming snow. The gates along the way, slabs of wood or the graceful joined semicircles of moon gates, were shut; here an iron gate, and there a sentry box. Once a black car slithered past.

"Feng."

"Sir."

"I need beggars."

The san-luerh slowed and stopped. Feng's face shone like ivory in the moonlight. "The gentleman is pleased to jest."

"I need Head Beggar really, but he is difficult of access."

Feng was disillusioned. "The gentleman keeps low company."

"Like ricksha men?" Burnham made teeth in the night. Pricking the snobbery of the poor was a rich satisfaction; solidarity was all they had, and they squabbled like warlords.

"The gentleman rebukes me," Feng said.

"It is the hour. I ask pardon."

They started up again and traveled in silence until Burnham said, "He may know what I need to know."

"Then you will pay for it."

"I planned to. Though I have heard that Head Beggar is a rich man."

"So they say."

"He will prove to be fat." Burnham sighed. "And he will quote the ancient books."

"Is he at the Ch'ien Men?"

"I have no idea. The first step is to find a collection of beggars. I thought perhaps Gold Street or Embroidery Street."

"At this hour?" Feng slowed. "The gentleman is indeed weary."

"Then where?"

"Whore Street."

"Then let it be Whore Street."

Feng took them into a dark and narrow side street out of the flow. A wineshop was open. A clam-and-mussel shop was just closing. Two women tripped along, bearing what seemed to be huge bundles of laundry. A late, forlorn noodle merchant noted the foreigner and stared. Above them a few stars struggled in a heavy sky.

Whore Street was brighter lit: bulbs, lanterns, windows. From the Nagging Wife Wine Place came a gust of laughter. Burnham knew the street and was worried only that there would be foreigners, perhaps one who knew him. Such accidents could spoil a day and evoke gossip.

Feng drew up. "If the gentleman would descend and display money."

"Why not?" Burnham asked, stepping down. He extracted his wads of paper money and made a show of riffling and counting. "Here, take a bundle. These ruffians may do me in."

Two beggars approached as if on cue, and beyond them more glided from crannies and doorways. Feng accepted the sheaf of bills, and tucked it away. The beggars did not touch Burnham, but whined. "I starve." "The great lord will take pity."

Burnham's flesh seemed to contract. This too was the smell of China, and not so romantic: pus, skin disease, the body's careless wastes. The men were skeletons in rags, one disfigured by pockmarks, the other by slashed scars. One limped. "I have money," Burnham said loudly.

The two became six, then more. Their soft whine was scary;

he wished they would jabber and shout. Through the robe he touched his pistol. "You listen," he said, "all of you." The whine continued. "There is money," Burnham said, "but first silence." Slowly the keening whimper subsided.

All his life Burnham had known beggars, and still they horrified him. Maimed scarecrows outside all law, scarcely human, yet reminding him what men and women might become. Dull faces, only the gleam of avarice; twisted bodies, hands like birds' feet.

"I have traveled a thousand li," he began. He had traveled thirty thousand li, but the number must be reasonable. "I have come a thousand li to speak with Head Beggar." He had said kai-t'ou; now he used the second name, "the chi-t'ou." They gazed stupidly. "There is money," he repeated. "But I must find the kai-t'ou."

One murmured, "Who knows the kai-t'ou?"

"You know your district leader."

The scarecrows stood silent, cold.

"Then your neighborhood leader."

They blinked and spat. Again Burnham was overcome by the night, the dreamlike street, sinister shadow. Somewhere a woman spilled silver laughter.

"There is no way," a beggar said.

"There is always a way," Burnham said. "Come here now. All of you."

They stepped closer, their stench with them. Quickly Burnham peeled bills: "Here. One each. For this you will do me a service. I am the only foreigner at the Willow Wine Shop in Stone Buddha Alley. The chi-t'ou may find me there. You will tell others, and they will tell still others. There are lives to be saved or lost, do you understand?"

They snatched at the bills. Burnham's breath came shallow, and he stood tense: if they jumped him?

"It is mysterious," one said.

"And irregular," another said.

"Still, it can be done," a third said.

"With luck."

The third said, "Very well. You have raised the wind, but do not hope for immediate rain."

Burnham breathed easy. "Go, then."

They melted away like phantoms.

"Yüü." Feng sighed. "It is perhaps not so bad to be a ricksha man." He raised his right hand; the knife gleamed faintly.

"A scary moment," Burnham said.

"They are evil men, and will take you by hidden ways. They will steal your money and send you to the house of the long sleep."

"That journey may be taken anytime," Burnham said, "though I confess I am in no hurry. Still, he who hunts the tiger must not fear stray dogs."

"If they send for you," Feng said, "you will take me along."

"No. If the worst is to be, then you must survive to tell the story later of the foolish foreigner who stood in Whore Street at night with a bag of gold."

"The gentleman is not foolish," Feng muttered, "and not a foreigner."

"I thank you for that, my friend Feng. If you believe it, then will you, in the name of all the gods, stop calling me 'the gentleman'?"

"But what then?" Feng protested. " 'Elder brother'?"

"It must be thought about. Meanwhile you may take me to the Beggars' Hospital in Rat's Alley."

"As the gentleman says."

Burnham descended from the pedicab and hesitated. His package lay on the seat. Accidents. A heart attack or a stray bullet, and Feng left to explain this odd parcel. Burnham tucked it under one arm. "Once again I may be some time."

Feng showed the open hands of acquiescence, pedaled toward the cumbersome two-wheeled wagon, ranged himself alongside and took the passenger's seat. Burnham saw the bright eyes roving: Feng liked to know where the exits lay.

Burnham too. He walked back to the open entrance and the admissions office. A distant machine gun clattered. He knocked and entered. In the glow of a feeble bulb he saw a desk, and at the desk, asleep, the dumpy woman of the sharp tongue.

From the shadows a figure glided to him: another woman, gray-haired, a surgical mask, a black gown of medium length over the padded black trousers. She placed a finger to her lips.

"Good evening," Burnham whispered.

The woman touched her surgical mask, and her forefinger said No. Burnham was annoyed; he had only whispered. But she pointed again to her own mouth, and he understood: she was dumb.

The sleeping woman woke. Her chair creaked. Burnham turned to see, and caught his breath. The woman might or might not be beautiful, but in the dreamlike wash of dim and friendly light her round face and soft features emerged from centuries of night, dynasties, millennia: symmetrical, almond-eyed, a face from a scroll or sculpture. With that face she should be tall and her body willowy.

She rose, peering, and he saw that glasses hung on a chain about her neck. She put them on. The woman was nearsighted and short. She might be willowy but that would be hard to say: she wore padded trousers and a short padded jacket buttoned in man's fashion. Yet she was lovely, and he smiled.

She was also sleepy, and still short-tempered. "What is it?"

"Good evening," Burnham said, only slightly offended, "and forgive me. I came some hours ago, and I am looking for Dr. Nien Hao-lan."

"Yes, I remember. And what do you want with Dr. Nien Hao-lan?"

Again Burnham was stung. " 'Little ceremony and less grace.' "

"Oh, for heaven's sake," she said in queerly reminiscent English. "You must be American. Where did you learn a phrase like that?"

"Aw, hell," Burnham said. "Everybody talks English here."

"And why is that wonderful? You speak Chinese."

"True. Will you tell me where I can find Dr. Nien?"

"I am Dr. Nien Hao-lan," she said. "Why don't you sit down and tell me where it hurts."

So he introduced himself, and they shook hands. Immediately there was much asking and telling, in a salty stew of Chinese and English, strangely intense talk, nervous, as if they had been introduced at a party where everyone else was handsome and rich and only they were uninteresting and homely. "I went west with the universities, I was just out of middle school," she said. "You know about the great migration? The great trek west?"

"Yes, of course. I went back to the States after . . . after Nanking, but I kept in touch." Then did-you-know-this-one-and-that, and he had once met Soong Ching-ling, the widow of Sun Yat-sen, and she remembered May 1938, when Chinese planes actually flew over western Japan and dropped leaflets, a moment of exaltation, like a great victory. She said wryly in Chinese that she was of good family—both parents dead now—and a brilliant student, and had proceeded from Chengtu to medical school in London. Burnham said, "Of course. That lovely accent."

"If you flatter," she said, "I will confine myself to Chinese," and he repeated what he had said to Tun the bicycle man—"He who lives by flattery works harder than the peasant"—at which she laughed a full, rich laugh and opened a box of Players to offer him one. He accepted the unaccustomed cigarette for companionship and because yes was more natural than no and refusal would chill the moment. He smoked and told her of his parents and his days in college and his war with and against the United States army, and how he had met the White Mikado and discovered in himself a disputatious tendency. She laughed again, a good round laugh and booming, almost a man's laugh, but his mind saw her in silks, that liquefaction of her clothes, though at the moment she was a shapeless and nearsighted bundle, and bad-tempered to boot, as he now knew at first hand. He remembered also the vigorous and colorful language of her rebuke to the police, and the bull of a cranky sawbones he had imagined. He could not say why this dowdy doctor called to mind princesses, canopied boats on the Yangtze and tinkling cymbals.

"Why do you look at me so?" she asked.

" 'The flowers blush, and the moon hides her face.' "

"Oh no," she warned. "That is dangerous. Besides, you have said it before."

"Two hours ago," he boasted, "the proprietor of a bicycle shop said it to me."

"An admirer," she said. "That is social success indeed."

"I rebuked him. This isn't an ordinary hospital, is it?"

"It is scarcely a hospital at all. Officially, the Children's Clinic. Unofficially . . ." She shrugged.

"Unofficially, the Beggars' Hospital."

"You know that?"

"I have heard."

"Then we come back to my question. What do you want with Dr. Nien Hao-lan?"

"I want to invite her to dinner," he said.

"Of course. Then a walk on the moon bridge, and a recitation of ancient poetry."

"Don't be difficult. Have you eaten?"

"No. I fell asleep."

"Then come to dinner."

"I'll have to change."

"Change? Is this the Nien Hao-lan who curses police?"

"You know that too. How do you know it?"

"Come to dinner," he said.

"I have no choice. Mother!" she called. "Mother!"

Burnham was alarmed. He had not intended to meet the family. The mute woman entered. "I must go out," the doctor told her. "Send Dr. Shen to me." The mute woman departed. "And now I will change," Dr. Nien said to Burnham. "Wait here, please." Her walk was brisk, not willowy. Not a princess but a doctor who knew more of him than he knew of himself: where his spleen was, for example, and possibly even why he wanted to smile like a child.

Dr. Shen shambled in, muttering, and stopped short. He was

a skinny young man and made white eyes. Burnham rose, and they introduced themselves and exchanged small talk, until a stunning, bosomy young woman, in a red-and-silver brocade dress slit well up both thighs, joined them, peered myopically at Burnham and said, "Claridge's or the Ritz?"

At which Dr. Shen gaped, and Mr. Burnham swallowed his astonishment and with difficulty subdued a savage pang of pure desire.

Outside he said, "No, no. This way. I have my own vehicle."

"A rich Yankee." She took his arm, and they walked to Feng, who scrambled to his feet and bowed.

"This cart here," Feng said.

Burnham glanced at it. A tarpaulin covered it. "Yes?"

"Perhaps the gentleman should look."

"Perhaps the gentleman should not," Dr. Nien said, but made no move to stop him. "Perhaps not before dinner."

Burnham flung back the tarp.

He did not understand. Piglets, perhaps.

He peered closer. By the light of the full moon he saw the cold, naked corpses of perhaps thirty newborn babies.

At the Black Duck he set his package on the table and ordered strong drink. Dr. Nien smoked with weary, ironic sympathy. "They cannot be left in the streets."

"You collect them?"

"Mother collects them. It is her career."

"She is not your mother. Your mother is dead."

"True. This one is only a mute with no home. The beggars also bring us babies. Mother takes them to the burial ground, pushing her little cart. Picturesque Peking."

They spoke Chinese now, in public, in a pleasant, dim restaurant of many tables and no chairs, only benches. The walls and ceiling were smoked black. The waiter was expeditious; Burnham poured two cups of hot wine and dried his own at once.

"It is worse in Shanghai," she said. "Here we expect winter. In

Shanghai winter seems to be a surprise every year, and the city is full of former country people who cannot cope."

"The war drove them in."

"As well starve in one place as another. But there are hundreds of thousands homeless."

"Well," Burnham said awkwardly, "drink up." What more could he say? Words failed: what words bore on death-in-life? Statistics, yes: in forty years the flower of civilization, East and West, had murdered sixty million men, women and children, and allowed to die how many hundreds of millions? And allowed to live in hopeless squalor and chronic hunger how many hundreds of millions more? What were thirty dead babies? Here diners laughed; dice rattled. A warm, subdued room, the smoky comfort of old wood, the lapping gleam of an open fire, the mellow odor of roast duck, the reassuring sight of fat birds on a turning spit. Burnham felt grossly foreign, and wondered who he really was.

"Please." She touched his hand. "It must be lived with."

His impulse was to cover her hand with his own, but he refrained. "There are simply no degrees," he said. "I have seen more dead men than I could count, as you have, but . . ."

"I know. Babies. Think of them as the lucky ones."

"In the house of the long night there is always room."

"You invent proverbs. You went to a Chinese school?"

"Yes. My father insisted. Age six to age twelve." He poured again and sipped. "Standing with Full Nose and Fat Ass—we all had nicknames—and shouting the classics. Then I would go home and my mother would teach me geography and English and Christianity and arithmetic."

"That was good luck. I learned English in middle school and college, from Americans, and then when I went to London I had to learn it all over again. Bung-ho, Burnham. Mud in your eye."

He raised his cup. "There's more old drunkards than old doctors."

"That's the stuff." They caromed from language to language. Her eyes were bright, her gaze clear and affectionate; she was enjoying herself. Burnham felt gallant and unselfish; he patted her hand, and let his own lie on hers for a moment.

"Before we go to hand-holding," she said, "you must tell me what you want with Dr. Nien Hao-lan."

"Oh yes." He sighed. "I was forgetting." And he told her.

"It's all such nonsense," she said. "In the first place, it's none of your business. Americans, I mean. You want revenge for Nanking? You had Hiroshima. And Nanking is not yours to avenge."

The duck lay sliced, and a platter of pao-ping, little crêpes that the foreigners called "doilies," to Burnham's disgust; and leeks, and two sauces. Elegantly, with chopsticks, Burnham plucked up a pao-ping, laid it flat, dipped a slice of duck in plum sauce, set it on the pao-ping, added a leek, and then, still with chopsticks and frankly showing off, rolled up the pao-ping, picked it off the plate, and bit it in two. The taste had not changed; he made animal sounds. The pleasures of Chinese cookery were always mitigated by the ironies—famine, malnutrition, dead babies— but apparently some gustatory life-force was unquenchable. In the midst of death there is duck. Dumplings thou art and to dumplings shall return.

With clinical precision, Hao-lan outdid him.

He admired: "You surgeon!"

"Pediatrician."

The waiter hovered, a slim, aged man with a cobwebbed face. Burnham tapped the cruet and he glided off.

"Who did what to whom is not my concern," Burnham told her. "Some rough justice is being done. I'm only a hunter."

"The hunters are always foreigners," she grumbled. "We Chinese could find the man."

"But we Chinese have not, and three years have passed." He made the flat face of empty courtesy.

"Now we have it," she said. "The corrupt Chinese, hiding this monster."

"Or only indifferent, or busy with other matters. All things are possible," he said. "Things have their root and their branches. Listen one listen, Doctor. I myself may be no more than bait for this big fish. I may already be impaled on Fate's hook. Lecture me no lectures." In English: "Honest folks like you and me don't know nuthin'." And back to Chinese: "Only tell me about the hospital."

"Well, there is more to you than flirtation," she said, and stabbed moodily at the platter. She constructed another duck roll, ate it in silence, and drank three full cups of wine with it.

"We are almost six hundred million here," she began then. "Just after the war there were fifteen thousand doctors. That is about one for every forty thousand people. There were also six thousand certified nurses and as many midwives. One nurse or midwife for every fifty thousand people. Do you know how many trained modern dentists we had? Licensed to practice? Three hundred and fifty."

She had begun a long story, but Burnham made no objection. He had started this day in another country, hung over, and life had improved by the hour: Yen's car, the Willow Wine Shop, tea in a defunct whorehouse with the last of the red-hot Manchus and an apprentice pimp. Wonders, freaks and prodigies. And here he sat, luckiest of men, at table in the Black Duck, the food and wine hot, and across from him shone the Lady Chrysanthemum, or Princess Snowdrop, who had journeyed around the world, performed wondrous feats and passed taxing tests, and returned to the Middle Kingdom bearing the magical caduceus. "It is, professionally speaking, a great balls-up," she was saying. In the firelight her cheeks glowed ruddy, her black hair lay soft and threw off auburn sparks; her eyes were deep and sad, and the line of her jaw was so graceful, the pout of her lips so lush, that he ached. Not with desire—not yet, not now—but with foolish bliss. He would not exchange Peking for any other city, or Nien Hao-lan for any other woman, or, he thought, champing happily at his leek, the Black Duck for any other beanery.

"So I came back from England in 1946," she was saying, "with my degree from the Royal Free Hospital and five years of Western civilization behind me. Rationing and the V-2s, but my own flat and a young man who was actually called the

Honourable, and you know what chaos I came back to."

"A young man called the Honourable," Burnham repeated in stuffy and offended tones.

"It is the best way to learn a foreign tongue," she murmured. Burnham began to wonder if this woman was more than he could handle; her face was all innocence. "My accent is upper-class in both languages, as you have surely noticed. Anyway, I came back full of lore and idealism and applied for government certification, endless questionnaires and examinations and paper work, endless insults from clerks—there was some error, women were not doctors, perhaps 'nurse' was meant, or 'midwife' or 'dispenser.' That was in the winter of 1946, and three years later I am still not certified. God damn them!" she blurted in English, then reverted to Mandarin for an extended blast: "Defile their fathers, uncles, brothers, and in time of need their younger sons. Also their kitchen gods, lap dogs and goldfish."

The waiter had returned with wine; he set down the cruet, and admiration settled on his wise old features as he backed off. "The lion roars east of the river!" Burnham said; it meant, for reasons he had never fathomed, "What a temper!"

He was rewarded. She laughed her deep tuneful peal and said, "Oh, you scholar. Oh, you show-off. I suppose you have about twenty of those and you rehearse them."

"For you only," he said, moved. "You are a fox in disguise." That meant "a bewitching woman."

"Next you will be wanting to hold hands again," she said severely.

"Humbly I retreat to my duck. Go on." He poured wine.

"Oh well, a dull story," she said. "The angry young woman. The furious rich bitch. The winter of '46, and the rice bowls empty. The five constant virtues notably lacking. The same wolves barred the roads, and it took a peck of gall—you know the term?"

"Great courage."

"Full marks, Burnham major. It took great courage to talk about medical care for the ordinary people or other such radical fantasies. And I was just back from England, where they'd fired Churchill in favor of fair pay and free dentures. So when my certificate was lost in the celestial swamp, and the marsh gas told us the government was rotting, I went to work at the Children's Clinic, where I can pretend to be a doctor. Half the time I feel noble and half the time I'd give anything to get out. When I think of a real hospital, with X-ray machines and labs—I'm wasted. My whole life could be wasted."

"Times are changing," he said.

"Ah, the Communists. They care more, I suppose. But I'm tainted with foreign heresies, and I'm not sure I want to be re-educated. I seem to be a woman of the world."

"A society girl," he said. "Spoiled rotten. Who pays you?"

"Nosy."

"Not the government."

"Of course not the government. Our doctors aren't certified, you see. I'm a woman and cosmopolitan. Shen's a suspected Communist. We have a colleague, Teng, who'll never be certified because his father was a Shanghai gangster who feuded with Chiang Kai-shek in 1928. The fact is, we're hardly paid at all. The beggars' union supports us as times permit. We beg of rich friends —missionaries and other foreigners."

"The beggars. Astounding."

"It is. You know about them?"

"That they're organized, yes. There are many odd stories. In other countries too. Beggars who each pay a penny to a kind of alderman who sits on the beggars' council. Beggars' committees to deal with the police or with famine or cold spells. Delegates who resolve geographical disputes: who, and how many, shall work Embroidery Street or Bead Street. And when a woman's time comes there are beggar midwives. Also, there's a Head Beggar. So. They contribute to your clinic?"

"As in America," she said. "Hospitals for crippled children, and so on. You have one group that collects eyeglasses for the poor, and one that fights tuberculosis. So why not Chinese beggars? There are so many of them!"

"I ask because both my leads to Kanamori touch on beggary."

"Then go to the beggars and ask."

"I may," he said agreeably. "Do you know Sung Yun?"

She tapped her cup impatiently with a chopstick; Burnham clucked an apology and poured. "I know of him," she said. "Rich and corrupt, and therefore important. If he's still in Peking it's a wonder. When the Reds come he'll be the first to be boiled in oil."

"A splendid fellow. Why is he rich?"

"The usual mystery. A little of this and a little of that. Gold bars in time of war. Shipments of rice diverted. Adolescent girls, opium, favors. The country's full of such."

"He has a connection with the clinic?"

She paused, shocked, chopsticks high. "Madness."

"All right. Inspector Yen."

Mouth full, she shook her head and mumbled, "Never heard of him."

"If he, or any policeman, comes to see you, please tell me."

"What are you dragging me into?" she complained. "Your Japanese is none of my business."

"I am beginning to think he's none of mine." Burnham sighed. "Things have changed around here."

"And are about to change more. I need some soup to wash this down."

Burnham cast about for the waiter. Other diners caught his eye and glanced away. Colors seemed rich and dim at once, the blues and blacks of gowns, here a red shirt, the smoked walls. Behind the open fire sat a cook, fat as a bonze, nodding and dreaming, a cigarette shrinking in his drowsy hand.

The waiter bowed, and Burnham ordered hot walnut soup. It was of all soups the most exhilarating, homely yet exotic, whetting the appetite it appeased. It was also expensive, and Hao-lan chuckled. "You're plying me."

Burnham nodded vigorously, and their eyes conversed. A welcome confusion warmed him: desire, but something more, much more, the watchdog's ferocious instinct, protective, brotherly. He hoped so. If it were merely the fucker's possessive jealousy? Unworthy. A rare woman indeed, calling forth quality and class, that best of oneself so seldom required. Her brows were straight and almost bushy. Her look was honest. So were her hands, a doctor's hands, no lies or false moves.

Now as if by accord they did a pleasant thing: took soup in silence, chatting only in half-smiles. Then tea, and Burnham called for the bill, and paid it, and they started downstairs. As always at the Black Duck, the waiter thundered the amount of the bill, and the amount of the tip—and Burnham had been generous, as was only fitting; it was taxpayers' money, after all—so a great roar of "Hao! Hao!" rose behind them: "Good! Good!" As they stepped into the cold, animating night air Hao-lan said, " 'With coarse rice to eat, with water to drink, and my bended arm for a pillow—I have yet joy in the midst of these.' "

"If a foreigner come with money," Burnham asked, "is it better for the poor that he keep it, or spend it?"

Feng rode toward them. The shadowed alley was home for an instant: must Burnham leave this woman? Desperately sad, he grumbled, "Well, back to the hospital, I suppose."

"Nonsense," she said. "You will take me to your lodgings, please, and seduce me."

He could hardly speak, only squeezing her arm and swallowing nervously, choking on walnut fumes. Finally he said, "How not?" tossed his package to the seat of the ricksha, took her by the shoulders and said, "Until this moment my life has been all sky and no sun."

"You talk too much and too well," she scolded, and said to Feng, "Your master is sodden and maudlin. We must wring him out, and restore him to his former childlike simplicity."

Feng gaped and blinked, then smiled like the dawn and said, "Simplicity indeed. 'What does a man need, but a bamboo hat and a gourd?' "

11 寶

August 1938. Even Kanamori's voice was at attention: "Sir!"

The colonel smiled. Kanamori's heart swelled. "My dear Captain Kanamori!" said the colonel.

Dizzied, Kanamori fought for control. A double promotion! How Kurusu would wail and stamp!

"You have fought well and bravely," the colonel went on, "but we are past mere brawling now, and have better use for our best."

Kanamori thought perhaps he should say "Sir!" again but stood rigid.

"At ease, my boy, at ease."

Kanamori stood at formal ease.

"Prince Asaka has suggested that you join us in military government."

Kanamori never forgot those words. The room pitched, and he almost staggered. Prince Asaka! Twice now, such distinguished notice!

"I think you must sit down," the colonel said kindly.

Kanamori sat, and heard the rest in a dream. Part of Kiangsu province was to be his, and part of Anhui. Thousands of square miles, millions of people. His own vehicle and a full company of infantry. He listened with the joy of a child. "You will be responsible to Military Accounting and not to Division. More directly, to Lieutenant Colonel Shizumi." Provinces? Nanking and Wu-hsi and Soochow? Who was this Shizumi?

"We are transferring you," the colonel continued, "to social services."

Kanamori's heart sank.

"More specifically, to narcotics."

"But, but—"

"Speak out, Captain."

"But I am not a policeman, sir! I am a warrior!"

"A warrior of renown. And your duties will not be a policeman's."

Kanamori bowed his head and waited.

"You will be in charge of the distribution of heroin cigarettes and processed opium. It is a tremendous responsibility, and a step toward the General Staff."

The General Staff!

"Opium will henceforth, in all public announcements, including shop signs, be known as kuan-t'u."

"Controlled earth."

"Or if you like," the colonel smiled, "government dirt."

Shakily Kanamori laughed.

"Let me explain further," the colonel said, and did so. Kanamori listened with respect, but an inner voice protested: Opium? But I am a soldier!

Some minutes later the colonel struck a bell on his desk, and an aide appeared. "The man Wang," said the colonel.

A Chinese entered; the aide vanished. The Chinese was a civilian, a tall man of large bones, thick shoulders and a peculiarly feline aspect: snub nose, prominent teeth, mustache like a cat's whiskers. His eyes were veiled, his manner bland. He remained standing.

"Wang is a leader," the colonel said. "That is, a man with followers." Wang was forty-five, perhaps a bit older. He stood smiling faintly; Kanamori scented false humility. "He will be your link with the Chinese world."

Kanamori said farewell to his platoon, his home. A family of brothers. They would return to the line. In the courtyard he assembled them. He announced his promotion. He introduced Lieutenant Nakasawa, who would replace him and who had asked, at their first meeting, if he might make one swipe with Kanamori's famous sword. An engaging boy. Kanamori walked the ranks and bowed to each man. In the silent morning no one spoke; his heart cracked. He returned to Sergeant Ito, who stood at ease front and center. Kanamori almost embraced him—an impulse, no more. He made a brief speech: if he was exiled to

Staff, they were the glorious Line. Asia was theirs because they had fought well. In days to come they would fight even better. In his oblivion he would envy them; in their triumph they must not forget him. He called them to attention and saluted them, then walked away. Behind him three banzais ripped the air.

A captain! Staff! But narcotics?

He did as he was ordered. The colonel represented Prince Asaka, who represented the Emperor, who represented Heaven.

The line between the Chinese and the Japanese was the line between Wang and Kanamori. Kanamori was importer and distributor; Wang was buyer and technician. The method was the same as in Shanghai. But there the apparatus, the bureaucracy, the commercial organization, had not been destroyed. In Nanking, in all of Anhui, officials had fled or been murdered. Rails had been torn up, bridges blown, vehicles demolished by the thousands, towns razed. Here they began painfully, with a skeletal administration. Wang did the donkey's share of the work, but his manner was always aristocratic. In Nanking he maintained a private ricksha, like the last of the mandarins. He and his minions roamed the two provinces. He reported faithfully to Kanamori and received nothing that he did not pay for. Kanamori never asked whence came the money. Their relations were correct.

At first they set aside special nooks in ordinary shops. They ordered signs painted: KUAN-T'U. They commandeered what remained of a cigarette factory and commenced the manufacture of heroin cigarettes, powdered heroin mixed with cheap tobacco from the uplands of Kiangsi. At Wang's suggestion they took two fish with one hook: they ingratiated themselves with young laborers, from ten to thirty, by supplying them with free cigarettes at the end of the workday, and at the same time began the process of addiction. The old-time dealers complained to Wang; the official dealers were undercutting them. Wang advised them to be patient: the official dealers were building trade for them.

Even when food was short, cigarettes were plentiful. Soon they opened special shops. Little signs above the door: KUAN-T'U. Smoothly Wang diversified, and they encouraged yen kuan, old-fashioned opium dens. Kanamori was sure that Wang invested in pipes, perhaps even couches, perhaps even lamps; no item was too small, no profit negligible. Wang lived for business. One local trader had turned up eight hundred pounds of ordinary charcoal and wanted to ship it into Nanking by dory. Only eight hundred pounds. Yet Wang, shuttling here and there in his silent, gleaming ricksha, arranged it and exacted a share.

By late fall local newspapers carried advertisements: this number on that street, kuan-t'u. A far cry from old men in obscure back rooms! Now it was an industry.

And the work! Combat was indeed preferable. Kanamori was "responsible only to Military Accounting," which meant that no one on his level or lower must see his records. He listed shipments by grade, by weight, by origin, by cost, by resale value. He listed distribution by region, district, town and ward, relying on Wang for information. Wang enriched himself, of course, but Kanamori received his price, and Wang's swindles were not his affair.

Kanamori's work was praised by his superiors. His dreams remained confused. Still he saw the woman in labor; still he saw the man-child spring full-blown and full-armed. But he dreamed those dreams in a pleasant house of four rooms with ginkgo trees in the courtyard. He went to his office in the morning and to restaurants in the evening. Wang hired a houseboy for him. This one was called Ping-ping; he was perhaps sixteen, and he in turn hired a cook who was comely and surely his woman. Each evening a woman awaited Kanamori, and sometimes two, and he would see one again if he expressed approval; yet he was not always interested. Often he assured Wang that the women were indeed gracious and not at fault, but the stress of work, the importance of his task, the responsibilities of the occupying powers . . . Wang understood, and the neglected women were not rebuked.

Kanamori traveled. Sometimes in a car and sometimes with a platoon in trucks, he visited towns and cities. Often he wore a

gown instead of his uniform, and purchased cigarettes unan-
nounced. He never found the prices unreasonable; if Wang was
skimming, he was enriching himself on volume and not on piracy.
Kanamori did not like Wang, who was dry, bloodless and always
correct, though occasionally his voice or his cat's face betrayed
enthusiasm—at a good month's take, a rich consignment from
Indochina, praise relayed by Kanamori. Wang wheedled, too,
mainly licenses—a ferryboat license, a monopoly of turnips in
some neighborhood, a travel pass for some anonymous and doubtless corrupt Chinese trader—in return for which he surely banked
handsome bribes. He made Kanamori exquisite gifts: a jade figu-
rine, a painting of a showy peacock, a small pheasant in bronze,
streaked with patina like feathers. Kanamori tolerated him, even
admired him. The man's manners were courtly, his suggestions
gentle; he was not ostentatious; he never complained about
money.

Three years passed. By 1941 Kanamori realized with only mild
chagrin that he preferred his trader's life. He was by now all but
Chinese. He preferred Chinese women and Chinese food. Among
the Chinese reconciled to the Japanese he had many friends. He
attended the theater, cock fights. At one cock fight he encountered
a fellow officer, one Okuhara, who took him drinking afterward
and then to a whorehouse. A fashionable place of good repute. It
was called the Snow Goose Pavilion because its madam was a
White Russian named Olga, and the local word for goose was a pun
on the word for Russian. Olga was a woman of understanding.
What there was to see she had seen; always Kanamori sensed an air
of weary contempt in her, of cynical resignation, but he assumed
that the contempt and cynicism were directed at men and not at
Asians. One of the girls—her name was Cropped Hair, and she
entered his dreams—rebuked him one evening for his drowsy lack
of interest, and he enjoyed the rebuke and found his interest
reviving. He instructed her to slap him, and then laughed and took
her joyfully, almost savagely, as if in revenge.
Kanamori was pleased, even lulled, by the spaciousness of

China: the plains, mountain ranges, river valleys, even the endless sky and the dry air of autumn. He began to think of himself whimsically as the last mandarin. One day he would perhaps wear a hat with a red button. It was not merely that he was a conqueror; he now felt like a superior man by virtue of accomplishment, residence, participation. So when the Japanese attacked America he thought, They have taken a great step—"they," not "we." Yet he wondered, and breathed quicker: would they need him now? Many nights he vowed to apply for transfer. Again his sleep was troubled. A lieutenant was assassinated. The authorities executed several Chinese, and Kanamori felt sorrow. He also felt disquiet, and kept an eye on Ping-ping, who was by now nineteen or twenty. He distrusted the parade of women: there were poisons. He distinctly preferred the girls at Olga's: the purchase money seemed to guarantee not merely satisfaction, not merely the occasional exhilaration of a light whipping and his subsequent revenge, but also his personal safety. Olga herself was a comfort. She understood his desire to experience pain as a contrast and prelude to exaltation. At first playfully and then more casually, as if they could both take it for granted, he made it clear to her that she would be held responsible for excessive pain or, as he added in jocular tones, misguided patriotism. He liked having her watch, and she raised no objection. It was odd, he knew, this foreign woman witnessing his pseudo-humiliation, but it was a source of banter between them, and augmented his pleasure. In time he ignored the women offered by Wang or Ping-ping, and when he spent an evening at home he was happier cataloguing his little collection of statues and scrolls.

In November of 1942 Kanamori inspected his retail outlets in the city of Yang-chou, a city heavily garrisoned because it was the confluence of a railroad line, a great canal, and Kao-yu Lake. As usual he wore the Chinese gown; as equally usual, his guard platoon, in field uniform and heavily armed, accompanied him on the truck. For Kanamori an opium den was now no more evil or notable than a wineshop. One entered, one greeted the pallid, unsmiling proprietor, one noted a few, or many, customers on pallets or wooden bunks. The sweetish, sickish odor was no more than an industrial effluvium. He scarcely ever saw faces, only the supine smokers or drowsers, so many rag dolls. In one den—a clean place, an air about it of reliability and domesticity—he had discussed price and volume with the proprietor and was warmed by the satisfaction of the honest businessman who feels that he has supplied a superior product at a reasonable price, thus buttressing the pillars of earth and the arches of heaven. Now he strolled the aisles, as if to ask, "Is all well? The service leaves nothing to be desired?" He stooped to retrieve a dead pipe lying at his feet, and pushed it toward the pallet, looking into the smoker's face with the instinct of the gentleman about to say, "Your pardon, sir; you dropped this."

The face was familiar. Before he recognized it he felt shock, shame, a wrench and a stab; he set his teeth together in a hissing grimace, and then his mind relayed the message: this is Kurusu.

When he could stir, he turned and left, with only an abrupt nod to the proprietor.

Once each year Kanamori traveled home, by train to Shanghai and by ship to Nagasaki and then by train again, an interminable journey with stopovers and switchings, and if it was summer he baked in the metal cars, the humming of paper fans like a chorus of winged insects, to Akita finally, and then by wheezing bus to the village of Saito on the River Omono near Akita.

In the village of Saito his father, white-haired but strong as an oak and stern, was the police force. When Kanamori entered the house, exhausted and dripping sweat, after his boots had been snatched almost from his feet by the servant girl, his father rose and stood like an emperor reviewing troops, eyes aglitter and the flare of his deep nostrils betraying grand emotion. Kanamori saluted; his father did the same. Kanamori then knelt at his father's feet, and received his blessing. The old man spoke gruffly; it was the voice of affection, but even more the voice of instruction, of command, of manliness, the voice of the samurai. The father praised the son. From the family altar the household gods approved. This old man who had risen to major over thirty years recited the son's successive promotions, and then spoke with rising satisfaction of their country's triumphs, first in China and then, after the glorious winter of 1942, in Hawaii, Indonesia, Hong Kong and the Philippines. The old man's voice was enriched by these victories; he spoke like a herald, or a narrator in an opera. He ordered the servant girl to bring wine, and to prepare a bath. Then he called to Kanamori's mother, who was at last permitted to behold her son.

Kanamori's mother did not age, except for the graying of the hair. Each year she showed him the same face, unwrinkled, placid, impassive, only an occasional flash of joy or submission. The father would ask for details of Kanamori's work in "military government," and Kanamori would invent whole administrations, elaborating on "the transport problem" or "flood control" or "public health," to his father's obvious pride and satisfaction. Then his mother would ask if he caught many colds, or if he was planning to marry. At this his father would laugh and scoff. The two men would stroll, and in the street the father would say gravely, "Military government," to Sugita the tinker, or "Political education," to Kotani the restaurateur, and once, when a subprefect traveling through stopped to say hello, "A captain now, you see, and on the General Staff in Nanking!"

All was serene in the village of Saito on the River Omono near Akita, but Kanamori's dreams were more frequent and intense there, as if in contrast to the cool dawn and the eternal peace, and after ten days he was restless, and yearned within for Nanking, as if he were firmly bound to the scene of his conquests and his sins. The village of Saito was a painting from an old scroll; Nanking was the world. He studied his mother. Perhaps he was in essence Chinese. Always in these years this notion teased him: he was at heart Chinese.

He said nothing ever of opium, of Olga's, of murder and corpse-lined streets, of rape, or of the man-child leaping from the womb in his nightmares: feint left, feint right, *Ima!*

12 獅

Burnham sauntered into the Willow Wine Shop late at night with a hundred pellets of Grade A Laotian opium in his right hand and a severe infatuation on his left arm. Sea Hammer scurried and hissed, but too late. Burnham walked in on a Chinese cop in a gray sharkskin double-breasted and an obvious gangster in purple rayon.

He reacted like a trouper. He slew Sea Hammer with a dirty look: some protection! He shoved his door shut with the small package, bowed and smiled at the two men, warned Hao-lan of incipient snakes and scorpions by tightening the ring of his fingers on her wrist, and said, "Do not be a guest."

Yen saw the joke. "The landlord objected, but in the end admitted us. Official business. I hope I may be forgiven."

"There is nothing to forgive. The police are always welcome here."

"Hsü, now you are fooling." Amused, he was inspecting this woman. Burnham took a moment to catalogue the gangster. Perhaps twenty-five; the suit tailored; sunglasses; a gold ring, intertwined snakes; a white shirt and a pale gold necktie with a pattern of small red crowns. A ready smile, a hairline mustache, flat eyes. "May I introduce Ming Chang-wei," Yen said. "He is the trusted friend and confidant of Sung Yun."

"How do you do," Burnham said.

"Hello, Joe, whaddya know?" Ming said. "Sung Yun sent me because I speak English."

"An exquisite courtesy on his part," Burnham said. "This is Anna May Wong. She has manifold talents but speaks no English, aside from a few coarse expressions. I suggest we confine ourselves to that language." To her he said in Chinese, "Take off your coat and have a chair. Ashtray and cups on the chest. Whiskey in a drawer. A few moments only." He asked the others, "You have news? It's an odd hour for a social call."

"We came earlier, of course," Yen said, "and so waited. We had wonder if your news. Also, Sung Yun would urge you to call by."

"I've been working," Burnham said. "Renewing old ties."

"Ah, contacts!" Yen approved.

"At least one old tie," Ming said, "is worth renewing. A slick chick. Built for speed and not for comfort."

Burnham blinked, recovered, forced a smile.

"You heard guns?" Yen asked.

"Several times."

"Your safety. I am responsible."

"You must not think so. I must go here and there alone. There is no help for it."

"Still," Yen said, "one feels such bad host."

God damn these fools anyway. "Nobody wants me to find Kanamori," Burnham said. "Everybody tells me to go home."

"Sung Yun wants you to find him," Ming said, "and that's the straight goods."

"And I too." Yen paused, groping for words. "He is remind them of war, you see. Most people rather forget. Also, your danger embarrass others, who lose face and feel guilt."

"Watch your step," Ming said. "Kanamori is one tough baby. If he ain't croaked by now."

A stylist. Burnham grunted. "I think I'm being used to draw fire. Or at least to stir up the snakes."

"Not by me," Yen said. "I want only the man Kanamori."

Hao-lan complained in Chinese: "Is this to last all night? Time is money."

"My sweet singer." Burnham's voice oozed. "A moment more only."

She mouthed a noisy kiss.

"Oh you kid," Ming said, and to Burnham: "If we don't pull him in now, he's gone for good. You're the last hope. A fresh bloodhound."

Yen slipped into Chinese: "There is so little time, and you work alone. Suppose you disappeared? What then?"

"It must be done my way," Burnham insisted. "I seek a paw print here, a bent blade of grass there; I sniff the wind, and listen to birdsong."

"You will hear more than birdsong," Yen said gloomily. "You have already heard gunfire. The city is aboil. The students march. Your grass will be trampled, your paw prints obliterated. By tomorrow, perhaps."

"Then I must fail," Burnham said.

Yen drew smoke and calmed himself. "Forgive me. Perhaps it is as well. You have done this before, and with success. I hope I have not been unpleasant."

"You have been indispensable. Without your report I would wander in darkness."

"You have my number. You will call me each day?"

"At least once."

"My prices are going up by the minute," Hao-lan said. "Russian princes do not keep me waiting. Or American bristle merchants."

"My wild pigeon," Burnham said.

"I will stay for breakfast," she said decisively. "For breakfast I like cold salt fish and hot rice."

Ming cleared his throat. "Sung Yun says to drop in tomorrow. Okay?"

"You said it. What time, kiddo?"

Ming beamed. "Around eleven in the morning? Can you dump hot stuff here?"

"Where'd you learn English?" Burnham asked reverently.

"In college."

"In the States?"

Ming melted, suffused with joy. "No, no, right here. That is, in Chengtu, during the war. I majored in the American vernacular or mei kuo pai hua, and I hung around with GI's. Have I the gift of gab?"

"A richer gift than mine, old buddy. You're hip."

Ming frowned. "I am not hep?"

"No, no, my dear Ming." Burnham was firm. "It is very unhip to be hep."

Ming sparkled. "Oh, that is swell. 'It is very unhip to be hep.' I am hip, pops, I am hip."

Hao-lan stood up, threw her fanny out of joint, slapped it and said, "Doss ah hip."

"Not now," Burnham said. "Please remain seated."

"Not now, now now!" she cried. "Then when? Am I not lovely as the night sky? Am I not fragrant as the jasmine? Must I suffer rejection and indignity at the hands of tourists?"

"Tourists!" Burnham was outraged.

"Well, we go now," Yen said. "Not much to report, you or we. Good luck."

"Bring him back alive." Ming jiggled his brows. "Sleep tight, and—"

"Don't say it," Burnham cut in. "Just this once, don't say it."

He bolted the door and stepped to Hao-lan. On her face he saw a confused agony of need, love and gentle mirth, mirroring his own; he kissed her lightly on the mouth and said, " 'My heart is a silver bell, and my blood peals your name.' " She sighed happily and tugged him closer, and he wrapped her in a huge hug, and they kissed again, lips alive and flesh singing. Burnham went out of himself, and wandered remote, dark regions; it was an aching, obliterating kiss, a fusion of two ghosts, annihilating time and place, a chaos of thunder, sea foam, stars, tropical winds. He drew her head to his shoulder, and stroked her hair; he was overcome by a rude desire to cry out, to spill his love in speeches, but he kept silence and listened to the tremor of their blood. They clung as if drowning.

In time they surfaced. Neither spoke. Her mouth quirked; she had perhaps thought of a small joke, not worth the telling, as he had thought of a waggish rebuke for her shameless and stylish performance, and found it not worth the saying. They did what lovers do. He kissed her eyes, her nose, her lips again; she ruffled his hair and stroked his face. He sat on the bed and pulled her to him, laid his head between her breasts, stroked her back and her buttocks. She pressed his head to her, tilted it back and bent to kiss his face.

They paused, and smiled foolishly.

With fingers like melons he fumbled at her cloth buttons, and they laughed aloud, because all buttons everywhere resisted lovers' untimely ineptitudes. In time the buttons, indulgent after all, relented, and he drew the brocade from her and kissed her soft and silky breasts; one, and then the other, and then the one again, and the other, until she pushed him away and put him to shame by springing his own buttons in a jiffy. When his shirt was off she spoke: "You are a hairy bear."

His throat was thick, so he only nodded. She untied his blue sash. He flipped his shoes off and stood upright; his padded trousers fell about his knees, and he laughed clownishly, stepping out of everything and standing naked before her. He went to his knees, stripped her quickly, and planted a lingering kiss on the warmth of her mound. "Why, you are indeed a redhead," he murmured. Already he was huge and tremulous. Her touch instructed him to stand. She stared frankly, made a little girl's wide eyes and grinned in greed, mischief and open delight.

He stumbled backward to the bed, sprawled, plumped back onto the pillow and extended a hand. She took the hand and carried it to her lips. He saw sorrow in her eyes, and remembered that she was vulnerable. He pressed his fingers to her mouth, met her gaze and tried to show her his own defenseless melancholy. Setting a knee on the bed, she leaned to kiss him. His hands cradled her breasts; the kiss endured; her nipples budded, and she slipped down into the crook of his arm, body to body as he turned to meet her. They lay together, and were warm.

He stroked her sleek flank, and she his. They panted gently in rhythm, kissed, again, and he saw that she was happy and trusting. "In debauchery," she murmured, "haste is a sin." She spoke Chinese. Heeding her, and the poets, he lingered. Glaciers formed, covered the earth and melted away. Floods followed, and centuries of sunshine kindled their flesh. His breath deepened, hers quickened. His flesh throbbed, hers rippled. He grazed plains and meadows, and knelt groaning, his nose muffled in russet tufts. She cried out, hummed, chanted. Her body writhed and arched.

After a lifetime she took him in. At the sudden sleek, silky, wrenching heat he gasped; yearning scalded his loins like hot tears, and they strained together, rocking and pounding. When she purred, sang out and finally sobbed, he grew giddy with joy and relief, and soon his own fervor overwhelmed him; he burst within her like a summer storm, riding her, spending love, desire, ecstasy in throb after throb. He heard his own voice: "Unh! Unh!" and hers: "Nnn."

They lay like moist sleeping pups for some time. Speech struggled to his lips and died; sweat mingled and trickled. Burnham shifted; for an instant Hao-lan's embrace tightened, and she sighed complacently. Burnham growled. They nuzzled. He kissed her lips and breasts, slipping from within her, and rolled onto his back. She scrambled to her knees and bent to kiss his wilting flower. She pouted and bemoaned the loss: " 'When the hare dies, the fox is sad.' " He seized the moment to swing her round rump into range, and kiss each swelling moon with a loud smack.

"Decadent foreigner," she said.

"Like your Russian princes and American bristle merchants."

She giggled, and hopped off the bed to stand gazing down at him. She ran a finger along a ridge of scar over a rib. "A bullet?"

"A knife. A bullet here."

She kissed his scars and left him. Weak with love and gratitude, and scared half to death by both, he watched her walk, drank in her small body so beautifully formed, sleek and unwrinkled, golden in the low light. She sat naked in an armchair, and smoked, and they did not speak for a time—only looked and smiled and shook their heads as lovers do who cannot find the words.

They shared a drink then, and tried feebly to find the words, and slowly the sadness came, drifting into the room with hints of tomorrow. They did not speak of this future; there was no need. Later Burnham's manhood stirred again and they spoke of the mystery, awkwardness, homeliness and inefficiency of the human body, and yet, and yet. "Four legs would be so much better," she maintained. "Good for the back and the balance."

"But then we could not make love face to face," he said.

"Seen in that light," she said primly, "the suggestion loses force."

"Seen in this light," he said, "you acquire force. Come and lie beside me. Soon enough it will be time for cold salt fish and hot rice."

She did, and he rose on one elbow to gaze upon her body. Bliss surged into him at the sight, the exhilarating geography of sex, the rounded hills of breasts, the cavern of an armpit, the soft slope of the belly, the tangled grove of love-hair and the invitation of thighs. He remembered his father preaching on eternal bliss. To Burnham this was the only bliss. He tried to imagine eternal orgasm. He sensed the noisy simmer of his blood, rushing and clanging, oh breathless love, the prickling and longing, but also —God, will you never learn mercy?—the agonizing foreknowledge, the bone-deep anguish of love's end, suppressed and denied but always impending: here or at the horizon, now or at the hour of death.

He was thirty-five, and all he knew about the heart told him that love was more vulnerable and evanescent than dew, was killed quickly by a word, a look, a smell, or slowly by the years, dying nastily, screeching out its life, withering, blowing away, ash. The fear of that, the secret pain of it, kept pace with love; great love was twinned to great torment.

He could hardly believe that he was in love, but he saw no other explanation. For once the word did not embarrass him. He was suddenly mortal, and it was worth the anguish. Chills and fever, pangs and spasms, and yet this sense of natural discovery, of permanence, of belonging.

He spent a moment of pity for men who died without ever loving, and he touched Hao-lan's cheek. "Shameless," he said, to dispel the sorrow. "A wanton."

"Oh yes," she said. Her hands roamed his body; again she bent to kiss his manhood.

"You are merely trying to soften my heart," he said sternly.

"Wrong on both counts," she said, and they did not sleep that night, but made spring showers until dawn admonished them, and a fresh fall of lacy snow. They stood at the window entwined, and wished the world lost.

On a summer afternoon in 1943 Major Kanamori and Citizen Wang were celebrating Kanamori's promotion with a cup of Dragon's Well tea in Kanamori's garden. The hum of bees was loud, bucolic, comforting. Kanamori wore thin cotton Chinese trousers and a silk shirt open at the neck. Wang was his customary dry and deferential self, though he had ventured a joke: if the war lasted long enough, Kanamori would be a general. "If the war ends unexpectedly," Kanamori answered, "I shall be a civilian, and Chinese at that." He was tired these days, and inordinately jumpy. His visits to Olga's had become more frequent, his abasements deeper, his ecstasies sharper. Mornings after, he was shattered. He was ashamed now to be seen without a shirt. He understood that debauchery was taking a toll, but it was after all only a habit, like wine, that could be broken if his light anxiety turned to fear.

"Ah well, if the war ends sooner," said Wang, and let the thought drift between them. American forces were progressing westward across the Pacific. Tokyo had actually been bombed over a year before—shocking news—and while the Japanese had continued to advance, occupying some mysterious islands in the far north near the icy wastes of a land called Alaska, the Americans had now retaken those islands, as well as some of the Solomons, and had won—if communiqués were read carefully—two or three considerable naval battles. Wang invariably asked Kanamori to locate these exotic spots; Kanamori suspected that Wang's geography was not at all deficient, but supplied the information anyway.

Kanamori was not so fierce now, and heard himself saying, "I suppose we could lose this war."

"The prudent man," said Wang, "fills his pocket with coppers and lines his shoes with gold."

"If we lose this war I will be stripped of my shoes too," Kanamori said.

"In the jails of Chungking," Wang mused, "cockroaches thrived. The administration set the prisoners a quota: ten roaches per day per man, or no food. The roaches disappeared. Now the quotas could not be met, and the wardens laughed as they divided the food appropriation, and the prisoners starved."

"So?"

"So the prisoners founded cockroach farms. Assets, exchangeable. In effect they lined their shoes with gold."

"Parables and proverbs," Kanamori said. "You are about to sell me a cockroach farm."

"No, no, no," Wang said, and they went on to speak of other matters: Communists in the northwest, and the local Vermilion Society, which had proclaimed itself responsible for several assassinations and promised more. But as the sun westered and conversation flagged, Wang said, "You know Ho Tzu-kai the master steamfitter?"

"Of course." Ho Tzu-kai the master steamfitter had not done a day's work in four years: he was a licenser of steamfitting projects, and was fat on bribes.

"His parents are in the unoccupied zone. They are old. He fears they will die before he and his wife and their four young ones can make proper obeisance."

Kanamori took this news calmly, but among the lees of his samurai's soul contempt stirred. The first rat was fleeing the ship. "Surely he can find a way across the lines."

"Ah, but he is a man of substance."

"And wants to carry the substance with him."

"You understand."

"Let him convert it to gold, and line his shoes with it."

"Generations of household goods? Ivories? Old porcelains? Furniture? Think of the loss, should he sell at panic prices."

"Then let him stay." This Ho annoyed Kanamori.

"Well, it is not merely the going," Wang said. "And it is not merely the salvaging of his possessions. For that alone he has a porcelain chicken."

Kanamori laughed. The laugh subsided, but a residual giggle bubbled to the surface.

"This porcelain chicken is painted green and yellow."

Kanamori waited.

"It is perhaps a thousand years old."

Kanamori said slowly, "A T'ang porcelain."

"He also owns a porcelain peasant woman, hauling water by means of a yoke." Wang was almost jolly now. "So great is Ho's filial piety that he will give a chicken to cross the lines, but he will give a peasant woman for a warrant."

Wang was too clever. Irritating. "What is this warrant?"

"A warrant for his arrest," Wang said, "denouncing him as a Chinese patriot and hero of the resistance. Perhaps even posters in the public square."

Kanamori grinned like a thief. "Why not kill him and take his baubles?"

"Because," Wang said patiently, "there are others. Would you destroy the cockroach farm?"

Kanamori's collection grew. So, he assumed, did Wang's. Yu Tsung-huang the cement king was denounced for communication with Chiang Kai-shek's armies. He disappeared; his poster graced the Central Post Office in Nanking, and Kanamori was the richer by a winged pedestal cup, of wood, lacquered, possibly an imitation, but priceless if real. Jung Meng-yu the coalyard king remained in Nanking, but his wife, a former opera singer, was denounced; shortly she was said to be in Chungking starring in patriotic dramas. Kanamori was fond of the gilt bronze bodhisattva that sat like an icon smiling at him; it was only four hundred years old but rare enough, after all. Chou Chun-yi the chemical king (sulfuric acid, nitric acid, hydrochloric acid, caustic soda, soda ash, sodium sulfide) remained in place, but a false dossier was prepared with care and filed away; should the Chinese actually win this war he would be found to have "sheltered criminal elements," "maintained criminal contact with the Chinese government," and "transmitted information of a confidential military nature." Kanamori received a bronze oil lamp in the shape of a ram. His favorite piece proved to be erotic and Japanese: a topknotted samurai grimacing in glee as he plunged into an acquiescent maiden from behind, horse upon horse; the figures were of painted hardwood, and the woman, her head upflung, seemed to be screaming in joy. After some days he noticed that her hands were not flat, but clawed the earth, that the cords of her neck strained, and that her scream might not be joyful. He was momentarily depressed, even sullen, but the features, limbs and joints were so delicately carved, the figures in such flowing balance, that his annoyance ebbed. Even when this piece invaded his dreams he cherished it. More, he became superstitiously attached to it, and stared at it for long minutes, as if in penance.

Kanamori had no notion what he would do with these treasures; Wang presented him with another every month, and dimly Kanamori realized that they were not easily negotiable. But by now he was in the grip of a curious fatalism, as if suspended: he had his house, his servants, his work (which all but accomplished itself), his amplifying obsessions at the whorehouse. Day followed day, none much different, and what was to become of him seemed unimportant. Now and then he wondered if he was falling into madness. He was courteous always to the Chinese. He was incapable of sex save with whores and when beaten. In 1944 he concocted excuses and declined home leave. The Americans swept westward across the Pacific: Tarawa in the Gilberts, Saipan in the Marianas, Hollandia in Dutch New Guinea, Peleliu in the Palaus. In Burma the Allies took Myitkyina. The bombing of the Japanese homeland became commonplace. Toward the end of the year, American forces invaded the Philippines.

"There is someone I want arrested," Wang said testily. Today he was more nervous than Kanamori.

"My pleasure. Who is it?"

"A man called Sung Yun." Wang wrote the characters on a scratch pad.

"And what shall we arrest him for?"

"He agitates among the Chinese, urging sabotage and general

resistance. He slanders men like me, who keep the peace and maintain order. He seems to have singled me out, and I do not like it."

Kanamori was indifferent to this: "Write up a description, and you shall have your warrant."

"Thank you. He may be hard to find. I hope you will set spies and informers at his heels."

"Whatever you say."

"A troublemaker," Wang muttered.

"A Communist?"

"No, no," Wang said quickly, and paused, frowning. "No, I do not believe that. Though . . . no."

"Write him up, write him up," Kanamori said. "I shall have a fat price put on his head."

Olga dressed his wounds herself, with buttery unguents compounded by old-fashioned pharmacists. Kanamori was thoroughly at home now with this henna-haired, sharp-beaked ex-countess. He had met few White Russians who were not ex-counts or -countesses, or dukes or princes, but was happy to give Olga the benefit of his ample doubt. "Ya, ya, ya," she murmured. "You heal quickly, but in time this will be scar."

"I am less than human," Kanamori said sadly.

"The Orient," Olga said. "Dans l'Orient désert quel devint mon ennui!"

Kanamori understood no French and so was even more fascinated by this harpy. She was little more than fifty, but the veins in her nose were disintegrating beneath the rice powder, and no makeup could clear her bloodshot eyes. He was also fascinated by her wrinkled neck and parchment chest, and the crab-apple breasts beneath the watered silk of her Western evening gown; always she wore a long dress, like a diplomat's wife at a prestigious function. Kanamori did not desire her. He was aware of her body as an alien and faintly disagreeable presence: how dismaying, almost sickening, to realize that this sharp-nosed, scrawny snob grew hair between her legs, presumably made the beast with two backs, had in her time moaned and shrieked and whimpered! These days he was most often repelled by the human body, at best intrigued when it was exotic like this one. He had seen so many bodies used and thrown away. Yet he was sensitive to fluctuations in his own pulse: a bellyache frightened him; the recurrent failure of his manhood depressed him; he did not smoke because the swelling of his nasal membranes and the consequent snuffling, hawking and spitting alarmed him as portents of malfunction and dissolution.

With Olga he drank vodka and felt international. "My father," he said, "fought Russians."

"Fate moves in circles. The stars rule all." Olga's Chinese was fluent but her accent deformed. "And now we are friends. Even intimate friends."

"That is true. No woman knows me as you do."

Olga waved off the gratitude.

"Nevertheless," Kanamori persisted, "I am grateful. You will one day allow me to be of service."

"Absolutely," Olga said, surprising him. "Today. I want to leave here soon."

"Ah." Kanamori's heart ached, as if a young love had spoken of some other man. Nanking without the Snow Goose Pavilion? Where would he find ease? A young woman could perhaps be trained, but would she understand? Or would contempt show behind the eyes?

"Let us say the war ends," Olga grumbled. "Let us even say it ends badly. In Nanking I am Madam Olga, friend to the Japanese. In Peking—for example—I could be Madam Olga who quarreled with the monkeys, Madam Olga much persecuted. You forgive my frankness."

"Of course. Between you and me . . . but I can promise nothing. I must think."

"Think all you like," she said, "but one promise you must make me: if you are called back to the home islands for defense, you will arrange my . . . well, my own transfer, before you leave."

"That I promise," Kanamori said, and brightened. "Such a

recall might be the making of me. Now I am only an edgy bureaucrat suffering nightmares."

"It might indeed be the making of you. I cannot say what would be best for you. Your soul does not exist. I have seen men in all conditions and states of lust and madness—fetishists, syphilitics, even Americans. But there is something especially empty about you."

"Madness," Kanamori repeated peacefully. "Yes, I think I am mad."

Wang said, "If the worst happens, we must not be taken in this city. We must be anonymous. You could pass for Chinese."

"I too have thought so. I know where I want to go."

Wang cocked his head.

"To Peking."

"Ah. The mother of cities."

"Madam Olga also wishes to see Peking."

Wang grimaced elaborately. "The foreign bustard."

"My friend."

"And I honor her for it," Wang said quickly.

So raddled red-haired Olga, waving a long Russian cigarette (luxuries ignored parties, armies, boundaries), left Nanking by train, taking with her an old servant and four lovely, accomplished whores. The platform was thick with officers, many of whom had brought flowers, some real and some of paper. Olga smiled a wooden smile and blew regal kisses. Kanamori was there, strutting like the rest and making a soldier's jokes, but nervous within, abruptly homeless. The Americans were fighting in Manila, Tokyo had been devastated by B-29s, and here was Kanamori with his filing cabinets and objets d'art and no one to whip him.

"Perhaps," Wang ventured diffidently, "we should all prepare a move to Peking."

"But you are rid of that bustard," Kanamori said lightly. "Can you be in such a hurry to rejoin her?"

"I have given this some thought. A businesswoman in Peking,

with a house of her own . . . In the north, foreigners sprinkle themselves more evenly among the populace, and are less noticeable." Wang smiled, cheerful and guileful. "A place to go! What man does not need a place to go? With a bit of space in the basement to store the household gods—"

"Those priceless household gods," Kanamori murmured.

"And a room in the attic," Wang continued, "where a man may live quietly for a time while life's storms subside."

"Peking!" Kanamori mused. "Perhaps I shall be a mandarin after all."

The Imperial High Command played the card for them: after a few judicious hints, Kanamori was seconded to Peking. Much of the Peking garrison was posted back to the home islands for defense; in a steady drift northward, or toward Shanghai, Japanese officers and men responded to forces dimly perceived and not truly comprehended. Kanamori was ordered to destroy all his records. The work took a whole day; the bonfire blazed high. "All those years of life and labor," Wang grieved. "Up in smoke."

Kanamori admired the man's sense of humor. "I can make copies of your own records, if you wish, to reminisce over in your old age."

"No, no," Wang protested; both men laughed. "Will your baggage be limited?"

"Personal belongings, but most officers have accumulated souvenirs."

"Souvenirs indeed. As I am a Chinese civilian, my own baggage would be subject to examination and even pilferage."

"We shall consolidate your things with mine," Kanamori said.

"I hoped you would say that."

"But we have been partners for six years. Think of it!"

"I think of it often," Wang said, "and always with gratitude."

Such a conniver! But Kanamori was more amused than wary.

I have killed and raped and plundered, Kanamori thought, and now I must crown my work by betraying my own country. And yet, which country? I have conquered the one and now I shall cheat the other. There seemed to be two Kanamoris these days —one half-witted, doing as instructed by Wang; the other shrewd, detached, observing and understanding Wang's every gesture and intent. Also the dreams were more frequent and more horrific, as though the imminent end of the war was also to be a reckoning, a climax: *now* the nervous breakdown, *now* the impotence, *now* a gibbering Kanamori locked away by righteous, vengeful victors. Yet what remained of his mind worked like a fine watch.

With his goods and Wang's crated together, a narrow heart was advisable. Wang's pieces, he noticed, were less valuable than his own, more humble, deferent, ordinary. They were predominantly bronze and porcelain lions, with also a lacquered Ming box, much Ch'ing porcelain and several scrolls and paintings beyond Kanamori's ken. Wrapped and buried in straw, the entire collection occupied four large crates. Kanamori was impressed by the probable value of all this; yet part of him shrugged. He could not know that his bronze oil lamp in the shape of a ram was not a gift from Chou Chun-yi the chemical king but was the last of a series of extortions and trades—trading up, indeed!—effected by Wang and was virtually priceless, surely beyond the means of all but a handful of collectors; he could not know that the collection as a whole would never be negotiable except to governments and museums; but he did know that Wang coveted the entire lot. He warned himself to be cautious. Wang smelled of greed as other men smelled of sweat.

At the station Wang sat in his well-sprung, brass-mounted ricksha like a lanky prince; when he required forward motion he touched the ricksha man with a foot. In all these years Kanamori had never noticed who, or how many in succession, pulled the ricksha. Nobody ever sees the ricksha man. It was a true ricksha, beautifully balanced, not a pedicab.

The crates were duly sealed, placed in Kanamori's compartment and guarded by two Japanese infantrymen personally known to him. (Not Tateno or Kyose; those days were gone.) Wang expressed satisfaction, even affection. They would meet again in a better place: to wit, Peking. Kanamori admired the man's audacity: staking his all—and a large all it was—on one grand throw. Nevertheless, Kanamori's final farewell was to a captain of military police, whom he instructed to follow Wang, arrest him and see that he died quickly and in silence.

Then Kanamori settled into his compartment, and watched the countryside fly by as far as Yang-chou, where he and his crates left the train and were escorted to a comfortable, not to say luxurious, canal boat for a leisurely trip north by water. So when Wang's spies boarded the train at Kao-yu, they discovered the bird flown and the nest bare.

But when the captain of military police halted Wang's ricksha, he found it empty. The faceless coolie had no idea where Wang was. Under a new identity, and with impressive credentials, Wang the patriot was making his own journey north, in the shadows and by crooked paths.

Kanamori arrived in Peking sure that Wang was dead, and did not hesitate to store his personal effects at Madam Olga's on Palisade Street. Madam Olga was expecting him, not because she took for granted her madam's powers or his perversity, but because the wily Wang had instructed her carefully and bribed her generously.

Yet in the end Kanamori won.

Possibly man's most intense and memorable amusement is a sleepless night with the beloved. Burnham, aged thirty-five and passing painfully through a prolonged adolescence, wondered how old or stupid or brave a man had to be before he abjured this sweet slow suicide. Morning brought its own rebukes. No regrets, but the bruised flesh cried out, the scrambled brains begged for rest, the taste buds died of overwork. Furthermore, he found himself lonely, and decided that he was born to be monogamous. The gods had commanded him to love, and he saw no reason now to be without his dumpling even momentarily. He would bury her waist-deep in diamonds, rubies, emeralds and sapphires; offer her whole provinces; share with her all the jokes, music and sorrows, yes, even sorrows, that life had taught him. And she would teach him to be patient, wise and steadfast.

Meanwhile he was half dead, sprawled behind Feng and groaning intermittently. They were riding north on Morrison Street, and first the Union Church and then the old Salvation Army building stared down at him reproachfully. "Yü, I am punished," he said. "Social calls."

"The superior man does not murmur against heaven," Feng said, "nor grumble against men."

"Neither does he preach to the afflicted," Burnham scolded. "Wake me when we arrive." He thought perhaps Feng was laughing.

Sung Yun's house, near the East Four P'ai-lou, was grand, with a moon gate. Even exhausted, Burnham was fond of moon gates. To enter one's home through a perfect circle! Doors were dull, ordinary—carpentry and not architecture, for ciphers and not creatures of flesh and blood. He noted the spirit wall within, simple and blank, obdurate, forbidding, faintly screened by falling snow. He also noted the courtyard:

trees and shrubs sunken and withered, stone benches uninviting beneath the gray sky, the light layer of snow roiled and slushy. The area was crowded with crates and cases and young men in black padded trousers and short jackets. When these young servants ceased their tapping and hammering to observe Burnham, they were transformed into flat-eyed gangsters in uniform. Sung Yun would sport fine hair in his ears, maybe a silky beard or an embroidered skullcap. And a million bucks in the basement. Burnham would disappear down a trapdoor and be nibbled to death by carp.

Burnham exaggerated. To stay awake at all, some exaggeration was necessary. Two hours' sleep. Before that, noodles and tea. Before that, escorting his weary Lady Doc home by the dawn's early light. They were forspent and leaned together in Feng's chariot, nothing so undignified as cuddling, but flesh to flesh beneath the padded gowns, keeping awake on nervous energy and imbecile rapture. At the clinic they maintained a desperate decorum, desire flickering still as they mouthed inanities: See you later, a most pleasant evening, and Nurse An polite and remote. An ancient truth: those who flamed in need, whose souls shrieked for flesh, whose blood simmered in the anguish of desire, were not the resentful and deprived but manic lovers, gorging and starving at once on unremitting lust, the appetite that grows by what it feeds on.

And now he must be polite and cagey to the eminent Sung Yun. Who was on his way out. Shanghai, Formosa maybe. Packing the household gods, the photograph album, the high school yearbook and the golf clubs.

Ming cried, "Greetings, gate!" with a sparkling smile and a serpent's eyes.

Shambling though the moon gate Burnham muttered his own greetings.

"Oho, the morning after," Ming said.

A glow of rage died quickly in Burnham. "Does the eminent Sung Yun speak English?"

"Not a word." Probably a lie, but it was what Burnham wanted to hear. Enough American vernacular was enough. "Then let us confine ourselves to Chinese," Burnham said.

"That is proper and courteous," Ming said smoothly, and then they were across the courtyard and entering a spacious salon. Lamps flickered against the winter gloom beneath shades of many colors. Couches, rosewood tables, chairs, more crates. Two small gongs. On the walls, scrolls and calligraphies, and several bare spots. On the tables, a few jade carvings, a Chinese book with blue boards held in place by ivory teeth through tiny cloth loops. Burnham saw a small ceramic woman in a green and yellow gown, her hair in two horned peaks. Also a lo-han, a bodhisattva in ivory. Whatever else he was, Sung Yun was a man of taste. And money.

A door opened and Sung Yun entered. Burnham was too tired for shock, but experienced surprise. The man was about sixty, with a full mane of white hair and a broad, leonine face, the white mustache too springing wide like a lion's. He was rawboned, tall and vigorous. So much for Burnham's squat mandarin. Sung Yun's hands joined as if in prayer as he bowed and said, "You honor my rude hut."

"To enter it is an honor," Burnham said mechanically, and bowed in turn.

"Its simple ornaments are sadly diminished." Sung Yun's hand fluttered vaguely at the bare spots, crates and uncluttered tables.

"What remains is breathtaking," Burnham said. His heart was not in it. A fine time for troublesome inner winds and lacquered eyes! Either he should not have met Hao-lan, or he should not be chasing this wild Japanese goose. He roused inner reserves and made a painful effort to appear sociable.

"The merest knickknacks," Sung Yun said mournfully, "suitable to relieve the gloom of a tumbledown shanty."

"May I stand a moment and look?"

"But of course. Do not be a guest."

Burnham admired a painting—a fisherman in a small boat beneath a towering, misty mountain. "It is surely late Ming?"

"Why yes!" Sung Yun's tone was rapturous. "A connoisseur!"

"And this ivory lion. A work of art."

Sung Yun sat languidly on one of the couches. "Please. Do not fear to touch."

Burnham smiled appreciatively, and did what connoisseurs do: he picked up the ivory with reverence, and peered at the base and head to verify that the narrow brownish nerve ran through the center of the piece, and that its owner had therefore laid out many bundles for it. "I envy you," he lied, knowing the cost of these arts: slavery, misery, a land fertilized by the bones of the hopeless and reaping the surplus that made lo-hans possible. Chinese culture. The porters at the airport were also Chinese culture, and the woman who made coal balls, and beggars and bandits and Feng and civil wars. His own father in Nanking, years before: "Everything is God, even war." And Burnham flaring, "Everything is politics, even art." Well, he was older now, and calmer. This morning everything was love and the rest superfluous.

A woman entered, young, flowing, a beauty, and behind her another, almost identical; at their heels scampered two tiny tawny dogs.

"But here are two flowers who will perfume our morning." Sung Yun's skin was taut; his face was almost fleshless, and when he smiled, as he did now, he seemed glossy. The two women were indeed flowers; lovely round faces, lively dark eyes, their bodies cloaked in gauzy blue gowns, hemmed and piped in black and red brocade. "Miss Mei and Miss Ai," Sung Yun identified them; the women bowed. He spoke of tea; the women departed, and idly Burnham noted the flow of flesh beneath the silk. Old Sung lived right. Burnham's mind, drowsy but unquenchably prurient, leaped to orgies: Sung and Ming and these two slick chicks. Impossible. "The most winsome of women," he lied.

Sung Yun shrugged. "One appreciates beauty. It is the glory of China. Poetry. Painting. Works of art."

Of course. Miss Mei and Miss Ai were knickknacks. "The art of China is the envy of the world."

"That is true. But please. Be comfortable. Sit."

Burnham sat on a couch opposite his host. Ming took a wooden chair and looked alert.

"So how goes the hunt?" Sung Yun asked amiably.

Burnham was truly shocked at the question: he had expected several minutes of frothy roundaboutation. Sung Yun must be worried. Burnham weighed his answer; this smooth mandarin knew of the foreigner's nocturnal hijinks, but how much more did he know?

"I have paid several courtesy calls," Burnham said, "seen some old comrades, and tested the breezes."

"Yes, yes," Sung Yun approved, "immersing yourself in the atmosphere of old Peking."

"True. It is slow and careful work. Before the rabbit stew, I need the paw print in the snow."

"I know of Inspector Yen's report," Sung Yun said. "More than one paw print, but they vanish. They are obscured by drifts, or fresh falls."

"So I must begin again, and sniff the eight winds."

"And where will you begin?"

"In old and disused paths," Burnham said. "I am the fox who returns to the forest when the tigers have left. I must trot the narrow trails and not the beaten track."

"And how does one spot these narrow trails?"

"One touches noses with other foxes." Probably there were more ways not to answer a question in Chinese than in any other tongue. Burnham cheered up. He cheered up further when Miss Mei or Miss Ai tripped into the room again, followed by Miss Ai or Miss Mei; they bore tea trays, and busied themselves like ancient dancers, setting out the cups, wiggling gracefully, pouring, serving, distracting. Oh, Burnham! he thought. Your eyes are bigger than your— Well, never mind. One looks inevitably. Miss Mei's breast brushed his arm; he wondered if their bosoms also were identical. He imagined the lap dogs huddled in the bedroom, gazing curiously at monstrous copulations.

Sung Yun produced cigarettes; Burnham declined courteously. The ladies flirted and poured, and he wondered if these cookies too were bound for Shanghai or Formosa, or if Sung would leave them with a string of cash, counting on local talent later—cookies everywhere, stamped out by the great cookie cutter of population, poverty, corruption. China, the golden age. Philosophy. Acupuncture. Ephedrine. Spaghetti, brought to Italy by Marco Polo. Old men with four-inch fingernails. Cookies.

"We have not much time," Sung Yun said. "You could move in here, you know."

Burnham was startled.

Sung Yun waved a languid hand. "My poor home. Dismantled now, but livable. A room, servants. Miss Ai and Miss Mei to make music. Though of course you do not lack company of your own."

"A keen bimbo," Ming murmured. Sung Yun ignored him, and Burnham held his peace.

"You honor me," Burnham said. "It is far above my merit." For a moment he became what he knew they thought him. "True, I am alone, with a full purse, in this greatest of cities."

"Messengers also would be at hand," Sung Yun said. "Bodyguards if necessary. The swift coordination of all intelligence."

"It must be thought about." Burnham allowed a doleful regret to sadden his features. "You see, I will be in and out at all hours. I must communicate with my own consular people."

"Consular people?" Sung Yun in turn allowed his brows to arch infinitesimally. "It was my understanding that your country would, ah, defer officially to my own."

"Your understanding is remarkable," Burnham said. "My government, like any government, need not be informed of every sneeze. Nonetheless, the safety of even its meanest citizen is of natural concern."

Sung Yun understood.

"Moreover," Burnham pressed on, "I may need to receive visitors of a quality unworthy of this room's serenity and beauty."

"Still, your demands would be as my own. Your safety, comfort, pains and pleasures."

"Alas. My instructions complicate the matter. Had my superiors known of your hospitable nature, I might have been spared the pains of discourtesy."

Sung Yun was appalled. "But there is no discourtesy! As you

may know, America has no more faithful friend than I. You are a foreigner and therefore incomprehensible to a degree; nevertheless, it springs to the eye that you are a man of good bones."

Burnham offered the witless half-smile of the grateful barbarian.

"My only concern is for you," Sung Yun emphasized. "You are —may I say so?—an unusual man and a pleasant surprise. You arrive speaking the language and wearing the clothes. You take a room in what can charitably be described as an authentic neighborhood. But in Peking, the mother of cookery, it will not do to subsist on steamed dough and maize rolls."

"Indeed it will not do!" Burnham said heartily. He was rapidly wearying of Sung Yun. "I have my restaurants. Old favorites."

"Ah, let me guess! The Peking Duck. The Tung Lai Shun."

Tung Lai Shun. A man of Peking would have said "Shuerh." His faint accent indicated other regions, but perhaps it was merely elegance of speech. Burnham nodded: "And others. As you say, the food of Peking is unequaled anywhere."

"Mm, the food of Szechuan is not bad. A bit peppery perhaps. The food of Hankow and Soochow is of a notable delicacy, they say."

"To serve many dishes is to be sure to please all." Burnham's back was stiff, and his behind ached. He inhaled the fragrance of his tea, and took a long sip, slurping loudly. This was not bad manners; it indicated that Sung Yun's hot tea was too delectable to wait for. Nor was Burnham a flatterer; the tea was in truth a rare pleasure, of the first leaf. A rich and tangy taste and a blossoming, teasing aftertaste. "This is tea for the gods."

"Boiled water and straw," Sung Yun protested. "Why is Kanamori important to the Americans?"

Whoa! Sung Yun was going for the throat. "Notions of justice. An obligation to his victims. Also personal feelings."

"You knew him?"

The innocent astonishment: a lie hovered like incense, and Burnham prickled. Beneath it lay a patch of truth, like a small mosaic or an aerial photograph. When complete, it would reveal city walls, foundations, grave mounds, public baths, armories and streets. Until then it was a shadow here and a streak there. This was a moment to be alert, sharp, shrewd, and here sat Burnham the Belly-Button Inspector, a mindless lump of ravished flesh. "Briefly. We spoke once. In Nanking."

For a tick Sung Yun's eyes widened. The effect was extraordinary, as if he had dropped his trousers or spilled farina on his vest. "A city I cannot claim to know," he said easily in his lightly accented Mandarin—the accent of Shanghai? or of the light and songful Wu dialect? Nanking? "And when did that unfortunate encounter take place?"

"In 1937."

"So early! So early! And you so young! During the sack of Nanking?" Sung Yun's good humor was restored.

"Yes."

"Then your desire to snare him is more than natural. Young Ming here was only twelve or so, but like all Chinese he burns with anger still."

"Sore as a boil," Ming snarled.

"Moreover, Kanamori may lead us to others," Sung Yun said. "Surely an interrogation by interested Chinese would be in order."

"Inspector Yen was emphatic on that head."

"I had hoped to interview the man myself," Sung Yun said. "Extraordinary psychological interest."

"For friends of America I shall do what I can."

"The whole world is in America's debt," Sung Yun said. "As you may know, I directed the distribution of much American relief—money and goods both. But we Chinese have our pride. Kanamori's crimes were against Chinese, not Americans."

Again. Burnham was beginning to feel unwanted. Such a gracious people: at the least discourtesy one felt clobbered.

"We do not ask custody," Sung Yun went on. "Only to interrogate."

"No objection. I have already made a promise to Inspector Yen."

Sung Yun grimaced like a bronze lion. "May I speak in confidence?"

"All between us is in confidence."

"Good!" Sung Yun meditated. He pursed his lips. His gaze took refuge in his teacup. At last he said, "Yen wants him for selfish reasons. He wants a prisoner of importance. This is a critical time, yet a slack time: where two tides touch, the waters may be calm, and large fish caught. Such a fish may be an offering. Should Yen float off southward on the ebbing tide, Kanamori might be his exit visa. Should he drop anchor and await the rising tide, Kanamori might be his credentials."

"Then he is standing on two boats at once."

"And perhaps sailing both on dry land."

The two shared a smile at this eloquence, and for a moment were old friends.

"Small heart," Sung Yun said. "If you and Yen should scuffle for Kanamori, look to your safety. You might be more secure with Kanamori hidden and spirited away. Justice would be served as well. Yü! He may be dead. He may be anywhere in Asia. There are hordes of Japanese, free and mingling, all over Asia."

"There are thousands in China alone," Burnham said mildly. "Many chose not to go home."

"That does not simplify your work."

"Frankly," Burnham said, "I am no longer sure of success."

"Why then, you will do your best, and what more can we ask?" Sung Yun touched a gong twice. "No more business today. Did you know that those monkeys put a price on my head?" He chuckled theatrically. "Such a compliment!"

And in tripped Miss Ai and Miss Mei, and cigarettes were passed, and more tea was poured, and the recent American election was analyzed, why Tu-I had lost to Tu-ju-man. "Thus it is in democracies," Burnham said. "Politicians and paintings are on public display, not for private collection."

Sung Yun sniffed for irony or hostility and chose to find none. "Your heritage is elections, and a certain mediocrity. Mine is scrolls and porcelain and, I confess, a certain injustice."

"The price of both heritages is high."

"It is, it is," Sung Yun agreed. "Vigilance. Courage."

A nest of madmen, Burnham decided. Sung Yun making speeches. Ming holding a cigarette by the tips of his thumb and forefinger, dragging deep, French inhaling. Miss Ai and Miss Mei serving, sashaying, parting and winking, bosoms and behinds bobbing against the flimsy cotton. Burnham in love, sick with love, yet noticing these creatures. The room bare, the walls discolored. Gone the Ch'ing calligraphy, gone the T'ang chicken, gone the Peking carpet, the celadon vase, the Mongol dancer, whatever booty this tycoon had plundered from life. All gone, and replaced by Burnham, prying and prowling at the end of the world.

Hungry, requiring strong drink, he made his excuses. "Ming will fetch the car," Sung Yun assured him.

"No need. I have a san-luerh waiting."

Sung Yun admired. "That is style, and the old way. It is sad to watch a civilization die."

"Yet what a noble fate, to be the last of the mandarins."

Again there was a swift alteration in Sung Yun's features, a hitch in the very air. Aw hell, Burnham told himself. You're not Chinese any more. You said something interesting and you don't even know what it was.

"But we are both that," Sung Yun said. "You, too, when you are in Peking, are a rich man in a poor time, for all your quaint native ways."

Burnham was annoyed but dredged up a proper smile.

"So you see that I must leave," Sung Yun went on. "Farewell to this city and this house, and my servants, and Miss Ai and Miss Mei."

"A shame you cannot take them."

"Take them? Miss Ai and Miss Mei? They would not transplant well. Their roots are here."

Burnham wondered whether this was a witticism in Chinese. Surely not.

"You may rely on Ming for whatever you need: intelligence,

transportation, a cache for your prisoner. We have a telephone here; you know the number?"

"Ming gave it to me."

"If a man answers, hang up," Ming said. Burnham's fatigue deepened.

"I have a right to him," Sung Yun said. "It was he who set a price on my head."

"Kanamori?"

"Kanamori."

"I was not told that," Burnham said.

"It is not significant. I was only bragging. But you must bring him to me. Yes, yes, bring him to me. And remember, small heart!"

Burnham said, "I intend to be careful. Between a bad man and a worse, it is better that the bad survive."

"You make fun!" Sung Yun appreciated the jest strenuously. Burnham was a social success. He bowed to the Misses Mei and Ai, and to Ming, whose eyes twinkled, and then he and Sung Yun shared a long look of almost affectionate distrust; each contributed half a smile, and they parted like dukes.

"I am dying, old horse." The snowfall had thinned; in the noontime light myriad specks of tinsel glittered slowly down, and tile roofs shone white. It was a new Peking, two for the price of one, and even tired and hungry Burnham blessed his luck. "Find us a noodle shop."

Feng commiserated. This was not his first debauchee, he informed Burnham. In his ricksha a woman had died, just like that, and lovers had touched, and a foreigner had vomited. A ricksha man saw too much, because no one ever noticed the ricksha man. "There is also the French Bakery," he said. "The gentleman could lunch on sa-min-chih and ka-fei."

"The gentleman does not desire sandwiches and coffee," Burnham said peevishly. "The superior man does not travel thirty thousand li to eat what he has left behind."

"Then it shall be noodles," Feng said. "The Sheep's Gut is not far. They offer an assortment of meats and garnishes."

"Gallop." Burnham sighed. "And do not talk. I need to think now; we will talk while we eat."

" 'We' is better than 'I,' " Feng approved. It was a delicate way of saying "I thought you'd never ask," and it brought a smile to Burnham's bruised and weary lips. Slowly the smile faded, and so did he; the next he knew, Feng was calling, "Sir! One has arrived."

"Indeed," Burnham said with dignity. "I was sunk in thought."

A table by the window; a solicitous young waiter to whom this foreigner was obviously a great adventure; a flyspecked vista of the Yangtze across one wall like a comic strip. Burnham preferred the dimming drift of dying snowflakes on Inside Fu Ch'eng Gate Great Street, or Fu Nei, as the street kids said. Across the way a pot-and-pan shop, a ready-to-wear shop, and what looked like a bank; the sign was eroded. Within the Sheep's Gut all was warm; customers chattered, odors mingled, and Burnham was happier but even sleepier. You scoundrel, he told himself. Betrayed your country for love of a foreign beauty. Haven't done a decent day's work yet. You will come to a bad end. "Feng," he said, "I have a strange story to tell you. I am in a peck of trouble."

He told Feng everything. This required two bowls apiece of noodles, one with flaked carp and the second with bits of pork; also two cruets of yellow wine and a bowl of sweet-preserved orange rind. Feng listened humbly, as if awed, lifting his gaze rarely from the bowl. He plucked or scraped every scrap of noodle from the porcelain surface, and Burnham did the same, almost embarrassed. "In sober truth," Burnham finished, "I do not know who is doing what to whom. You move among the mice and sparrows; have you heard a squeak or a chirp about any of this? or any of these people?"

Feng slurped up a mouthful of tea, gargled his teeth clean, swallowed and smacked his lips. "Of Yen I know only that he is a cop. The poor do not like cops, not even poor cops, because when a poor man becomes a cop he forgets that he was poor. He will kowtow still to the rich but now he coppers the poor, and that is the only change, by all the gods. So I have no more to say of Yen."

"The others? Do you smoke, by the way?"

"When I can."

"Then ask the waiter for cigarettes. I think one would wake me up, which is to be desired. But not Antelopes."

Feng had already clapped, once and loudly, and the waiter scurried to them. "You have perhaps a foreign cigarette?" Feng asked.

"In two minutes. Less. Which sort?"

"American. The camel or the bull's-eye." Cheng-chung, he said, and Burnham had not heard that before as the name of a cigarette: correct-middle, therefore bull's-eye, therefore lucky strike! How could anyone not love this land? The waiter fled.

"Sung Yun," Feng continued placidly, "is a motherfucker."

"Indeed." Burnham cocked his head, and watched for signs of a second Feng, a police spy or free-lance meddler, a hired hand of some mysterious kind, but all he saw in the face or heard in the voice was Feng the poor but honest toiler.

"Sung Yun is very rich," Feng pronounced, "and therefore a bad man."

This left Burnham wistful: if only life were so simple! "Is it dirty money?"

"When a war ends and a man is rich, that is dirty money."

"How simple is the truth."

"Rich men and soldiers haggle hard and pay slowly."

"What is said of him?"

"Well, he is not of the government but above it. He is a trader. He is a friend of the Americans. That last is not in itself evil."

"He speaks with the accent of Chekiang or Anhui."

"So." Feng heard this with evident satisfaction. "He is not a Pekinger." An afterthought: "The gentleman has met Sung Yun?"

"That was his house we just left."

"So, so, so! A fine address to know. But too late. He appears to be moving away."

"Fleeing," Burnham said.

"While the gentleman was within, cases and chests were removed by cart."

The waiter pattered quickly in and slammed the door. Ceremoniously he set the packet on the table, rubbed his hands and blew hot breath on them. "Thank you," Burnham said. "It was good of you to brave the cold for us."

"But what else?" The waiter was regal. "Within these walls you must want for nothing." He withdrew, stepping backward two steps and bowing, as if taking leave of majesty, but hovering, matchbox in hand.

Feng spoke: "And the gentleman wishes to take this Japanese to America?"

"To Japan. But my heart is no longer committed." The waiter darted forward, bearing fire, and Feng and Burnham smoked.

"I am unhappy," Burnham went on. Feng did not reply; perhaps he was unused to talk of happiness. Perhaps simpler matters —the belly, the cold—took precedence over such high-class vaporings. "It is not what I expected, and not customary. I have been here a whole day and I have killed no one. No rascal has bopped me in a dark alley. No schemer has offered me a bribe. All is decadence, and thugs wear silken shoes. All I do is eat and talk and . . ."

Delicately Feng glanced away.

"I suppose you think I'm crazy," Burnham said.

Feng was appalled. "Of different ways, only. Fish do not make fires."

"What would you do?"

"This one? You ask me?"

"I ask you."

Feng asserted himself. He drew deeply on the cigarette, pursed his lips and expelled smoke thoughtfully, tilting his head back, seeking wisdom in the rafters. Burnham was much encouraged. This poor but honest toiler was a strutting ham like all of us. "I would kill Kanamori and Sung Yun," Feng said.

"That sounds reasonable."

Feng, whose moment had passed, sipped tea and smoked.

"Now," Burnham said, assailed suddenly by heartache, "tell me about the hospital."

"Well, it is a good place, they say. Beggars and the poor may be treated there. All. Those without funds, riffraff."

Burnham made the sign of eight, and looked his question.

"Oh, as to that, who can say? These days . . ."

"Let us go there," Burnham said, "and while I make my visit, you snoop."

"Snoop," Feng said, bemused and flattered. "Snoop."

15 獅

In the spring of 1945 Kanamori's collection was stored in the basement of Madam Olga's International Hospitality Center at Old Number Twelve-and-a-Half Palisade Street. Kanamori's superiors never questioned his baggage or his mode of travel because he was a hero. His subordinates never questioned anything because they were Japanese soldiers. While the coolies offloaded into the basement, Madam Olga absented herself with the discreet aplomb of the true aristocrat; she drank vodka, shook her head lugubriously and pitied this Japanese madman in a long soliloquy of theatrical Russian. The goods—she did not know their nature but sensed their value—were here, Wang would follow, Kanamori's days were numbered, and the sooner all this ended, the better. The Americans now owned Okinawa. She hoped they would occupy Peking, for a time anyway; she would charm them with her continental ways and long record of anti-Communism.

Madam Olga was astonished and outraged when, not two weeks later, her house was briefly occupied not by handsome and courtly Americans but by Japanese military police, and she herself, with her colleagues, was politely but firmly herded to the upper story. She ranted and invoked the protection of Major Kanamori. The captain in charge assured her that Major Kanamori would be sent for.

Kanamori had found himself assigned not to narcotics but to the termination or dismantling of various Japanese military enterprises and establishments within the city of Peking. His luck had held. Within ten days he had been detailed to retire a grenade-and-demolition practice range in the Cemetery of the Hereditary Wardens of the Thirteen Gates. In this cemetery stood several stately tombs, a few of them truly ornate mausoleums. Scattered among the tombs were concrete bunkers built by the Japanese to simulate their standard defenses. Within each bunker was an ammunition well about eight feet by four, and four deep. The lids of these wells were counterbalanced concrete slabs which, when latched shut, were simply part of the floor.

Kanamori giggled at the beauty of it. Already outside the tombs and bunkers grew tangles of planks, scrap metal and assorted garbage, including animal and human bones. The cemetery itself was forbidding, rutted, overgrown and gravelly; it would be mud in a winter thaw and in spring. Nor was the cemetery fenced. Only a low stone wall and a malevolent aura, and of course the presence of death, protected the premises. All decorations, ex-votos and gewgaws intended to accompany the deceased to the great beyond had been stolen decades, perhaps centuries, before. The casual thief or busybody would not be attracted. Furthermore, the well could be cemented shut, and the outer door could be rendered unpropitious and obstinate by a few iron bars strategically planted in the earth and buried under trash.

So Madam Olga's was shortly closed for repairs: not to the building or the women, but to Kanamori's crates. His two coolies, one a mason's apprentice, worked quickly and with enthusiasm; he had promised high wages for a job well done, and the apprentice, just nineteen, wished to marry, and his girl friend would not marry until he had bestowed upon her the san-chuan, or three-things-that-go-round: a watch, a bicycle and a sewing machine.

Soon the three were roaring through the golden summer afternoon to the cemetery, with the major himself at the wheel of a half-ton truck and several footlockers loaded behind. At the cemetery the coolies worked quickly and well. They mopped their brows and chattered gratitude for the cool of the concrete bunker. Their wages proved to be death. The garbage gathered, the footlockers stowed, the cement mixed, Kanamori shot First Coolie between the eyes. When Second Coolie popped out of the well to keep up with events, Kanamori shot him too between the eyes. Then he shut the slab over them and hemmed it with cement, leveling and trimming carefully with the trowel and feeling rather professional. After removing all tools and equipment to the truck, he slammed the outer door and wedged it shut with a few iron rods, on which he dumped the remaining cement, followed by a choice selection of rusted metal, bones, splintered boards and ordinary gravel. Upon all this he then relieved himself.

He returned to the barracks, showered, changed and had himself driven to Madam Olga's. He strode upstairs feigning wrath, rebuked the captain in charge, freed the women and apologized profusely. Olga was mollified by this intervention; in these tense days the unexpected had shaken her aplomb. Now she expressed delight, opened a fresh bottle of vodka, and was pleased to serve ice. She and Kanamori drank and exchanged gossip. The girls served them and flattered the major. Kanamori lingered, happily intoxicated.

Later, customers circulated. One of them, for seven years a loyal ricksha man and factotum, had been instructed to assassinate Kanamori at a favorable moment of his own choosing. Kanamori resolved to make a night of it. Intoxicated by vodka, by success, by a surge of unaccustomed lust, by a momentary release from years of acknowledged nightmare and unacknowledged self-contempt, he saw himself as the last of the mandarins, and decided that he owed himself a mandarin's revels. "I will stay," he announced. "I wish a grand supper, with hsia mi." Hsia mi were tiny shrimp, delectable, from the southern seas. "I will then frolic with two women." He thought he might enjoy hara-kiri later in the evening: what a gesture! Olga greased the whips, plied him with vodka and encouraged his fantasies. She was frightened—the man was insane, and lunatics were notoriously capricious—but the stakes were high. The Americans were bombing Japan savagely. The tiger heat of July lay upon Peking. Surely the time was right.

In the late watches Kanamori enjoyed his punishment. He crooned and yipped with each lash, he sang, he shouted boisterous laughter and sobbed exultantly. Like an animal he swilled. Like an animal he took one of the women. Like an animal he was beaten again. Toward the end he was briefly puzzled and perturbed by a certain sense of excess, by flashes of true pain replacing the exhilaration, by waves of dizziness and nausea, by flashing colored lights within his head, but Olga reassured him—friendly and reliable Olga, who understood him, who would shelter him and see that he was pleasured and kept safe, and later soothed with ointments. So when his senses failed, and even the taste of his own blood faded and the night closed in, he swooned away in peace, as if cradled in his mother's arms.

16 愛

Cots lined both walls of the long whitewashed room. Near the door stood a hot potbellied iron stove; its pipe ran the length of the ward, radiating softer heat. Burnham and Hao-lan stood in the aisle holding hands. Many of the children lay still; others played gravely with wooden blocks. "Trachoma," Hao-lan said. "Manges and eczemas. There is no beriberi now but there is kala-azar."

He raised her hand to his lips, and for an incandescent moment their eyes married. "Insane," she murmured.

"Both of us. Don't fight it. Whatever happens, we have plenty of sadness ahead. What's kala-azar?"

"Visceral leishmaniasis. Hyperplasia in the reticuloendothelial system."

"The stone drops into the well," he said glumly in Chinese.

"Oh God," she said, and hugged him. "How funny you are! I love you for that."

Lost, goofy, he smiled down at her.

"I suppose it's nothing to be funny about." A schoolchild's complicated joke, and he had been showing off: in Mandarin "I do not understand" was "Bu doong," and what is the sound of a stone dropped into the well? Bu-doong! A schoolchild's joke and she loved him for it! "But I really do not understand. I've never heard of it."

"An internal infection caused by a parasite, borne by a fly. It used to be a problem in Szechuan and the northwest. With the war, and all the shuffling, it spread. A protozoan. No fun."

"No fun." Some of these tots were skin and bones, others more potbellied than the stove. At least one girl seemed totally blind. The walls were streaked, the old floor waxed dark. Odors rose and mingled: urine, alcohol, a faint overlay of rot. The blind girl seemed to listen; was this strange language a menace?

"What happens," Hao-lan said, "is that these little Leishman-Donovan bodies muck about with the spleen and liver and phagocytes." This was gibberish to Burnham but he knew the information was nothing and the tone was all, bitter and flat, an absence of passion that had set in long before, when anger was exhausted. "This causes anemia, emaciation, irregular fever and a sharp drop in the number of white corpuscles. The liver swells and the spleen balloons. If you want, I'll let you feel a spleen. I have one so badly swollen that it runs all the way from the stomach down to the crest of the pelvic bone. The girl is eleven. The best way to diagnose is to stick a long needle right down into the spleen and—"

"Stop it now," he said, and slewed her gently, his hands firm on her shoulders; he kissed her forehead and held her for some moments. "It's necessary work. It's noble."

"It's miserable and I hate it." Her voice was like iron; she muffled it, pressing her face to his chest. "It's mostly nursing care. We need something called a Romanovsky stain for diagnosis and we have none and the government won't give us any and we have to beg it from the national hospital or the missionaries. And kala-azar isn't all." She pulled away and the words tumbled: "There's simple malnutrition and battered children and girls raped. *Little* girls. And there are some with dysentery and some with meningitis, and we haven't even started on *normal* diseases and accidents. The lucky ones are the little dead ones Mother brings in, or the beggars—twenty, thirty, forty a day." Her voice had rung shrill, and Burnham tightened his hold: on her, on himself.

She felt his anger. "We needn't stay here," she said. "The children amuse themselves."

"No need to flee."

"But it bothers you."

"Christ, yes, it bothers me! I don't like hospitals. I don't like sick children. I don't like a world where . . . ah, the Lord works in mysterious ways!"

"The Lord."

"A notorious bungler," he said. A boy of ten or so offered him a block. Burnham released Hao-lan's hand and knelt to make a house of blocks. Children drifted closer. The house rose tier by tier. There seemed an infinity of blocks, wooden blocks, stone blocks, tiny concrete blocks.

"From various demolitions," Hao-lan said. "The beggars loot old sites. They bring pipes and wire, too, and tiles; they can be sold to the scrap merchants, and the money buys food."

Burnham's house was waist-high. Enough. He stepped back, forcing a smile. Immediately a boy ran forward, buzzing like an aircraft, his arms wings, and flung himself onto the house, razing it with a great clatter. A shout of laughter rewarded him. Half a dozen kids commenced reconstruction, chattering and conferring. Many of the little heads were shaved. Many of the little eyes were caked. Many of the little faces were marred by sores. Ragged shoe soles flapped. The blind girl listened.

A vast dismay chilled Burnham, a numbing horror. Swept by obscure shame, he wished for whiskey. What fun it was to gallivant through China! What a romantic, exotic life! Guns and drums and wounds and women! "I think I want to go now," he said. Hao-lan touched his cheek.

In the office he met Dr. Teng, lean and silent, nodded to Mother and a nurse, and sat with Hao-lan. The chill vanished; between them a dizzying, unquenchable joy seemed to leap and spark. "At this late date," he said, "the foolishness of first love is embarrassing."

"Nobody will laugh at you," she said shyly.

"I'll come for you tonight," he said, "but I have things to do and I may be late."

"Things?"

"I don't really care much any more. Yesterday I saw mysteries, plots, wheels within wheels. Today I see a lot of tired, sick flesh and blood. Sung Yun even, with his dirty money. Yen playing cop while the world blows up around him. Ming from the funny papers."

"You're tired."

"And whose fault is that?"

She dimpled with the guilty, gleeful smile of a sinful girl, and he laughed at the innocence of it. "I'll give it one last try with the beggars," he said.

"Be careful."

"I will. I wish . . ."

They were silent for a moment. "So do I," she said. "Did you sleep?"

"A little. I'll nap now. You?"

"A little. I wish we lived on some other planet."

"Just the two of us."

"Fields. Lakes."

"Fat fish."

"And no nasty protozoa."

"Poor girl. What a hell of a time you must have."

"It could be worse," she said. "I could be a patient."

Feng took him home. "I saw nothing."

"Perhaps there is nothing to see. Perhaps it is all foolishness. The man may be dead. Back in Japan. Out west and a bandit. But come for me at six, will you? We must toss one last stone, to see if the sleepers wake."

But it was not Burnham who tossed the stone; Burnham was the sleeper who woke. He woke in gloom, confused, haunted by the last tatters of a bad dream: assassins, exile.

He knew that he was not alone in his small room. He cursed Hai for a bungler. As usual, his weapons were not handy. He lay in the half-darkness, unmoving, barely breathing.

A match flared, and lit the stub of a candle. Burnham saw two men. He saw only one knife but it was sufficient; its point approached and pricked his neck. This was annoying, and Burnham felt that resentment was justified, but the other thug held Burnham's .38 affectionately, and the instant did not seem propitious for heroics.

Knife said, "Come along now. Rise slowly, and dress warmly."

Pistol made big gray teeth.

Burnham obeyed. His blood jangled, his brain creaked, and he wanted to brush his teeth. It was bad form to be abducted with hairy lips, an emery tongue and a head full of sawdust. "How did you enter?"

Knife said, "The alleys and the window. One man's out is another man's in. Hsü! You are a big fellow."

"Who are you?" Better off without weapons. Do not stir up the natives. He would use his wits: a rare opportunity.

"The scum of the earth," Knife said.

Burnham's roll of bills seemed intact.

"The hat," said Knife.

Burnham donned the fur hat. Knife grinned, and pricked Burnham's chin. Later Burnham realized that Pistol had sapped him with his own .38. Now there was only an explosion of light, and then darkness.

Shadows ebbed and surged like waves. Burnham saw a vast flat field and a red swastika. A crowd whispered.

He lay on his back. The shadows ceased to ebb and surge, and only flickered. Lamps. He was in a room and staring at a wall. The red swastika was painted on the wall, the color of fresh blood. The crowd buzzed and hummed like bees.

Burnham's head ached slightly but he was glad enough to be alive. He was not bound; he rubbed his face and sat up. The voices died. His head throbbed.

It was a left-handed swastika and therefore Buddhist. This was good news. Sufficient unto the day was the evil thereof without Nazis. Furthermore the Buddhist swastika signified good luck.

The room seemed to be a disused restaurant or shop. A couple of dozen men and women watched him, some sitting on wooden benches along the wall and most smoking. To the rear a kettle sat on a stone stove.

Burnham had been lying on a stone bed. His pistol and knife had not been restored to him. We'll have to scrape by on charm, he told himself, and bobbed a nod at the men and women.

Beggars all. "Is there water?" he asked. "I am always thirsty after being beaten about the head."

The others gazed at a scrawny man of middle age, who nodded. A woman moved to pour water, and brought it to Burnham in an earthen bowl. He drank it off. It was pure and sweet. "Thank you," he said. She took the bowl and withdrew.

"Our visitor is a gentleman," a scratchy voice intoned.

The speaker stood beside a large table concocted of planks and bricks. Burnham rose and stepped toward him. On the table lay stacks of documents and heaps of currency, and a couple of ballpoint pens, still rare in China; this was a modern enterprise. There was a lamp too, the old-fashioned standard oil-for-the-lamps-of-China lamp. It cast a trembling light on Head Beggar.

The kai-t'ou was a rooster of a man, in padded trousers and a short padded jacket. He sported a rooster's sharp beak and bright eyes, and instead of a comb, a monstrous growth on the left side of his scrawny neck, a reddish-purple tumor or goiter like an external liver, running from the ear down the jaw and neck. Having noticed it, Burnham could not look away; the growth could not be ignored. He made the best of a sickening moment, and examined it frankly. His stomach yawed.

The rooster approved. "So you are not too busy to look."

"How could that be? My business is with you."

"So I have been told. And how do you know who I am?"

"One divines the quality of a man," Burnham said. "One senses leadership."

The rooster crowed briefly. "Also, you saw them look to me for permission."

"That too is true." Burnham tried a friendly smile. "A blindfold would have sufficed. There was no need to slug me."

Head Beggar showed palm. "But what is life without dependable rituals? Who are you, after all? And what are you?"

"I ask myself often."

"A cigarette?" From some recess of his gown, Head Beggar whisked a pack of Antelopes.

"Thank you." For a special occasion one made sacrifices. He

accepted fire from Head Beggar, who then lit his own cigarette. They blew smoke companionably. "I have not much experience of beggars. If there are special forms and courtesies, you must forgive my ignorance."

"Nonsense," said the kai-t'ou. "It is a trade like any other."

"That would surprise me. Truly like any other? Not colder, not hungrier? You eat no more bitterness?"

The kai-t'ou spat on the floor. "And what would you know of it?"

"Nothing," Burnham said. "I have never even been poor. That is why I asked."

"Never had to beg, hey?"

"Never."

Now the kai-t'ou shrugged. "Then what can pass between us? Who can discuss ice with the summer insects?"

"Yet I know that poor men's bones bend."

"Tell us what you want," Head Beggar said impatiently. "Women? You have come to the wrong place. Are you perhaps a journalist? A tourist? Do you find us fascinating? Will you return with a camera? Are you pleased to feel superior?"

"I feel only luckier," Burnham said, "and I am not a seeker of curiosities."

"Well, then? Speak, speak. Do not be a guest. You need a hundred beggars, perhaps, for a funeral procession? Or to swell a riot? This is a new thing, a rich foreigner importuning beggars. You must forgive my rude questions."

Burnham said, "I believe we have a common enemy—"

"Nothing else in common," the kai-t'ou muttered.

"—and I need your help."

"And when we need you?"

Burnham experienced an odd flare of simple annoyance. Why was he held personally responsible for all evil? Gloomily he contemplated Head Beggar: bright eyes, scanty white hair, skin glossy and little lined. "I have done what life asked of me without whining or kissing feet," Burnham said. "I have tried to do no harm to the weak. I have fought side by side with

Chinese for China. More than that I cannot claim."

"It is something," the old man allowed.

"Listen one listen," Burnham said. "This is no foreigner's prank. It is a question of the rice bowl, the larger rice bowl and not the smaller. Wolves and tigers guzzle our blood, yours and mine alike. There are foxes in the city walls and rats upon the altars."

From across the room a voice rose: "Yi! His speech is clear water."

Another spoke, a woman: "In clear water there are no dead fish."

Burnham scanned his audience in the lamplight. They seemed more whole than most beggars, less deformed. The stench of sickness, decay and neglected bodies was less strong. But one, he saw, lacked a nose; he had only two cavernous, scarred holes.

"Three years ago," Burnham began, "here in Peking, a beggar called One Foot One Hand went to the police station off Lantern Street. He had recognized a fellow beggar as a former Japanese officer, a killer and a rapist, by name Kanamori Shoichi, wanted by the authorities of China, Japan and the United States. The police beat him and threw him into the gutter.

"Kanamori has been tried for his crimes and convicted, and sentenced to death. I have been sent here to find him and take him back. I cannot find him without help."

"And why should we help?"

"Were the Japanese kind to you?"

"No less so than the Chinese." The others murmured, "True, true." "The insults were perhaps milder: to the Japanese we were proof of Chinese inferiority, and they humored us. We are not often humored. To the other foreigners we are of course picturesque but morally deplorable. And what do you believe?"

"I believe that my head aches," Burnham said wearily.

Head Beggar cackled, stepped forward with a dancer's grace and slapped Burnham hard.

Burnham jerked his head back, and restrained himself. Thoughtfully he puffed at his corrosive cigarette.

"Explain," Head Beggar instructed him.

"Is there an ashtray?"

Impatiently the rooster said, "Yü! On the floor. This is not the Six Nations Hotel."

Burnham tossed away the butt. A beggar darted forward, squealing in mock delight, snatched it up and marched across the room puffing vigorously. Head Beggar and his tattered chorus laughed heartily.

"Explain," Head Beggar repeated.

Burnham reflected. "You did that not because you hate me; you are beyond hate. And not because I am a foreigner," he said slowly, "because all men but beggars are foreigners here. So you did that because it gave you pleasure; or to remind me that I am not in the world of ordinary men and women; or to see if I possess understanding."

"Not bad. Go on."

"To see if I would respond to the blow, which was real but transitory, or to the insult, which may be a delusion. Or perhaps you struck me to remind me that there are causes without effects and effects without causes: that not everything follows. Or that my headache—I had just complained of a headache—was without significance."

"Ah. Better. Yes. Between you and a Japanese criminal there is not a hair's difference to us. Your quarrels out there"—his gesture encompassed the world—"are meaningless."

"And the world we try to make?"

"Pah! A world without beggars, you mean. It is not our work to move the world. It is our work to survive this day. We are specialists in survival. We exaggerate limps. We exacerbate running sores. We make stinks. What your world has not mutilated in us, we mutilate. We use filth as those who wrap the head— you know who they are?"

"Yes. Men who play female roles in the theater."

"Yes. We use filth as they use makeup. We are nothing!" The rooster was screeching. "For many centuries, nothing! No work, no home, no family! Only what we build among ourselves.

Even the collectors of dung despise us! Do you understand? For the others we do not exist. We are what real people walk on, piss on, shit on!" More calmly he continued: "We prey on all who are not beggars. On all who hope. If we ourselves begin to hope, then we begin to show affection and mercy, and we do not survive."

"But soon your world will change. Surely you know that."

Head Beggar said, "Yes. These are new times." He squinted: "Are you a Communist?"

"No."

"We tend to prefer the political right," the rooster said almost whimsically.

Burnham showed puzzlement.

The rooster crowed again. "With the right"—he was impish now—"we are not only tolerated but inevitable, perhaps essential. The left has a deplorable tendency to do away with us."

"Then you love what you are?"

"No one else loves what we are."

"That is true. I do not love the beggar folk," Burnham said. "Or running sores. Or washed babies."

The sudden silence was absolute; Head Beggar's eyes flashed. Again Burnham was bewildered: what had he said?

Head Beggar seemed to consult his cohorts.

"Survival is your business," Burnham said. "If I offered money?"

"To sell one of our own?"

"Then he *is* one of your own?" The question was too direct, the tone too eager, and Burnham cursed himself. He fought to recover ground: "One Foot One Hand tried to sell him."

Head Beggar replied dryly, "One Foot One Hand is not."

"Ah. Is not. So." He tried once more: "If I offered money to the hospital?"

That silence again. The kai-t'ou seemed to freeze; his trapped eyes sought help, and his friends murmured.

Burnham plunged ahead. "Tell me this, then. Why did you . . . send for me?"

Head Beggar laughed. "How gently put! And how I distrust elegance of speech!"

Burnham waited. Again Head Beggar consulted the others. "Why not?" a voice asked. "He is after all our prisoner. We are three-legged dogs, but we have bayed this stag." The others approved. Burnham took heart. They were curious about this bizarre foreigner.

"Kanamori entered Nanking on the first day," he began, and he told them all he knew of the man. He told them also about Nanking. And he let Kanamori stand for the Japanese army; he heaped it all on Kanamori. The women. Twenty thousand women raped. The number was unmanageable. Better to have shown them, shown them even one. He told them of the forty-three technicians at the power plant. Of beggars shot on sight, and for sport. Of ordinary men roped hundred by hundred and doused with gasoline and burned alive. Of fathers ordered to rape their daughters. Of families drowned, under compulsion and sometimes by choice. Of hundreds more lined up on the banks of canals and machine-gunned. Of thousands upon thousands executed and buried with their wrists wired together in violation of all spiritual instinct and religious precept. Of a woman of eighty raped and her throat slit. Of babies bayoneted because their cries annoyed their mothers' rapists. Of two hundred thousand men, women and children, officials, teachers, laborers, soldiers, beggars and shopkeepers murdered in six weeks and buried by numbed survivors.

A woman came forward to touch Head Beggar's shoulder.

Burnham was sweating. He wondered what time it was. The question was senseless. Time did not exist here; it ran forward as usual but was not marked in any usual manner. How old was human beggary? When would it end? Had it begun with a big bang or was it a steady state?

"And that is all?" Head Beggar asked.

"It seems enough," Burnham said.

Head Beggar sniffed, frowned and showed palm to the others. A gravelly voice rose, flinging words angrily; it was street slang and beyond Burnham. Another speaker interrupted. Soon they were all jabbering. Head Beggar spoke sharply; they shut up.

"And what do you offer?" Head Beggar asked.

"There is always money. But I do not believe you want me to offer money."

"Such a prince! Such delicacy! The last mandarin!" But the kai-t'ou smiled. "Ideals, is that it? Justice?" In the lamplight his tumor glowed, rich as burgundy.

"No. You would only reproach me for that." Burnham smiled back. "Well, I have come a long way, and I have been rapped on the noggin, and there are others, perhaps less deserving, who also seek Kanamori. I offer you only the need of an honest workman."

"Hsü, what talk!" Head Beggar spoke again to the others; they answered, chattered, fell silent. Head Beggar paced. He rubbed his hands. He snorted. He spoke to his friends: "Go away."

They protested.

Head Beggar waved angrily. "Go away. Leave us."

Slowly the others filed out, glancing back. A woman called, "Narrow heart!"

"Nonsense!" Head Beggar cried. "Be careful of what? If he budges I will slice him!" His hands made a dazzling pass; a knife flashed and disappeared. He grinned at Burnham; his tumor trembled. "Odd, odd," he said when the room was empty but for the two of them. "Except to beg I have never before exchanged speech with a foreign devil. The Japanese are, after all, not so foreign. But you—you are the first big nose, and I confess that you seem to me a man of understanding. I have taken a liking to you, young fellow."

" 'Old friends are better than new, but new are not bad,' " Burnham said.

"Well said. But the Kanamoris of my world are, in a way, old friends." Head Beggar squinted. Burnham met his gaze, forcing himself not to see the tumor. "What you have just told us—well, we knew and we did not know. It makes no difference."

Burnham returned to the stone bed and sat. He heaved a sad sigh.

"You are unwell?"

"I need a drink. Never mind."

"But of course," Head Beggar said, every inch the embarrassed host. He scooted to the small table. "Whiskey?"

"A miracle."

Head Beggar filled two earthen bowls.

"Whoa," Burnham said.

"Wo?"

"That is English for 'too much exhilaration by wine and even the emperor pees on his shoes.' "

"An economical language," Head Beggar said. "Well then, sip slowly."

They touched bowls.

"This is good stuff," Burnham said.

"Swiped it from the Six Nations Hotel," Head Beggar said proudly. "A crazy foreign bottle with dimples. We refilled it and sold it."

"Refilled it with what?"

"Urine and shellac."

They laughed like cronies and drank off a mouthful. Head Beggar slumped to a bench and exhaled briskly. "Strong spirits. Now listen. In the spring of '45 two beggars went out to dinner —downtown, of course, as downtown is more fashionable. They proceeded to the south garbage dump off Whore Street. They beat the dogs away and found the usual chicken bones, fish heads and assorted tripe. They therefore concocted the customary picnic. While snacking they noticed that the dogs had congregated elsewhere and were worrying a heap of possibly meat. They investigated. The dogs were gnawing at a human body. This was in itself not novel, but the dogs were also licking at fresh blood. Humanitarian as only beggars know how to be, our two friends drove the dogs off once more, and determined that the human body was still alive. It was a naked man who bore welts and stripes, the marks of scourging. The man was skinny. Now, a skinny man who has been badly beaten may well be a beggar. Moved by the three primary virtues—"

"Human-heartedness, sympathy and affection."

Head Beggar beamed. "The sheer joy of civilized converse! Precisely. They brought him here."

"Not to the Beggars' Hospital?"

"The Beggars' Hospital did not exist then. At any rate, we cleaned him up and applied ointments, and he did not die. He raved. He said, 'Sergeant Kanamori' and 'Lieutenant Kanamori' and 'Major Kanamori' and he would wail his name: Kanamori Shoichi. All this was translated by one of my colleagues, an eminent bathhouse specialist since deceased, who would catch you as you arrived—afterwards he would be merely a disgusting contamination, but beforehand the sight of him induced such relief that you were about to become clean . . ." Head Beggar clucked. "The man was brilliant with dirt. Ashes, simulated scabs around the eyes and corners of the mouth. Ah, well. At any rate our guest seemed to be one Kanamori, and we soon enough found out who he had been."

"And you did not mind."

Head Beggar's brows floated in soft surprise. "But we have discussed all that. He also spoke Chinese quite well. A mystery."

"I can solve that one for you. Kanamori's mother was Chinese. What did he say?"

" 'The last mandarin.' He kept saying that. 'Dead and buried. The last mandarin.' Does that mean something to you?"

"Nothing. Did he say more?"

"No. In time he recovered his forces, but he was addled. Once fully conscious he never spoke. He smiled much. He did odd jobs. Later he begged. He was scrupulous, and never held back on his daily take. He accepted cold and hunger well. He was excessively polite to women. More than polite." Head Beggar's tone was reflective, puzzled. "He seemed to worship women, but not as a man adores them, not to flatter and please and touch. He was himself sexless. A ghost. A man of perhaps thirty-five, but a phantom.

"And like any phantom, he disappeared one day. About a year ago. He was one of us. We missed him." Head Beggar brooded briefly. "We beggars scarcely exist, but this was as close to nonexistence as any man I have ever known. He was an example for some philosopher: non-being within being. I believe Lao-tzu speaks of such matters."

"Disappeared." Burnham's disappointment was a true pang; his belly ached. "Yet you would lie to me if it suited you."

Head Beggar's eyes were opaque. "Another bowl of whiskey." He poured; the gurgle was familiar, and comforted Burnham. "Yes, I would lie," Head Beggar said. "And even when I tell you I would lie I may be lying. Perhaps Lao-tzu speaks of that also."

Burnham accepted the bowl; they nodded a brief toast and drank.

"You are an odd fish," said Head Beggar. "An engaging sort of whale." He was grumbling, complaining, in the tone of a man about to make a grudging concession. Burnham took heart. Head Beggar went on: "I find myself thinking, After all, I am Chinese. Imagine! I am acquiring a nationality."

"Perhaps it is the presence of a foreigner."

"Yet not so foreign."

Burnham acknowledged the compliment, saluting with his bowl.

"Here we sit like diplomats," Head Beggar said, "toying with others' lives. Drinking strong waters and negotiating."

"I have nothing to offer."

"You offer good bones and a steady eye."

"I too could be lying."

"No. Shall I tell you why I trust you?"

"Tell me."

Head Beggar grinned a villainous grin, and his tumor stretched, expanding and shining in the lamplight, and he patted it. "Because you did not ignore my little companion—this unfortunate blemish!—and gaze in all eight directions and make polite mumble. And also because when you woke up you checked your pistol and your knife"—again the grin was impish—"but not your money. This argued virtue."

Burnham laughed. " 'In practicing the rules of propriety, a natural ease is to be prized.' "

"More talk out of old books," Head Beggar scoffed. "Listen, even I do not understand all things. Change is upon us, as you know. Signs and portents. The crust shatters, bubbles rise, dark matters come to light. Well, well, why not?"

Burnham held his breath, but after a moment sipped.

"What would you do with this Kanamori?"

"This evening I cannot tell," Burnham said softly. "Yesterday my way was clear: take him back and see him hanged. But . . ."

Head Beggar's gaze hardened. "The truth, now."

"Yes." Burnham downed another mouthful. "The truth is," he said weakly, "that I have met a woman, and nothing else seems important."

"Oh, women," said Head Beggar morosely. "I loved a girl long ago. She belonged to another man, so I had her only once. I suppose I should thank the gods for small blessings, but I miss her."

Burnham was moved. A tug at the heart. This freak—grotesque, deformed, outcast—had shown him a soul like that of other men. The true humanity, the common misery, love and its tangles, crossings, impossibilities, cruel revenges. A glimpse of the human condition.

"I still love her," said Head Beggar.

They drank in silence, bereaved, friends.

Head Beggar heaved an enormous sigh; his tumor bobbled. "Your Kanamori works at the Beggars' Hospital. He wears women's clothes and is mute. He is a receiver of washed babies, which he buries in the Cemetery of the Hereditary Wardens of the Thirteen Gates."

Head Beggar returned Burnham's pistol and knife and escorted him to the west mouth of Arrow-Maker's Road.

"No blindfold?"

"I have already trusted you beyond such minor matters. But you will forget this place."

"I have already forgotten. But not the kindness, nor the truth."

They had come to the Street of the Female Flutist, and it was like a new world: a few lights, a policeman, a porter pushing a two-wheeled cart, a drunk across the street warbling softly. Head Beggar shouted for a ricksha; one approached. It was not Feng; Burnham felt cheated.

Head Beggar clapped Burnham on the shoulder. "Listen, my friend. Kanamori is no butcher now, nor even a man. You will follow your own heart, and kneel to no princes."

"I will. But I must first listen to my heart," Burnham told him.

"Well, I cannot say 'See you again' but I can wish you luck. May the lord of all under heaven grant you ease, warmth and a full belly."

"Some luck is indeed due," said Head Beggar, "and the same to you." Then, his face closing like a gate, he said, "Go home. Let the dead bury the dead."

Their eyes locked for a dark moment before Burnham hopped into the pedicab and the kai-t'ou vanished into the night.

"Not by Ch'ien Men," the driver protested before Burnham could speak. "There is shooting in T'ien An Men Square, and a curfew is declared. We have but a few minutes. The police will beat me."

"A fine way to drum up trade," Burnham grumbled. "Then I will go only to Stone Buddha Alley, and I will make it worth your while. I have just been bludgeoned and am in a good humor."

The man made a sour face and took him home. Burnham pondered Kanamori and Sung Yun and Yen. Then he surrendered and thought of Hao-lan. For an hour he had not truly thought of her. He had been doing his job, and he felt cleaner and purer and stronger, and less full of spices and spirits and rare meats. Still, he wished dolefully that Hao-lan's face would cease rising before him; he had come to a moment of decision and wanted at least the illusion of keen judgment uninfluenced by youthful emotion. It was time now to sharpen the knife and breathe fire, and half of him was sniffing peonies and murmuring ancient poetry. He groaned. "Oh Christ," he said aloud. "What a hell of a time to fall in love." Probably at his age there was no good time. He tried to say, "Oh, women," like the kai-t'ou, but there was no harshness left in him. He decided to concentrate on Hao-lan's imperfections, but for the moment failed to find one. He tried to evoke the faces of previous loves, and like all lovers decided that he had never truly loved before.

He recognized this for a lie, and heard Hao-lan's mocking laugh, and that eased the moment. He grinned at his own foolishness. Well, say it: why not take your woman home? I know where you can get a flying machine and all.

Halfway down Stone Buddha Alley the pedicab braked; the driver said, "There is a car, and no room to pass."

"Then leave me by the car." Burnham overtipped as usual. The car was Yen's rickety Packard.

"Some landlord!" Yen said. He perched on Burnham's chair, his manner jaunty but his face unhappy in the reluctant lamplight.

Burnham sprawled back on his bed. Her bed. "Your foreign spirit-cart is blocking the alley." Was Yen friend or foe?

The inspector shrugged. "Curfew soon. You know?"

"I heard."

"If you need to move about, I can drive you here and there."

"Thank you, but no. Have you any news?"

"Nothing. I came to ask you that."

"Who is the last mandarin?" Burnham asked.

"Why, I never heard of the fellow," Yen said.

"Then I am a tourist. I have seen picturesque sights, met natives virtuous and vicious, and sampled the tonier noodle shops. What was that about my landlord?"

Yen clucked. "Well, it was apparent even yesterday that he knew I was a cop and that I knew he was a crook, so by tonight we were old friends. He asked me if my medal was for desertion or killing civilians."

"That bit of color in your lapel?"

"Yes."

"Which medal is it?"

158

"The Paoting. The Precious Tripod. 'For meritorious service in time of war against foreign aggression or internal rebellion.' "
"Doubtless hard earned."
"Thank you for 'earned,' " Yen said dryly. "I got it for arresting students."
Burnham remained cordial: "My landlord is a Sea Hammer."
"I might have known. Well, I will not hold it against him."
"How goes the war?"
"It does not go; it comes closer." Yen sighed. "I imagine they will take away my button and feather."
That was what the Manchus had done to cashiered officials; Burnham warmed to this show of style. "I hope not. All societies require policemen."
"True. Well, this is a pleasant chat but we are a long way from Kanamori. What do you propose to do?"
"Quit," Burnham said. "Give up. The rumors were of interest. We have made an honest effort."
"You surprise me. By the way, you met Sung Yun?"
"I spoke with him today."
"And?"
"Nothing. He offered full cooperation, but we cannot make ice without water. I cannot say that I liked him."
"He is not likable. You told him you would quit?"
"No. I decided later." Burnham's head throbbed.
"And the beggars? The hospital?"
"Nothing," Burnham said. "Cold trails and empty warrens. Kanamori may be dead. If alive he may be anywhere in Peking, or, by now, Tientsin or Mukden or Harbin or back in Japan. It would take a dozen men ten years."
"Ah well." Yen sighed again. "Shall we mourn together in a restaurant?"
"Thank you," Burnham said, "but I cannot. I have yet one call to make."
"Then you fill me with regret," Yen said. "To know you has been interesting."
"In other times . . . "

"Yes. Other times." Yen rose. "I am now and then overcome by sadness."

Burnham too rose, and their eyes met, and Burnham knew that Yen had not believed him.

"You will leave?"

"Perhaps tomorrow."

"If you will allow me to drive you to the airport . . . "

"When I know, I'll call you. There remain personal matters."

"Ah. Personal matters. The women of China. Another sort of imperialism."

"That's unfair," Burnham said.

"It is, and I withdraw the remark." Small, cool, ill-dressed, his face tight, Yen offered a hand, Western style; Burnham grasped it. "Please call me. In any case, good luck."

"Thank you," Burnham said. "See you again."

"What an odd idiom, for the circumstances," Yen said.

"True," Burnham said with a wry smile. " 'The future lies beyond the waters of oblivion.' Yet after a long swim, who knows?"

"Who knows? Therefore, see you again."

Burnham bolted the door behind him and packed. Upon reflection, he did not pack the pistol or knife. Upon further reflection, he did pack his small kit of smokers' requisites. Laotian yen was not easily come by, nor to be casually discarded.

Outside his room he paused and called into the silence, "Sea Hammer!"

Sea Hammer padded stoutly toward him, bearing a lamp. "The cop has shown heels?"

"Yes. He says you walk crooked ways."

Sea Hammer shrugged. "I fence stolen goods."

"Goods must move," Burnham approved.

"Commerce is the sinew of the nation." Sea Hammer noted the bag. "Yi! So soon?"

"Once again the sadness of parting."

"Well, yes, it is sad."

"The room is yours," Burnham said.

"No gutted brigands within?"

"No, nor beggar footpads either. A cricket would be a better watchdog. My room is always full of surprise parties, chiefly cops and jackals, and this evening I was clubbed and abducted by a committee."

"The gods!" Sea Hammer blinked in dismay. "But all is well?"

"All is well."

"I am fat and slowing up," Sea Hammer said mournfully. "I have brought shame upon my house."

"The house holds pleasant memories too," Burnham said. "No harm done. By the way, the police have no interest in you."

"Good news, for which I thank you." Teeth gleamed in the shadows.

"Well! A horse grows horns! A Sea Hammer says 'Thank you.'"

"Old and sentimental," said Hai Lang-t'ou, "but my gratitude is real. Think of my good luck. Once more I have worked with you and survived."

"Third time unlucky," Burnham said, "but probably there will be no third time."

"I could almost regret that. And your Japanese?"

"Found him," Burnham said.

"And now you will take him out?"

"Maybe. Maybe not."

Sea Hammer groaned. "Further complexities. Disturbances of the middle air."

"Possibly a surprise or two," Burnham agreed.

"O gods," Sea Hammer said. "I prefer not to hear this. It is Tsitsihaerh all over again. But I suppose you must hurry now."

"No. No hurry. Perhaps even . . . ah, defile it! Perhaps even reluctance."

"Hsü! Complexities indeed."

Burnham hesitated, and then paid old debts: "He was a beggar for two years, then vanished. He is at the Beggars' Hospital now and goes as a mute woman. They call him 'Mother.' Most of that the kai-t'ou told me. If this soup curdles, use the information as you will."

"Again I thank you. The kai-t'ou? You spoke with him?"

"Old friends," Burnham said. "Who is the last mandarin?"

"Bugger! I thought you were. Otherwise I never heard of him."

"Kanamori mentioned him in delirium. Our Japanese tiger was beaten and stabbed and became a kitten. Apparently he is mad, and has never spoken again."

"Yü! A hard hunt, and no tiger at all for the bag, but only one sick mouse. The kai-t'ou! You spoke to the kai-t'ou? Truly?"

"Truly."

"The company you keep!"

"Like fat fences."

Hai Lang-t'ou laughed aloud. "Indeed and indeed. Listen, old soldier, you said 'reluctance.' "

"Your own words of wisdom," Burnham said. "Perhaps the wily Chinese should be left to find their own destiny."

"Ah. They were your words, as I recall. Either way, it is a wise man who gives good advice, and a wiser who takes it. So what will you do?"

"I may steal a plane and kidnap someone else," Burnham said. "For the sake of form."

"And practice." Now Burnham laughed aloud.

"And pride, and mischief. A prank. My bones tell me further madness is afoot."

"No, no, no, old Hammer. It is love!"

Sea Hammer groaned again. "I condole with you. But the demented must be humored. It is at least a woman?"

"It is indeed a woman."

"Nothing new in that. You were always falling for a moon face and a sparkling eye."

"Never!" Burnham said. "This is the first time, I give you my word."

"Yü! Worse and worse. Who is this princess?"

"You saw her last night."

"Yes, well, yes." Hai Lang-t'ou groped for suitable expression.

"A surpassing beauty," he said, and cleared his throat, "and a, hm, woman of the people. But surely there are, hm, professionals in all lands."

"Not like this one. Her presence is my noon, and her absence is my midnight."

"A rare creature surely," Sea Hammer mumbled. "Why then, good luck and much happiness and prosperity and many handsome sons and even daughters."

"Thank you, thank you," Burnham said, restraining mirth. "Anyway, you are out of this alive, and once again you have done much for me. Beyond thanks, truly."

Sea Hammer made a rude noise. They loitered awkwardly, large men with much to say and none of it sayable. At last Sea Hammer spoke: "We are in the hands of the gods, and the future is an empty glass waiting to be filled."

"Then I wish you good hot wine," Burnham said, and Sea Hammer echoed him, "Good hot wine," and they stood for a moment, hands on each other's shoulders like wrestlers. It would be a long time between drinks, and Burnham loved this fat scoundrel; his eyes warmed, and he nodded once sharply, and so did Hai. In silence they crossed the restaurant, and as Burnham stepped out into the dark street he heard the door whisper shut behind him.

He stood alone, forlorn, dismal; these farewells were farewells to China too, and not to temples and pagodas, not to opium and singing girls, not to duck and walnut soup and fish lips, but to people no better or worse than others, yet his own; yet not his own. To avenues and alleyways. To Peking carts and canal barges. To black shop signs flaunting gaudy gilt characters, to prestidigitators who performed in bazaars; to puppet shows and dreamy Taoist priests; to family societies and student unions; to spice shops, tea shops and shops called The Seven Sages of the Bamboo Grove that sold herbs and elixirs. But not to Nien Hao-lan, by God! He perked up, and swung the duffel bag over his shoulder.

From the shadows surged a san-luerh, and Feng cried, "Is it my gentleman, or his ghost?"

Resisting the impulse to embrace him, Burnham only flung up a hand and called back, "How can I not survive? Imagine dying before Chiang Kai-shek. It would take half the fun out of life."

Feng glanced about nervously. "The gentleman must not joke. All is well, then?"

"Thank the gods. All is well."

"No damage?"

"No. Bopped on the head, but it is not a part I use much."

"The gentleman is never serious," Feng reproached him. "And has the gentleman found his Japanese?"

"I have found something better. Take me to the Beggars' Hospital."

"Well, it is not what I would advise," Feng said.

"Nor any sane man. Nevertheless."

"Nevertheless," Feng said. "Well, we will take the prudent way."

Burnham said, "Gallop, old horse."

Feng said, "You know of the curfew?"

"Yes. Make a friend of shadows."

"But if they shoot first?"

"At a san-luerh? I doubt it. Here, fold the top down. And I remove my hat, so. With luck they will see the foreign face and think twice."

"In reasonable times once would do," Feng said.

獅 II

The Watches of the Night

"The man is not precisely a fool," Sung Yun said. "He is like one of those strapping bandit rebels of the old chronicles, doomed to fail and die because the strength of the ox and the courage of the lion are insufficient. Wit is essential. Cunning."

"And a sense of timing," Ming said. The two sat in Sung's lamplit study, a modern room, a businessman's desk with drawers, a telephone, leather chairs, the smoke of Ming's cigarette. Sung Yun was not a smoker, but sniffed hungrily at the rich odor of American tobacco.

"Timing. If only Manchuria had held . . ."

"We lost thirty divisions. The Sixtieth Army simply turned coat."

"Yunnanese!"

Ming shrugged; he liked to think himself above regional prejudice. "If the Americans had entered in force—"

"Always the Americans. But they are better than most. Many times they converted me. Oh, yes. I have been a Roman Catholic and a Methodist and a Baptist. For the bowl of rice and the thin soup and the night's shelter. I was poor, Master Ming. I grew up in true Chinese poverty, and I am not enthusiastic about it. Once I ate human flesh. Once I was kicked by a foreign soldier. I saw with my own eyes the sign at the great park in Shanghai: 'Dogs and Chinese Not Allowed.' That much I can say in perfect English: 'Dogs and Chinese not allowed.' On the whole I found the Japanese far more civilized. Men of finer clay."

"These confidences do me honor."

"They pass the time. Listen, now: an American once told me that poverty was our national disease. Well, I have survived it, and am henceforth immune." True. He had learned well the way of his world: one fought tooth and nail, but mere brutes lost. Superior men won, men quick of eye and flexible of mind. At each stage of the battle certain rewards accrued. The businessman was entitled to a profit, the policeman to petty squeeze, the magistrate to respectable bribes, the provincial governor to a distinct fraction of taxes. Thus it had been, thus it was yet. Generals receiving full pay for vanished regiments! He enjoyed those reports. The cockroach farms in Chungking had amused him vastly. The way of give-take and buy-sell! The road of life! Thus it was yet; thus, they said, it was no longer to be; yet this was the only road on which Sung Yun could read the signposts and milestones. He would follow that road whither it led—even out of China.

But if Kanamori lived? If his hoard was not lost? Sung Yun sighed again. Only once had he underestimated that Japanese madman, but once was enough. He had himself gone underground, but had sent Liao, loyal Liao, and Liao had killed Kanamori.

And yet, these reports and rumors! Sung Yun was tempted toward false beliefs: omens, phantoms, unlucky stars. Revenge and retribution. The malevolence of fate.

"Keep watch," he said. "You have sent for Liao? Good. Time is short. Too much at once. Half a million Red Bandits closing in on Peking."

"Protest is rising," Ming said. "There will be no resistance."

"No. General Fu is a brave and frugal man and a good soldier, but he will not risk Peking. The city itself is a work of art. Now then, I leave you to direct operations. Report to me each hour, even if nothing occurs. And be kind enough to knock."

"As you say, Master Sung."

Sung Yun felt his years. He hoisted himself wearily to his feet. Twelve years of work, hope and frustration, and the future foggier than ever. Communists outside the city, anarchy rising within, and Kanamori neither dead nor alive.

Women, he reflected, were less baffling, less refractory; he would console himself with Miss Ai and Miss Mei, who answered his less complicated needs, who made agreeable whimper and moan. Affection, training, simpleness of mind? Sung Yun could not know, and cared little; there had been Miss Ais and Miss Meis in other cities, and they were the least of life's problems—though, paradoxically, the sharpest of life's gratifications. Money was a gratification, and influence, and objects of art, shrimp out of season, and a bin full of coal balls; but what were all these without the gratifications of the couch? The harmony of the body's humors. The smooth circulation of its airs and liquors. The humming of desire, which hummed in him now, stilling even greed. The sweet anguish of fulfillment to come. In ten years Sung Yun had not entered a cold bed except by his own choice.

But as he crossed the doorsill the thought of Kanamori chilled him again. Not merely Kanamori's hoard, but also Kanamori's revenge.

18 獅

Burnham and Feng were halted once, by a nervous young soldier rabbity in the dark and inordinately relieved at Burnham's plausible account: an American missionary, compelled by politics and war to bid sad farewell to this greatest of cities, had lingered overtime at the whorehouse and been nipped by the curfew. Lutheran, Burnham specified. The soldier depressed the muzzle of his machine-pistol and waved them along.

Feng was severe: such frivolity would draw the lightning of the gods. A fine joke was one thing, pissing in chalices another. Burnham protested: "And if I had told him the truth? He would have scoffed and been grossly offended, and you and I would even now be eating vinegar in a police house."

Feng grumbled and huffed but admitted the justice of Burnham's view. "The base motive," Feng said, "rings of truth. How odd!"

"And how sad. And listen to us, making philosophy on a cold night, with gunfire to mock us and my head still sore."

"Those are mortars."

"Far from the city, but sound carries. The small-arms fire sounds like T'ien An Men."

"As usual," Feng said. "It is the municipal battlefield. Will the gentleman be much abroad tonight?"

"No, my friend. We shall shelter at the hospital."

"They will permit me?"

"They will welcome you. And I will need you."

"More journeys?"

"No. I need your right hand, and the knife in it."

Feng drew up and twisted in his saddle.

"My Japanese is there," Burnham said.

Feng showed fangs and hissed.

"No. I believe he is mad, out of his mind truly, and docile. Only be ready."

"Which of them is he?"

"No," Burnham repeated. "You will stare, or go for the throat. Wait. I will say his name when the time is right."

"I shall wait," Feng said as a distant burst of fire split the night. Burnham felt anger: somewhere the poor, the frenzied, the bewildered were milling and shouting and probably dying, and in a week or two it would be all over, so why bother?

In minutes he would see Hao-lan. His heart banged, swelled and shrilled. He breathed with difficulty. "Good Christ," he said, and to Feng, "Giddap," which he promptly translated.

Feng pounded at the gate. "Who is it?" "It is I." The gate creaked open. Burnham hopped out of the pedicab and waited near the door; Feng parked beside the baby cart and joined him. In the admissions office Dr. Shen waved hospitably and said, "Nurse An, fetch Dr. Nien."

"You are kind," Burnham said, setting his duffel bag against the wall. "Dr. Shen, this is my friend Feng."

"Have you eaten?"

It was polite for "hello," but Burnham chose to take it literally. "Not since noodles at noon."

"There is steamed dough and plenty of cabbage soup, but little else."

"To the hungry man an egg is a chicken," Burnham said. "Are you all here? Dr. Teng, and Mother?"

"All here." Shen seemed cheerful but skinny in the lamplight, hollow-eyed, hollow-cheeked.

"Firing in the street. Will they bring the wounded here?"

"Probably not. They take them to government clinics for interrogation, and later trial. Some they simply jail, still bleeding."

"Modern times."

Shen shrugged. "In ancient times—well, not so long ago, in my own lifetime—public execution entertained the populace. Men were tied to stakes and mutilated, and there was betting and gossip, and cheering for a refined stroke of cruelty, and vendors sold meat patties and hot rolls."

172

"No end to it. How go the children?"
"They would be better off dead," Shen said.
"Surely not."
"We have so little for them."
"Have you a corner for Feng, this night?"
"We turn no one away," Shen said, "not even the healthy."
Nurse An returned, and behind her Hao-lan, who paused in the doorway, obviously tired but to Burnham unspeakably lovely in her shapeless quilted garments. "Good evening," Burnham said. "Good evening," she answered in a warm and singing whisper, and came to him. He met her, and they looked deep, surrendering and only a little wary, and gently he bent to kiss her.
"Yü," said Nurse An. "Such carryings on." Nurse An was thin, twentyish and bucktoothed, and her reprimand was a benediction.

Later they congregated in the warm kitchen, with a coal stove heating both the room and the soup, and when his gown was off Burnham felt snazzy in his striped cotton shirt, handsome for Hao-lan, man-about-town and crack shot, but he kept his mind on Kanamori and took the head of the table, not because he was an honored guest or comfortable and domestic with these friends but because his heart was pumping fast and he wanted his arms free.
He gestured Feng to the foot of the table; this too was socially normal, but Feng was jumpy, the eyes hopping, so Burnham said, "Easy does it," and Feng grew calm. Hao-lan glanced curiously from one to the other. Dr. Teng, skeletal, smacked his lips and looked ravenous. Hao-lan sat by Burnham, and Shen padded in and relaxed audibly, sniffing at the mist of soup, and Nurse An busied herself about the stove, and finally Mother shuffled in from the children's wing. Burnham shot a quick look at the face and recognized it, though barely. Mother bobbed her head and seemed to smile behind the surgical mask. She hurried to help Nurse An, and passed close by Feng, who was popeyed with impatience and uncertainty.

Mother served Hao-lan first, and as she drew back after setting down the bowl Burnham rose carelessly and grasped her forearm. Feng seemed to flow; he stood at Mother's side, and his knife was ready.

Dr. Shen said, "What is this foolishness?"

Burnham said, "Kanamori Shoichi," and then stopped because he was not sure, even now at the critical moment, what it was that he had to say to this Japanese.

Appalled, confused, even frightened, the others were silent until Hao-lan began: "Burnham! What—"

Kanamori made owl's eyes and quavered "Eeeee, eeeee, eeeee" as Burnham's grip locked tighter, "eeeee, eeeee, eeeee" as Burnham bore down, forcing him to his knees, "eeeee, eeeee, eeeee" as the Japanese peered up just once, and for a brief instant Burnham saw, behind the eyes, the empty horror of Kanamori's mind, the hell he inhabited. Then Kanamori's head drooped forward, his throat seemed to close, he hawked and rasped and croaked. Burnham held tight, and some of the man's anguish flowed to him; they were like a statue, victor and vanquished, two yet one.

Benches scraped. Hao-lan protested, but without conviction: "Burnham! You're crazy! She helps me with my bath!"

Burnham twitched away the surgical mask. Kanamori's face was hairless, slightly wrinkled, Japanese or Chinese—well, what had he expected? A full beard? A rising sun on each cheek?

Kanamori was panting now, euhuh, euhuh, euhuh. Burnham bent to undo the buttons of the gown. Between them he and Feng stripped the gown from the upper body, and then the tank top of white cotton, and for a fleeting moment Burnham saw this Japanese loitering in summer on Fisherman's Wharf, smoking a cigar in his undershirt like any workingman. Beneath the tank top, no breasts, no woman: a man's body, lean, downy on the chest. Burnham said, "Helped you with your bath, did he?"

"She was like a grandmother. The gentlest soul—"

Feng said, "Look at his back."

Burnham forced the Japanese head to the floor. The man's back was a crisscross of scars, white alternating with pink, ridges and slashes. "This the kai-t'ou told me." He released Kanamori's head. The Japanese did not move, only remained kneeling in the eternal kowtow, forehead on the bare floor.

Hao-lan plumped down heavily on the wooden bench and blurted "Bugger!"

"None of you knew?"

Dr. Teng shook his head, and Dr. Shen, and Nurse An. Perplexed, recoiling from this unclean masquerader as if he embodied an ancient curse, they looked to Burnham for wisdom. This nest of vipers was his discovery, and it would be his hand that sorted them. But Burnham only showed sour anger.

Kanamori stirred then, and Feng tracked him cautiously as the Japanese crawled to the wall like a roach and huddled, keening "Aaawww" and "Aaahhh," clutching his flanks and rocking from side to side. Yes, like a grandmother.

"We should examine him," Shen said finally.

"Me first," said Burnham. He set a firm hand on Hao-lan's shoulder. "It's all right now. He never hurt you?"

"She never hurt anyone," Hao-lan said.

"Once upon a time he hurt a few."

"But he . . . the babies. He buries the babies."

"As indeed he should." Burnham's voice was low and calm, and he was astonished at the lack of resentment in his heart—no anger, not even annoyance that he had been balked of a hot chase and a fierce fight. "Back off," he told Feng, and bent to speak. "Major Kanamori," he said in Japanese. Kanamori hummed and rocked. Burnham tried again and failed again, so fell back on tradition: he slapped him and called out, "Major Kanamori! Attention!"

Kanamori giggled. Burnham's hand rose again.

"Don't hit him," Hao-lan said. "We're doctors here."

"Yes. It does no good anyway. A world full of incompetents. Look at this killer, this savage. Look at me, last of the big-time headhunters. He giggles and I scream and shout and the soup cools." Burnham squatted and tried to look Kanamori in the eye. "Kanamori Shoichi, do you remember

Nanking? Do you remember Ginling College in Nanking?"
Kanamori squealed and whimpered, then grinned.

"Kanamori," Burnham said, "do you remember your sergeant
breaking my nose?"

Kanamori hummed and blinked, but Burnham caught a gleam.

"Kanamori," Burnham said, "what is the last mandarin?"

Kanamori was silent, and his eyes were steady. Then he
frowned ferociously, grimaced and wheezed out a windy breath.
His mouth contorted; the cords of his neck swelled. His voice was
at once a scream and a whisper: "Nan-ching!"

Nanking. Burnham took him by the throat and hauled him to
his feet. "Kanamori, who is the last mandarin?"

Kanamori gasped and made a fish mouth; Burnham slacked off.
"Kanamori, where is the last mandarin?"

Kanamori grinned and cocked his head; he was trying to speak.
He failed, slumped, and panted like a runner.

Hao-lan came to them and said, "Mother, where is the last
mandarin?"

Kanamori laughed like a crone, and said on a strangled cry, "In
his tomb!"

"Oh, forget it," Burnham said.

"What's this last mandarin supposed to be?"

"I don't even know. It was something he said in Chinese when
he was delirious once."

"I killed the baby," Kanamori said in conversational tones. "I
killed the little baby. Hai-ju. Hsiao-haerh. Hai-ju. Hsiao-haerh."
White-eyed, he swayed.

"He raves," Dr. Shen said. "What is this about a babe at the
breast?"

"No idea. Kanamori, who is the last mandarin?"

"The cemetery," Kanamori said. "I killed the little baby. The
baby. The mother and baby. The little baby. The father and
mother and baby."

"Kanamori," Burnham said, "will you go home and bow before
your mother?"

The Japanese took them all by surprise; he cried "Yaaaah!" and struck like a boxer, snapping Burnham's head back hard, then screamed and plunged and flailed. Burnham shouted "No, Feng!" and the knife hung suspended. He socked Kanamori gently with a straight right hand and bounced him off the wall. Kanamori screeched and sprang, but Burnham pushed him back. Kanamori weighed all of a hundred and twenty pounds; Burnham was close to two hundred and felt gross now, a barbarian.

Kanamori seemed to be brandishing an imaginary club. He feinted to his right. He feinted to his left. He raised the club high and shouted "Ima!" and chopped down savagely. Then he stood panting and white-eyed, a trickle of blood on his jaw, panting hoarsely and bending an evil eye on Burnham. "The unborn babe." His voice was rusty. "The unborn babe."

"Hold him," Dr. Shen said. Burnham saw the needle, and he took one arm and Feng the other, and Dr. Shen gave Kanamori peace with morphine.

愛 19

His room warmed by lamplight, Sung Yun reclined on the vast, comfortable bed, beneath him a mattress of genuine feathers and beneath that intricately tooled wooden springs. Miss Ai sat beside the bed; they were playing chess and drinking hot yellow wine. Miss Mei, on a couch in the corner, embroidered. When young Ming knocked and entered, he was struck by the hominess of it: a snug room bathed in golden light, a man and his women in calm recreation, the faint spicy odor of wine, Ming himself like a son come to chat. "Ah, the domestic pleasures!" he said. "How remote from strife and calamity!"

"Archery would be more classic than chess," Sung Yun said, "but the season and the hour keep us indoors. I agree, however, that the note of bliss is antique and pastoral. You have brought Liao?"

"I have. And news."

"Tell me."

"The American went to the beggars. He then returned to his room, packed his traps, and made haste to the Beggars' Hospital."

"The Beggars' Hospital! Again! We have perhaps been remiss. Where did he, ah, interview these beggars?"

"At their union hall in Arrow-Maker's Road."

Sung Yun shuddered. "Arrow-Maker's Road! Off the Street of the Female Flutist, where that silversmith was dismembered?"

"Between that and the Street of the Aged Midget, where the three fishmongers were found."

"An elegant neighborhood. This American is not only resourceful but courageous."

"Foolhardy."

"He is at the hospital now?"

"He is."

"Let Liao enter."

Ming clapped once. A spare man, perhaps thirty, of pinched

features and wearing a policeman's uniform, entered and stood at attention.

Sung Yun dismissed Miss Ai, who glided to the couch and plumped herself down beside Miss Mei. He rose, sniffed thoughtfully and rubbed the tip of his nose. "Ah, Liao! Do stand easier. Do not be a guest."

With obvious effort Liao relaxed fractionally.

"You killed Kanamori," Sung Yun said.

Liao made no answer.

"Well then, you were sure once that you had killed Kanamori."

"I was certain," Liao said. His voice was soft and musical, little more than a sung whisper. "I am certain still."

"Tell me again. In detail."

Liao recited like a student. Now and then he frowned, and strained to remember. "I made my way from Nanking with the two sets of papers. I rode the train to Hsü-chou and Chi-nan—"

"Less geography," Sung Yun said, "and more killing. You reached Peking safely. You found the Russian woman's brothel." Poor Madam Olga, now dead. The crab in the belly, they said. Orange hair, painted mouth, the long cigarette dangling always, and her eyes flat, empty, inscrutable except for flashes of weary scorn. For men; for Orientals? Blue eyes! A woman of brass and cheap lacquer. Sung Yun imagined the scene: the parlor with foreign publications and sheaves of erotic prints, even the lampshades pornographic. Bottles of brandy. Probably a White Russian or two sitting about, chunky and superior, and perhaps other Japanese. The women in their silks urging Kanamori upstairs. The monkey disrobing as women mistreated him. Grinning. Those teeth. Chattering in Chinese. Always with the women he spoke Chinese.

"It was she who supervised," Liao was saying, "and limited the injuries. I heard his cries. I saw him beaten. It was a large peasant girl with a Northeastern accent who whipped the monkey."

Sung Yun imagined the lash descending, Kanamori wincing and crying out. On all fours, Liao was saying, and his sex hanging

like a goat's. And the whip itself? Leather? A bull's pizzle? And
the other women watching. Kanamori insisted: See, see!
"He cried for his mother, and urged the girl on. Welts rose.
Blood flowed."
The features twisted in anguish, Sung Yun could see this now;
the tears running, the large teeth mangling the lower lip, and the
women cheering one another on: "Beat him! Monkey!" And
Kanamori in the lamplight swallowing his own blood.
"He called for a girl and mounted her as the peasant woman
whipped him."
Miss Ai said "Yüüü!"
Miss Mei set down her needlework.
" 'The last mandarin,' he shouted. He was laughing. 'The last
mandarin is the richest of all!' "
Sung Yun clapped his hands in vexation. "It means nothing!
It was a joke! Go on, go on."
"After the monkey completed his act he collapsed on the girl.
He whispered 'Enough.' The peasant girl hesitated, and at a sign
from the Russian woman continued. Kanamori cried out, and
struggled to rise. I entered the room then, and with both hands
and all my strength, pressed his face into the other girl's belly. It
seemed fitting that such a one should suffocate so. The peasant
woman whipped and whipped. The others turned away; only the
Russian woman stared. When Kanamori was limp and at least
unconscious, perhaps already dead, the woman cleaned him off.
I picked him up. The Russian woman looked sick. I carried him
to the dumping ground south of Whore Street and dumped him
among the dead things. Then I drew my knife and stabbed him
in the chest. Then I cleaned my knife as well as possible in the
dark. Then I listened for a heartbeat or a breath, and none came.
Then I went away, and never came back, not to that house and
not to that street. I went to the address in Pig Market Alley and
awaited my lord's arrival."
Sung Yun made teeth like tiles. "Oh, what a rascal you are,
Liao! You did well, you did well."
"I am so pleased to be a woman," Miss Mei murmured, and

the others glanced at her, startled, unsure how to take this original remark, this independence of thought.

"As indeed you should be," Sung Yun said finally. "Both of you. The world of men is a world of brutish horror, but you women are all beauty and light. So," he said to Liao and Ming, "if more than that happened, or less, it is fate and cannot be altered. Thank you, Liao." His gesture dismissed the man, who bowed and marched out. "Yi, so much depends on this!" He brightened, as if struck by a comical thought. "And Inspector Yen. What has the virtuous and talented Inspector Yen done with his hours?"

"What he usually does," Ming said. "He spent most of the day at his office, eating sunflower seeds, smoking cigarettes and complaining that he had no personnel. He then quarreled with his car, which eventually yielded and deigned to locomote. After dark he paid a visit to the American's room. Then he went home."

"Splendid. His customary civic accomplishments." Sung Yun rubbed his hands. "I begin to think again that Kanamori is long dead. That all this is merely a fuss of righteous bounty hunters, adventurers and frustrated authorities, and that we must resign ourselves to the loss. We have all been taken in by false reports."

"Nevertheless," Ming said firmly, "Liao will proceed. I believe the American to be less foolish than he appears."

"He could scarcely be more so," Sung Yun said. "Good. Liao will indeed proceed. A brief enlistment in the local constabulary." Sung Yun enjoyed a moment of imperial joy: he was a glossy spider at the center of an intricate web. Each hour a new strand. He glanced complacently at his wall, where hung three painted scrolls, priceless if genuine, by Ma Fen, Ma Lin and Ma Yüan, a family unequaled for seven hundred years. His wine was served him in exquisite porcelain cups. Miss Ai and Miss Mei were incomparable, except to each other. His clothes were tailored by Old Silver Needle himself, and in his kitchen the rarest red peppers from Szechuan sat opposite the rarest top-leaf tea from Chekiang. Financially he missed his collection; sentimentally he missed only the lions. He was particularly partial to lions, porcelain or bronze. A shame to leave all this, with the Red Bandits swarming closer by the minute. Still, the man of character is at home in a hut. A hut! It would never come to that. One ivory, shrewdly sold, would keep him for years. "If he lives, we must have him," Sung Yun said lightly. "However faint the spoor, we must follow. How I want that one! What an opportunity: to kill him twice!"

"If he lives, we shall find him," Ming said. "My bones tell me it is a matter of hours."

"You will report to me throughout the night."

"You will remain watchful?"

"I shall remain awake," Sung Yun said. "The mind paces, you understand."

Ming allowed himself a small smile. "I understand."

"Do you know what I miss in winter?" Sung Yun asked. "Tangerines. A tangerine would be interesting at breakfast. A tangerine and good news." His face fell into the smooth sad lines of inexpressible sorrow. "Think, Ming, one day soon, my last breakfast in Peking."

20

At the hospital Kanamori was asleep, locked in his own tiny, bare room. Feng had volunteered to play sentry, sleeping on the doorsill, but Burnham assured him that a quarter-grain of morphine would subdue even the craziest Japanese for some hours. So again they gathered in the kitchen, where soup might now be served at leisure and with decorum, but Burnham set them all at sevens and eights by rolling in like an unruly and purposeful bear, stepping right across to Hao-lan and saying, "I believe I have learned something of value. I do not want this Kanamori. They can elect him emperor for all I care. All I want is you. I want you to come away with me tomorrow."

Nurse An served soup while Hao-lan and Dr. Shen argued, Burnham having shot his bolt or at least suffered a flash of good sense that enjoined some minutes of silence: the decision was more momentous for her than for him. But not much more, by God! Feng was tranquil now, placid, full of wonder, and sat at his end of the long wooden table shy and impressed, though sucking up noisy gouts of soup. "Whatever happens," Shen said after a time, "you will be Ch'en wearing Li's hat. When the Communists come, you will be a daughter of the upper bourgeoisie and a lover of things foreign."

Burnham's brows twitched. Shen saw his own joke and apologized. "At least I too am bourgeois," Burnham said. "I am not hoping to marry above my station in life—though far above my merit," he added immediately.

"Well," Shen said, "and what are your prospects?"

"Well sir," Burnham said, "I am an electrical engineer and a good one, and there is always need for such. I seem to be a failure as a hunter of Japanese, but that is a declining trade. I promise that Hao-lan will never go hungry, and will have her own key."

Shen smiled in embarrassment and Teng laughed frankly. Feng caught Burnham's eye and timidly revealed the package of Lucky

Strikes; Burnham nodded, and Feng, after offering one first to Burnham, then to Hao-lan and Nurse An, and then—he was observing some strict personal protocol—Shen and Teng, ignited a cigarette and inhaled voraciously.

Hao-lan sighed. "And legal complications? Will I be welcome?"

"Yü," Burnham said, "I shall tell them that you are Kanamori."

"Not funny," Hao-lan said. "And how is it all to be accomplished? A visit to your consulate with my passport? I have one, you know."

Suffused by mischievous joy, Burnham meditated this possibility. At this season the gentlemen would sport ties and waistcoats. They were men of breadth and sympathy, in danger of transfer to Africa or Iceland if they told the truth about China, and consequently a touch higher-strung than the diplomat's exterior would indicate. Also about half a million Red Chinese troops were knocking at the gates: a busy time for all. And here comes old Burnham without a visa, bearing pistol, knife and Luxury Pipe Pack, and on his arm this myopic dumpling who claims to be a doctor, and Burnham wants a license and a preacher and two first-class tickets to Niagara Falls, and mumbles an apology about some Japanese nobody ever heard of.

"I am about to make a splendid impression," he said, "so listen, all. Where is your telephone?"

"At my desk," said Nurse An.

Burnham beckoned them into the admissions office. Behind him they crowded through the doorway.

He hoped the damn thing would work. Clicks. Buzzes. Shrieks. The demons of the upper air. Disembodied go-betweens. Burnham's impulse with Chinese telephones was to hold the receiver some inches from his face and shout. Voices twanged and jingled: hobgoblins, busy signals, the spirits of ineptitude and treachery, the gods of the short circuit. "Patience," he advised his audience.

A voice: "Number, please."

"Liu erh wu, liu pa liu."

Silence. Bravely he smiled at Hao-lan, who obviously mistrusted this performance.

A sharp click, a businesslike American voice: "Yankee Stadium."

"Hello, Yankee Stadium," Burnham said. "This is Babe Ruth."

"Son of a bitch," the voice said. "You work fast, Babe. Whatcha want?"

"I want the player bus for ten ack emma tomorrow."

"You're lucky, boy. We're terminating that franchise. We'll have a bus all warmed up. Listen, you any use in the right-hand seat?"

"Had about four hours."

"Good. We're short a man here. You wouldn't believe what we've been ferrying where."

"I don't even want to hear about it."

"Good thinking. Hey! You mean to say you got your home run?"

"You bet your sweet ass I got my home run. Seoul or Tokyo?"

"Seoul, buddy. Don't worry about it. Once you get through the tubes it's all Bridgeport. Nice goin', old son."

"Thanks," Burnham said. "Over and out."

"Over and out."

Burnham hung up and waved in airy triumph. "I have just reserved a private aircraft."

Teng said, "Americans! A people of miracles!"

"A people of gall," Hao-lan said.

Burnham shooed them back into the kitchen. "It is for Seoul only, and the clerks there will wear out a brush or two before letting us go further. We shall tell them you are Chiang Kai-shek's daughter."

"A patriot," Hao-lan said. "An officer and a gentleman. You lie to your superiors."

"They are not my superiors," Burnham said, "and they will be angry, but not at you. At me"—he knew a moment's shame—"because I did not do my job."

"That I understand," Hao-lan said. "I too have a job, and cannot do it."

Shen dismissed the question. "Listen to your heart. In time there will be doctors here aplenty, and nurses too, and dentists."

Nurse An served another round of soup, steamed dough and tea. Smoke hung blue. Savors and odors mingled, and winter was forgotten. "I myself would go," Nurse An said, "and not because of the distinguished visitor, whom I hardly know, though he is not unpleasing in appearance and speaks a proper local tongue, but because I have never left Peking, and the world is a carnival place. To see even Mukden or Shanghai!"

"It is not only leaving my own people," Hao-lan objected. "It is living among Americans. More than once I was insulted in England. The assumption was made that a woman not English lacked morals." Her eyes flashed suddenly at Burnham. "Did you make the same assumption? You grew up among us; was the easy little Chinese maiden always at your beck and call? Was it less a sin than with Miss Blue Eyes?"

This was not a question to evade, and Burnham did his best. "It was more a sin. Because heathen Chinese, they told us, were like untutored children, and were in our charge, and to take advantage of a Chinese girl would be heinous, like striking a servant. Oh, how I burned! And yet—yes, the Chinese were lesser. In America too you will be insulted. You will be asked if you are Japanese or Siamese or Eskimo. As here I am called a Russian sometimes by men of the northwest, and pointed reference is made to my nose." She winced lovingly at the bad pun. "And some will offend you by good cheer and tolerance. They will speak clearly for your poor foreign ear. They will touch you —your hand, your forearm, a kiss on the cheek—to show that they accept Asian skin and fear no contamination. We have many black people, and there are still Americans who believe that the black rubs off, that white is clean, that yellow is cowardly. You are tan and in places ruddy like an apple, but to them you will be one of the yellow people.

"All of this will lessen," Burnham said, "but in our lifetime fools will abound. All I can say for sure is that I will love you as long as I can—I think as long as I live, but tonight I am not reciting romance—and will keep harm from you. But the important reasons are not these."

"Why then, tell me the important reasons."

"Never, before others. You have no shame. Morals indeed!"

Shen and Teng laughed; Nurse An tktked. Feng seemed not to understand, quite, and sat diffident, silent, prepared to smile.

Hao-lan said, "The future here. It matters."

"Yes, it matters. There will be more and better medicine and much to rejoice the social soul. That too is irrelevant."

"Well, I am impatient to hear what is relevant. You are all smoke and no fire."

"A bold and forward woman," Burnham grumbled. "Very well, then, before the world: I love only you. How this happened remains a mystery. Without you I will be only what I was: a foolish boy. And without me, you—you—ah, it is not for me to say, but together we can be the only one that is more than two," and he slipped into English, saying softly, "a very singular plural," and she translated, so that Nurse An and Teng and Shen said, "Ah, pretty, pretty," and Hao-lan herself, though she tried to look too wise for elegant flattery, only glowed.

For some moments then, as if they were all overcome, they focused on food and drink. Shen muttered, "A disgrace that we have no wine."

With a trace of misery in her voice but no real conviction, Hao-lan said, "I must think. It is all so final. I would no longer be Hao-lan. I would be Helen. *Helen,* they called me in England" —her laughter dissipated much of her anguish—"and in Chinese that is hei-lin, which can mean black bladder trouble. Imagine being called Black Clap."

"Or Hei-lung," Burnham smiled. "I did some fighting up in Heilungkiang." It was a province of Manchuria and meant Black Dragon River. "You will be my Black Dragon, and breathe fire upon me."

Her full lips parted slightly; she breathed fire upon him,

and retreated almost blushing to her cabbage soup.

Feng astonished them all, evidently including himself, by speaking. "In Peking are people of all nations and degrees. There are Mohammedans and Cantonese and foreigners like the gentleman, some with yellow hair, and older foreign women, those with immense bosoms, and the foreign priests, and once I carried foreign sailors with buttons atop their hats like chrysanthemums. Surely it is so elsewhere. And surely a Pekinger in a foreign land would be superior. Pekingers are superior to Shanghainese and Nankingers, so it must follow." He subsided in confusion, and slurped tea.

"There you have it," Burnham said. "Must we take a vote?"

Hao-lan laughed again. "Nurse An?"

Nurse An nodded, her eyes gleaming; gently she touched Hao-lan's arm.

"No, no, no!" Hao-lan cried. "It is all too beautiful, but I must think. And we two must speak alone."

Burnham only gazed upon his girl and sighed.

21 獅

Inspector Yen Chieh-kuo admired the English word "flatfoot."
He thought often that he would have made a good flatfoot in
some progressive country with microscopes, fingerprint kits and
electric chairs. He was a Peking man, born and bred in a quiet
quarter near the Lama Temple up by Tung Chih Men; his father
had been a supervisor of streets, roads and alleys for the municipal
government, first under the Dowager Empress and then under
various warlords and republics. Yen thought of himself as an
oppressed civil servant, with immense tasks and no resources,
hunting fiery dragons with a paper sword. He was married but
childless, and not for lack of effort; it was a tragedy but no longer,
in modern times, a shame. His wife was unlettered, and his house
was a man's house; when colleagues came to dinner, they left their
wives home, and Yen's woman ate alone. They kept one servant,
a scolding old cook. Yen's wife had little to do. Yen assumed that
she had her interests and hobbies. He was wrong; hers was a
wasted life, and that was all that could ever be said about her. No
one bothered to say it.

When he left Burnham, Yen went home. He was not expected;
neither was he unexpected. This was his house; when he arrived,
a meal was started. He ate pork dumplings, drank tea, and finished
with steaming pig's-ear soup. He brooded. He needed a department, at least a squad. He had rank; his pay was acceptable; bribes
and confiscations eked out a comfortable domestic treasury. But
he was a flatfoot. He liked his work and felt that he should be
doing more of it. Normally it was cut and dried. A malefactor was
found, apprehended and punished. But this chase for Kanamori
depressed him. His files had told him more than he had told
Burnham: for example, that the price on Sung Yun's head had
been set by Kanamori himself. Or that Sung Yun's enemies,
foreign and domestic, had a way of stumbling over trouble. One
simply did not tell everything to foreigners.

Burnham had lied to him only tonight. The nature of the lie eluded Yen, but he had been a policeman for more than twenty years and the music of a lie was flat to his ear; he knew. That Burnham was leaving he did not doubt. Still, he would enjoy setting hounds on Burnham's trail this one night. Unfortunately, he lacked hounds. He knew—he had known before he asked— that Burnham had seen Sung Yun. Had he actually spoken to the beggars? What was it he had said? "Cold trails and empty warrens."

Yen shrugged. A frosty night, and a flatfoot was better off at home. Still, if Burnham was leaving, there remained Sung Yun, who could not have been idle.

Inspector Yen came to a decision. He would sleep for some hours; he would then cast in small circles. If by tomorrow noon there were no fresh corpses, he would close the books and banish this Kanamori from his mind. There was an abundance of trouble without Japanese ghosts. The Red Bandits were everywhere. Fu Tso-yi's Thirty-fifth Army had been destroyed, two of the best divisions in North China. Lin Piao—that turtle's egg!—was sweeping down from the northeast with thirteen columns. To the south, the news was even worse: army after army wiped out on the central plains. Grudgingly Yen admired the enemy. Why were all the military geniuses on the other side? Chu Teh! Liu Po-ch'eng, the old one-eyed tiger! Chen Yi! Teng Hsiao-p'ing! And Lin Piao, worst of all because closest.

Perhaps I should have been a soldier: better to stand and die for Peking than to spy upon foreigners, or to bow and scrape before that gangster Ming.

Inspector Yen cursed them all, and then himself, and went to bed.

At four in the morning Peking was almost silent, and Inspector Yen was grateful: no armies in the distance, no roaring mobs or chattering gunfire in the streets he loved. His lemon, as if lulled by the city's repose, responded amiably and chugged away from the curb with a minimum of resistance. Yen tried to complain—

Why must I do everything alone? Where are my subordinates, my planners, my staff, my communications?—but admitted to an odd happiness, as if the city belonged solely to him for this hour, as if he alone ruled, guided destinies, maintained order.

He traversed the Imperial City north to south. At Ch'ien Men he was halted, recognized, saluted and waved on. Slowly he drove past the Willow Wine Shop: darkness and silence. He proceeded to the Beggars' Hospital: silence, but within the walls a dim gleam. The streets were almost deserted; in one doorway, he glimpsed a solitary figure, and by the peripheral glow of his headlights saw that it was a policeman. Reassuring and comforting. Peiping, the old name: northern peace. Well, this city had known little peace in his lifetime.

He drove back to Ch'ien Men, the only gate open at this hour, and once more was passed through. He set his course for the East Four P'ai-lou, and swung off to to inspect Sung Yun's house. What was there to see? A wall. A gate, closed and surely locked.

Thereafter he drove aimlessly and marshaled thoughts. The simplest: Kanamori was alive, Burnham had found him, lied about it, and was taking him out. Entirely possible. As they both knew, Burnham's promise to allow Yen an interview had been an empty promise.

One thing Yen knew for sure: the Americans wanted Kanamori for more than a simple hanging. And he knew the why of it. He wondered now, as he had before, whether Burnham did. In China, with his language and his delicacy, Burnham seemed canny, knowing, even powerful; perhaps to the Americans he really was only an errand boy, as he had said. Could Burnham believe that Kanamori was merely a thug? Kanamori's public crimes had been committed by thousands of Japanese officers and men, and many of them had remained in China, settled, married, melted into cities and villages unmolested. Surely Burnham must know this.

But perhaps it was not a simple case of lost-and-found. Perhaps Burnham had truly burned the boats and bridges, given up in despair or disgust.

Or had found Kanamori, learned what he wanted to learn, and had no real interest in the man himself.

Or Sung Yun had found Kanamori—in which case Kanamori was already dead, and Inspector Yen was wasting yet another night. Yen knew Ming well; he knew many Mings. No heart, no scruple, a killer almost frolicsome in his vocation. Sung Yun and his minions! A platoon of hirelings. There was one feeble consolation in a Communist victory: farewell, Sung Yun!

The thought of such a victory depressed Inspector Yen. He saw himself in uniform, demoted, directing bicycle traffic or apprehending fornicators.

He was at the West Lower P'ai-lou now, and he was hungry. Soon the noodle shops would open. He realized abruptly why the city was empty. Curfew! He had forgotten entirely. Such peace! How beautiful Peking would be unpopulated!

An inexpressible melancholy swept over him. An aging cop prowling through the night, his talents, his mind, his very life, all wasted.

22 愛

Ming's knock was more respectful than his expression. The two Pekinese frisked at his feet, rousing his more murderous instincts.

Sung Yun's response was quick. The women were dozing.

Ming said, "Kanamori lives."

Before his eyes Sung Yun aged, then recovered. "Very well. Report."

"The American alerted his compatriots at the airport. In a complex spoken code he announced the capture of Kanamori, and demanded transportation for ten in the morning."

"Then Kanamori is at the Beggars' Hospital?"

"That we cannot know. We do know that Burnham is there."

"Bad, bad," Sung Yun groaned. "I do not want this American killed."

Ming shrugged.

"Pour wine."

Ming stepped to an inlaid cabinet, and returned with two cups of kao-liang wine. "It is cold, but it is wine."

"We will not dry these cups," Sung Yun said. "We will sip like philosophers, and savor and think."

The dogs leaped to Sung Yun and licked at his hands; absently he scratched their heads.

Ming waited. This old man was a riddle. His mane was gray but his face was shiny and unlined, his body limber and loose-jointed. A riddle, with his Miss Ai and Miss Mei, his transactions, his hearty commercial friends, his Sino-American Amity Association. Ming himself was only twenty-five, and impatient.

"I think I must have my horoscope cast," Sung Yun said. "I sense emanations. Quiverings."

"This American—"

"Ah, the American!" Sung Yun flapped a dismissive hand. "Invaluable. The brain of an egg, but he did our work for us: he charged into the tiger's lair in the name of justice. A true hero. But you know them so much better than I."

"The language only. A few customs. My acquaintance was with soldiers, rude and vigorous, and not with the lords and princes."

"Lords and princes! So many sides of beef! A strange tribe, Ming, lacking all delicacy and sensuality. They have no history. They swarm like demented nomads; they cross all borders, and when they see a peacock they take up a gun and slay it, and eat it raw. But," he conceded, "they accomplish great tasks, and they ignore the laughter of their critics. Invaluable, as I said."

"Is he to die?"

Sung Yun shrugged. "I think not. An unnecessary risk. Also I am now cautious about premature killing. When I believed that Kanamori was dead, and his secret with him—"

Ming said, "The American is a loose end alive."

"But dead he could be an embarrassment. These are delicate matters in delicate times. Hsü! Not to know who knows what: that is the true ignorance."

Ming inclined his head. "As you say."

"I shall miss these tables," Sung Yun said, suddenly glum. "In rosewood I find a special gleam and warmth. Also walnut." He tossed off his wine. "Kanamori is of course the business of the moment, but I am concentrating poorly. To leave Peking! Think, Ming, how sad! There will be rosewood in other cities, and lovely ladies too, but all stability is of the past and a dream. I shall be an exile. Once, my dear Ming, men of talent made this city a corner of heaven. Men of my stamp were archers and musicians, horsemen and lords. Have you heard of Fu Hsi?"

"No."

"In the time of the Six Dynasties. An ordinary man but a son of Han, a Chinese! He invented the revolving bookcase. I told this once to an American, and he laughed. Gunpowder, he said. You Chinese invented gunpowder, and that was more important. No, I said, no; the compass, perhaps, but not gunpowder. After gunpowder the archer faded."

Ming listened respectfully. Sung Yun must be humored, and the Japanese could wait; the hospital was under close watch. Fu

Hsi indeed! This old man was shrewd and elegant but also full of bowl. Ming smiled slightly. For years he had said "full of bowl" until an American had corrected him: "Bull! Bull!"

"Now then," Sung Yun said. "Fill my cup, will you?" Ming rose and complied. "Enough culture. I think now we must act, and act boldly. You will take the car and find Liao. Yes." Sung Yun chuckled, clapped hands, nodded happily as he continued. Liao would rule the rear seat and do the heavy work. Kanamori was not to be incapacitated. Speed was essential. Perhaps Ming should mask himself. A few of them would play the pedestrian and slow traffic—perhaps Huang the Tinker would maneuver his cart strategically. The moment must be perfectly chosen. Had Ming any questions?

Ming had no questions.

Sung Yun seemed pleased. He clutched the dogs to him and kissed them in turn. "We must discuss these canine friends. I cannot take them with me."

"I shall care for them as my own," Ming said. Dogs!

"I think not." Sung Yun was sleek and cheerful now, almost merry. "You will destroy them painlessly."

Limb from limb, Ming thought.

"I do not wish to think of them harried and starving in the new Peking," Sung Yun went on, "or dropped alive into some savage's cooking pot. Well, there is yet time. But if we succeed, I shall leave soon. Kanamori! I wonder if he can stand torture."

Ming inclined his head. "Not Liao's."

"Go now," Sung Yun said. "Do this quickly, and do it well. My house will be yours. Miss Mei and Miss Ai will be yours."

Miss Mei and Miss Ai slept on as Ming departed. The house, and Miss Ai and Miss Mei! And perhaps something more, by golly! Sung Yun was mortal: his collection was immortal. Ming warmed to the excitement of this. A-number-one; all was A-number-one. He was pleased at the turn of events, and with himself. A sharp article. It was not merely that the house would be his, or even the women, or even the hoard, whatever it consisted of; after all, the house would have to be sold, and for a song, with the Red Bandits at the gates; treasures were severely discounted; a woman was only a woman, though in time of need he could pimp these two broads all the way to Taiwan.

No, Ming's pleasure was artistic. He had used his bean. He was hip.

23 寶

In Hao-lan's room they embraced and clung. Nurse An padded in and out like some Oriental Cupid bearing not bow, quiver and arrows but a basin, a pitcher and a chamber pot. "Our love nest," Hao-lan said. "Do you know Yeats? 'Love has pitched his mansion in / The place of excrement.' "

Burnham said in lofty and offended tones, "You have no sense whatever of *occasion*. This is a time for champagne, flowers and fiddles, not urinalysis. God almighty, what have I done?"

"I imagine," she said carefully, "that you have proposed to me."

Nurse An stood in the doorway blessing them again, and then the door clicked shut. They were alone in a weak bath of amber light.

"Yes, I've proposed to you."

She left him to sit morosely on her iron bed, which shrieked and jingled. "It's unfair. I'm exhausted. I can't think."

"Then don't. This may be the one time you shouldn't. Impulse is a fresh horse; ride him."

"Is it that easy?" The smile was wan and almost tearful. "Listen: I know you love me. It's obviously impossible. I could have been betrothed at three and married at sixteen, and here I sit at the mercy of a foreign devil without even a chaperon. Oh"—she laughed shakily—"we are so silly, you and I! Tell me one thing anyway: do you love *me*, or China? I'm not a pagoda, or a picturesque corner of Peking, or the Western Hills or a rice paddy or the classics or the world's best cuisine. I'm a doctor. I want to practice medicine. I used to play the piano. I'm cranky for three days before I menstruate. I hate tapioca and the kind of music they play in hotels. Someday I may get fat. When I have a cold my nose turns scarlet. I don't ever want to find myself alone because my impulsive man feels another impulse and chases off to Hong Kong to find his China again in some silken chippie."

"All I ever wanted to be," Burnham said, "is monogamous.

The few times I really cared for a woman I was miserable in the company of all others. Why, I remember one squab of a girl with spots—"

"In the end I will strangle you," she said thoughtfully. "If you can't maintain a decent romantic tone, then you shouldn't be proposing at all. And if you can't establish your monogamy without a long history of sentimental high points—"

"Well, I am a terrible fellow," Burnham admitted. "I drink a bit in moments of stress, and I hate neckties, and I wake up like a bear in spring and growl until about noon. My old father is recently bald, and it's hereditary. I like a cigar from time to time. And about that girl with spots—"

"Oh, shut up!" She choked on a warble or a sob or a laugh; Burnham wanted to step to her, yank her to her feet and enfold her, but knew that he must not touch her for a few moments more. He himself was shaky, his heart plinking and twanging like a banjo. "I really thought I loved my Honourable," she said.

"Ah. And did you love him because he was the mysterious Occident? Piccadilly and the Yorkshire moors and the changing of the guard and the roast beef of England?"

"I think so now," she said, "and I'm half afraid that you love me that way."

"Is that how you love me? Do you love the burly American with the crooked nose and the gift of gab? The citizen of the world, the conqueror, the old Yankee can-do?"

"No," she said passionately. "No! And that's how I know what it was about him. It was—believe me, believe me—nothing like this."

"I believe you," Burnham managed, strangling, "and I wish you'd believe me. I simply cannot tell you why I love you."

"Thank God!" she said fervently. "You don't mean you're speechless for once? Oh, what are you doing to me? Don't you know there's a war on? And all these children, all these children!"

"I worry about that. Do you see it as necessary and noble work? Does it tear at your heart?"

"It's miserable work. Without equipment and medicine it's mainly nursing care and post-mortems."

"Then for God's sake let me take you away from all this." Even as he spoke they laughed at the absurd phrase, and then he did go to her and tugged her upright and held her close, and spoke in Chinese because without the music the words were stale and abused: "Listen to me. I have thanked many women, and most were fair and some were tall like the willow, but none showed the peony's smile or the river otter's grace, none dizzied me with the fox's sweet musk, none brought me youth and love in a cruet—"

"Like the Lady Ch'ang," she murmured, "who stole the elixir of youth and fled with it to the moon, where she was turned into a frog."

"A frog! And you complain because I mention a girl with spots! You are the least romantic woman I have ever met. You had better marry me because you stand no chance otherwise. You have muddy eyes and a big nose and no upper lip—"

"I do not have a big nose! I have a beautiful upper lip!"

"—also you are too short and your breasts are walleyed and you peer and blink like the summer owl. Who else would have you?"

She tightened her embrace and rebuked his chest: "And you. Your skin is pink and scaly. Your nose is zoological. Some ancestor was a mastodon."

"An eagle. Besides," he explained, "the nose is merely symbolic, an indication of—"

"An *anteater*," she said. "And you are incorrigibly lecherous. You talk of love, but in truth you only hanker."

"Oh yes," he said. "I hanker all right. I plan to hanker all our lives. I could walk through hellfire and it would not burn away my hankering for you."

"There," she said. "Hellfire. That is another thing. I cannot marry a Christian."

"My God," he said, "you're Jewish."

At that she laughed, a gusty, wailing bellow, and he too, and they rocked together, safe, safe at last, and annihilated the world in a kiss, their first, it would always be their first; the kiss of love, the kiss of peace, the kiss that passeth all understanding.

Liao was short, mean, wiry and pinched of feature. He was deficient in the Five Constant Virtues, but of the secondary virtues he was strong in loyalty and tenacity, and he had worked for Sung Yun since 1937. Like many of his compatriots, he had survived inhuman poverty, and by sixteen his normal state of emotion was a dull, chronic bitterness. Belief was alien to him; intermittent flashes of ill-defined hope relieved his brutish acrimony, but always he had sunk back into the sullen despair of the dispossessed. With Sung Yun he had found purpose: decent work, good food, steady pay. Sung Yun was not personally a tyrant but a man of shrewd ways, who did not bluster and did not require his men to cringe and fawn. Liao knew that Sung Yun would leave Peking. Liao would miss him. He could make no certain plans but saw himself as perhaps a policeman, under any regime.

At this moment, late in the middle watch, he was wearing the black and stolen uniform of a policeman of Peking. In his holster rode a 13-shot, 9-mm. Browning High-Power Automatic Pistol, manufactured (Ming had deciphered the markings for him) in a place called Canada. The pistol could be adapted to a shoulder stock and used as a short rifle, but Liao possessed no such stock, and his work did not require a rifle. While he would have been pleased to kill a Japanese, he understood that he was to spare this one for the time being. The thumb safety was on: it would be a long night, with perhaps a long day to follow. He had Luger ammunition with a flat point, so at need he would destroy, not merely pierce. The finality of this warmed him. He saw the tiny bullet holes of entry, the mangled organs within, and the gaping gully of exit. Perhaps when this Japanese had supplied the mysterious information Sung Yun sought, Liao could then dispatch him. The Japanese! He could almost taste blood. He saw them again, heard their jabber.

A car approached; he pressed back into his doorway. He could pretend to be strolling a beat, but he preferred invisibility. For years, as Sung Yun's ricksha man, he had been invisible. A clear night now, and the firing over; quiet, no wars, no commotions. He would shelter in this doorway and hope for a quick resolution. He was cold, but he had been much colder in Nanking, unforgettably cold, blue after those hours in the Yangtze. The Japanese. If this Japanese never emerged? Or if he emerged in midmorning, with the streets thronged? But Ming would come before then, and perhaps new instructions.

He would warm himself with memories. He owned a good store of them, and they roused hate and anger, both conducive to inner warmth. He remembered eating unspeakable scraps, begging, stealing, sleeping in the streets, but his serious memories began at the docks off the Chiang-pien-lu in the Hsia Kuan district of Nanking. With four of his companions, all young boys, he had hidden in a shed full of stinking hides, and they had been routed out by snarling Japanese soldiers. He remembered them as bow-legged because of their puttees. Animals. They had pricked the five boys with bayonets, bound them with wire and hung them by the armpits on a long wooden wall through a cold December day.

That was cold. This was only the friendly frost of a winter night in Peking. But that day in Nanking his bones froze, and not only from the weather but from the target practice—exquisite Japanese war games, the object being to outline each man without drawing blood, with special attention to the inner line of the leg. Half-Wit was struck once in the thigh and cried out; the Japanese made fun of the poor marksman, and cried encouragement. The soldiers wore boots, warm uniforms and wool hats or metal helmets.

In the afternoon, with Half-Wit almost dead, the five were taken down. Liao was frozen stiff; his legs would not support him, and his hands and feet refused response, as the wire had cut deep. The five lay in a heap. The Japanese chittered and giggled. Now a new pain was kindled, in the wrists and ankles, as if spikes were driven through the flesh again and again: the pain of his own blood flowing. The five were dragged to the riverside. With much clatter and bounce oil drums were rolled off a truck. The men were bound securely to these drums, face and belly out, and then rolled onto a boat. Rolled. Liao could remember the thwack of his face against the gangplank, the weight of the drum, the blast of pain in his hands and feet. Engines throbbed, and the boat cast off. Liao wished for death. He could see only a scupper. His wrists and ankles were afire. He hoped that he would find an afterlife, and in this afterlife he hoped to find Japanese. His pains eased then, as his vital humors ebbed and his spirits guttered.

The drums were tossed overboard, one by one, into the swift current. Liao was sucked under; the drum rolled; he popped up. The water and air were freezing. A bullet pinged into the metal beside his head. The Japanese were true devils, and thorough. The river itself might drown or freeze a man; the drums might fill and sink; meanwhile the troops of the Son of Heaven improved the hour with rifle practice on moving targets, and not merely moving but rolling, pitching, yawing and even vanishing. Targets worthy of divine warriors!

He was helpless, unable to alter the drum's motion. He expelled all air, hoping to roll beneath the surface like ballast, but popped up again. As well. A man must breathe. Why was he not dead of cold? A poor boy and scrawny, yet still alive.

Shortly it seemed to him that he had been napping. Time had passed. He had been ducked in a regular rhythm, taking breath above and holding it below; he seemed to be in midstream; he was no longer oppressed by rifle fire. The world seemed white; perhaps he was seeing heaven and not earth. He wondered if he would drift to sea, and thence to lands unknown. He thought of monstrous fish. He lost consciousness peacefully.

He was restored to consciousness by Chinese voices. This happened more than once. Dimly he sensed that he was no longer in the river.

Later he learned that he was on the great island of Pa Kua Shou. He had been rescued by a launch. The business of this launch was the nocturnal ferrying of rich Nankingers. On this marshy island the rich Nankingers huddled, praying for transport farther west. Still later he learned that they had prayed in vain, but by then he was back in Nanking. The launch was owned by a man called Wang, whose crew had taken pity on him. Wang himself was a stranger to pity, but he saw Liao's rescue as a good deed, and Liao as a mascot. "We shall keep this little fish," Wang said. "This minnow lives by our virtue." So Liao became a ricksha man and learned that no one sees the ricksha man; he also became an errand boy, and in time a collector of fees and a runner of opium. To Liao, Wang was a man of good bones, whose charity exceeded his greed; who healed his wounds and nourished him and gave him work and set him free; and who should say that Liao was wrong?

So now in Peking he would bear the cold. With luck, he was about to take and torture a Japanese.

Just before dawn Ming arrived in the black sedan with new instructions. They discussed these instructions at length. Liao went so far as to smile.

After noodles and tea, Inspector Yen watched the streets fill; his private Peking was ravished. He drove here and there, as if saying good-bye. The city walls seemed immense this morning. He knew how frail they were, and that they would not be stormed but sold. Near the Temple of Heaven he spotted a known pickpocket, and found himself indifferent. Of what interest were petty felons in these times?

He felt seedy. He drove to the public baths near East Station. He found a patrolman, identified himself, and ordered the man to watch his car.

He emerged refreshed, and less pessimistic. He would brace Burnham one last time.

Hai Lang-t'ou was up and about, and wrinkled his nose. "Lotions and essences," Yen explained. "I have just bathed."

"It is like early spring," Hai said politely. "Have you eaten?"

Yen almost chuckled at the fat man's wary expression. "I come only to speak with the American."

"Ah." Hai showed relief. "But he is gone. A sad parting."

"Gone? To the airport, perhaps?"

Hai said, "Nnnn," and fluttered a hand. "Farewells. He spoke of women."

"So. The hen rules the morning, with such men."

Hai said, "It is a hobby like any other."

Yen made a courteous departure, and sat for a time behind the wheel of his lemon. Which then declined to function. Yen pounded here and tickled there; he raised the hood and slammed it shut. He turned the key and pressed the starter; the engine roared. "Defile it!" Yen muttered. "A monster of inconsistency." He wove his way through pedestrian traffic toward the Beggars' Hospital. Someone somewhere would have news of Burnham. If not, he would drive to the airport and prowl. Prowling like a demented cat with ten mouseholes! Briefly Yen wished that he had been born rich and handsome, or huge, a bulky and imposing man. Near the mouth of Rat's Alley he was halted by a band, of all things: flutes and gongs and ceremonial gowns—a wedding. Irrepressible mankind! At the very moment of Peking's fall—a day from now? a week?—a wedding would be in progress somewhere. Men and women would be making the fish with two backs. Drunks would ignore the making of history.

The Packard stalled, and Yen swore. He lowered his head to the steering wheel and shut his eyes like a man accursed. The gods would spare him no humiliation this day.

When he looked up he saw the black sedan a block away. He prayed, and once more pressed the starter. His prayer was answered. He backed around the corner and paused for thought. He turned, circled a block, and eased to the curb. Should he investigate this black sedan now? Its occupants might be of interest. But then, he might be of interest to the occupants. He would sit. He could see the sedan, and beyond it the Beggars' Hospital. Perhaps the sedan was waiting for Burnham.

"We ought to sleep," Hao-lan said.

"This is murderous," Burnham agreed, richly complacent, "but I have decided that I am quite a fellow." He kissed her navel. Burnham the fetish king—her navel, her toes, anything. "One day you will dance for me in a blaze of light, wearing only baubles."

"One day you will stop reciting foolishness."

"I can't stop," he said, and then in Chinese, "You are an inexhaustible felicity, and my happiness is infinite. I have never been happy before—"

"Except for that squab of a girl with spots."

"—and it requires expression." In English: "Thy navel holds an ounce of ointment. Thy belly is like an heap of wheat. Do you realize the luck of it? Not just that I was sent here, but every step I ever took, everything I ever did or that ever happened to me, good and bad, decent and indecent. If any least bit of it had been different we might never have met."

"Which justifies the war."

"Nothing justifies the war. But if there has to be war and misery, this is what had better come out of it. They died for us, all of them."

"You babble."

"Of course I babble. You have no idea what it is to be a man and to love Hao-lan."

"You have no idea what it is to be Hao-lan and to put up with Burnham."

"It will take some getting used to," he admitted. "In time you will slake the fires."

"Now you go too far," she said; she tugged at his hair and kissed him on the lips. "No slaking. Slaking is absolutely out. I can't believe this is real."

"It's real," he said. "It's real, but you can't see or hear or even imagine the most real part of it. It's like the speed of light. A constant. We hold the universe together. Everything that ever happened made this miracle, this ultimate blessing."

"Someday," she suggested, "we may even be friends."

"Friends!" Burnham was aghast but recovered. "All right. Later." He kissed her, then again and again. "You cast a spell. You stole two hairs from my head, boiled them up in a pot and muttered incantations in ancient Chinese."

"And turned you into a pig."

"My truffle."

"Rooting and snuffling."

"Indeed," he said, "an interesting suggestion."

"Just lie still," she said sternly.

They lay warm and silent, and the lord of all under heaven smiled.

In the morning they gathered again in the kitchen, Burnham and Hao-lan exhausted and somewhat sheepish, the others amused and polite, until finally Burnham gave way to wholehearted laughter and they all rollicked for some moments. The wedding breakfast was cabbage soup and steamed dough, but Dr. Shen had stolen out to purchase a cruet of wine, and they raised a toast, Feng going so far as to demand many children of them. After breakfast Burnham remembered to pay for the wine, and pressed more money on Shen and Teng for the hospital and the children—American money and no one in America would miss it. Shen and Teng passed it back and forth, riffling the bills and blinking in embarrassed gratitude, a gratitude that might have broken Burnham's heart if his heart had not been so full, so whole, thumping and walloping like a bass drum, that he almost forgot about Kanamori. Burnham was in his American togs again, knife, pistol and smoker's requisites all tucked away in his duffel bag. Hao-lan too had packed what life had left her, all in one suitcase; her little black medical bag sat forlorn on a shelf, supplies being short here.

Feng restored his sanity: "And the Japanese?"

They all stood silent for a time, each looking into another's face. Then Shen said, "I believe he is harmless. Perhaps he should be Mother for the rest of his life. Perhaps he *is* Mother."

Burnham pondered. "He means nothing to me now."

"Well, then." And Shen showed palm.

"I am a bit uneasy," Burnham said. "I suppose it is an archaic sense of duty. Feng, can you forgive Kanamori?"

"My tenth Japanese," Feng said sadly. "If the gentleman can forgive him, how can I not?"

"He broke my nose, not yours," Burnham said with a small smile. "And yet I remain uneasy. There were hundreds, perhaps thousands, who did what Kanamori did, and who were not sentenced to be hanged, and not even tried. So on the one hand he is no more guilty than those thousands, but on the other hand, why was he tried? Why was I sent here?"

"To find the lady," Feng said primly.

"For that I was sent by the gods," Burnham said. "But why would the gods work through the American military?"

Hao-lan laid a hand on his cheek, but did not speak. She had made her decision; this was his.

"Well, go fetch this monster," Burnham said. "Small heart: a night's rest may have changed him."

"I will go with you," Shen told Feng, "and examine him."

The others waited, gossiping of the war and the future. After some minutes Feng and Shen reappeared, flanking Kanamori. As if denying the previous night, Kanamori was once again Mother: the gown, the surgical mask. He stood quietly, his eyes on Burnham; at least he was sane and calm this morning, and knew in whose hands his fate lay.

Burnham asked in Japanese, "You are Kanamori Shoichi?"

After a long moment Kanamori shook his head.

Burnham asked, "You are Mother?"

Kanamori nodded.

Burnham sighed. "You ask much of me."

Kanamori whispered in Chinese, "No. You ask it of yourself."

"Yes. That is true. And what do you ask?" Burnham tried to

208

remember the agony of Nanking. It seemed remote, an ancient massacre, a primitive rite.

Now Kanamori sighed. "In three years I have not spoken. In three years I have not wept." He hunched and bowed his head. "In three years I have not thought. Each day I live my punishment; each night I dream my punishment. Do with me what you will." Then he giggled, and they were shocked. He blinked rapidly and moaned.

"What will you do here?"

"Bury babies."

"Who is the last mandarin?"

Kanamori raised his head; his frail chest heaved. "A dead one," he croaked, "in the Cemetery of the Hereditary Wardens of the Thirteen Gates."

Another victim. Burnham was weary of old mysteries, vendettas, riddles. Kanamori had killed a man. Now he punished himself by trundling dead babies to the cemetery where that man lay. It made sense. As his calling himself Mother made sense, as his becoming Chinese made sense. As taking him to Tokyo and seeing him hanged would make no sense.

"Kanamori Shoichi," Burnham said, "go in peace."

Kanamori did not move for some seconds, and then stepped forward to Hao-lan, and knelt and touched his forehead to the floor.

Hao-lan said, "Go in peace, Mother."

Well, it was no crazier than any of the rest of this, Burnham decided: Mother joined the party, and ate soup and even drank a cup of wine, and shortly Burnham had begun to think of him —her—as Mother again. When the moment came there were tears and laughter, and soon there was a small assembly in the courtyard, Nurse An and Mother openly weeping as if this were the wedding, and Shen and Teng entertained and exhilarated but also much moved. Burnham said, "Here we are in China, and there is not even a grain of rice to throw."

Feng fetched his pedicab and stowed the bags, and Hao-lan

embraced the others, including Mother. When Burnham had shaken hands with Shen and Teng and kissed a dizzied Nurse An, he stood before Kanamori, looked him in the eye, and then, obeying what anarchistic impulse he never knew for sure, stuck out his right hand.

Kanamori's rose to meet it, slowly and stiffly, and Burnham clasped the slender, papery Japanese hand.

"The war is over," Feng said softly, and for a moment they all believed it.

Then Burnham and Hao-lan boarded the pedicab, and Feng cried out, "All aboard for the airport!" and the others cheered and shouted "Hao! Hao! Good Luck! Long Life!" and Shen and Teng opened the gate with grand gestures, and Feng drove out yelling "Make way! Make way!"

The crowded street seemed indifferent to this triumph of the higher passions. Carts and rickshas creaked and maneuvered. A tinker cried his wares and repairs, dodging traffic and beating vigorously on a shiny frying pan with a small mallet, and the shimmering song of his trade clanged above the alley's busy bawling. Feng was compelled to dawdle, cursing cheerfully. Children scampered and shouted. To crown the confusion, an automobile growled slowly behind the pedicab.

Burnham was barely aware of all this; he had turned to his love, and she to him, and they murmured. Feng slowed and halted. Annoyed but indulgent, Burnham saw a skinny cop with a pinched, angry face waving Feng to the wall, and heard the car rev up to pass. At the same time he saw a gang of coolies surge out of the crowd. The car gunned into the pedicab; Burnham went flying, bellowing and clutching for Hao-lan, and Feng was pitched into the wall, and then the pedicab tilted and crashed down on Burnham and Hao-lan screamed once. Burnham lay there pinned and yelling with a face full of spokes, and heaved and strained in fear, not for himself but because he saw the policeman grasp Hao-lan around the middle and toss her into the car, and his heart burned away, his heart and blood and bones, and all he could do was heave at the wreck and shout "Hao-lan!

Hao-lan!" as the black car picked up speed and wove through the crowd. The coolies vanished like magic, and the car found the mouth of the alley and vanished also.

And among the ashes of his heart and blood and bones Burnham saw again a round pockmarked little fellow in a dunce cap trimmed with squirrels' paws, and he remembered that the man had said not "You will die in China" but "You will lose your life in China."

III

The
Last
Mandarin

狮 27

Burnham bulled his way free and blundered to the mouth of the alley, gulping for air. He saw nothing and his heart stopped. No cop, no coolies, no car—only the avenue, vendors, shoppers, kiddies, an early juggler drawing a small crowd as if the heavens had not just fallen. The pain was immense, crushing, the stab of loss like a branding iron. Sucking at the breeze and howling inaudibly, he ran back to the hospital and burst into the admissions office. "They took her!" he choked. "They took her in a car!" He waved blindly. "Yen," he said, and grabbed the telephone. Miraculously an operator acknowledged him. Kanamori made snarling hoarse sounds. Burnham gave Yen's number and stood heaving. A voice. "Inspector Yen. Emergency. Yen Chieh-kuo." Inspector Yen was not on the premises. Burnham left a message. Kanamori was mouthing gutturals in his other ear. Burnham rang off and said, "Shut up."

"It was me they wanted," Kanamori croaked.

Insanity. Burnham's shattered world shattered again. "You? Who wanted you?"

"Wang."

"*Wang?* Wang who? What Wang?"

"Wang Hsi-lin."

"Who the hell is Wang Hsi-lin? Fifty million Wangs out there and you tell me Wang!"

Kanamori struggled visibly to gather his wits. Burnham took him by the throat, which was no help: "Say it, you murderous spawn of a syphilitic turtle! Who is Wang Hsi-lin and why does he want you?"

Kanamori wheezed and struggled. Burnham plucked him off the floor and shook him until he flopped like a hooked fish. "I'll kill you. I'll kill you. I'll kill you. I'll—"

Dr. Shen said "No, no," grasped both Burnham's middle

fingers and bent them back sharply. Burnham roared "Yow!" and let go.

Kanamori gasped and rattled. "The last mandarin," he wheezed.

"Yes. I am all right now and will not kill you, so listen, Kanamori, or whoever you are. Someone has taken Nien Hao-lan. Do you understand? You will tell me who and you will tell me why." Burnham was aware that his pitch was rising again, but he could not seem to control his own sounds or meanings. He stood there huffing like a blown horse.

"Oh yes," Kanamori said. "It is Wang. I stole his hoard."

"His what? He took Hao-lan for *gold?*"

"It was me they wanted."

"Oh Christ, of course." Burnham groaned. "I found you for them! Anybody leaving Peking with the American!"

"You found me for them." Kanamori nodded as this profound truth sank in.

"Oh, yes." And I forgot all the simplest rules. Business before pleasure. Trust nobody. Cover your flanks. "Sung Yun," he said. "Do you know the name? Sung Yun."

"Oh yes. Sung Yun."

"Take off that mask. Let me see your face."

Kanamori removed the mask. His lips twitched. "Sung Yun. I know the name. Oh yes."

"Speak up."

"I cannot remember."

"Then this hoard. Where is the hoard?"

"At the cemetery," Kanamori said.

"They cannot want Hao-lan," Burnham said rapidly. "They will discover their mistake and send her back. They cannot know that I have found you."

Shen said, "Perhaps they will ask her."

The gates of hell swung open. They would not ask politely. Somehow Burnham spoke calmly. "Kanamori, I will give you to them if I must. I will sell you to them for her."

"Oh yes. I must be punished."

"Is there still wine?" Burnham asked. "I want wine. And Feng. Where is Feng?"

"There is wine but no Feng," Shen said.

"Then find him."

"I set a price on his head," Kanamori said brightly.

"*Feng?*"

"Sung Yun. A troublemaker and a famous enemy of Japan."

Weepy Nurse An brought wine; Burnham drank from the cruet. The cemetery. Yes. Hao-lan would remember. He lunged for the telephone. He waited like a man praying. He gave Sung Yun's number.

Sung Yun answered, and Burnham offered fervent thanks. "Good morning. This is Burnham, the American."

"My dear Mr. Burnham! An exquisite pleasure so early in the day. Good news, I hope?"

"The worst possible, Master Sung. Someone has stolen my good friend and woman."

A pause; he pictured Sung Yun, a baffled lion, taken aback by the mad foreigner.

"But that is impossible! Your good friend and woman? A tragedy! I confess that I was unaware of her existence. But surely some error . . ." Sung Yun's voice trailed off.

"Error indeed," Burnham said. "She was taken for Kanamori."

The lion roared. "Taken for *Kanamori?*"

"Yes, and in the name of all the gods you must help me."

"Yes, yes! Only tell me how!"

"I cannot say how. Only pass the story everywhere, and find her for me, and bring her safe and well to the Beggars' Hospital. Her name is Nien Hao-lan. Go to anyone who cared about Kanamori and tell the story."

"In the name of all the gods I will."

"And hurry."

"I shall hurry. You are there now?"

"I am. She is my life, Master Sung."

"It will be done," Sung said. "And Kanamori?"

Trust nobody. "Nothing."

"You have informed Inspector Yen?"

"He is not to be found."

"Then much depends on me."

"All depends on you."

"Be easy, my American friend. And now to work."

Burnham hung up. Be easy! Shen trotted in. "Feng is nowhere, nor his san-luerh. But here are your bags."

"Nowhere! That misbegotten fry chose his time well! A villain and traitor like all the others! With my fifty dollars! The humble, faithful ricksha man!"

The force of his anger and the shock of the event stilled them all. Burnham sat unmoving, wrapped in chains.

Teng asked, "What does it mean?"

"It means that every alley is Rat's Alley," Burnham said miserably, "and a thousand eyes have spied, and a thousand feet have trod my tracks. It means that I was sent to frighten the tiger so that others might make the kill. Only Old Man God knows what it means. They may even know that Kanamori is here."

"We must wait here," Kanamori said, "and they will bring my lady when they come for me. It is my punishment."

"No, we will not wait here," Burnham said, "lest they bring a battalion and raze the walls. Major Kanamori, you are now a man of prime importance. If they do not know that you are here, then they must not know it. If they do know, then they will not have you until I have her. And maybe not even then." Burnham's blood was sprinting again. "Let me tell you, my samurai, I am now angry. I want my girl back. I want to know what you have out there in the graveyard. I may yet slice a gizzard. The cemetery is where you bury the babies?"

"Oh yes. The Cemetery of the Herditary Wardens of the Thirteen Gates."

"Then let us go there," Burnham said. "Damn that Feng! Where is he anyway? He hasn't run off. I know he hasn't. But we need him."

"Not Feng," Kanamori said. "If they know that Kanamori Shoichi is here, then another departure by ricksha would be imprudent. Or if they do not know, but have discovered their mistake." His voice was hoarse and cracked but no longer a madman's voice.

Trust nobody, Burnham thought again, but he waited for more wisdom.

"Anyone leaving with you," Kanamori said, and showed palm.

"Then we must smuggle you out."

"You would let me leave alone?"

"No. I will carry you out in a sack if I must."

"And be followed. You are unmistakable."

"But I will not sit here stewing and dying slowly," Burnham said. "Somehow we must smuggle you out."

"No," Kanamori said. "We must smuggle *you* out."

All great ideas are simple, and most are unworkable. Burnham showed his appreciation, but said, "How? In a hamper of laundry? In a coffin?"

"Nurse An," Kanamori called.

Nurse An was sniffling into a kerchief. "I am here."

"You can shave a head?" Again the tentative, rusty voice, the words emerging after ponderous effort but making sense.

She blew her nose. "I can shave a head."

"Then you will shave this Japanese head. Dr. Shen, is there an old tattered jacket? Perhaps a pair of trousers?"

"Yes. And a gown and a hat?"

"No gown and no hat. So!" It seemed for a moment that Kanamori was about to rub his hands in satisfaction. "My punishment continues!" He giggled once more and darted to a cupboard.

Burnham was too shattered to understand, but he sensed that forces beyond his control were converging on a situation beyond his control, and his instinct approved. He watched fascinated but impatient as Nurse An clipped and lathered and shaved, and when Kanamori stood before him bald as a bean, all one hundred and twenty pounds of the man in rags and tatters, Burnham saw the eternal scrawny coolie. He went to his duffel bag and extracted the knife, which he dropped into a pocket, and the pistol, which he checked, and the shoulder holster, which he strapped on outside his shirt. He then said feebly in Japanese, "All right, Major. You command. Where will we go?"

"Why, to the cemetery," Kanamori said, and handed him a hammer, a chisel and a box of matches. "You must meet the last mandarin. *Him* you may trade for my lady. Kanamori is nothing."

"My luck!" Feng spat. A fat man all in black, with a mandarin's hat, a fat man reeking of money, had hailed him, but Feng could not stop. The fat man's look of dismay was a consoling touch of humor, but it could not be good luck to pass up such a fare. Feng sighed, and bent to his work. Red Head Street. Good. A warmish morning, the breeze wet in his face and a film of slush on the streets. The false spring. In January always a few days of false spring. Feng's skinned elbow ached and his head throbbed, but on the whole he was sound. A morning already full of event and mystery, and within Feng a morose griping. He too was heartsore. That good woman!

At the Willow Wine Shop he knocked. His san-luerh was undamaged, which was perhaps a favorable omen. No one answered his knock. He pounded. In time he heard an angry voice. He pounded again. "Who is it?" "It is I." A bolt screeched; the gate creaked open an inch or two. "We need no san-luerh," the voice said. "At this hour! We are a hotel and a restaurant, not a railway station!"

"The American sent me," Feng said.

The gate swung further and a round head emerged. "And who are you?"

"I am Feng his horse."

"His horse! I have never seen you."

"No one sees the ricksha man."

Hai Lang-t'ou squinted fiercely, but opened the gate. "You have some token?"

Like a lizard's tongue after a fly, Feng's hand produced his credentials from his pocket.

"Hsü! Fifty American dollars!" Hai held the bills to the morning light.

"Few ricksha men carry so much."

"You could have stolen it," Sea Hammer said.

"Only to show it to Hai Lang-t'ou? Does a thief wear bells and carry a torch?"

"Come in here and tell me what is afoot," Hai said grimly.

"Come out here and step into my san-luerh," Feng said. "He has found his Japanese and lost his woman."

"Curse his Japanese. I know about that. And what does he want with that woman anyway? A fancy whore."

"The woman is a doctor," Feng said, "and they were to fly off together, over the water to America."

"Nonsense. Women are not doctors."

"Nevertheless. Hai Lang-t'ou, time fleets. Trouble calls. The American is an essential man. When we abandon essential men, the heavens fall."

"Do not scold me," Hai grumbled. "Who are you to rebuke a fat man?"

"Only the ricksha driver. I am not essential."

"And my belly yet empty," Hai complained.

"You must come."

"Come where?"

"To the Beggars' Hospital in Rat's Alley."

"Oh gods," Hai groaned. "Tsitsihaerh."

"Come."

"Without a weapon? Wait here, ricksha man." Sea Hammer turned away.

"My name is Feng. And Master Hai—"

"What is it? Are we in haste, or are we not?"

"My fifty," Feng said.

"Ai-ya," Hai cried. "Such absence of mind! Forgive me. In times of crisis, you know . . ."

"I know."

寳 *29*

Inspector Yen was not an excitable man. He was a bad shot with
the pistol, but this derived from faulty coordination of hand and
eye, not from tremors or sudden surges of hot blood. Nevertheless,
he chewed his lower lip now and when he was not cursing he
invoked the aid and protection of the supernatural. He was tailing
the black sedan at a respectful distance, over the canal and north
through Ha Ta Men, and every time he slowed for a cyclist, a
honey cart or a gaggle of pedestrians he risked stalling. Moreover,
to remain inconspicuous he could not lean on the horn, and the
siren was unthinkable.

He took a chance: cutting away from Hatamen Street, he raced
for Sung Yun's compound. If this was Kanamori! Again he imagined himself a true policeman in an ordinary city. "Sergeant Shih?
Inspector Yen here. I want twenty men fully armed, here and here
and here, and roadblocks in this place and that place, and in
precisely thirty minutes you will place a telephone call to the
venerable Master Sung . . ."

Instead of which, one weary if barbered inspector was racketing
through grimy alleys, heart and engine knocking. If this was
Kanamori . . . The wolf hunts in packs, and shares his kill; the
tiger hunts alone, and gorges.

"Fly now," he said to his Packard. "Fly to Sung Yun's house,
and let me look one look, and if it is Kanamori I shall commandeer
a new ignition for you."

30 狮

"Just man the telephone," Burnham said. "Anything whatever, including Kanamori's head or mine, for Hao-lan."

"Of course," said Dr. Shen, "but what you are doing is insane."

"Not if they know he's here."

"Oh yes," Kanamori said. The Japanese major had vanished again, and the simpleton Kanamori stood beside the cumbersome wooden cart, bald as a melon and tatterdemalion. He was not playacting. He seemed to slip in and out of sanity.

"We should call the police," Shen worried.

"Ah, the bureaucracy! No. The beggars, maybe. I can go to the beggars, who hear everything. But not before I see this hoard. I need to know what I must trade. One hour. I need to know what is at stake, and I need to meet these villains on my own ground and not thrash about Peking like a blind man. Do not negotiate. Only tell them I await instructions, and what they want they can have."

Kanamori bobbed his head. "Oh yes."

"Now let us go," Burnham said.

There were perhaps forty corpses in the wagon. God bless you all, Burnham thanked them, God bless you and keep you and let us do this one thing right.

They cleared a space in the bed of the wagon, and Burnham climbed aboard and lay prone. He waggled the pistol. While Kanamori and Shen heaped the babies about him, Burnham's flesh crawled. "More," Kanamori said. "All my babies." A tiny foot dangled over Burnham's right eye. The little bodies were frigid to the touch, cold and smooth as slate in winter. Hands, blind faces, smooth bellies, little porcelain people. Burnham swallowed his gorge.

"It is well," Shen said.

"Invisible?"

"You have disappeared."

"The tarp, then. Open in front. Kanamori: between the shafts."

"Oh yes."

Burnham sighted on the small of Kanamori's back. But the Japanese would be no trouble. Within the madness a samurai's obsessive mulishness dominated; he would stand fast. "This is for Hao-lan, Kanamori."

"Oh yes. For my lady."

Shen flung the tarp and laced it in place. Burnham lay in gloom. Now he could not see Kanamori's head. "Be good, Kanamori. Stay between the shafts and pull like a donkey."

"I do this for her," Kanamori said.

"Then move."

"Good luck," Shen said.

"You too," Burnham said.

"I do this for the dead swordsmen," Kanamori chanted, and leaned into his work. The cart rumbled forward. "I do this for my mother, who was a daughter of Han. I do this for my father, in the village of Saito on the River Omono near Akita, who was a warrior."

Outside the gate, and into Rat's Alley, Burnham said, "A brisk pace but no unseemly haste. You are a workingman doing a job."

"It is the job I do best. I am Kanamori Shoichi."

And I am Jack Burnham, and if this goes sour I will kill a few. My fault. If they touch her! That face!

The face wavered, dissolved. Burnham panicked. He squeezed his eyes shut and concentrated; feature by feature Hao-lan returned. Hello, he said. Be strong.

My fault. International clown. Self-declared mythic hero. Guns and drums and wounds and women. Brainless!

The cart rumbled to a halt. "What have you there?"

Burnham could not see the speaker.

"Only look," Kanamori said.

A corner of the tarp rose. "Hsüüü!" The tarp slapped into place. An ugly laugh. "You come from where?"

"From the Beggars' Hospital."

"So that is what they do at your hospital. Kill babies."

Silence. The pistol was suddenly slippery in Burnham's hand.

"Go on, then. Where do you take them?"

"To the burying ground," Kanamori said, and the wagon inched forward.

Burnham breathed. A cop? A bad guy?

"It was a coolie in black," Kanamori said. "We are alone now."

Burnham could see both sides of the street far ahead but his range narrowed nearer the cart. A winter morning in Peking. There is a shoe, sock and legging shop, and there kitchenware. Gilt characters on black or red signs. There a beggar, and a man-pulled ricksha. And a woman with three small children. No ravens or foxes skulking in doorways. No roadblocks. No beady-eyed dragons loitering conspicuously.

And in all those shops, behind all those walls, lived love, hate, hunger and gallstones; the mandarin with his four-inch pinkie nails or Head Beggar and his goiter. And this flyweight here is Kanamori! Ah, Hao-lan, Hao-lan! Half a billion in China suffering cancer, athlete's foot, beriberi, torture by secret police, annual famine and annual flood, but Burnham inhabited his own hell. Only he knew what hell was: the absence of that woman with muddy eyes. Well, we all want love, a warm room, a full belly and children. The luxury of love—no, the necessity. Without it we are less than human. That is why the wheat grows, why the heart pumps blood, why Yen gumshoes and Sung Yun collects pieces. It is what Feng awaits and what Head Beggar mourns. In some titanically perverse way it is probably why Kanamori killed. It is why Hao-lan fights the kala-azar. And all my own bullshit, my wise-ass jokes and my truant prick and those voracious blondes, that was all to disguise the absence of love, and now I have it, my small but perfect other half, and I wish I believed in God or somebody who could lay a hand on her shoulder and lead her out of her torment.

They proceeded eastward, Kanamori Shoichi and his forty-one passengers, forty dead and one dying slowly.

*   *   *

"Tell me what you see," Burnham said. "Speak as if singing, and do not turn."

"I see the observatory, high upon the wall," Kanamori sang.

"And in the street?"

"In the street I see men and women and children. I see a seller of corn in the ear. Where does he find corn in the ear at this season?"

"And why do we turn now?"

"To approach the Eastern Handy Gate, where there is a guard, and each day this guard greets me."

"You are no longer Mother," Burnham reminded him. "He will wonder."

He did wonder. Within the massive, arched stone gate Kanamori halted, and a deep bass voice rumbled, "What have we here?"

"The poor dead little ones," Kanamori said, and Burnham feared that the guard would recognize the voice, until he recalled that the guard had never heard it.

"Why, so it is: the baby cart. And where is the mute woman?"

Kanamori said, "She is dead."

"Hu! A good woman she was, and hard-working. And how did she die?" Burnham could not see the guard but imagined a barrel-chested sergeant.

"She took her own life," Kanamori said.

"That is evil, and bad luck even to speak of. So you will come each day?"

"If the gods wish."

"Well, go along then." Burnham heard the canvas rattle. "A big load today." The buttery tones of a born gossip.

"And not the only baby cart in Peking," Kanamori said.

"Hsü, it is a sorrow. The old woman gone too, and the bandits at the gates."

Burnham dreamed of Hao-lan. His mind flickered like a newsreel. It was odd what a man remembered. A swimming pool in Tokyo, the YMCA, and Burnham aged six half drowned at the deep end, and no one noticed and he could not shout because of the water in his gullet, so he grabbed a passing Japanese foot and was towed to the shallows; he could still see the astonished Japanese face, the crew cut, the teeth. A quarter century later, ice on the Sungari and Burnham's boot full of water. Hai told him to remove the boot and build a fire lest he lose his foot, and when Burnham protested—no time, danger—Hai and Lou sat on him, tugged the boot off, built a small fire and lectured him sternly. But how could you lose with lieutenants named Hai and Lou? Maybe that was Kanamori in the swimming pool. Maybe that was Lou guarding the gate.

Burnham realized uneasily that the world was now unmanageable, that good and evil were, like all old couples, coming to resemble each other. He offered a bargain to the gods: only let him pluck her out of this coil, and he would—well, what? Be faithful? Responsible? A decent man? Foolish promises without meaning. Fate and history made no deals. Life was a slow fire, and events were the chips and kindling, and the end was always ashes, which was what they would all be in fifty years. But oh those fifty years!

Dr. Shen was helpless. He sat at Nurse An's desk and smoked while rage warred with grief. He knew he was smoking too much, but each day taught the same lesson. Life was heartbreaking, so what mattered a day more or less? Death was sure, so why not make a friend of it? It was no philosophy for a doctor, and he knew that he was wrong. Life was indeed cruel; its joys were therefore triumphs over great odds. And death was indeed sure, which was the best of all reasons to love life.

He should report this abduction. All well and good for the foreigner to prowl off like some bandit hero, but the police would be better, with their weapons, resources and informers. Yü! One asked only to heal children. One did without food, without sleep, without the comforts and pleasures of a hearth. One suffered senseless wars, venal politicians, greedy overlords. And now this irruption of foreigners, with plots and schemes and private wars!

A Japanese! He had scarcely noticed the "mute woman" at all. And this large, imperious American, plucking a flower of China! Dr. Shen's heart ached. He had admired in silence, had felt his soul awaken at her entrance or her voice, and now . . .

Rat's Alley was no longer simply an alley; it was a battlefield. If he told the police? He was to keep the telephone open. If Teng sat by the phone, and Shen braved the roadside wolves and walked quickly to the police station?

Who could say what web had been woven? He imagined himself speaking to the police. I am a doctor from the Beggars' Hospital. For three years we have harbored a Japanese war criminal.

You have *what?*

Unknowingly, of course.

Continue.

This morning an attempt was made to abduct him.

One may hope it was successful.

It was not. A woman, a doctor, was abducted instead.

A woman? Abducted for a man? Women are not doctors.

The Japanese had lived as a woman. The abductors were in error.

Error, indeed. And who are these abductors?

We do not know. The ricksha man may have seen them, but he has disappeared.

What is this story of Japanese and doctors and abductors and ricksha men? What ricksha man?

The American's.

Now an American! Who is this American?

He too sought the Japanese.

By now the desk sergeant would be crooking a finger for help, and within minutes Dr. Shen would be a guest of the municipal constabulary.

He decided to omit the police. He would be a good soldier and sit by the phone. He was pouring tea when Feng and Hai burst in. He spilled tea and scalded his hand. "Feng!"

"They are here?"

"They are not here. Who is this?" Startled by his own shrill tone, Dr. Shen fought down rising alarm.

"A Sea Hammer and the American's friend. Quickly now," Hai urged, "where are they?"

"That I do not know," Shen said.

Sea Hammer came to him, angry and businesslike, and placed a fat finger on Shen's nose. In the other hand he waggled a pistol, a huge weapon. Dr. Shen flinched. "Now, you listen," Hai said. "You are a doctor, but even so I have killed more men than you have, and I will dispatch a few more for his sake if I must. I owe him a life."

Dr. Shen made a stubborn mouth. He had never before been called upon for heroics. He rose to the occasion. "I will tell you nothing."

"You will tell me where they are, and right now," Hai said.

Feng said, "Good Doctor, we must know. These are a good man and a good woman and we must go to him and recover her."

"We do not know you," Shen muttered. "It is a matter of the woman's life."

"It is that!" Hai said. "And no time for debates."

"You do indeed know us," Feng said. "You know me; we have taken food and drink together. We have raised a toast to the bride and groom. Now I bring this man, who is his friend and owes him a life."

Teng and Nurse An had stepped into the room; Hai showed the pistol. "Fools!" he cried to all. "It was in my wineshop that they sealed their love!" His brown eyes flashed above his fat cheeks, and he loomed tall; the room seemed small and crowded. "This man and I killed Japanese for one whole winter on the frozen plain. Each stanched the other's wounds, and we shared all, food and warmth and women and danger. I knew then that he was an essential man because he had crossed half the world to fight by my side, would not lie even in war and killed without hesitation but with reluctance. I was a skinny dog then and not worth a worn cash, but never did he hang back in my time of need. So I found that I could not hang back in his time of need, and for that season I too felt essential."

Sea Hammer's voice boomed. In his mind he heard the northerlies whistle down across Heilungkiang, saw a Japanese truck explode in flames, rejoiced again as a butt-plate bruised his shoulder. He could almost taste again a fat sturgeon caught and fried one frosty, clear morning, and he could almost hear Burnham gobbling the flaky hot fish and cursing because there were no onions and the barbarous Chinese grew no coffee. "We made no vows, because there are things we Chinese do not say aloud to foreigners, but he knew that his women and children would be my care as mine would be his care, and that one's trouble would always be the other's. Well, time has cooled the warriors' blood, but the unspoken vow is the one we must not break, and what will the world think of me, and of us all, if I cannot find him now? Must I beg? I will beg. Must I plead? I will plead. Must I kowtow? I will kowtow. Must I beat it out of you? I will beat it out of you."

He made tiger's teeth, and roared gently. "By the gods, this makes me young again! No use to play a lute before an ox," he said to Feng. "I must thrash this fellow."

Nurse An asked, "You are Hai Lang-t'ou of the Willow Wine Shop?"

"I am, by the gods! Have you more sense than these mules?"

"She spoke of you," Nurse An said, "and of your exploits, and if you will tell me where you blew up the power plant—"

"Tsitsihaerh! Tsitsihaerh!"

"So she said." Nurse An pleaded silently with the two doctors.

"They have taken the baby cart to the Cemetery of the Hereditary Wardens of the Thirteen Gates," Dr. Shen said, and Hai raced out; Feng snatched up the bags, as if they were all about to catch a train, and ran after him.

In traditional fashion, Inspector Yen left his car around a corner and lurked. If he was wrong . . . But a black sedan was a black sedan, and Sung Yun owned one. Sung Yun, sprung from nowhere, without history, born of some postwar egg. Inspector Yen, with plenty of time for theory and supposition, had long since assumed that Kanamori himself was nothing. A major? Who cared about majors? Generals, admirals, princes were hanged, not majors. Hence Kanamori knew something, possibly about the honorable Master Sung; or possessed something, and Yen imagined the range of choice: incriminating documents, a bag of diamonds, or the bones of Peking man. Yen was a proud professional policeman, but in the famous and baffling case of the sinister and mysterious Kanamori Shoichi he had played the frustrated, bumbling amateur detective. To his desk had come rumor, report, and endless lists of private treasure stolen or confiscated —genuine lists from the truly bereft and spurious lists from canny opportunists, all demanding action or compensation. For a year or so the police had drowned in such lists. Bureaus had been established. Little had been recovered. Japan was awash with ancient works of Chinese art. In Paris and Bangkok dealers advertised ruby-eyed phoenixes and jade Buddhas in the great postwar rummage sale. T'ang horses grazed in Swiss vaults. Yen wrestled shadows. One man, when whole governments despaired!

Now he sheltered in the recessed doorway of an astrologer's shop. On the door a single character gleamed gold: *chan*, prognostications. Today the shop was closed. Perhaps forever; perhaps its master had indeed read the future and fled the city.

He saw the black sedan and pressed back.

A policeman emerged. A policeman? Yen peered, but the face was unfamiliar, a hard face, pinched, without animation. Ming emerged. Yen held his breath. A woman emerged, and Ming grasped her arm roughly.

A woman! She tried to pull free of Ming's grip, and for a flash Yen saw her face. It was a face he knew, but his memory, shocked and surprised, failed him. A young woman and pretty, and he had seen her not long ago. Images tumbled: Kanamori's face on a poster, Yen's own wife, Sung Yun's two dumplings, Burnham— *What?* Burnham's whore here?

They passed through the gate.

Inspector Yen despaired.

Still, Burnham might follow. Perhaps this was the whore of whores. Perhaps young Ming was consumed by passion. Perhaps the woman was not a whore. Nonsense. He remembered clearly; the woman had reeked of sensuality.

He felt a pang of nostalgia for the students he had hosed, clubbed and—well, interrogated. Life had once been admirably simple.

狮 33

Within the graveyard Kanamori grunted his way along a rutted slushy track. Burnham parted the mantle of dead babies and scrunched forward. He saw tombs, concrete bunkers, a dusting of snow, low mounds and shallow ditches. Kanamori proceeded to the northern end of the cemetery and halted at an open trench. Burnham scrambled out.

The ditch was deep, six feet and more. A wooden shovel leaned against one corner: all wood, it seemed, and made of one timber. So this was Kanamori's work. Each day or each week, he dug out the next day's or the next week's mass graves. Each day he prayed over another sad contingent. God knew how many cubic yards he had shoveled, how many rows of trench this penitential maniac had dug and filled.

The trench was muddy. A January thaw would ease the digging. The sun was well up now, though balked by clouds, and rivulets of melted snow purled through the muddy slush, trickling and spurting to the bottom of the ditch, where a pool rippled gently. No tiny limbs or heads peeped through the mud: Kanamori was a neat, careful workman in the best Japanese tradition.

Burnham spat away the bleak aroma of frozen corpses. Kanamori was plucking at his sleeve and indicating one of the bunkers, a squat concrete vault streaked now and mottled. Burnham checked his perimeter: not a soul. No reverent strollers, no thugs come to tuck away a spare corpse, no soldiers. Unreal: so much space and so few creatures, less than a mile from Peking.

Kanamori was scuttling crabwise through the slush, brandishing his hammer and chisel and beckoning him along like the elf in charge of the gold when the prince beheads the dragon. Burnham was slowed by a dreamy wave of unreality: here he was, in a cemetery in the ancient capital of an ancient kingdom, drifting through a clammy thaw beneath cloudy skies, trudging after a loony troll toward an obsolete bunker. One day he would take

Hao-lan sailing, he decided, on a bright blue afternoon, the boat spanking along on a silver-sequined sea beneath a blaze of California sunlight.

He shook the mood, and loped to catch up. Kanamori was scampering to the rear of the bunker. When Burnham arrived the Japanese was scattering debris, rocks, old bones, rusted scraps. The door hung aslant, neglected, jammed. Together they strained and heaved; with a raucous creak it inched open. Kanamori slipped through. It was a tight squeeze for Burnham; he braced and bucked, and the door flapped wider.

At first he saw only gloom, and stood as if waiting for daylight to follow him in. Some did so, faintly. Before him more light filtered through a long horizontal chink, a gun port or an observation slit. Beneath it a shape loomed and took outline; a concrete bench or platform along the wall. The bunker was empty, not even a discarded ration box. Burnham shivered. A cold, empty bunker.

Kanamori had dropped to his knees. "Step away," he chirped. Now Burnham saw that he was standing on a concrete slab six or eight feet long and perhaps four wide. He crouched beside Kanamori and saw the Japanese smile, the teeth as on a poster. Burnham had found his war criminal and been lured to an abandoned bunker in a deserted graveyard, and this ruffian knelt beside him with a hammer and a chisel. He saw himself lying dead, chisel through the heart, naked and anonymous, a mystery for the conquering Communists.

Kanamori ignored him and tapped away at the cement that sealed the slab. The clangor echoed, and cement crumbled on the borders of the slab; so it was counterbalanced. An ammunition well or storage bin? Kanamori tapped; a flake of cement stung Burnham's cheek.

Finally the Japanese set down his tools and leaned forward, pressing his hands on the slab. It rotated, grinding harshly. Burnham's flesh prickled. Kanamori reached down and fetched up a small oil lamp. He set it at the edge of the well and struck a match. His shadow swam against the concrete wall, then grew sharp, still and immense in the small room as the lamplight flared and steadied.

Heads together, Burnham and Kanamori stared into the well at two fully clad skeletons lying together like lovers: coolies' trousers, coolies' shirts, cloth shoes.

Kanamori lowered himself into the well and hoisted the two unfortunates to Burnham. Bones spilled and bounced. Burnham tugged them to a corner of the bunker and piled them out of the way.

Again the hammer and chisel. Burnham heard wood splinter. Kanamori was muttering in Japanese. "Yes. Hello. Hello, pot." To Burnham he said, "You take these. Small heart, please." Kanamori was standing shoulder-deep in the well, his cheekbones and bald head glistening. He handed Burnham what seemed to be a soup kettle on a tripod. What seemed to be a toy chicken. What seemed to be a ram's horn. What seemed to be a drinking bowl. Carefully Burnham ranged them on the concrete bench. Kanamori muttered, chuckled and excavated. Burnham sensed the answer to many riddles and grew excited. He began to guess what he was handling and took even more care in the grasping and placing. "Small heart," Kanamori warned again, and Burnham gently accepted a little woman—pottery or porcelain he could not tell—with a yoke across her shoulders and buckets dangling. A horse, small but heavy. A lion or tiger or snow leopard. An old man, bearded, the ivory smooth, almost oily, to his hand.

Piece by piece the collection grew. The bench became a museum. Kanamori had stopped twice to open footlockers. Now he paused again, as if thwarted or in prayer, then took up his tools, hammered and pried. Wood splintered. Burnham heard the intake of breath—a true, classic Japanese hiss—and in the silence that followed he prickled again, sensing not mere animation, revival, passion, in Kanamori but a fierce reverence, so that he would not have been surprised if the man had said "Here is God," but knew that he would say instead, "Here is the last mandarin."

Kanamori stood and, like a priest, raised a slab of wood on

which lay a shining doll that glinted green and gold. Burnham took the slab from him and saw that the doll was fabricated of many platelets sewn together. The hands and feet were shoes and gloves contrived of many small, flat greenish oblongs, and the face was not snub-nosed and rounded like a human face but constructed of similar oblongs, the nose cruelly sharp and the chin square, the head earless and the eyes sparkling a deep, fiery green.

Burnham made this doll the centerpiece. He was dazed and overwhelmed. Kanamori came to stand beside him. Twenty-odd pieces. This minor Japanese thug. Burnham was not truly a connoisseur, but expertise was unnecessary. His awe was enough. If these were genuine . . . Of course they were genuine! The skeletons alone proved that: coolies rendered forever discreet.

Kanamori's expression of utter sorrow startled him. "There is not money enough—" Burnham began, but desisted before the man's silent tears.

For some time they only gazed. The ram's horn was not a ram's horn but a drinking horn wrought from a single block of onyx, its narrow end an exquisitely carved bull's head. The chicken was of porcelain and was painted. Burnham touched these. He raised the bowl; it was bronze, and of obvious antiquity. The horse was also bronze and unmistakably a T'ang horse.

Burnham did not touch the doll, but peered closely. He turned to Kanamori in disbelief.

"It is the jade funeral suit of a prince's son," Kanamori said. "The rectangles of jade are sewn together with gold thread, and the eyes are emeralds."

My son, my son! Hundreds of years ago, perhaps thousands.

The ivory gentleman was a lo-han, a bodhisattva, smiling tolerantly. Beside him a gilded Buddha meditated. A jade owl glared, about to hoot. A ferocious dancing warrior, of wood painted red and yellow, lay helpless on his back. A horseman of painted pottery sat tall in the saddle, stiff-backed; behind him on the crupper his hunting cheetah lay curled in repose. A ceramic lion champed its leg in search of fleas. A bronze lion reared, rampant.

"How?" Burnham asked. "How did you—"

"Wang," Kanamori said. "Wang Hsi-lin. He bought cheap; these were traded for life itself."

"He sold freedom," Burnham said. "It is always costly. But this! There is not money enough anywhere. How did you think to—"

"We did not think so far," Kanamori said. "There is always a way. Piece by piece, for money. Or not for money but for immortality: the guardian of all these would be a national hero, to the old government or the new. Or not for money or for immortality but again for life itself; I might have traded these for amnesty. Wang might have taken them anywhere in the world and lived in peace and plenty." Kanamori was certainly not addled now. He spoke melodiously, like a man shedding years.

"And those bastards never told me," Burnham said. "They knew, somehow they knew, but I was not to know. Just find the Japanese and bring him out. Or maybe not. Maybe you were to be delivered up . . . Maybe they thought somebody *owned* all this . . . Maybe . . ."

Then Burnham seemed to see four things at once. He saw Hao-lan in the hands of evil men; he saw the face of a colonel in Tokyo; he saw a lowly Japanese major, no more and no less guilty than a thousand others, condemned in public and hunted in secret. And he saw an ivory lion at the end of the bench.

"Kanamori, what did Wang look like?"

Kanamori considered. Slowly his round face smoothed, and for a moment he seemed almost jolly. His shoulders squared, his head rose, his mouth opened in a soundless snarl, his hands combed back a heavy mane. Before Burnham's very eyes he became a lion.

34 愛

Hao-lan had suffered many indignities in her time but had never before been popped into a bag. One moment she was preparing to cuddle, gazing soulfully into the ardent, bloodshot eyes of her deranged bridegroom; the next came a sharp jolt, and she was derricked out of the pedicab, enveloped by darkness and harsh, stinking cloth, and flung—dumped—into the back seat of a car. She cried out and tried to claw at the cloth, but a drawstring at the bag's mouth pinned her arms.

Cold fear stilled her then, terror compounded by the resinous reek of the jute gunnysack, and then she was struck on the head, just once, and knocked back against the upholstery. The car veered and she was pitched against her tormentor, who slammed her upright. "Stop it!" she bellowed.

A voice said, "Silence, monkey."

Monkey!

She coughed. "Air. I cannot breathe."

A second voice said, "Give him air."

The drawstring slacked.

The second voice warned, "No tricks."

She knew the voice, but whose was it? And what had they done to Burnham? She drew a shallow breath, then another, and almost sobbed. Burnham! This nightmare, men and their mysteries, cops and robbers and war!

Steady on, old girl. What to do about a nightmare? Wake up. "Where do you take me?"

A smug trill of laughter, then the familiar voice: "To a reunion with your business partner."

Madness. "And who is my business partner?"

"He is Sung Yun now."

Sung Yun! Now she knew the voice. Yen, was it? No, Ming. This Ming spoke English. Slang, sunglasses, a tie pin. Hao-lan dared fate: "You're bonkers."

"No Japanese," Ming said. "You will speak Chinese only. You are famous for the purity of your Chinese."

"My dear Ming," she said, "my dear chap, that was not Japanese. That was English."

"So you know English too." Ming was almost convivial. "And you know my name. Interesting."

"What's this Japanese jazz? No savvy Japanese, buddy. You got a bum steer somewhere."

"A bum steer! How well you do it!"

She bowed her dizzy head toward the mouth of the sack and drew an enormous breath. Her vital signs fell to human levels. "What do you want with me? Who do you think I am?"

"I think you are Kanamori Shoichi," Ming said, "and I want you to make me rich."

Bonkers indeed. Two psychopaths in one week—three, if you counted Burnham.

The car slowed, swerved; a blast of the horn, full speed ahead.

"What is this 'bonkers'?" Ming asked.

"British slang. A new field entirely for you, rich and historic. Bonkers means you're crazy, nuts, section eight."

"And how would a Japanese officer know this?"

"I am not a Japanese officer." Carefully Hao-lan suppressed hysteria, speaking in patient, gentle, medical tones. "I am a Chinese woman, and a doctor. You have made a serious mistake, and you had better take me back, or Burnham will nail your hide to the wall, if Sung Yun himself does not."

The long silence allowed hope.

"Listen to me, Ming. I am Burnham's friend. You and I have met. We met two nights ago at the Willow Wine Shop."

The car slowed, then stopped. "Release her," Ming said.

The gunnysack was plucked away. Within the sedan the air smelled of petrol and exhaust, but was infinitely sweet. Hao-lan smoothed her hair, met Ming's eyes, then glanced at the other —a policeman, impassive. The same everywhere: an outcast's outrage shook her.

"A doctor? A woman, yes, but a doctor? Who was that doctor

I saw you with last night? That was no doctor, that was a floozie!"
Ming chortled. "A whore playing whore's tricks. If you're a good
one maybe Burnham will swap you for Kanamori. You know the
word? 'Swap'?"
    "I know the word."
    "And you know Kanamori?"
    "I do not know Kanamori."
    "Burnham did not tell you?"
    "Burnham and I speak of other matters," she said demurely.
"I think now you must take me back to the hospital."
    "Not on your life."
    Hao-lan shivered. The policeman seemed to be smiling.

    Sung Yun hurled thunder and lightning. "Mule and blockhead!
Oaf and dullard! Numskull and half-wit!"
    "I followed orders," Ming said stubbornly. "Do not berate me
before the woman."
    But Sung Yun had paused in his tirade and was bowing again
to Hao-lan, a ghastly smile writhing upon his face. He radiated
humility, he oozed apology. "Please be seated, please be seated."
He returned to Ming: "If I sent you for leeks, would you bring
me pig's feet? Did it never cross your mind—mind! mind! the
compliment is undeserved!—that this beautiful"—he bowed
quickly to Hao-lan and the lion's smile flashed—"elegant, young
Chinese lady was perhaps not a scrawny, aging Japanese officer?"
    "There was no time to verify. One could scarcely demand
papers of identity."
    "Silence! There is no explanation possible. No excuse is accept-
able. You have offended this exquisite creature. You have
offended our American colleague Burnham, whose betrothed I
gather she is. You have offended *all* my American friends unless
we can set this right. That you have offended me is unimportant.
Yü!"
    Hao-lan perked up. The presence—the tailored, barbered,
laundered appearance—of this elderly gentleman had defanged
Ming and rendered human the silent steely man in policeman's

uniform. The master of these premises was not a white slaver, an international spy or Dr. Fu Manchu. At Sung Yun's parody of a grin she had feigned outrage: "How the white teeth shine through the artful smile!" Now she said, "All you need do is drive me back to the hospital. Burnham is a man of understanding; moreover, his happiness, like mine, will leave no place for anger."

"Yes, dear lady, yes, but this . . . there have been . . . Ming!" Sung Yun the obsequious was replaced by the leonine Master Sung. "If this is a diversion? If he is even now on his way to the airport with Kanamori?"

For one molten moment Hao-lan admired the notion. Ah, you sly fox, Burnham! Anger churned, anger at this false mandarin for daring to make the suggestion, anger at herself for accepting the possibility, anger at Burnham and the world because, yes, it would make sense; it would be no more vile than war, kala-azar and famine.

"Sisters!" Sung Yun clapped.

Sisters? Hao-lan's spirits prepared to rise.

"We must confer," Sung Yun told Ming. "I am displeased. You and Liao will await me in my study."

Ming removed his sunglasses to clarify the dirty look he cast at Hao-lan, and followed Liao out of the room, squeezing aside for Miss Ai and Miss Mei, who were entering. Hao-lan dismissed Ming from her mind and struggled with disbelief at this brace of quail, so obviously the introductory painting on a long and classically pornographic scroll. She warmed, and sketched a smile in a first effort to weave some frail bond of womanhood, to evoke the common sympathy of underdogs. The corners of their mouths rose, but these were figurines, and even their smiles seemed carven.

Sung Yun was once more courting and appeasing. "So the lady speaks English! Alas, that I do not!"

"I am not a lady. I am a doctor, and attended medical school in London." Hao-lan inspected the courtesans for traces of joy or awe, but saw only the ivory smiles.

"Medical school in London! So remote! The antipodes! My

songbirds," he addressed his mopsies, "you will attend to this lady's every need. You will serve tea and the little ginger cakes, and set out the better cigarettes. The lady's knowledge of English literature is extensive; there is reading matter in Ming's room. The breadth of culture!" He rejoiced in Hao-lan's existence. "That such a lady should be discommoded!" He almost fluttered, his hands soared and swooped, but Hao-lan noticed that his body and eyes were serene. "I leave you now, to resolve this lamentable confusion. Should my dear friend Burnham call, you will of course speak to him? Good. Forgive me. You will be alone for a matter of seconds only. My lady."

Sung Yun bowed and backed out of the room. Hao-lan was indeed alone. She drooped. On a shelf beside her a ceramic lion ramped and roared—ancient, painted, once a gaudy trinket, now priceless. Otherwise the room seemed forlorn—faded rectangular patches on the walls, few knickknacks, bare tables. She blinked away the delicate sting of unshed tears. This was only stupid, and not dangerous. Some foolish people had made a mistake.

This *cannot* be a trick! Burnham?

Still. The faint prick of doubt.

Miss Ai returned, bearing books and magazines. It served Dr. Nien right: here she was in a waiting room, and the nurse was clicking and smiling, and at any moment the podiatrist would emerge. She murmured thanks and examined the books. *The Silken Lash. Chained in Soho. The Reader's Digest.* She smiled gratefully. Miss Ai dimpled and cast down her eyes. Hao-lan opened a book at random. Heaving bosom, swollen lips, senses reeled. Dear God, am I like that? I suppose so. Burnham too, twirling villainous mustaches. Trust him whatever. A constant, he said. No, he is not hurt, and no, he has not gone to the airport. Big crooked nose, greedy eyes. How he loves to look at me! Goofy. That fat smug grin!

Miss Mei materialized. A tray, teapot, cups, the little ginger cakes. How do you do. A fine winter morn, is it not? Indeed, Vicar, and how goes it with you? A lot of clap in the parish at this season.

In the magazine Hao-lan read that she should decide now precisely what she wanted to be doing five years from now, and should do nothing that would deflect her from her goal. She invented herself: five years from now I want to be a pediatrician in private practice in a place called California, my name will be Helen Burnham, and every night, and perhaps even every morning, a burly, hairy man with a broken nose will hug the bejesus out of me. So I must do what will lead me there, and not be deflected. For example . . .

She could think of nothing. Escape? Recruit these two doxies? Start a fire?

Miss Mei offered pumpkin seeds.

And there they sat when Sung Yun returned: three women, one sipping tea and hoping for the best, the others smiling at unpredictable intervals.

"Your Burnham has gone," Sung Yun announced, "and no one knows where."

"He is doubtless conferring with the police."

"Frenzied and distraught! I may sit? Thank you. Tea, my peony." Miss Mei hastened to pour. "The estimable Inspector Yen, perhaps. You know Inspector Yen, of course."

"I have heard the name."

"The inspector too seeks Kanamori."

Hao-lan sat silent.

"You know about Kanamori. Perhaps you have met him." Sung Yun sipped, and sighed his delectation.

"I know nothing of this Kanamori."

"As well you may not! A villain of deepest dye, my dear Doctor. My dove, will you fetch Ming and Liao?" Miss Ai departed swiftly. "So!" Sung Yun offered a fatherly smile. "How romantic! In the best tradition of the classical novel. The barbarian and his Chinese maiden. The spark of love. Rocky going, the jealous fates, the angry princes, confused identities, but at last all is well, and in palanquins the happy couple is escorted to the Great Wall, and disappears into the desert holding hands and blushing."

"Nothing so grand," she said carefully. "Only an aircraft, and surely difficulties with the immigration service."

"An aircraft! How imperial! A man of importance, our Burnham. Aircraft at his beck and call."

"He is important to me."

"Nobly said! I could envy this Burnham, were it not for Miss Ai and Miss Mei. Incomparable beauties. I am truly attached to them. You must not be deceived by my age, dear lady; there is snow on the roof, but fire in the hearth. Believe me, I rejoice for you. Another small cake? The coarsest flour, but these are straitened times."

"The cakes are delicious, thank you, but I cannot."

"As you wish. A brutal shock to the nerves. I can only hope that time will efface the bad impression."

"I am sure that none of us will want to remember it."

"I trust my men were gentle—ah! and here they are! Ming and Liao, do join us. A fascinating conversation." Ming sat, looking affable, and Liao stood sentry near the door. Hao-lan noticed that Sung Yun's windows were casements, with leaded panes, foreign, almost English. "You will scarcely believe this," Sung Yun went on, "but our dear Dr. Nien has, in the space of two days, met our friend Burnham, fallen in love, and accepted his proposal of marriage. And all the time we thought he was tracking a Japanese butcher! By the way, Ming, in these two whole days Dr. Nien has not met Inspector Yen, and knows nothing of Kanamori."

Ming was hearty and prankish. "But there has surely been a mistake! In my own presence, and in Burnham's very room, the doctor met Inspector Yen."

Again this trouble breathing. "Oh, that was Inspector Yen? Then I have of course met him, though you must forgive my little charade. It is Burnham's elfin sense of humor."

"A sense of humor! So valuable in trying times!" Sung Yun was positively expansive. "And never once speaking of Kanamori— that too was his little joke. He told you that he had come to Peking only so the gods could unite you."

Hao-lan tried to smile. "Government business, he said."

"What a coincidence! Unknown to you both, his government

business concerned the very man about whom you—his gift of providence!—had been interrogated not a month ago."

"Yü," she said faintly. "Was that the name? Kanamori?"

"You see!" Sung Yun said in triumph. "We all make mistakes. Careless errors of identity, often leading to extreme embarrassment and confused misunderstanding. You will forgive me? Good, good. Now then, Ming, and you too, Liao, let us thank the gods for this curious and enchanting encounter, and restore Dr. Nien to her indulgent lover." He ran on for some seconds about long life, many children, richly merited bliss. Hao-lan's smile grew feebler, but finally she was in the courtyard, and Ming ushered her smoothly, deferentially, to the black sedan, assured himself that she was comfortable, and then said, "My dear lady! My dear Dr. Nien! Thass a crock, honey. I'm going to take you for a ride."

35 寶

Inspector Yen was famished. He was also chilly. Moreover, he was tired of standing in doorways like a cop on the beat. He could not see through the wall of Sung Yun's compound, and could hear nothing from within. He reviewed his predicament, then abandoned his doorway and proceeded to his car. He turned the key and pressed the starter.

The motor ground and would not catch. It ground again, then whined. "All I ask," he said, "is to edge this lemon to the corner, where I will have a view of the gate." He pressed the starter again, and was answered by silence.

Hong Kong, he thought. I will transfer to Hong Kong, where the vehicles are of commendable modernity. Or I will adopt another trade. Pedagogy: a teacher of the martial arts in a middle school. Or suicide. Why not suicide? How reasonable!

He banged the dashboard in anger and stepped out. He returned to the shop and dug into his pocket for a small jimmy. The lock yielded and Yen's eyes widened: something had gone right! He stepped into the shop and closed the door. In the dim light he glanced about. On a table he saw facsimiles of fish, fowl and pig's heads, used in divination. On the walls he saw charts of the planets with their elements and characteristics, charts of the cycles of the years, and bunches of paper strips covered with calligraphy and hanging like horsetails. On a shelf he saw tortoise shells and small bones. Also many bowls. He shrugged. Superstition.

At the small window he commanded a fine view of Sung Yun's gate. Superstition or no, he thanked his household gods that he had not delayed: within minutes a squad of black-clad coolies, chattering and joking, but knaves to a man if he knew his business, came marching up the street and pressed through the gateway. A large household, Sung Yun's. Ming the snake, the false policeman, the whore, Sung's women, and now the riffraff.

Yen grinned. He was not accustomed to grinning, but this might yet prove a fascinating day. If Burnham should follow along, he would walk into a fine nest of vipers.

He wondered if Kanamori was truly in Peking. He wondered again if Kanamori was even among the living.

When Ming and Liao escorted Burnham's whore through Sung Yun's gate and into the black sedan, Yen stopped wondering anything, cursed himself for a triple imbecile and prayed to the god that ripens grain, as well as to the righteous phoenix, that his unaccommodating automobile would reform.

He barely waited for the black sedan to move. Before it reached the corner he was racing for his Packard. The engine obliged him on the first try, but he forgot to thank the god or the phoenix.

36 獅

Below the East Single P'ai-lou Ming eased the sedan to a halt and cut the motor. Hatamen Street was thronged, midmorning bustle, clusters of agitated rumormongers and argufying shopkeepers. Hao-lan looked at the glacis where the foreigners formerly played polo, and south to the city wall and the legations, where men in neckties and wingtip shoes spoke English, French and Italian. West of the glacis was the Peking Hotel and its French Book Store, and she ached for civility, order, learning, courtesy, for a bobby unarmed and polite, for the might and majesty of the Crown.

"The whole time you did not smoke," Ming said.

"I forgot."

"You were frightened. Have a cigarette now."

"Yes."

They might have been tourists, or brother and sister.

"If Burnham's taken a powder," Ming said, "then you don't matter a damn."

"He has not."

"I need to know one of two things: who and where Kanamori is, or who and where the last mandarin is. I think Burnham knows."

"But I don't. Sung Yun won't like—"

"The hell with Sung Yun," Ming said, and leaned to pat her hand. "Of course you know something. You must have heard of Kanamori, and you couldn't have forgotten Yen, so you were lying."

"These are awful cigarettes." Hao-lan's voice struck her as reedy.

"Camels. From the American navy. They were waterlogged somewhere about three years ago. We got five thousand cartons cheap."

A fire brigade trotted by, a dozen or so men pulling a wooden cart, straining like mules, chanting their ancient lament. On the cart was a huge metal tank brooding over a border of buckets like a monstrous sow with her farrow.

"It's only money," Ming said. "It's not as if empires were falling or people being wiped out, so we have to assume that everybody knows more than he ought to."

"This is hopeless," Hao-lan said. "I truly do not know why your Kanamori matters."

"Trouble is, it's *lots* of money. Bags of gold, honey. So I'd ice Burnham in a second. I might rub him out for the hell of it if I got sore. Maybe if I cut you up a little? Liao knows how. Then Burnham loses his head and charges into the china shop."

Ming wore a cheap cotton shirt, pinkish with a maroon pencil-stripe. A seedy boy in jacket, silk tie, sunglasses, his mustache sparse and unhealthy. A shaky beginner, a man of no bones, no permanent name, with not yet a true face. His immaturity frightened Hao-lan, and reminded her of dangerous fish and snakes, which strike by reflex and cannot be reasoned with as can bears and even the great cats.

She found it impossible to speak of Kanamori. Perhaps for doctors human life was simply not expendable. "I really know nothing." A beggar peered into the car, raised two claws, saw Liao in uniform and vanished. "One thing only I heard. I believe it was Inspector Yen who told this to Burnham." It was an improvisation, but it felt right. "The last mandarin is somewhere in the Cemetery of the Hereditary Wardens of the Thirteen Gates."

Ming pressed the starter, shifted and turned the wheel in what seemed one motion. The sedan bucked and shot into traffic. Rickshas wobbled to a stop, pedestrians shouted. Ming cut east, leaning on the horn. Hao-lan saw a cartful of caged chickens loom and shut her eyes, and felt the veer and sway. She looked back: the livid chickenmonger stood with both fists raised high, but his cargo was intact.

She could not imagine what Sung Yun wanted with a corpse.

A relative? Well. Perhaps she had saved Burnham's life. Her bones seemed to soften, her lips to curve. She would remind him of this in moments of stress and domestic turbulence. Soon they would share a san-luerh again, soon they would ride in loving state to the airport, soon—

She believed none of this, and buried her face in her hands.

Burnham and Kanamori repacked the hoard, set the dead lamp
on a crate and swung the slab back into place. Outside they
rammed the door shut and replaced the debris. Burnham was
explaining that there was no time to bury the babies. He remembered Head Beggar saying, "Let the dead bury the dead." He was
groping for a way to tell the Japanese that he must now be
exchanged, and all this loot with him if necessary, when a pedicab
wheeled through the south gate and started up the rutted track
toward them. He rushed Kanamori behind a bunker, flung him
to earth and hit the deck beside him, tugging at the pistol. A
mocking voice blared, "Up, you fool!"

"These are friends," Burnham said.

"Friends." Kanamori's eye was wistful.

Burnham tucked the pistol away and slapped slush off his
jacket. Feng let the pedicab coast to a swampy stop and asked,
"Sir, is there news of my lady?"

"I know where she is," Burnham said. "We are in plenty of
trouble, and my brain is like one of those thousand-year-old eggs."

"The famous Kanamori." Hai squinted. "You look more like a
plucked chicken than a butcher. So," he said to Burnham, "you
have found your man and lost your woman and there is no time
to squander. What now?"

Burnham saw no way to lighten the blow, so looked Kanamori
in the eye and said, "We take him to Sung Yun and swap him."

"Sung Yun!" Sea Hammer flung up his hands. "Explain."

"The wily Chinese. He has bamboozled the whole American
army, and they have bamboozled me, and all to find our plucked
chicken here."

"Patriotic fervor?"

"Loot. In that bunker."

"Goods?" Hai brightened.

"Plenty goods."

"Then you cannot hand him to Sung Yun."

"I would hand *you* to Sung Yun for that woman."

Sea Hammer scowled.

"What does that mean, that look of an angry boar?"

Sea Hammer lost some fat. Fleetingly Burnham saw the cold gaze, the cruel intent visage, of the old guerrilla. "You traveled half the world for this one," Sea Hammer said. The words boiled out angrily. "You took the prince's gold piece. You oiled the string and strung your bow and sharpened the arrow and trimmed the feathers. Now you will swap him for a musky fox, and in three months you will wake up one sunny morn and she will be just another stale vixen."

"Not true, defile you! Can you not see a difference?"

"A difference! Each one is new and different. You smacked your lips and scratched your crotch over every peasant girl in Heilungkiang, and your eyes gave each the face of a princess— but the prick is blind, man, the prick is blind!"

"You fat bastard! Have you never loved? This is not a night's work for the long bone! It is the sun and the moon!"

"That is true," Feng said. "It is the sun and the moon."

"Ah, the ricksha man!" Sea Hammer said. "Another authority."

Kanamori startled them: "It is the sun and the moon."

"Naturally," Sea Hammer said. "You save your own skin. Why go back and be hanged?"

"It is the sun and the moon," Kanamori repeated, "and Wang also will kill me, after slow torture."

"Wang! Which Wang?"

"Sung Yun," Burnham told him. "His name was Wang Hsi-lin, and he was a great collaborator down Nanking way. I thought I heard the Wu accent but did not trust my ears."

"Worse and worse! You sell a villain to a villain and call it justice. Do you not understand, man? This touches your warrior's honor! What are the sun and the moon to a man of no bones? What is long life with shameful regrets? What is love to a coward?"

"Coward! And who but a coward would leave a woman in villains' hands?"

"Hsüü," Sea Hammer crooned. "You have another hard bone, you fool—namely, the head. Who speaks of leaving her? You grow old. Where is the archer I knew? Listen, you poor sad fornicator: you will take them both out."

And leave you with the goods, Burnham thought, almost laughing. The man was breathtaking. Once a Sea Hammer always a Sea Hammer. The graveyard snapped into focus: bunkers and tombs, the muddy slush, the low mortared wall, streaked and mottled. "If we fail I will have your gizzard."

Sea Hammer mocked him. The tiny brown eyes sparkled, embedded in the fat face like shiny currants in steamed dough. "What a squad we are! One lovelorn foreigner, one fat restaurateur, one ricksha man and one loony monkey."

"Huuu," Kanamori said, and pointed, but they were already on the move when the black sedan nosed through the west gate. Instinct prevailed: soldier's for Burnham and Kanamori; guerrilla's for Hai; assassin's and car hater's for Feng. They scattered and dove for cover.

Later, after Burnham had been shot and gone pleasantly woozy, he grew muddled, and for the rest of his life the precise order of events during the next few minutes escaped him. He drew his pistol behind a tomb and mindlessly, out of inertia, frustration and heartache, was preparing to squeeze off a round at the windshield when he heard Feng shout, "My lady! My lady!" He heard Ming's voice at about the same time—"Burnham!"—and heard doors slam. Slush trickled into his left sleeve. Without looking he knew that Hai was cutting a circle.

Burnham eased around the corner of the tomb, chin in the mud —take your peek at ground level, they'll be watching for you up above. He saw the black sedan. He did not see Hao-lan. Nor could he see Ming, but he assumed that the sedan was cover.

The first shots were fired by no human agency but by Yen's

lemon, which came barking in, popping and backfiring like a whole platoon. The Packard swerved toward Burnham in a slithering rush as if terrified by the oversize sedan. It plowed into a patch of mud. Wheels spun, tires whined and possibly some buried babies were ground to hash. Yen hopped out brandishing a pistol, and all of a sudden everybody was firing at everybody else. With half China out for midmorning target practice, Hao-lan chose her moment: she slipped out of the sedan and dashed toward Yen's car in a low skimming crouch, until she bogged down.

And Burnham found himself *smiling*. By God, there she is!

He could not have said who was shooting at what. Ming and Liao were careless about cover in their excitement, and he saw them both. They could have been firing at him or Yen or the scuttling Hao-lan, or even Kanamori—but where *was* Kanamori? Yen could have been blasting away at Hao-lan or Ming or Liao or all three. There seemed to be considerable shooting on general principles.

Burnham took temporary leave of his senses. He regretted this later—he would always regret it when he remembered Sea Hammer—but he applauded it too. It was fitting. He had lost his heart; why not his head? Waving the pistol like some demented pirate, he charged toward Hao-lan.

As soon as Yen swerved away from the sedan he knew that he was losing traction, and he quickly realized that he was only digging himself deeper—into his grave perhaps. He hopped out of the car and came up shooting—or almost: the woman was in his line of fire. Hsü, to die for a whore! He held fire, adjusted his aim, recalled disappointing hours at the pistol range, and scored a near miss on Liao. He had no idea why anyone was firing, or at whom. Perhaps it was simply more useful than not firing, or more bracing to the temperament. Perplexed, he paused and glanced about. He saw a fat man surge up out of the ground some yards away. He saw Ming peer in all eight directions, hopping about like a marionette. He fired at Ming—it seemed reasonable —and missed. The woman was lurching and flailing on the soft slippery ground.

*   *   *

Burnham, too, was skating through the slush like a runner in a dream, but he saw only Hao-lan. He was aware of the skirmish, but it lacked importance and even reality. He seemed to be running in slow motion. Possibly he was committing a cosmic blunder, but that too seemed irrelevant, and also unlikely. It was the most Oriental moment of his life. The upshot of all this was ordained. The universe and its two powers, three principles and manifold events were truly in the hands of the gods, and man was but a derisory and powerless speck.

It was also his purest moment. He had no name, age or nationality; for those few seconds Hao-lan was his whole existence.

Hai had dived for a bunker, vaulted heavily into what he thought was a slit trench, and landed hard on concrete, paining both feet severely. By some magic, his pistol had leaped into his hand. This pleased him. Three years had passed, and while the warrior may pretend to long for peace and rest, there lingers always the heady memory of real life—that is, life at risk. The paradox had long troubled Hai. Presumably life was to be lived in normal ways: namely, in filling the belly, pursuing jolly sport with agreeable females, playing cards, cursing the government and gossiping. But all that was life lived unawares. Life fizzed and sparkled and the blood hummed like hot wine only when rivers rose, arrows thrummed and war horses whickered, when danger flushed the spleen, when mind, heart and hand were one, and death's cold breath raised the hackles.

So when he saw Hao-lan break for freedom he glowed with the first true happiness he had known for years. He was young and slim and deadly again, and death's cold breath cut shrewdly and roused him from a long sleep. To risk death for a whore, and another man's whore at that! Now there is style, by the gods!

He was scouting for a suitable target when he saw Burnham gallop forth.

He shouted, "Down, you fool!" but it was useless, and before he knew it he had leaped from his trench and was sprinting toward the sedan, firing as he ran, knowing that at this distance it was luck and not skill that aimed the weapon, but knowing too that any diversion favored the moving targets— Burnham, the whore and himself. His feet still hurt. He frowned fiercely. He flew, exulting, and heard himself cry "Haaa!" like the warriors of old, and felt his heart thunder.

Then the mud sucked at his cloth shoes and the thunder of his heart dulled to a painful hammering. The cry died in his throat as he labored for breath. He plunged on, but the world had slowed, and death's cold breath no longer animated him but rendered him sluggish. O gods! I am an old man and fat! Panting, he veered toward Yen's car. He saw the nasty young fellow in sunglasses firing at him. Hai Lang-t'ou returned the fire, but his vision was clouded and his hand unsteady.

Yen ceased fire and quickly checked the fat man, who had altered course. He recognized Sea Hammer, and tried to cover him by firing wildly in the direction of Ming and the sedan. The woman was half in and half out of his line of fire now. He was cursing her under his breath when he heard Sea Hammer grunt.

Hai was hit, and knew it: a hammerblow high in the gut. His mass, and the remains of his exhilaration, carried him some steps farther. The woman was nearing the car. He had hoped for a close look at her, to see what nature of woman could reclaim a weasel like the foreigner from flowered and willow-lined lanes. Curse the foreigner! I am dying and it is his fault! And curse his whore too!

He touched cold metal, clutched at the car's frame and dropped his pistol. He slipped down, scrabbled at the mud, knew that he had fallen beneath the car, heard a great rushing wind, saw the world spin and darken, and had just time to savor the last spark of hot pride.

Yen watched the fat man fall beside him, and turned quickly back to the fight. The uniformed policeman, he saw, was ranging on him, and it seemed to Yen that he saw the bullet leave the muzzle and fly toward him. He felt a flash of fire and slumped sideways into the slush. He did not believe that he was dead, but he was suddenly quite tired. He had earned a rest. He slept. Even in his sleep he heard gunfire.

Hao-lan too saw Hai fall. She was sobbing, slipping, fighting her way toward Yen's car. Each shot refreshed her terror. She saw Yen fall. Burnham was somewhere; she had seen him. Her legs betrayed her, frozen and enfeebled by fear. Exhausted, she ran blindly. It seemed an hour since she had bolted; it was perhaps ten seconds. She hurdled Yen and lurched against the car, wailing Burnham's name. Hai had slumped beneath the car. Hao-lan stopped wailing, stooped swiftly, groped for a trailing wrist and felt for a pulse. None. Her vision blurred by tears, she wrenched open the door and tumbled into the driver's seat. The steering wheel was on the wrong side. She slammed the door, saw a key and turned it. She trod the accelerator: nothing. She saw Burnham hit and saw him fall, and her heart died within her. Then she saw him struggle to his feet. She jabbed at a button: the siren shrieked.

Ming drew down again on the struggling Burnham, drew down carefully and with deep satisfaction, but at the wail of the siren jumped a foot so that his shot went wild. Liao too was startled. They leaped back behind the sedan and crouched.

The bullet had torn into Burnham's forearm like a spear and spun him half around. He dropped his pistol, fell, groped for the weapon with his left hand and hauled himself erect to see Ming and the cop hoping to finish him off. He hit the deck rolling as the siren wailed. Ming and the cop scurried out of sight. Burnham shouted Hao-lan's name. He heard a motor catch and chug.

Feng and Kanamori crouched behind a bunker. Feng's knife was out and he was praying. A few yards off stood his pedicab with the two bags. All was at sevens and eights, the heavens had fallen, and Feng did not know what to do. He crouched beside Kanamori. All this was Kanamori's fault. His tenth Japanese, perhaps. If worse came to worst . . .

Hao-lan shifted gears; the car bucked backward. She shifted again; the wheels spun. Snow in Devonshire, and the Honourable's Humber; she remembered, and rocked Yen's Packard. At the third swing forward the rear wheels found traction and the car pounced ahead. Grinding in first gear, she set her course for Burnham, who was up and firing. She skidded and slithered toward him, and swung the car at the last moment to put the rear end between them and the enemy. Burnham tugged the door open and flung himself on the seat beside her. "Go!" They roared forward. "Hai is dead!" she cried. She cut behind a bunker and almost ran down Feng and Kanamori. Burnham shouted "Stop!" and she kicked at the brake pedal. "In, in, in!" Burnham shouted. Kanamori tugged at a rear door. "Oh Christ, locked!" Burnham said. "I can't! My arm!" Hao-lan dived for the rear door and loosed the lock. Kanamori scrambled aboard, wild-eyed. "Feng!" Burnham cried. "God damn it, Feng!"

Feng came racing. He tossed the two bags into the back seat and cried, "Go now, my gentleman! Hurry!"

"Inside!" Burnham roared.

"Here, the money." Feng held forth Burnham's fifty dollars.

"I am shot and cannot take you by the throat," Burnham said, "but if you are not inside and the door shut within two seconds—"

Kanamori reached out to grasp Feng's wrist, shifted his weight slightly and twisted. Feng cried "Yai!" and sailed aboard.

"Now go!" Burnham told Hao-lan. They plunged ahead. "Feng! The door!" Feng hung out over the mud, caught the door and slammed it shut. As they jerked and skidded north, Burnham caught a last glimpse of the mass grave, the baby cart, Kanamori's bunker, and then they were through the gate.

"For God's sake, shift!" Burnham said.

"I don't know how! I found reverse and first but not second. It's an American car."

"Clutch," he said. She clutched. With his left hand he shifted into second. "Again," and they were in high, and on an avenue, and Burnham said, "Don't stop for anything," and punched at the siren—*rree-ee! rree-ee!*—and all the cosmopolitan traffic of a Chinese street parted like the Red Sea. They might yet see the promised land. "Go like the wind," he said.

"You're hurt."

"Right arm won't work. I'll live."

"The hospital."

"Hospital, hell. The airport, madam, and step on it." He craned to scout behind. "Kanamori, can you still fire a pistol?"

"I should not. Oh, I should not!"

"Defile it!" Burnham said. "In time of need you will. Ah, Hai! They killed Hai! Feng, are you all right?"

"I am unhurt, but you must set me down."

"Set you down?"

"My san-luerh," Feng said. "It will be stolen."

Burnham ached all over; his arm was on fire and he noticed that Hao-lan was tear-streaked. "By the gods, what is a san-luerh now?"

"The gentleman is surely right," Feng said, "but it had a brand-new tire."

Inspector Yen struggled to a sitting position and felt his head. His hand came away bloody and matted with hair. He seemed to be alone. Shakily he came to his feet. The graveyard was deserted and silent: tombs and bunkers, a two-wheeled cart, forlorn. Yen took an unsteady step, stumbled, almost fell, broke the fall with his hand and felt flesh. The fat man lay on his face in the mud. Across his back the tread of a tire stood out like a pattern in the cloth of his gray gown.

My car! Yen shook himself awake. They have stolen my car! They have stolen the car of a police inspector! They have stolen a car that will not even start!

He gathered up his pistol, saw Sea Hammer's and took that too, and wondered why there was all this fuss over a whore. She was surely a woman. She was not, for example, Kanamori in disguise.

Kanamori! All these connivers and marksmen must know something! Inspector Yen ran.

For some minutes no one spoke while Hao-lan dodged through traffic. It was not ordinary traffic. Today the hum of the city was a din, an irregular chorus of whoops and outcries and occasional gunfire. Squads of troops and police seemed to be out for late-morning sprints and drill. Here and there a shopfront gaped, splintered. "Disorder, not true chaos," Hao-lan said. "Greed and small revenges."

They were breathing normally now and Burnham had knotted a bandanna above the wound. "I need a doctor."

"I suppose it will always be like this," she said. "I never planned to marry a juvenile delinquent."

"And I never planned to marry a doctor," Burnham said. "I suppose the phone will ring all night. Cheer up. Things will quiet down after the honeymoon. Keep to the right, for the love of Christ!"

"Of course. That's what it is. A honeymoon. In my whole life I have never driven on the right."

"Haven't driven since merry old England?"

"Not once."

"No speed limits here, you know. How's the gas?"

"Petrol. It reads empty."

"God almighty. Probably broken." Burnham was in high spirits. He recognized the onset of delirium. "Damn these bicycles!"

"The siren."

Burnham obliged. Indignant faces bloomed and faded. Peking raced by. Hai was dead. Sea Hammer. Burnham saw the old Sea Hammer, slim and hard, saw the white teeth flash in joy at a good explosion. "I like explosions," Hai had once said, "and twice-cooked pork, and women too are amusing. I do not like clerks, policemen and foreigners."

Nothing behind them yet, and a straight run to the airport. But Ming knew where they must go; would he also know a shortcut?

*   *   *

Inspector Yen had hailed a bus, and now stood, feeling cracked, leaky and slightly nauseated, holding his pistol to the head of an indignant bus driver.

"This bus does not go to the West Gate," the driver insisted. "This is a number seven bus and goes from the Altar of the Earth in the north to the Altar of Heaven in the south."

"Hsi Chih Men," Yen repeated. "I am a policeman and this is official business."

"Some policeman," a passenger hooted. "In foreign dress. Policemen wear uniforms."

A general grumbling arose. The streets were crowded with demonstrators, students, left-wingers. Tentative looting had begun. Here and there a shop was fired, and the Communists were not even in sight, so why were the police gallivanting about on buses? It was not as if they purchased tickets.

"Nevertheless," Yen said. They were rattling westward. Yen had not much hope of answers—he scarcely knew how to state the riddles—but a poetically just rendezvous at the airport, where he had first met Burnham, was as likely as anything else. He thought almost longingly of the Communists, who would know how to run a police department. Of course there would be questions about his previous affiliations, but he was, after all, a man accustomed to—devoted to—upholding the established order. Did it really matter who established it?

"I am doing this because I must," the driver said, "but I call upon these witnesses: I do it under coercion."

"I will descend along Hsi-nei," a passenger said emphatically, "by the Horses of Heaven Porcelain Shop."

"And me?" another called. "I am to select and purchase four hundred feet of eight-inch stovepipe at Mu's in Feng-t'ai. In winter stovepipe cannot wait."

"You will all be liberated at the West Gate Police Barracks," Yen said. He was faint. Perhaps he would pass out and be torn limb from limb by these irate citizens. "Make speed," he told the driver.

"Speed! Look about you, man. This is a Ming Dynasty omnibus."

"Nevertheless," Yen repeated. It seemed to him that all his life he had been saying "Nevertheless." Perhaps that was how matters were ordered in China: all was accomplished "nevertheless."

Burnham was still mourning Hai Lang-t'ou, a scoundrel and a rogue, a cutthroat of the first chop but one who stood fast, and who now had died for him. Not to rescue Hao-lan and not to snare Kanamori, but because Burnham had failed him. Yet there was some deeper success in this.

He looked gratefully upon his girl and forgot Sea Hammer. A bullet in your arm and two hoods after you, and she is driving to endanger, and what shall I do about Feng, and here is a Japanese war criminal goggling at the countryside, and I am about to betray my mission and in a way my country, and I am happy as a tick on a beagle because this smallish creature is beside me and I can gaze my fill at her face. A grown man. I am supposed to be doing important things like working and voting, and instead I sit here composing valentines.

Burnham knew that he should make some effort to organize the rest of this unusual day. Here was the familiar stretch of road where he had seen the Peking cart pulled by a pony. Soon he would see the teahouse, and then the airport. The same road crew would be tamping the same earth.

Hao-lan's face, that very face, was haggard. Hell of a courtship. "Cheer up," he said again. "They can't shoot down an airplane."

"I'll cheer up when I bloody well want to."

"That's the trouble with China. The women wear the pants." His arm throbbed and streaks of pain shot up into his shoulder. Hai was dead and the top of Burnham's head was floating away. Plenty of time for fits and vapors when we're in the air. Much to be said for marrying a doctor; a man can have fits and vapors whenever he bloody well wants to.

Defile it, Hai, I'm sorry, but I'd have cut your throat myself for this woman.

He saw Hai, scornful, crabbed and full of spleen, heard him snort.

"Kanamori," he said, "tell us what-all under heaven has befallen you these last dozen years."

And Kanamori recited, at first halting and apologetic, then running and jumping. In the end the picture was clear, a sordid but not extraordinary portrait of degradation and inhumanity, and Kanamori's face was grim but his voice only calm and weary.

All along the way knots of people were gathered at the roadside, and men made speeches, and bands of demonstrators carried banners, and one shop burned unattended. Soldiers marched and trotted, and convoys passed, transporting sullen troops into the city. The outskirts were furling inward; the old rulers were retreating, leaving a vacuum of power into which the new rulers would rush.

There was no sign of the black sedan.

The airport was in disorder. Senile pursuit planes huddled, some guarded by frightened sentries: P-40s, P-47s, two Zeroes. Crowds swirled about the sheds and godowns, prospecting and shoplifting. A line of frantic travelers besieged a DC-4, and Burnham saw crates, trunks, sacks, baggage in mounds, Chinese pilots shouting instructions.

Hao-lan steered them through the chaos. Twice they were slowed by hostile groups; twice Burnham made the foreign presence known; twice they were waved on. "There. Just past that hangar. The one with two engines."

The DC-3 was idling with the door down, strictly against regulations. From the pilot's window a man shook a fist, then waved for haste, and Burnham recognized Captain Moran. Hao-lan pulled up and they piled out. Burnham waved a salute. Moran seemed to be cursing him, but the voice was lost in the engine noise. Burnham turned to Feng and Kanamori. A decent farewell. His arm ached and his brain swam, but a sense of safety, of arrival, of leisure, warmed and eased him.

*   *   *

Ming cut a man down to reach the aircraft. He sped into the airport from the Hai-tien road and shot straight across baggage areas and runways, toward the American—or by now perhaps ex-American—operations shed. He saw Yen's car, and when a boisterous band of lcoters, or just shouters, surged up to block his way he swerved very little, blasting through, and caught one on his right fender, hurling him high and away. He saw the four travelers standing in casual conversation, saw an American hanging out the pilot's window and gesticulating. "Liao. That pilot. Ground them first."

Liao ran down the window and steadied his pistol on the frame. The pistol jolted and clattered. He raised it and aimed free. Better. He waited. He knew pistols and their limitations. In time he fired.

The pilot flopped forward, his arm swinging like a pendulum.

Ming shot past the plane, stood on the brake pedal and skidded into a turn and stop. He and Liao scrambled out on the far side.

Burnham saw the sedan fly past and shoved Hao-lan to the ladder. "In! Keep down! Feng! Kanamori! Run!" He turned to signal Moran and saw the inert body, the red hair, the arm dangling. He leaped up the ladder. "Hao-lan! The pilot!" He tugged at the door's cables, and was dizzied; his hand slipped and he fell to his knees. He groped for his pistol, fumbled it, picked it up. "He's dead!" Hao-lan called, and came running.

"Co-pilot?"

"There is no co-pilot."

"Keep down. Christ, I'm going to pass out."

"Lie down. Head down. Oh, God."

He took a deep breath of cold air and was grateful for winter. The smell of oil and metal was familiar. Pain tore at him, but it was pain for Hao-lan. "Damn you," he said, "I never used to be afraid before I fell in love."

*　　*　　*

At the Hsi Chih Men Police Barracks, Inspector Yen thanked
his bus driver, commended his fellow passengers for their patience
and patriotism, and left the bus to a chorus of imaginative Chinese razzing: "The turtle squad." "Go annoy a criminal now."
"Go redeem your uniform from the pawnbroker." He trotted into
the barracks and explained quickly to the duty sergeant. "Explained" was perhaps inaccurate; how could this be explained? He
rapped out a splendid fabrication: Communist agitators, foreigners, a bank robbed. The sergeant had already called for his captain. Yen showed identification and they set out at a brisk walk
for the barracks motor pool, which was, this being Peking, three
blocks away and consisted, this being Peking, of an antique Fiat,
a prehistoric Daimler and a monstrous American hybrid. All were
equipped with sirens and floodlights, and were therefore police
cars.

Within a commendably short time two armed men manned
each car, and the cars were on the move. From Yen's vehicle, the
hybrid, several pieces of metal dropped clanking to the road, but
the car persisted in its forward motion, and Yen nodded gratitude.
After a moment he activated the siren. Grudgingly the populace
made way. It was a small satisfaction.

"We must rush them," Ming said.
"We should wait. Cover the door and wait."
"For what? These mobs? Soldiers? Other interested parties?
There were four. Four! One of those two Chinese was Kanamori."
"Kanamori is Japanese."
"Fool! Now listen: you will dash out at some distance, di-
rectly opposite the door. Dash out beyond Yen's car. I will
slip beneath the tail. You will fire and keep them busy. I will
slip along the fuselage and take them at close quarters. You
understand?"
"The risk is great."
"When the reward is sufficient, risk is not a factor. You under-
stand?"

"I understand."
"Then go!"
Liao moved out.

Burnham saw the uniformed policeman—Liao was his name, according to Hao-lan—and recognized him vaguely: once in Sung Yun's courtyard, a glimpse when they took Hao-lan. The man scuttled toward Yen's car and Burnham tried not to hurry his shot. He braced his left arm against the doorjamb. Now, Hai, grant me a double measure of your spirit, and a Sea Hammer's eye.

Liao went down hard, skidding some distance on his face before he came to rest. His weapon skipped and clattered.

"Thank you, old friend," Burnham breathed just as Ming wrenched the pistol from his hand.

"Step down," Ming said. "Have no fear. I shall not kill you. I want only Kanamori. Both of you—down."

"Leave her alone," Burnham said, descending the ladder.

"Both of you," Ming said pleasantly.

Hao-lan stepped to the tarmac and took Burnham's good hand. "Not your average honeymoon."

Ming jeered. "Honeymoon! Where is Kanamori?"

Ming stood aft of them and so could not see the tail assembly. Burnham could, but did not believe his eyes. Hao-lan's hand clenched on his wrist. "Kanamori is dead," Burnham said.

Ming showed impatience. "Do you want me to hurt her? I could shoot out her kneecap, for example. Would you talk then?"

"Kanamori's right behind you," Burnham said.

On the tail assembly Kanamori heard his name and smiled.

"Wise guy," Ming said. "Where is he?"

"Leaning on the rudder," Burnham said. And when Ming turns, then what? Rush him, with one arm? He'll empty the magazine and kill Hao-lan.

Ming edged away, three or four mincing steps, keeping Burnham and Hao-lan well in sight, and turned to glance up.

Kanamori vaulted lightly from the tail assembly, floating, landing in a crouch before an amazed Ming, and raised an imaginary sword. He lunged and feinted left, lunged and feinted right as Ming stood hypnotized.

Kanamori shouted *"Ima!"* He tightened both hands on the imaginary hilt—his knuckles whitened—and raised the sword high. His face was young and eager, his brown eyes were lustrous and joyful.

As Ming raised the pistol, Feng darted out from nowhere and grasped Ming from behind, left forearm beneath the chin. Kanamori leaped to clutch at the pistol, and one wild shot ricocheted whining as Feng cut Ming's throat.

"My tenth Japanese," Feng claimed. "More Japanese in spirit than my Chinese friend Kanamori." Kanamori acknowledged the dubious compliment with a wry bob of the head.

Hao-lan returned briskly, slightly dazed in manner but still professional: "Both are dead. Now let me bandage our innocent bystander here." Burnham was seated on the ladder. The bleeding had freshened, but his house physician now assured him that he would survive. "Whether I survive is something else again," she complained. "This is not what I am accustomed to."

"A rare half-hour," Burnham said.

Hao-lan spoke for both: "Feng and Kanamori, we owe you more thanks than can be uttered."

Feng was overcome by embarrassment; his eyes seemed unable to focus. Kanamori stared at the ground.

Burnham asked, "Feng, why should you not come with us?"

Feng made owl's eyes: "Come with the gentleman? But I am a Pekinger."

"We can take you to Korea or Japan, and then Shanghai or Taiwan."

"Japan! Japan is an island! And so is Taiwan, and they eat undersea creatures that cling to rocks. Come with you!" Feng clapped hands twice in wonder. "Only think, I have sported about an aircraft, and almost been beheaded by its propellers, and have slain my last Japanese, and been invited abroad! The world is indeed a place of marvels."

Feng looked back at the city. Not much could be seen from here because of Yen's car, various aircraft in the way and clusters of excited citizens droning in the distance like swarms of bees, but some suburban houses and shops were visible, roads and vehicles, a few billows and plumes of black smoke rising and thinning—and the city was a presence. The mere certainty that Peking stood—Burnham felt it too. "No, good sir, I will not come," Feng said. "I am a man of Peking and a san-luerh driver, and the streets and alleys are my old friends."

"They are mine too," Kanamori said, "and I will miss them."

"But you have not been invited," Burnham said.

Kanamori screwed up his face and strained to understand. "I must be punished."

"I do not believe they ever wanted you," Burnham said. "Moreover, Kanamori is dead. Even the mute woman called Mother is dead; I heard it this morning by the Eastern Handy Gate. So I am not sure who you are, but you have saved my life and the life of this unfortunate, deluded woman shortly to become my relative. I owe you thanks, now and forever, and to hang you would be bad manners. Besides, I am on my honeymoon."

Hao-lan's work was finished. "There. Try not to move that arm."

Burnham inspected the job. "What's this sling?"

"Moran's scarf."

"Dig my money out of my pocket, will you?" He rose.

"No charge," she said. "I'm not licensed to practice here." She extracted the sheaf of bills.

"Peel off a hundred for us, and present the rest to Master Feng and Citizen Kanamori."

Feng backed off in alarm.

"You fool," Burnham said, and embraced him awkwardly. Feng stiffened and said "Yü!" and Burnham squeezed his shoulder.

70

"I owe you more than this. It is no one's money, and now it is yours and Kanamori's."

"It is riches!" Feng said, and grasped the wad. "A year's money and more!" He and Kanamori both seemed somewhat addled now, and passed the bills back and forth.

Burnham himself was experiencing a certain vacancy of mind. He disliked lecturing friends, but felt he should say more. "Use this money slowly and do not show it about—and remember, now is no time to become a capitalist. Money can be trouble. Narrow heart."

"Money cannot be trouble," Feng said. "It is we who owe the thanks, now and forever."

"To think that all this was ordained," Kanamori said, "and now it has come to pass."

"About the bunker," Burnham said.

Kanamori understood. "We are custodians only."

"When the time comes, go to the highest-ranking army officer you can reach," Burnham said. "The army is sure to rule for a year or so, and while they may execute you they will not cheat you. About politicians only the gods can say, but their army is not corrupt, nor afraid to offer thanks where thanks are due." Out on my feet and preaching about a world that is not mine. "And now we must leave you. More brigands may follow after, and I do not propose to linger. Go now. Go to the hospital, and drink tea."

"The hospital is not a bad place," Feng said.

They all touched hands and shared inadequate glances, and suddenly Burnham was heartsore. This should not happen. When a man made friends in far places he should be permitted to attend their weddings, bless their children, share needs and sorrows and drunken laughter.

Feng found a word, and made happy teeth: "We shall take a san-luerh into Peking. A commodious double."

Kanamori said, "We have a car, if I can remember how to drive one."

"You have not!" Burnham warned. "Only disappear, do you understand?"

"I understand." Kanamori raised a hand in benediction. Feng started to imitate the gesture but clapped the hand to his head instead, dashed to Yen's car, came running back with Hao-lan's valise and Burnham's duffel bag, and raced up the ladder with a mischievous grin. The others cheered. Feng leaped to the tarmac and shouted, "I have flown!" He joined Kanamori then, and they waved farewell and walked off holding hands in the manner of Chinese men who are friends.

39 獅

"And how do you propose to leave?" Hao-lan asked. "I think we should go to your legation and proceed more legally."

"Proceeding legally is the Burnham tradition, but we begin badly. We have just committed two murders."

"Bad form and embarrassing."

"Furthermore, there may be a dead cop somewhere in Peking, and guess who drove his car to the airport."

"Our own Robin Hood and Maid Marian."

"Furthermore again, Sung Yun lives. Suppose he is at the legation right now playing gin rummy with somebody from army intelligence? They knew about that hoard, and they never heard it from Kanamori."

"Then make a suggestion."

"All aboard."

"*All aboard?*"

Two interesting events then scared the life out of Burnham. He heard a distant siren, and the engines of the DC-3, which had been idling all this while, erupted in thunder. "What the hell!" he hollered. He took the ladder in two steps and ran forward. The aircraft shuddered and rattled; the thunder swelled. Moran's body had slumped sideways; beneath his head the throttles were wide open. Burnham yanked him away and throttled down, then dragged the body free and out of the cabin. "That takes care of run-up," he said. "Jesus!" He checked the brakes, scooted back to the door, hopped to the tarmac, yanked the chocks free and hustled Hao-lan aboard.

"You're crazy! The pilot's dead!"

"One experienced man can fly a DC-3 alone. Help me with the door now. Set your feet. Pull on that cable. Hard!"

"I'm pulling! How much experience?"

The door slammed shut. "Well, a couple of hours, twice. But

I paid attention. Bear down on the lock. Put your back into it. Good. Follow me, lady."

He slipped into the pilot's seat. "Sit down there, fasten your seat belt and do what I tell you. I helped you drive that car you stole; the least you can do is help me drive this truck."

"I'm hungry," she said.

"God damn it, woman, no jokes! By your right hand. Two round dials. The one on the right: what does it say?"

"Eight hundred fifty."

"Good. Up there, fourth and fifth switches from the left, bottom row: off. Jesus, they never made any two of these planes the same."

"My God," she said. "Off."

"I've only got the one arm, and it's the wrong arm. Battery switch, I got it here. That indicator on your side of the box—no, not that one, yes, there, what does it read?"

"Right main."

"Good. Those two red levers on top. Set them on auto rich."

"Auto rich."

"Ammeter's okay. Flaps half. Radio, who cares, altimeter, who cares, clock, who cares, gyros set and uncaged, controls seem to move all right, tail wheel unlocked—hell, this thing ought to fly all right. I want you to put your fingertips on each of those two black knobs marked T—and you need a surgeon's touch here, all right? Now push them both forward the least bit." She did; he eased up on the brakes.

"We're moving!"

"Hell," he said, "this is the hard part. Any child can fly it, but only a pilot can taxi it."

Inspector Yen flipped the siren on, let it shriek, led his clowns' squadron of antique cars through the maze of happy pickpockets, airport vehicles, retired aircraft and ordinary potholes, and arrived at the American operations lot in time to see the DC-3 trundling across a ramp toward the head of the runway. He also saw two bodies, and recognized Ming and the strange uniformed policeman. The sight was gratifying and a favorable omen. "Quickly," he urged the chubby captain at his side, "down this taxiway! They can be stopped!"

The chubby captain said "Yü" and gunned the motor. Yen made sure the other two cars were following.

Clear ahead. Burnham glanced out his side window and saw the burning shop: smoke straight up, no wind, heavy air, moist. What the hell; heading east of south, about one seven oh, why not? Take off straight ahead and worry about the turn if we make a hundred feet. Make it? Of course we'll make it, man! God loves a lover. They lumbered toward takeoff, steering with the throttles. "Ease off on the left. A blast on the right, now. Not so much—easy! Good." Well, here we are. Ready set go. "Clear on the right?"

"Clear."

He glanced left and saw three cars racing down a parallel taxiway. Now what? Forgot to pay my bar bill. Too late. "Equalize the throttles. Hold it there." Props full forward, okay. "Those first two switches you touched: on."

"On."

"That knob under the box there, in the middle. Turn it clockwise. Push it in hard."

"In hard."

Tail wheel locked. What have I left out? A dozen minor matters. "There's a big red handle to the left side of your seat. Yes. It's the landing gear control. Remember it. Now ease the throttles forward. Slowly. Good. Welcome to Amateur Airways Flight One." Manifold pressure, where are you? Forty-eight, perfect. "Hold them there."

They were picking up speed very nicely. Well down the runway the three cars raced ahead.

"Now!" Yen cried. "Sharp right!" They squealed and bumped onto the runway. "Now again! Halt!" He cut the siren, and the chubby captain jammed on the brakes. "Out!"

They tumbled out. Behind them the other two were screeching

and slowing. Yen ran, waving. He was dizzy. "Back!" he called. "Block the runway!" They understood, maneuvered into place and scrambled out. "Run!" Yen shouted, and led the way.

Keep her on the line. Air speed fifty, fifty-five—
"What the hell are they doing?"
"Burnham!"
"Good Christ!"
"Burnham! Stop!"
"I can't stop now! Dumb sons of bitches!"

"He must brake or swerve," Yen panted.
The chubby captain grunted doubts. "Will it blow up?"
"Courage," Yen said. "O gods."
"He is neither braking nor swerving," a lieutenant said.
"A madman!" Yen cried.

"Eighty," Burnham said. "Tail's up. Hold on tight, m'love." His blood was ice. He eased back on the wheel and they rose, eighty was not enough but they rose, sluggish as a wounded goose but they rose, and one instant the cars loomed below and then he had flashed over them, hunched and wincing against the fatal shock of undercarriage on obstacle, a shock that never came. They were up and over but the plane was settling; he eased off on the wheel, called "Hang on!" and they hit. They bounced. He was flung forward and his right shoulder blazed. They bounced again, a great jangle and rattle, heroic shrieks and groans from the tortured metal, and then they were rolling once more, and their airspeed was eighty again and then eighty-five, and somewhere out there was the end of the runway, and then the airspeed was ninety and the tail was still up and he eased back again and the runway vanished beneath them. They were airborne.

Mutely Hao-lan reproached him. She was speechless. She tried to breathe, and managed only an airy sob.

"On your side of my seat, down on the floor there's a latch. Release it."

Hao-lan groped. "It's up."

"Now, that red handle left of your seat: pull it up."

A rumble, a thud.

"Now put it back where it was. Not past that point."

"Damn, damn!" she sobbed. "Now what? What happens now?"

"Why, we're in the air," he said. "At this point the co-pilot usually kisses the pilot."

Far back at the edge of the tarmac Feng and Kanamori stood astonished. "I always believed such machines rose directly and without interruption," Feng said. "Apparently it was reluctant to leave the earth, as I too would be."

"The bouncing is not customary," Kanamori said.

"It was those automobiles," Feng said. "Automobiles are a menace, and should be confined to foreign countries."

"I would never have believed it," Yen said softly.

The chubby captain groaned. "I am a policeman, not a human sacrifice. To feel such fear is belittling."

The six men watched the aircraft rise and recede.

"We have lost," Yen said.

"At least we have not lost the cars. Are there further orders?"

"Take me back to my car and those bodies," Yen said. There remained a riddle or two.

"I gathered up these pistols," Feng said. "One for you and one for me. You will instruct me in their operation and maintenance."

Kanamori accepted Ming's short-barreled .38. He hefted it and snapped it open. The feel of it was familiar but saddening.

"What is this character here?" Feng asked.

Kanamori looked, and said, "Canada."

"And what is Canada?"

"A place across the water. A cold place, near where the American lives."

"A good omen," Feng said.

*   *   *

The six policemen examined the two bodies. Yen groaned and muttered. He preferred order, regularity and brutalizing students.

"This must be reported," the lieutenant said.

"I shall report it," Yen said. "A complicated case, and now further complicated."

"We must send for a meat wagon," said the chubby captain.

"No. Pile them into the back seat of my car. Odd, odd. Two corpses and no weapons. A policeman with an empty holster. Do you know him?"

They did not. They dragged the bodies to Yen's car and loaded them.

"Stand by," Yen said. "This spirit-cart is a lemon and unreliable."

"A lemon?"

"That is a technical term," Yen said, "for an automobile of fugitive moods." He took his seat, turned the key and pressed the starter. The engine whined and coughed. Yen performed the customary rituals, banging and cursing, and tried again; the motor caught, even purred. "Perhaps my luck has turned. Well, thank you. It was a brave attempt."

"We shall make our report."

"By all means. I shall make mine, and commend you all."

Bearing his grisly cargo he set his course for Peking. A gift for Sung Yun. He also had a question or two for Sung Yun. Perhaps the tycoon would reward silence, or tip Yen well for the delivery of these two cadavers. Another in the long series of unsolved crimes and mysteries that were called, in the aggregate, police work in Peking. Inspector Yen fails again, and is reassigned to a middle-school traffic crossing.

At the edge of the tarmac two coolies were walking hand in hand. Irritated, giving vent now to years of anger and days of frustration, Inspector Yen pressed the siren. The coolies leaped out of the way in alarm.

Yen felt gray within. Coolies. In a matter of days the whole city —Peking! Peking!—would be theirs.

* * *

"That was Inspector Yen," Feng said, with the air of one who has traveled in the first circles.

"Yen!" Kanamori blinked like a tortoise. "I am a stranger to him, but he knows you."

"Nobody sees the ricksha man," Feng said. "But this Yen is a policeman, and he was present in the cemetery."

Kanamori hissed.

Feng said, "Sooner or later he may . . . snoop."

"Snoop." Kanamori mulled this. "Well, we are now the custodians of the cemetery."

"Indeed. Should this Yen come prowling, we must be faithful to our duties."

"It would be a shame," Kanamori said. "I am accustomed to peace."

"A shame, yes. This Yen seems not as bad as some. Nevertheless, he is bad enough."

"I know just the place to bury him," Kanamori said.

Burnham flew at a thousand feet, in the sweet solitude of his own heaven, with his own angel. His enemy now was a light head. He had survived on adrenaline and love, but the adrenaline was ebbing. "Talk to me. Keep me awake. I'm faint."

"*I'm* supposed to faint."

"Nonsense. You're a doctor and a car thief. And don't make fun of me. I've been shot. I suppose there's a first-aid kit, but I don't know where."

"You need a psychiatrist."

"The least you could do is carry aspirin."

"You swore at me," she said. "And you called me *woman* as if I were a domestic animal."

"Tell you what: you be my domestic animal and I'll be yours. This damn arm! We can't even hold hands."

"You just drive," she said.

"If I put her on automatic pilot we could go back and lie down."

"You're wounded. You're faint."

"I am indeed. Keep talking. That reminds me: under one of these seats there ought to be a thermos bottle. Hot coffee."

Hao-lan rummaged, and came up with an odd rubbery contraption. "What's this?"

"A relief tube."

"A man's world. Here, coffee! How did you know that?"

"Always. American aircraft run on high-octane coffee."

"It tastes awful," she said, "and this plane scares me. It's noisy. Creaks and clatters, and the wing flaps up and down."

"That's called flex," he said. "A famous aircraft. Squeaks and groans, runs rough, leaks oil. But it's the most forgiving plane in the air. You have to work hard to make an accident. Safety first is the Burnham motto."

"I've noticed. You are not what I would call reassuring to be with."

"I thought you cared," Burnham grieved. "This always happens. I spend all my money and sexual energy, no sacrifice too great—"

"Can you think of nothing else?"

"Certainly," he said woozily. "I am a man of the world with many and varied interests. We are now over the Yellow Sea. Passengers on the starboard side may look down and see Shantung, home of the world's most famous silk. We are flying at one thousand feet to avoid the waves. Our cruising speed is one hundred and ninety miles per hour. All gauges and dials are normal—at least those I recognize."

"Stop babbling and breathe deeply."

"Yes, Doctor. But speak to me from time to time."

"This version is called the C-47," he said affectionately, "but to us early barnstormers it will always be the DC-3. They used to carry whole fighter planes, with the wings slung below the fuselage and everything else inside, dismantled."

"You really ought to shut up. How's your head?"

"Clear and light. I know I ought to shut up, but I'm afraid I'll snooze. Keep an eye on me. If I droop, whack me."

"Oxygen!"

"Sorry. Maybe a walk-around bottle somewhere. I'll be all right. If I get sleepy we can sing some of the great old songs. 'I was eatin some chop suey,'" he caroled, "'with a lady from Saint Looie, when there come a sudden poundin at the door.' That's Yeats."

"Stop it! Stop talking too. Just take deep regular breaths."

"Yes ma'am."

"It isn't over," she muttered. "I know it isn't over. Something terrible will happen."

"Well, we could ditch and drown. You only live about thirty seconds in that cold water down there."

"Shut up. Where are we going?"

"To the first frozen bean field in Korea. Or a straight stretch of road without donkeys."

"You mean we have to land this thing."

"Nothing to it." He grinned, goofy again. "My Christ, what a beautiful woman you are! Only a boor could fall asleep with a face like that beside him." Her eyes warmed, and he fought to swallow his swelling heart.

"I have never seen a fatter, smugger, more imbecilic smile," she said.

"I need a kiss."

"Watch the road," she said, but shortly relented.

Burnham dozed fitfully during the third hour. Hao-lan took the wheel, and read her own altimeter. "This is *fun!*"

"You'll have work to do when we land." Flight instructor Burnham rehearsed her. Higher flights to come. We supply all transports, including the amorous. She repeated his commands like a cadet. "Better give me the wheel now."

"Aw, why?"

"Company."

She gasped. Four fighters, well apart, converged on them. "Shooting Stars," he said. "Ours." The fighters flanked them, two on each side, one on their level, one above.

"Radio," she said. "Call them. Tell them who we are."

"The hell with it. No free hand. They know who we are. We're Moran." The Korean coast broke the horizon. Off his port wing a pilot waved: follow. Burnham acknowledged. The upper fighters shot forward and altered course, left about ten degrees. Burnham followed. They would not freeze to death in the Yellow Sea, and they would not need a long road or a farmer's bean patch. Soon he saw roads and farms. "Hell," he said, "I just thought of something."

"That girl with spots."

"Oh, shut up. Was Yen killed?"

"I have no idea."

"If he's still alive he's going to wonder about that cemetery."

"Have faith," she said. "Trust Feng."

"A young man of sterling character and infinite resource. Just the same, I wish I knew."

The F-8os led them to an airfield, a long, shiny, modern airfield with a control tower and fire trucks. "A relief. I admit it. Never landed one of these, and I wasn't looking forward to some dried-up pig's wallow in the middle of my runway."

"How's your head?"

"Clear as a bell, except for the customary exhilaration in the presence of my musky fox. Let's go to work now. I'll circle the field once, if they'll let me." He banked and leveled. "Throttle back now. Slowly." Lazily they went around. "Back a little more. Good."

Hao-lan shifted the mix from auto lean to auto rich. Carburetor air cold. "Cold." Fuel booster pumps on. "On." RPM: "Twenty-two fifty." Tail wheel locked. "Locked." Parking brake off. "Now, that handle by your seat."

"The landing gear control."

"Terrific. Push it all the way down." Again the rumble and thud. "Now back to neutral."

"Neutral."

"Now that latch over here. Slide it forward. Locked?"

"Locked."

"Now look out your window."

"I see the landing gear."

"You don't say that. I told you. You say 'I got a wheel.'"

"I got a wheel. Burnham, I *love* this."

"I got a wheel too. You got a green light?"

"I got a green light."

"Now that upper lever. Swing it out of the slot. I want it full down."

"Flaps down."

He turned carefully into his approach leg—too carefully. He overshot and corrected. "Speed ninety. Well, kid, all we got to do is land it. I thank the spirits of the middle air, and crave the indulgence of the spirits of the lower air."

"Amen."

They hopped, skipped and jumped a bit, and ran too far, but Burnham jammed on the brakes and they hauled up well short of ditches, rice paddies and interested spectators. He had Hao-lan turn off every switch in sight and cut a few himself. "Cheated death again. I'm tired."

"You look like hell."

"Damn little sleep this past while. Too old for sex."

"Then I'm going back."

They sat gazing straight ahead, as if some sacrament had been successfully administered and further orders from the gods were necessary. Slowly they became aware of motion and commotion outside: sirens, men at the run. "Uncle Sam really cares," he said. "Look at that: trucks, jeeps, fire engines, lots of soldiers. Makes you feel all warm and squiggly inside."

"No band," she said. "I'm glad you came to China."

"Wouldn't have missed it for the world."

They stirred then, undid their seat belts, shared an easy kiss, filed past Moran and stood at the door, almost reluctant.

"They have guns," he said. "You go first."

"I can't marry a man who talks like that."

"Got to now. We crossed a state line."

"Stand aside," she said, and wrenched at the lock.

The infantry were deployed in a semicircle, some kneeling, some prone. Fifty weapons bore on Burnham and Hao-lan. Outside the ring trucks and jeeps idled.

Two officers approached. "Take it easy, now," one called.

"We're all right," Burnham said. "You folks appear to be in some trouble."

"Who the hell are you?"

"Jack Burnham. American major." A useful half-truth.

"You don't look like a major to me."

"I'm on vacation. Also, I have a bullet in my arm."

The captain wavered; he and the lieutenant holstered their
.45s. "You look like an American and you talk like an American."
He wheeled: "Ground your arms!" Then: "Where's Moran?"

Burnham jerked a thumb. "In there. Dead. A riot at the airport. By the way, I want to thank his ground crew."

"Dead? God damn it! These crazy countries! You want a doctor?"

"I got a doctor," Burnham said. "What I need is a bellhop."

During a jouncy ride to Seoul Burnham explained to other
officers that Hao-lan was Chiang Kai-shek's daughter, whom he
had rescued from Communist scoundrels. "Hang on to the bags,"
he muttered to her.

"What now?"

"Something in mine they probably shouldn't see."

"Pornography."

"I have no further need of pornography."

"Horny slob."

They were placed under house arrest—"temporary detention"
—after a military surgeon extracted the bullet and dressed Burnham's wound. "This is a pretty fair dressing. Who did it, the little
lady?"

Burnham said gravely, "Dr. Lindholm, Dr. Nien."

"Very funny," Lindholm said. "But it's clean and that's a good
bandage. We'll give you a booster, and a little local, and a couple
of stitches."

"What booster?"

"Tetanus."

"I wasn't shot in a barn."

"Be quiet," Hao-lan said, and to Lindholm, "Shock. Exhaus-
tion. Nothing in moderation."

Lindholm smiled professionally and looked from one to the
other with curiosity. They let him wonder.

"You seem to check out," the lieutenant colonel said. "Major
Myers says he poured you aboard that same plane only a couple

of days ago. We'll put you up in the BOQ, but you're still under detention. The lady can sleep in nurses' quarters."

"No sir," Burnham said politely. "Where the lady goes, I go. Orders. You call Tokyo."

"I've already called Tokyo. Nobody tells me a damn thing. A colonel said a firing squad would probably be best, but then he said 'Correction, correction, treat him right.' They never heard of any lady, and Chiang Kai-shek has no daughter."

"Sorry," Burnham said, "but she's my prisoner and I will not let her out of my sight."

"Oh, God damn it," the lieutenant colonel said. "You mean sleep in the same room?"

"It's bigger than both of us," Burnham told him. "The same *bed.*"

"I can't let you do that. What kind of army you think we're running here? You know what they'd do to me—"

"Colonel," Burnham said, "fetch me a chaplain, will you? A Unitarian or a rabbi or some other atheist."

41 寶

On the sixth floor of the Dai-Ichi Mutual Life Insurance Building in Tokyo Burnham faced a battery of brass, including a general he had met before. His arm was out of the sling and he was, on the whole, presentable: woolen trousers, khaki shirt, field jacket. At a necktie he had rebelled; civilians must cherish their privileges, else we are all conscripts. Beside him sat Hao-lan, a vision of beauty and brocade. The colonels were skeptical and peeved, though restrained from excessive discourtesy by a lady's presence. Burnham's original colonel was the thorniest of the lot. "Reliable sources! A madam and a beggar!"

"And a police inspector. What do you want from me? I told you his mother was Chinese, and that checked out. And I told you where and when and how he was killed, and you say that checks out, though I don't see how the hell you could know it. What more do you want—his ears or his dog tags?" Damn these offices, these conference rooms! Damn all metal furniture and colonels like robots. And the general! Sunglasses like Ming's.

"We lost a captain," one colonel said.

"I suppose you'd rather have lost me. I lost a captain too."

"What's that mean?"

"Nothing." Burnham set his face in serious, helpful lines. "An old friend of mine helped out and paid for it."

"An American?" The general was stern.

"A Chinese."

"Oh. And that's absolutely all you have to tell us?"

"Listen, I'll recite it all again if you want, but that's it."

"Well, if the Jap's dead, he's dead," a colonel said.

Burnham's colonel spoke to a lieutenant seated near the door. "Bring him in."

Burnham never even twitched, but his stomach yawed. *Bring him in?* He shot a glance at Hao-lan, who looked queasy. This world of lies! What now? Infinite possibilities. Feng was with military intelligence. Kanamori had followed on the next plane. Oh Christ. Leavenworth. Alcatraz. From the wall Harry Truman smiled down on him, bow tie and all.

"No disrespect, ma'am, but this marriage is irregular. You had no permission from the military."

"I required no permission from the military," Hao-lan said.

"We're civilians and over twenty-one," Burnham said angrily. "And we were married by a preacher." He strove to be amiable. "Also we are married in the eyes of God."

"And you maintain, ma'am, that you have no other connection with all this?"

"None whatever," Hao-lan said.

"Oh, come on," Burnham told this colonel. "She is a doctor of medicine and we fell in love and did the honorable thing. It's the American dream. Every American mother wants her child to marry a doctor." *Bring him in?*

"Well, she checks out too," another colonel said. "College in London and all."

"I'm glad to hear that," Burnham said earnestly. "Could have been a pack of lies. But you know how it is. A well-turned ankle." He beamed upon her. She scowled.

"Christ," someone muttered.

The door squeaked open. Casually Burnham glanced up.

Sung Yun was pale but composed.

Burnham rose at once, all affability. "Why, it's Sung Yun! Hao-lan, it's Master Sung!" He managed to stride forward with enthusiasm and extend a hand.

Sung Yun had begun a perfunctory bow but caught himself and observed the American custom. His hand was dry, light, nerveless. Burnham pumped it like a salesman. Sung Yun did bow then, to Hao-lan. "My dear Doctor. My dear Burnham." Again Burnham heard the now unmistakable Wu accent.

Behind Sung a diminutive Chinese announced in English, "My dear Doctor. My dear Burnham."

A colonel showed Sung to a chair, and the interpreter stood close by.

Hao-lan was furious. Her glance asked Burnham, *More?* Burnham made scared schoolboy's eyes: the stone drops into the well. "This is the eminent Sung Yun, of the Sino-American Amity Association," he explained.

"We know that," a colonel growled.

The interpreter murmured in Sung's ear.

Burnham pulled himself together and sat easily. Always Sung Yun's presence seemed to demand a dim-witted smile of him.

"My dear lady!" Sung Yun seemed affectionate. "My heart rejoices to see you safe and well, and by the side of your betrothed. Did I not promise that?"

Hao-lan subdued obvious exasperation. "We are now married," she said primly. Helpful old Burnham patted her hand.

"My felicitations!" Sung Yun was overcome. "My most heartfelt wishes for long life and prosperity, not to mention handsome and properly filial offspring."

"You will put me to the blush," Hao-lan said. "I hope your own ladies are well."

The interpreter spoke and looked like a parrot. The colonels fidgeted.

"Alas!" Sung Yun was now the soul of grief. "How could I ask them to share a lonely and impoverished exile? No, they are women of Peking." He nodded complacently, this benefactor: "I left them well provided for. They will surely find useful occupation under the, ah, new regime."

A colonel harrumphed. "Excuse the interruption, but there seem to be some loose ends."

Burnham's hand lingered on Hao-lan's. The interpreter murmured.

"Ah, yes," Sung Yun said. "Tragic. Surely you recall my secretary Ming."

"His English was extraordinary," Burnham said. "And how has he fared, these latter days?"

"I regret to divulge misfortune. He was dear to me, as you

know. The poor boy was slain at the airport on the day of your departure."

"Sad news of old friends!" Burnham said. "The heart brims with sorrow."

"And also the man Liao, my servant for a decade and more."

"Worse and worse!" Burnham said. "The turmoil of those last days! Unruly mobs at the airport, loafers and beggars, all manner of irreverence and anarchy. We were barely able to take off. Our pilot, as you may have heard, was shot to death."

"As were Ming and Liao."

"Barbarous. You found them there?"

"Inspector Yen found them."

Damn! "Ah, the good Inspector Yen."

"He bore the bodies home to me. Picture my distress."

To Hao-lan Burnham said, "Is this too much for your delicate nature, my good wife?"

"Shocking," she muttered.

"Surely Inspector Yen illuminated this disaster."

"Unfortunately, I was too upset to discuss the matter," Sung Yun said. "I asked him to return; I needed some hours of repose and reflection."

"Only too understandable. And when he returned?"

"He did not return." Sung Yun fell glum. "Repeated inquiries elicited only puzzled disclaimers. His colleagues had not seen him, nor had his wife. He was a man of routine and a servant of the people, and his disappearance was considered most irregular."

"Perhaps he turned coat."

"Yen? Never!"

"Evil times."

"Evil times indeed!" Sung Yun burst out. "My automobile has also disappeared! It was a Hotchkiss of great value, formerly owned by the Swiss consul."

"But so much has disappeared," Burnham said smoothly. "At this very moment someone in Peking grieves because Sung Yun himself has disappeared. So much gone for good! A thing as large as a whole government! A thing as small as the least ivory lion!"

Sung Yun's face dried. "The least—"

"Even Wang Hsi-lin has disappeared."

Sung Yun shriveled.

"Who's this Wang?" a colonel asked.

Burnham held Sung's gaze. Sung's eyes showed white; his lips parted. "Just a mutual friend," Burnham said. "A man of low repute—of no bones, as we say."

"Dead, I believe," Sung said. Color returned to his face, and the glister to his eye.

"Possibly," Burnham said.

"Well then," Sung said, "we can only deplore these sad events and be thankful that we remain alive and well."

"That seems reasonable," Burnham said.

"Look here," a colonel said. "You three can gossip all you want later." He looked to the general; therefore everybody looked to the general.

The general granted them speech. "Burnham, the colonel has a serious question for you. I ask you to think carefully. This is a service you can perform for your country. Afterward I want you and Mrs. Burnham to forget that the question was asked. Do you understand?"

Burnham said, "Absolutely, sir. It's my wife's country too, now."

The general nodded majestically to the colonel.

"Any scrap of information may help here," Burnham's colonel said. "Think back, now, and take your time. On this whole mission did you ever hear anything whatever—rumors or questions or significant remarks—about an art collection, or any kind of works of art?"

"Of course I did!" Burnham said. "Master Sung is a connoisseur, and showed me some superb pieces."

"I mean other than that," the colonel said. "Damn it, Burnham, think hard and tell the truth."

"I wish you'd mentioned this before I left," Burnham said. "I would have paid more attention." He thought hard. He clasped Hao-lan's hand and said, "To tell the truth, Colonel, I don't know much about art," and he favored them all with his patented sunny smile, "but I know what I like."

The brass trooped out finally, the general glaring like an eagle with chicks, then recollecting himself and touching his forehead to Hao-lan. "Madam. My compliments." The colonels, en masse, left Burnham in no doubt of their displeasure.

Sung Yun dismissed the interpreter. "Wait in the corridor."

The three refugees sat in neutral silence. Sung Yun seemed to be meditating. Finally he said, "So Kanamori is dead."

"As dead as Wang Hsi-lin," Burnham said. "How heartwarming that Master Sung has found a haven among new friends."

" 'Old friends are better than new, but new are not bad,' " Sung said dryly. "I believe I understand what you have done, but not why. You are surely not a Communist?"

"I am surely not a Communist," Burnham said. "It's not folks like me who bring that on; it's folks like you."

"Such outlandish logic defeats me. If I understand you—which is not certain—you have flouted orders and betrayed your superiors."

"They are not my superiors," Burnham said, "and their orders were a lie, as you know. As for betrayal—"

"I believe you have betrayed more than your army," Sung Yun said. "I believe you have betrayed civilized man, and hastened the night."

"That night never comes," Burnham said. "It is merely that the sun sets for some and rises for others. A commonplace and daily occurrence."

"Someday we must discuss your quaint notions of honor," Sung Yun said.

Remembering Head Beggar, Burnham drew himself up. "Who can discuss ice with the summer insects?"

Sung Yun's face closed; he too drew himself up, and said, "Barbarian." He bowed one cold bow to Hao-lan, padded to the door and left them.

*　　*　　*

"I am truly angry for the first time," she said.

"I know a nice Japanese restaurant."

"I suppose Tokyo is famous for them."

"Don't be angry," he said.

"That man ought to be hanged."

"Which is what they said about Kanamori."

"Four men died."

They were walking through a light fall of snow. The Japanese street was more muted than Peking's avenues and alleys. Western clothes did not predominate but were noticeable. Former robed and topknotted samurai were now men of business, with silver pins to hold the collar down beneath the knotted tie: small men overtrousered, skinny legs flailing at floppy cloth, tiny feet freezing in leather shoes. Before a low, homely shop building of no national character one of these solemn commercial gentlemen greeted a respectful robed woman; she bowed, he bowed; he walked off, and she followed a step behind.

The screen of snow reminded Burnham of their nuptial chamber at the Willow Wine Shop, and again he invoked Sea Hammer's spirit: Help me to tell her this. Tell her what? That horror is fundamental and permanent? She knows that; it's her work. That love is what we salvage? She knows that.

She too had been reminded. "Sea Hammer will be our household god," she said. "On the mantel. To resolve our quarrels, and to make good luck."

"Stop it. You barely met him. We will resolve our own quarrels and make our own luck."

"I know."

"He was a good man and my brother," Burnham went on, "but he smacked his lips over that bunker. He was a man of sound bottom but mischievous tendency, and he was a good guerrilla because he loved the sport but also because he was a born opportunist. In the end he might have killed Kanamori and even Feng. He was a great killer, you know. A Sea Hammer first, and then a friend." Forgive me, old brawler, but I cannot let her mourn you. We will have troubles of our own, and you would scorn to shadow our days.

"All the same, he died for us."

"Fair enough. He knew what I was after, he knew it wasn't Kanamori, and he knew I'd found it. He wanted all us nice ordinary people to find our lovers, bake our bread and watch the sunset in peace."

"Everybody wants that. It cannot be."

"Then if everybody can't have it, nobody should? Listen, whatever you do, you do it for love or it goes bad. If you do it for the left or the right or even the middle, you wind up in a red shirt or a black shirt or a collar and tie, and nothing inside. He knew that. You try to make love possible. For those kids of yours, and that little girl with the chancre, and the whole sad squalid world full of hungries and sicks and crazies, and people everywhere with somebody's boot on their neck."

"Master Burnham the philosopher." Her eyes were calm and bright; her breath steamed among the falling flakes.

"You will make me grumpy," he said. "There's no way to tell you how I love you, so I have to dress it up in fancy talk."

"That's better."

The Snow Princess: silver flakes on her fur hat. For a moment he doted on her profile and smiled sheepishly, as if he had practiced some monstrous, funny deception on the world.

"No more opium," she said.

"I'll just smoke up those last hundred pellets."

"No. I don't want it around."

"Fool. Never again. In time it diminishes desire and accelerates impotence."

"Then no more ever," she said. "Where is it?"

"I left it for the general. You know how he likes his pipe."

"You'll be arrested."

"Never. They don't want to hear another word about this. They want Burnham retired from public life." He flung up a hand. A ricksha tracked through the snow and halted. A commodious double. He issued instructions and they settled in. He kissed her and wondered if he would ever not want to.

They rode through a Tokyo frosted white, a strangely silent Tokyo, and they held hands in an immense calm.

"Someday we'll be unfaithful," she said.

"I know."

At the restaurant he handed her down, and overtipped. He held the gate for her. If it was possible for human beings to feel this way, then they ought to. There, a moral imperative: Burnham's law.

"That ricksha man looked just like Feng," Hao-lan said.

"Really?" said Burnham. "I didn't notice."

About the Author

STEPHEN BECKER was educated at Harvard, in Peking after the war, and in Paris, where he lived for four years. Among his nine novels are *Dog Tags* and *The Chinese Bandit*; among his translations, *The Last of the Just* and Louis-Philippe's *Diary of My Travels in America*. He has also published biography, history, short stories, magazine articles, reviews and columns; has lectured in China, France, Alaska and Mexico, and taught now and then, most recently at Bennington College. After many years on a farm in New England, he recently moved to the Caribbean.